Praise for

THE PACK

"Guys' night out takes on a droll new meaning."
—*The New York Times Book Review* (summer pick)

"In this tightly written werewolf suspense thriller, crime writer Starr succeeds in keeping readers on the edge of their seats. The book brings werewolves to the streets of New York City and manages to seem completely believable. A great read; recommended for any paranormal suspense fan."
—*Library Journal* (starred review)

"An unusual, fascinating horror thriller."
—*Midwest Book Review*

"Manhattan receives a lustrous varnish of black, black humor in this sly urban fantasy thriller . . . Starr once again shows a real gift for satiric humor and capturing the contemporary New York scene."
—*Publishers Weekly*

"*The Pack* is pure Jason Starr, and it is one of his most gripping novels yet."
—*Spinetingler Magazine*

"Smoothly written and tweaked with humor, this urban fantasy supplies a seductive adventure that will appeal to wives as well as husbands."
—*Yahoo! Shine*

"Brings a few new elements to the concept and—thanks mostly to Starr's skills at character and suspense—is an engrossing and entertaining story . . . [an] alluring blend of supernatural and suspense."
—*Bookgasm*

continued . . .

Praise for the novels of Jason Starr

"From the first page . . . you know things are going to get worse, but you can't stop reading."
—*Newsweek*

"The ultimate page-turner . . . brilliantly blends psychological and physical suspense."
—Michael Connelly, #1 *New York Times* bestselling author

"[Starr] is a hard-knuckled writer [who] seems to have given a lot of thought to those tricky existential notions of fate and free will."
—*The New York Times Book Review*

"[A] fearless, pitiless writer . . . [and] a prodigious talent."
—Laura Lippman, *New York Times* bestselling author

"Jason Starr's got a hip style and an ear for crackling dialogue . . . [with] characters so real we feel we know them."
—Jeffery Deaver, *New York Times* bestselling author

"Starr [is] a terrifically taut writer."
—*The Baltimore Sun*

"Irresistible and truly terrifying."
—Joseph Finder, *New York Times* bestselling author

"Starr is such a polished writer that once you start reading, it's painful to tear yourself away."
—*Time Out New York*

"Demonic, demented, and truly ferocious, and a flat-out joy to read."
—Ken Bruen

"Relentlessly clever . . . mesmerizing . . . Starr has total control of his plot . . . an unsettling read, but hard to put down."
—*Booklist*

"Starr delivers a wild ride."
—*Publishers Weekly*

Ace Books by Jason Starr

THE PACK
THE CRAVING

THE CRAVING

Jason Starr

ACE BOOKS, NEW YORK

THE BERKLEY PUBLISHING GROUP
Published by the Penguin Group
Penguin Group (USA) Inc.
375 Hudson Street, New York, New York 10014, USA
Penguin Group (Canada), 90 Eglinton Avenue East, Suite 700, Toronto, Ontario M4P 2Y3, Canada
(a division of Pearson Penguin Canada Inc.) • Penguin Books Ltd., 80 Strand, London WC2R 0RL,
England • Penguin Group Ireland, 25 St. Stephen's Green, Dublin 2, Ireland (a division of Penguin
Books Ltd.) • Penguin Group (Australia), 250 Camberwell Road, Camberwell, Victoria 3124, Australia
(a division of Pearson Australia Group Pty. Ltd.) • Penguin Books India Pvt. Ltd., 11 Community
Centre, Panchsheel Park, New Delhi—110 017, India • Penguin Group (NZ), 67 Apollo Drive,
Rosedale, Auckland 0632, New Zealand (a division of Pearson New Zealand Ltd.) • Penguin Books
(South Africa) (Pty.) Ltd., 24 Sturdee Avenue, Rosebank, Johannesburg 2196, South Africa

Penguin Books Ltd., Registered Offices: 80 Strand, London WC2R 0RL, England

This is an original publication of The Berkley Publishing Group.

PUBLISHING HISTORY
Ace trade paperback edition / June 2012

Library of Congress Cataloging-in-Publication Data

Starr, Jason, 1966–
The craving / Jason Starr. — Ace trade paperback ed.
p.   cm.
ISBN 978-1-937007-55-3
1. Werewolves—Fiction.   2. Fathers—Fiction.   3. New York (N.Y.)—Fiction.   I. Title.
PS3569.T336225C73 2012
813'.54—dc23
2012001026

PRINTED IN THE UNITED STATES OF AMERICA

10   9   8   7   6   5   4   3   2   1

For Chynna

THE CRAVING

ONE

When Diane Coles heard the creaking footsteps in the hallway outside the bedroom, she knew it was one of them coming to get her. She sat up in bed and screamed so loud it hurt her ears, but this didn't scare away the intruder. The footsteps got louder, and then the doorknob rattled and the door shook. Oh, God, this was it, the moment she'd feared since she'd left New York and moved back in with her parents in Grosse Pointe. He—well, if it was a *he*—was going to break in and kill her. She had no idea how many of them there were. She knew there were at least a few, including her best friend— well, former best friend—Olivia.

Still shrieking, she grabbed the nearest object, a lamp, yanking the cord out of the wall. Yeah, like a lamp would protect her. Still, she raised it above her head, ready to fling it at whoever, or *whatever*, came inside.

"Diane, what's going on? What's wrong? Diane, open this door right now . . . Diane."

It took a few seconds before it registered that it wasn't one of *them* after all; it was just her mother.

"Diane, can you hear me?"

"I'm fine, Mom," Diane said, aware of her pulse pounding as if she were in an all-out sprint.

"You can't stay in there all day again," Barbara Coles said. "This is ridiculous. You have to get on with your life."

Diane remained with the lamp above her head for several seconds, then replaced it on the night table. She lay down again in bed and pulled the blanket up to her chin.

"Diane, will you please open the door?" Barbara shook the door a few more times.

"I'll be right down, Mom."

"What?" Barbara asked.

"I said I'll be right down."

Diane heard Barbara let out a long, frustrated breath, and then her fading footsteps as she marched downstairs.

Diane had been lashing out at her parents since she'd moved home, and she felt bad about it. She was thirty-two years old, but lately she'd been acting like a spoiled, angry fourteen-year-old. She'd thought moving back home would make her feel safe, protected, but if anything, being isolated in a small space had increased her paranoia.

If she knew who exactly was after her, it would make things a little easier—at least she'd know whom to avoid—but it really could be anyone. Maybe it was the dark-haired guy in the black Honda that had been parked in front of her parents' house the day before, or that older blond woman in the Delta terminal at LaGuardia who'd stared at her weirdly. Or maybe it was the very old guy, maybe ninety years old, who'd grabbed her in front of the apartment in the East Village one evening and said with a foreign accent, maybe German, "You must leave, before it's too late." The way the guy had looked at her with his intense dark eyes had scared the crap out of her. Before she could ask him who he was or any other questions, he ran away, with surprising speed for such an old man. Maybe he was one of them, or maybe there were others she didn't know about, but now she was certain of one thing—she wouldn't be able to avoid them forever.

Her parents, meanwhile, had no idea about the danger she was in, or the possible danger *they* were in. It would be so much easier if she were able to open up about it, get some genuine support, but she knew they wouldn't believe her. They'd have the same reaction as the police; they'd think she was crazy, disturbed, making it all up. Besides, they were getting older—both in their midsixties—and she didn't want to cause them any stress, especially since her father had had bypass surgery recently. So Diane had no choice but to keep all the stress to herself, and it had been taking its toll. She was losing weight and couldn't sleep, and her thoughts were so scattered it was hard to focus on anything.

She'd considered leaving Grosse Pointe, but where else would she go? If she stayed with another friend or relative, in Michigan or some other part of the country, she'd be endangering someone else, and she didn't have money to travel far or stay in a hotel. In New York, she'd been making decent money as a publicist for a financial services firm, but with rents the way they were, she had been barely able to save.

So, for better or worse, Diane was stuck at her parents' house. During the nearly three weeks she'd been here she hadn't gone outside at all. Her parents thought she was depressed—which was probably at least partly true—but as far as they knew she'd moved home because of a bad breakup with Steve, a jerk lawyer who'd dumped her with a text message, and because "the whole living-in-the-city thing just wasn't working out."

She shuddered as the memory nudged into her consciousness, but she refused to let her mind fully go there. Denial was her new mantra. Maybe it was a dysfunctional coping mechanism, but it had been working so far; after all, at least she wasn't in a mental institution. She wanted to believe that if she didn't think about what had happened in New York, the experience would eventually vanish, like a bad dream. Or, maybe if she just stayed in bed and hid her head in the darkness under her pillow, like she'd done when she was a kid on days she didn't want to get up to go to school, they wouldn't be able to find her and she would be safe, protected. The flashbacks—in vivid, horrifying detail—were still coming, though, but it had been only a few weeks. Maybe one day she'd wake up and it would all be gone, forgotten completely, as if it had never happened. She couldn't wait for that day.

Sitting at the edge of her bed, leaning over and kneading her scalp with her fingers obsessively, she'd never felt so out of control. She wondered if this was what insanity felt like. She didn't think she was insane, but wasn't that part of the definition of insanity? Didn't all insane people think they were sane? She was definitely *acting* insane—staying in bed all day, neglecting her appearance and hygiene, starving herself, virtually paralyzed by extreme paranoia. She had to admit, when she analyzed her behavior this way, as an outsider would, she didn't seem like a portrait of sanity. While she thought she had a very good reason to be behaving the way she was, if she was insane how could she trust her thoughts? Maybe nothing had happened to her in New York—maybe it seemed like a nightmare because it had been an actual nightmare, or some kind of hallucination. It was true she'd been under a lot of stress lately and had never really adjusted to life in the city. Maybe the breakup with Steve had been the thing that had put her over the edge.

As she continued to rock back and forth, kneading her scalp with her fingertips, she whispered repeatedly, "New York never happened, New York never happened, New York never happened . . ."

Gradually, she started to believe that there was at least some chance that she'd made it all up, had had some kind of psychotic break, which gave her more hope than she'd had in days. Insanity was a good thing. Insanity could be cured. Insanity would mean that she could get through this. If she just pushed herself, if she stopped being the victim, she could snap herself out of this before it was too late and it took over completely.

She went downstairs, apologized to her parents, and ate all the food her mother put in front of her, even asking for seconds. Already she felt energized, convinced she could get through this.

Practically beaming, Barbara said, "I'm so happy you're finally eating."

"You and Dad are right," Diane said. "I can't live my life like this anymore. I need some things at the drugstore. Can I borrow your car?"

"Of course you can, sweetie."

Upstairs, Diane showered—unlike her other showers over the past few weeks, she managed to not see glimpses of that scene from *Psycho*—and then she put on clean clothes. She felt good. *This* felt good. If she could just get to CVS and back without having an attack of paranoia, it would be a great start, something to build on. She needed to prove to herself that the danger wasn't real.

The fear didn't set in until she was about to leave the house. At the front door she was so dizzy she almost lost her balance and had to grab on to the molding on the wall near the front door so she wouldn't fall down.

Her father was nearby and said, "Are you okay?"

"Yeah, I'm fine," Diane said, recovering quickly. "Just tripped on my heels."

She was wearing clogs, with maybe one-inch heels, so this didn't really make sense.

"Maybe I should come with you," Robert Coles said.

"Don't be ridiculous," Diane said, "it's a five-minute drive, maybe less. I'll see you soon."

Barbara came over and said, "Drive carefully."

"Don't worry," Diane said. "I will."

Diane went outside. It was a perfect November day—bright and sunny, about fifty degrees. Most leaves were gone from the trees and there was the smell of mulch in the crisp, cool air. She was enjoying being outdoors for the first time in days so much that she didn't get nervous and paranoid again until she was inside her mom's Ford Fusion. She felt like she was being watched. She looked around quickly in every direction, but that didn't mean they weren't there somewhere. Her heart was racing and she felt extremely dizzy, as if she'd just gotten off a merry-go-round. Her father was probably right—she probably shouldn't be driving a car right now—but she wanted to prove to herself that she could get through this, that this horrible paralyzing fear she'd been experiencing wasn't permanent.

She repeated out loud: "New York never happened, New York never happened, New York never happened, New York never happened. . . ." and she felt better—well, at least she didn't feel like she was going to pass out anymore.

She started the engine and backed out of the driveway onto the quiet, suburban street. Driving away, looking in the rearview mirror, she thought a black SUV, looked like a Lexus, was following her, but then the SUV turned down a side street.

In CVS, Diane hurried to get the things she needed, avoiding making eye contact with anyone. At the checkout line, someone bumped into her from behind and she turned around suddenly, maybe even cocking a fist, and said "Hey."

Then she saw that the person who had bumped her was an elderly woman with a cane, about eighty years old. The old woman could've been one of them, but it wasn't likely.

"Oh, sorry," Diane said. Then she closed her eyes and said, "New York never happened, New York never happened, New York never happened."

When she opened her eyes she saw that the girl working at the checkout counter was looking at her like . . . well, like she was a crazy person, but this was a good thing. Diane wanted to be crazy. If she was crazy, that meant she was safe.

Returning to the car, Diane was barely afraid. Her heart was beating much faster than normal and she felt clammy—especially the back of her neck—but she didn't feel dizzy or wobbly. She was proud of herself for doing so well. She realized a trip to CVS hardly constituted resuming her life, but it was a major step in the right direction. Maybe if, over the next week or so, she left her house every day to take a small trip somewhere—shopping, to the gym, maybe even see a movie— she'd get used to being around strangers again and eventually the fear—and the memories of New York—would vanish completely.

Driving home, she looked once or twice in the rearview mirror to check whether anyone was following her, but her paranoia had subsided significantly. At this point she didn't want to put too much pressure on herself, have unrealistic expectations. She needed to take it day by day and build on what she'd accomplished this afternoon, but it was hard not to fantasize about what a fear-free life in Michigan would be like. Maybe within a month she could move out of her parents' house into her own apartment. She had a lot of friends in the area. She'd fallen out of touch with some of them, and most of them were married, but she'd have people to socialize with. Eventually she'd be ready to date again and she'd meet a good, solid Michigan guy. He'd come from a good family and have a good job and, most important, he'd be normal. The idea of settling down in the suburbs used to terrify Diane; nothing had seemed more terrifying than living her parents' life. But now that was all she wanted—an easy, normal, safe life. And, really, was that too much to ask for?

She pulled into the driveway and parked in front of the garage. As she got out of the car she was absorbed in the fantasy of her future life—marriage, kids, a big house. It wouldn't be such an awful life. It would be a good, safe, easy life, and that was all that mattered to her now. She was through feeling that she had to be in the center of the action, that she had to be in a big city, going to the newest, hippest bars and restaurants and attending club openings and wine tastings. She didn't even like going to wine tastings, acting so self-important, having to think of new adjectives to describe the wine to whomever she was with. She was through trying to impress, being fake. She just wanted to go back to who she was—a simple, happy, laid-back Michigan girl. It would be so relieving to not feel like she had to go somewhere or transform into someone else in order to be happy. She could be happy being who she was and where she was. She could be happy right here, right now.

She was starting to smile, feeling better than she had in weeks, when she heard movement behind her. In the next instant there was a sharp pain in her head and she was falling forward into the darkness, and her mother was telling her to get her head out from under the pillow, it was time to get up to go to school, but she wouldn't go to school.

She would stay in the darkness forever.

TWO

In high school Simon Burns didn't fit in with any crowd. He wasn't a jock, a math geek, a theater person, a burnout, or a dork, and he didn't dress in trendy clothes, or drive a sports car, or date the hottest girls. He was just a nice, average, normal guy. His friends liked him, but most people didn't have an opinion of him one way or another. On most days, when he was walking through the hallways or having lunch in the cafeteria, he felt invisible and was convinced that if he actually disappeared most people wouldn't have cared or even noticed.

Now, as a thirty-nine-year-old stay-at-home dad, hanging out with his three-year-old son Jeremy on the playgrounds of Manhattan's Upper West Side, Simon had the total opposite experience. It seemed as if the moms and babysitters couldn't stop staring at him. Even when he didn't see them looking at him he could *feel* their gazes, as if their eyes were projecting lasers that were boring into his skin. Sometimes Simon enjoyed the attention—hey, what married guy in his late thirties didn't like an ego boost every once in a while?—but most of the time the staring and smiling felt intrusive, so he'd started listening to music on his iPod and wearing dark sunglasses, trying to appear as standoffish as possible.

On an early November afternoon on the playground near 101st Street in Riverside Park, Simon was in his usual spot, on a bench near the entrance, trying to be incognito. He was wearing his shades, and on his iPod the Decemberists were into "The Hazards of Love." There were ten or so women in the playground—most Simon recognized from previous playground visits—and they were all checking him out.

Jeremy started playing with a taller boy, probably a year or two older than him. Simon hadn't seen the boy before, but Jeremy seemed to like him a lot. They were chasing each other around, playing some sort of tag game.

At one point, Jeremy came over to Simon and gave him a big hug and said, "I love you, Daddy."

"I love you too, kiddo," Simon said.

Jeremy put his hands over his ears, and Simon realized he'd spoken louder than he'd intended because of the blasting music. They laughed together, and then Jeremy went back to playing with his friend.

Simon's adjustment to being a stay-at-home dad had been an adjustment, to say the least. Though he still missed his career in advertising and harbored resentment about the way things had gone down at the job from which he'd been terminated, at times like this he felt incredibly lucky. How many dads got to spend so much quality time with their children? This was something special, and he never wanted to forget how great this felt.

Simon looked to his left and saw Jeremy's new friend's mother looking at him and smiling. She was an attractive woman with dark wavy hair, maybe in her midthirties, a few years younger than Simon. Though she was sitting about ten feet away from him, he could smell her strong perfume and knew she'd recently had a cup of dark-roasted coffee.

Other times over the past few weeks, when women smiled at him, Simon smiled back politely. Usually this had been a mistake, because the women often assumed this meant he was interested and started hitting on him. So, not wanting to encourage her at all, Simon remained blank-faced, not acknowledging her in any way, and continued to listen to the Decemberists and watch Jeremy play.

"Excuse me."

Well, that had backfired. The woman was standing next to him.

Without taking out the earbuds, Simon said, "Yes."

"Sorry, I don't want to disturb you," she said. "I just wanted to say hello."

Simon probably shouldn't have been able to hear her so clearly over the music.

"Hi," he said.

"Our children, they play so well together," the woman said.

She had an accent—something Eastern European, maybe Russian. Her perfume was Marc Jacobs or Lancôme, definitely Lancôme, and he was pretty sure the coffee was from Dunkin' Donuts, not Starbucks.

"Yeah, they do," Simon said.

"Can I join you?" she asked

Simon realized there was a limit to how rude he could be without coming off as being a total jerk, so he said, "Um, okay."

She sat next to him, smiling widely, and said, "I'm Milika."

"Simon," he said hesitantly.

"It's very nice to meet you," she said, looking right at his eyes. Hers were blue and open very wide.

Simon nodded in acknowledgment but didn't say anything.

He was looking straight ahead again when Milika said, "You have a beautiful boy."

Until recently Simon had no idea what beautiful women went through every day, but now he understood exactly how it felt to have his personal space invaded; he just hadn't learned how to deal with it.

"Thank you," he said, without looking at her at all.

Still, he knew she was staring at him. He could feel her gaze.

Then he heard, "Can you turn off your music, please?"

"Sorry," Simon said, "is it bothering you?"

"No," she said. "I just want to talk to you, that's all."

She still had a toothy smile and was giving him that look. He'd seen the look lately from other women around the city. It was the longing, desperate, come-hither look that rock stars get from their groupies.

Simon didn't know what else to do, so he turned down the volume.

"You know, you're a very attractive man," Milika said.

"Thank you." Simon was a little taken aback. Women had been checking him out lately, but few had actually started conversations.

"I'm from Serbia," she said. "I'm divorced."

"I'm from America," Simon said. "I'm married."

Just to emphasize that he was very married and very unavailable, Simon placed his left hand on his lap, in an obvious way, so the woman could see his thick gold wedding band.

This apparently had no effect on Milika either. "You know, you have very beautiful, deep voice," she said.

It was true Simon's voice had gotten deeper. His voice had always been deepish, but the other day he'd realized he could do a practically dead-on James Earl Jones impression.

She added, "You should be in movies. You know the voice of the man who speaks about movies, in commercials, you know?"

"Oh, voiceovers," Simon said. "Maybe it's not such a bad idea. I mean, since I'm unemployed."

So now he'd told this woman he was married, and he was unemployed. What else could he possibly do to turn her off? Tell her he had syphilis?

"That's good you're unemployed," she said. "It means you have a lot of time to, you know, do things with your son, and maybe with other people too."

The way she was looking at Simon, she might as well have been screaming, *I want your sexy body right now!*

"Look, I'm trying my hardest to be polite," Simon said. "But there seems to be a very big misunder—"

She shifted closer to him on the bench and said, "I love your eyes. So many people, their eyes say nothing, but your eyes, they tell a story. A story of a very handsome man who meets a pretty woman one day in park. They talk a little bit, get to know each other, and then one day they—"

Simon stood and said, "It was very nice meeting you."

He wished he hadn't said that; it would only encourage her.

He went over to Jeremy, who was trying to crawl up the slide, and said, "We have to go now."

"I don't want to," he said.

"We're going," Simon said, trying to avoid raising his voice or losing his temper, as he knew how dangerous that could be.

Thankfully Jeremy got the point that Simon was serious and

didn't put up much of a fuss. He finished crawling up to the top of the slide and slid down on his stomach, and then Simon grabbed his hand and led him toward the stroller near the bench.

Milika's son had run over to her and—although this conversation was taking place about twenty feet away—Simon could hear him saying to her, "Why did he have to leave?" and Milika said to him, "I don't know, sweetie."

Like a snotty, aloof supermodel, Simon purposely didn't make any eye contact with Milika, pretending she wasn't there. But he heard her, walking toward him, her heels click-clacking, and her perfume was so strong, it was nearly overwhelming.

Then he heard, "Maybe you want to give me your number, no? We make a play date for the children."

"I'm sorry, we don't live in the area," Simon said.

"Yes, we do," Jeremy said.

"Okay, time to get into the stroller now, kiddo."

Leaving the playground, heading toward Riverside Drive, Jeremy asked, "How come we couldn't stay? I wanted to stay, Daddy."

"We stayed for as long as we could," Simon said.

"No, we didn't. You always make me go home too soon."

It was true; Simon had left other playgrounds lately when random women had started hitting on him.

"How about some ice cream?" Simon asked.

"Yay, ice cream," Jeremy said.

Score another point for the ice cream distraction strategy. Simon felt bad for evading Jeremy's questioning, but what choice did he have? He didn't want to lie to his son, but the truth was out of the question. After all, how was he supposed to explain to a three-year-old boy that his daddy was a werewolf?

*   *   *

If someone had told Simon just last month that he would be hiding his werewolfness, or werewolfosity, or whatever it was called, from his family and the rest of the world, he never would have believed it. The thought of werewolves actually existing had seemed insane, and even now there were times when the reality that he had actually become one seemed impossible to comprehend. He'd wake up in the middle of the night, thinking everything was fine, that he was just a normal Manhattan husband and dad, and then he'd remind himself, *You're a werewolf now*, and he'd shudder as he relived the horror of everything that had happened to him over the past several weeks, the way his body and perceptions had changed, how it had felt to actually transform, physically and mentally, into a half-man, half-wolf creature, and, most horrific of all, how it had felt to kill with his bare hands. Or, well, bare *claws*.

Simon took Jeremy to the Tasti D-Lite on Broadway and Eighty-sixth. Jeremy had a cone of Nutella and Simon had a double cone of Cookies 'n' Cream. Though Simon could have engulfed the ice cream and cone in a couple of bites, he forced himself to eat at a normal pace. Lately it took a lot of discipline not to scarf down his food. Sometimes he slacked off, letting his mind wander, and suddenly his food was gone. Still, he finished the ice cream well before Jeremy finished his. Unfortunately, the carbs didn't do much for Simon's appetite. He was dying to get home and cook up some burgers or, better yet, steaks.

When they got back to their apartment on Columbus and Eighty-ninth, Simon parked Jeremy in front of the electronic babysitter to watch *The Wiggles*. Although Jeremy had probably seen the episode dozens of times—even Simon knew most of it verbatim—he was as happy as only a three-year-old could be. Meanwhile, Simon satisfied his craving by cooking up four hamburgers. Though he preferred his burgers well-done, the smell of the cooking meat was so enticing that he couldn't resist snatching one from the grill when it was rare, and he polished the others off when they were about medium rare—medium, at best.

Simon was content—for the moment. Lately it had been nearly impossible to satisfy his appetite completely, and even when he was going about his normal daily routine—taking care of Jeremy, doing chores, running in the park—thoughts of his next high-protein meal always seemed prominent.

"Hello."

Simon was in the kitchen, cleaning the grill, and Alison had startled him.

"Hey," Simon said, immediately recognizing his wife's particularly pungent end-of-the-day natural scent, mingling with her perfume and deodorant. She was in a navy work suit, heels, and a nice pearl necklace. She worked as a sales rep for a large pharmaceutical company called Primus, currently working on selling a new oral contraceptive, and she always had to look her best for her meetings with physicians. Meanwhile Simon was in his usual daddy outfit—jeans and an old gray hoodie.

"What a day," Alison said. "I think I've been running around nonstop since seven A.M."

Since Simon had lost his job, Alison had been the financial provider for the family. She worked nine to five, though some days she left earlier and came home later, especially on days she entertained doctor clients—taking them out to fine restaurants, sporting events, and Broadway shows.

Unable to block out the wonderful aroma of her body after a long workday, Simon said, "I know, I can tell." He imagined grabbing her, putting her on the countertop, then pulling up her dress and ravishing her. If fantasies of steak and sausage were the main behavioral symptom of Simon's being a werewolf, thoughts of sex, particularly with Alison, were a close second. If it were up to him, he would be all over her all the time, making love to her multiple times every night. Sounded like the perfect marital situation except for one small problem—the last time he'd tried to seduce her, he'd nearly transformed into a werewolf and mauled her to death, so—at least until he figured out how to control his transformations—actual sex was out of the question.

"What can you tell?" Alison asked.

Simon was lost, distracted.

"How can I tell what?"

"You said you can tell."

"I did?"

"Are you okay?"

"Yeah." Simon realized he was actually panting. "I guess I, um, didn't hear you come in, that's all."

It was a lame excuse but the best he could come up with. He tried to strike the sexual thoughts from his consciousness, but it was nearly impossible. They say that men think about sex at least once every two minutes—well, for Simon it was probably every thirty seconds. Complicating things, he just couldn't seem to control his brain the way he used to. Sometimes he felt like a puppet, as if someone had taken control of his behavior and actions and he was just a defenseless observer.

Alison came over and kissed him quickly on the lips—he couldn't help getting a little aroused—and then her gaze darted around the kitchen and through the pass-through toward the living room and dining room.

"The apartment looks great," she said. "Thanks for cleaning up."

"No problem," he said.   ⌐

He purposely hadn't turned toward her and the bulge in his jeans was pressed up against the stove, hidden from her view.

"Hello, sweetie, Mommy's home," Alison said to Jeremy as she walked away, into the living room.

Simon knew he couldn't keep the truth a secret forever, and that this period of calm in his life was a last gasp that wouldn't, *couldn't* last forever. The tension was building, like a rubber band pulled to its extreme, and it was only a matter of time until everything went to hell all over again.

A fter dinner, as per their routine lately, Simon let Alison have some alone time with Jeremy. She'd had mixed emotions about working full-time indefinitely, and though she'd adjusted to her role and claimed she was happy, Simon knew that she still felt bad about the situation, and he didn't want her to feel like she was missing out.

While Alison played with Jeremy in his room, Simon, feeling pent up, was dying to go for a long run in the park. But he'd been trying to resist his animalistic urges lately, so he did maybe a hundred push-ups to relieve at least some of his bottled-up energy, and then he went online on his laptop and did some job hunting.

Although he knew that finding work was the least of his problems at the moment, and he doubted he was capable of starting a new job what with all the upheaval in his life lately, he still browsed want ads and corresponded with headhunters regularly. The search for work was a habit, but also a fantasy. He wanted to believe that if he could just get a job, everything would be okay, and the rest of his life would miraculously revert to normal. Simon checked Monster and a few other websites, but he wasn't particularly hopeful about anything. The job market in advertising was tough, especially for a thirty-nine-year-old at middle management level. After tweaking his LinkedIn profile and sending a couple of follow-up e-mails to headhunters who hadn't gotten back to him or had simply lost interest, he got frustrated and watched some TV—*The Rachel Maddow Show*, DVR'd—until Alison came into the living room and plopped down on the couch next to him.

"He's playing alone and I need a break." She let out a deep breath. "What a day. I'm totally zonked and my feet are killing me. Want to give me a foot massage?"

Throughout their marriage Simon had been giving Alison foot massages when they watched TV. But since he'd become a werewolf Alison hadn't asked him for massages, and he was glad because he knew that touching her feet, feeling the warmth of her skin on his fingertips, and breathing in that especially pungent aroma from such a close distance would be way too arousing.

Simon knew Alison could tell he was hesitant. "You don't have to if you don't want to," she said.

He knew if he turned her down it would lead to a big discussion— *Why don't you want to give me foot massages anymore? Don't you want to touch me anymore?*—so he decided to give it a try.

"What do you mean?" he said. "Of course I want to."

When she put her feet up on his lap and he caught the first whiff, he knew he'd made a big mistake. He was already getting turned on. Breathing through a corner of his mouth, he used his thumbs to knead her insteps.

It felt incredible enough; it didn't exactly help the situation when Alison said, "Oh God, that feels so amazing," practically moaning, like they were having sex and she was on the verge of a powerful orgasm.

Like a horny dog, Simon was suddenly aroused, but unlike when he was doing dishes, this time he couldn't hide his excitement.

"Wow, looks like I'm not the only one enjoying this," Alison said.

"Sorry," Simon said, letting go of her feet.

"You don't have to apologize. You're allowed to get turned on by your wife."

Actually he wasn't allowed to get turned on by her. If he got too turned on, he might transform into a werewolf and rip her head open.

"Maybe this isn't such a good idea," he said, shifting away.

"Why?" she said. "Don't you like it?"

Here we go.

"Of course I *like* it," he said. "It has nothing to do with *liking* it."

Alison got up. Simon was relieved that he immediately felt a little less aroused.

"Well, I'm not sure *what* it has to do with," she said. "I mean, I know you have a disorder, and you're going through a lot right now. But I don't get why it has to do with me, why you're afraid to have sex with your own—"

"Can you keep your voice down?" Simon said, gesturing with his jaw toward Jeremy's bedroom. Though Jeremy's room was down the hallway, when he focused he could hear Jeremy playing with his train set, saying, "Choo choo, choo choo . . ."

"He can't hear me," Alison said.

Simon realized this was probably true, as she hadn't been talking particularly loud.

"Look," he said. "The last thing I want is for you to feel offended. But, you know, I'm going through something very difficult right now, and it's going to take time."

"So what has Dr. Levinson been saying about all this?"

Dr. Levinson was a psychiatrist downtown whom Alison had

arranged for Simon to see, but Simon, unbeknownst to Alison, had stopped going after one appointment, knowing the whole thing was a farce and a complete waste of time.

"He says I have lyncanthropic disorder," Simon said.

"I know that, but does he think it's getting any better? Do you still think you're a werewolf?"

Simon shifted uncomfortably, then said, "Yes."

"Does he think you're making any progress at all?"

"Some." Simon was a horrible liar. His mouth was suddenly dry.

"He can't give you any sort of timetable?" Alison asked. "He can't give you a ballpark when—"

"No," Simon said.

Looking frustrated and confused, Alison said, "And you still think if we have sex you'll turn into a—"

"Yes," Simon said.

"And what about the medication? Isn't that supposed to be helping your symptoms?"

Levinson had prescribed Haldol, which is commonly prescribed for schizophrenia and other psychotic disorders. Simon had filled the prescription just in case Alison checked, but he hadn't taken a single pill.

"It's going to be a process," Simon said. "I'm sorry, Al. Believe me, I know how messed up this has all been. I understand why you're getting impatient."

"I'm not impatient," Alison said. "I just wish I wasn't so in the dark."

"I want to tell you more," Simon said. "I want to tell you everything. Believe me, I do. But I can't. That's impossible right now while I'm a . . . I mean, while I'm recovering."

"What does Levinson say about all your changes? How your voice got deeper, and how hairy you are?"

Simon had been shaving his face and trimming the hair on the rest of his body a few times a day—usually when Alison wasn't home—to keep his hair at a seminormal length.

"We haven't discussed it much," he said.

"But it must've come up," she said. "I mean, these are major changes. Does he really think it can all be psychological?"

"Yes," Simon said. "I mean, that's what he's indicated. You know, a mind-over-matter-type thing." Simon was eager to get onto another topic.

"Look, I'm trying not to get in the way of your therapy," Alison said. "I'm trying to give you all the space you need to work on whatever you need to work on. And I don't want to intrude. I mean, I get that there're things you need to work on privately with Dr. Levinson. It's just hard when you . . . I mean when I can't . . ."

Alison's voice trailed off. She was looking away.

Simon went over, put a hand on her shoulder, and said, "Come on, everything's going to be okay." He said this, he noticed, weakly, wishing himself it were true.

"Sorry, I told you I had a really hard day," she said. "I had appointments back-to-back, and I think I lost a big contract. And I haven't been getting enough sleep and I'm not spending enough time with Jeremy and then with everything that's going on with you . . . it just gets a little overwhelming sometimes." She collected herself; she was still upset but she wasn't crying anymore. "I just want things to go back to how they were before you . . . I just want a normal life, with my normal husband. Is that too much to ask?"

Simon wanted that too; she had no idea how badly.

"No," he said. "It isn't."

"I know it's unfair to put so much pressure on you," Alison said. "I'm sorry."

"Stop it," Simon said. "It's not your—"

"Yes, it is," she said. "I know you're trying as hard as you can to fix things, and I know these things take time. I mean, I can't expect dramatic changes overnight."

Thinking that dramatic changes overnight was exactly what he was so terrified of, Simon said, "I just feel bad that I can't give you what you want."

"You mean sex?" Alison said. "Well, I *have* been especially horny lately. Don't worry about me, just worry about yourself, but I'm warning you . . ." Suddenly she looked very serious, but in a sarcastic way. "If we don't start doing it again soon, I'm going to leave you for someone else."

"Oh, really," Simon played along. "And who's that?"

Still pseudoserious, she said, "His name is Toy."

"Oh, really?" Simon was deadpan. "Toy who?"

"Just Toy. He has one name, like Eminem."

Simon smiled. "So does Mr. Toy—"

"Just Toy," Alison said. "No *mister.*"

"Sorry; is Toy-no-*mister* a good-looking guy?"

"No, he looks sort of like . . . a hot dog."

"A hot dog, huh? Sounds very attractive."

"It's not all about looks," she said. "Toy has that extra something, that X factor. Toy's a real stud, actually. He knows what a woman wants and he delivers it every time. And things are just so less complicated with Toy. He's always there for me. He's reliable, dependable—"

"Toy sounds like a very solid guy."

"Oh, yes, Toy is a very, very solid guy."

They continued to appear serious for a few seconds, then at the same moment started laughing. It was great to let loose; it felt as if they hadn't laughed together in months. Life just hadn't been very funny lately.

Suddenly Simon had the urge to kiss his wife, make out with her. He put his arms around her waist, pulled her close, and then as he felt himself starting to get aroused, he pulled back and pushed her away. This killed the lighthearted mood instantly. All of a sudden Alison had the guarded, tense expression that Simon had become accustomed to lately.

"Sorry," Simon said. "I don't know why I—"

"I should get him ready for bed," Alison said, and marched down the hallway to Jeremy's room.

After Alison read Jeremy part of *The Phantom Tollbooth*—Simon, from the living room, could hear her reading clearly—she passed through the living room, not making eye contact with Simon, who was on the rug doing more push-ups, and then she continued to the kitchen, where she opened the fridge and poured herself a glass of water from the Brita pitcher.

Simon finished the set of fifty, not at all winded, and asked, "Sleeping already?"

"Like a baby," Alison said, still not looking at him.

"Wow, you're amazing," he said. "If I tried to put him to sleep he'd still be up."

"That's because you're the fun parent."

The comment was loaded with innuendos. Simon could tell she was angry, sad, bitter, jealous, and resentful because she had to work full-time and he was a stay-at-home dad. But he didn't want to get into a whole discussion about it, knowing it would just lead to more tension and stress.

"I think I'm gonna go for a run now," he said.

Alison gave him a look because he'd told her that the therapy was supposed to be helping him work on the excessive physical energy, another "symptom" of his believing he was a werewolf.

"Dr. Levinson said running's good for me," Simon said. "It relieves stress."

For days he'd been using this lame excuse to explain his excessive need to run.

"If you want to run, run," she said. "I'm so exhausted, I feel like I'm going to pass out." Then in a tone that couldn't have been more deadpan, she added, "Have fun."

She smiled, in a fake, forced way, and went toward the bedroom.

Again, Simon had a foreboding feeling about his marriage, and his life, as he knew things couldn't continue this way indefinitely. Eventually Alison would lose patience with him and his odd behavior and their marriage would be in trouble again, if it wasn't in trouble again already.

Simon was putting on his running shoes—he'd just gotten this pair of hundred-and-fifty-dollar Nikes a week ago but had done so much running the treads were showing serious wear already—when he heard Alison in the bedroom, getting it on with her new lover, Toy. When he honed in some more, he could hear her panting breaths and soft moans. He couldn't blame her for being sexually frustrated; he felt the same way, but it was worse for him because he couldn't relieve himself. He hadn't had an orgasm since he became a werewolf, fearing that even masturbating would lead to a full-blown transformation. One night, while sleeping on the couch, he'd had a dream about Alison—they were outside, maybe on a beach, or in the park, and they started making love—and he woke up, feeling the pains in his extremities and on his face, especially in and around his mouth, that he'd felt before he'd transformed—and he realized that he had a full erection and had almost had a nocturnal emission, but he managed to subdue himself under a cold shower.

Simon could hear Alison's panting getting more rapid; she was whispering to herself, *Oh, God, Oh my God . . .*

One of the worst parts about all of this was that despite what Alison had said, on some level she had to believe that Simon was avoiding contact with her because he didn't want to make love to her, because he wasn't turned on or didn't think she was attractive anymore, which couldn't have been further from the truth. He was dying to attack her, ravish her for hours, for days—just the thought of kissing and touching her was so arousing, it was almost unbearable—but how could he explain to her that he didn't want to touch her anymore because he loved her too much and didn't want to tear her to shreds? She wouldn't believe he was a werewolf until she saw him turn into a werewolf herself, which could cost her her life. Even more frustrating, because he was a werewolf and was exuding a werewolf scent and/or vibe, Alison was obviously more physically attracted to him than ever before, but, for the very reason why she was attracted to him, he couldn't return the affection. It was the Catch-22 to end all Catch-22s.

Just as Alison was starting to come, Simon rushed out of the apartment and didn't bother waiting for the elevator, taking the stairs down nine flights to the lobby.

It was dark at about seven o'clock on this early November evening. Most leaves were gone from the trees, but there were still a lot of dried-up ones whipping around the sidewalks. Simon jogged across Columbus Avenue, toward Central Park, forcing himself to go at a normal pace. He wanted to break into an all-out sprint, but there were people around and if he ran as fast as he could it would definitely cause a scene. Though he hadn't pushed himself fully—fearing that the exertion could cause a transformation—he knew he was capable of running extremely fast.

In the park, he followed the route he'd taken on previous recent nights. He ran downtown on the bridle path, which was pretty much dark, aside from some dim light from the streetlights on Central Park West, but with his exceptional night vision it could have been pitch-dark and he would've had no trouble seeing. On the empty path, Simon let it out a bit, extending his stride and pumping his arms.

While being a werewolf was often terrifying, Simon had to admit it had its positives. He had never felt as healthy as he had these past few weeks. With his improved sight and hearing and overall aware-ness, he could appreciate details of the world that he used to take for granted. He was also much stronger. He'd put on at least five, maybe ten pounds of muscle, and in the gym he was able to lift as much weight as the hard-core muscle heads. He had much more energy—he was never lethargic—and he seemed to heal faster from wounds. The other day he'd cut himself while shaving, and within a half hour the wound was gone completely. But of all the benefits of being a werewolf, the one that Simon appreciated and enjoyed the most was his ability to run exceptionally fast.

Whenever he started running, he felt instantly invigorated and energized. He loved the cold air against his face and how he moved effortlessly, his feet seeming to glide, like a hovercraft, just above the ground. And while he knew this behavior wasn't normal, that it was a symptom of his transformation, he couldn't stop himself from the need to run, to let loose. The need was a part of him now, an instinct, and how was he supposed to resist his instincts, especially the ones that were so pleasurable?

He cut over to his left at full speed, easily clearing a short fence and running along a grassy area. He slowed as he crossed West Drive, where many joggers and bikers were out, and then headed over a footbridge and along a path into the Ramble, the woodsy area in the middle of the park. The Ramble was the closest you could come in Manhattan to being in the wilderness. Old-fashioned lampposts lit up the path and, although he didn't see anyone around, he sensed the presence of humans. He wasn't sure how he was able to sense this, but he just could, and without giving it any additional thought he darted into the woods. It was pitch-black, but he somehow knew where all of the trees, fallen branches, and other obstructions were and how to avoid them. It was as if he had his own built-in GPS.

He continued, zigzagging through the woods, with seemingly boundless energy. Going uphill was as easy as going downhill, and he was experiencing so much joy he didn't want it to ever stop. Now he understood why dogs seemed so unabashedly happy when they ran around unleashed, and why wild horses loved to chase one another, and why dolphins leaped out of the ocean. It was amazing how it felt to exert energy for no reason, just for the sheer joy of it. What he was experiencing was so far beyond the rush from endorphins, the runner's high that some people feel at the peak of strenuous workouts. If people felt the way he did right now from physical activity, the whole world would be addicted to exercise. No one would be able to sit at a desk in an office or on a couch, watching TV or playing video games, and there would be no such thing as obesity. Everyone would be out running fanatically, burning thousands of calories a day.

Simon jumped over a stream and was heading up another hill when he sensed someone nearby. Normally, Simon would have simply altered course to avoid the person, probably using the same mechanism that bears and other wild animals use to avoid humans in the woods, but there was something different about this odor. To confirm his suspicions, Simon stopped and listened closely and breathed deeply, somehow able to decipher the specific scent amid the thousands of scents in Central Park. Sure enough, he was convinced that he wasn't imagining this—there was definitely another werewolf in the Ramble.

Was it Michael, one of the dads Simon had met at the playground in Battery Park last month? Simon had hit it off with Michael and his friends Charlie and Ramon, until he'd found out that Michael was actually a werewolf who wanted to bring the guys into his "pack." Michael had killed at least a few people, and the last time Simon had seen him they'd fought as werewolves on the rooftop of the old brewery in Brooklyn that Michael owned. That was the same night Simon had killed Olivia, the crazed female werewolf who was attacking him and the guys. Simon had been hoping never to see Michael again and to deal with his situation alone, but what if Michael feared that Simon would go to the police?

Well, if Michael *was* stalking him in the Ramble, Simon wanted to make the first move. Without giving it much thought, or considering any possible consequences, he took off in the direction of the scent. It was strongest down toward the lake, where there were also the intense aromas of mulch, algae, and whatever weeds were growing in the water and nearby. Simon could have cornered the werewolf near the shoreline, but he had to alter his course to avoid a couple of humans—a man and a woman—who were in his path. When he picked up the scent again it was fainter, and he knew the werewolf had probably realized that Simon had caught on to him—it was definitely a male werewolf; the odor was particularly pungent—and was probably sprinting away, toward the center of the park. Simon increased his speed as well, going faster than he had all evening, practically gliding above the rugged ground. He didn't seem to be closing the gap very much, though, if at all, and then he reached the park's East Drive and he had to reduce his speed to a normal jogger's pace as there were many people around.

Simon stopped at the edge of the road, trying to pick up the scent. A family of tourists—they looked European—were passing by in a horse-drawn carriage, gazing at him with wide-eyed expressions, probably wondering why this scruffy-faced man was looking around frantically in every which direction. There were so many human scents in the area that Simon found it extremely difficult to hone in on the scent he was pursuing. He thought it was coming from down-town, but it was so faint now, it had almost vanished, and then it set in that it was too late.

The werewolf was gone.

THREE

Almost every night when NYPD homicide detective Geri Rodriguez got off work, usually at one or two in the morning, she went to the Midnight Express diner on Tenth Avenue in Hell's Kitchen, around the corner from her apartment on West Forty-eighth, and sat at the counter and had black coffee, a BLT, and a bowl of split pea soup. The guy who worked at the counter, Carlos, was Puerto Rican like Geri and usually asked her a couple of questions in Spanglish—Catch any *banditos esta noche*? Still keeping *la ciudad* safe?—then left her alone. Most customers left her alone too. Though Geri was pretty and petite—she claimed she was five two, but was actually barely five one—most guys picked up on the "don't mess with me, I'm a cop" vibe that, after twelve years on the force, three as a homicide detective, she'd learned to exude effortlessly. So she'd just

eat her food, read the *Post* or *News* if someone had left a copy, and be
on her way.

But tonight when the two drunk club kids, both maybe twenty
years old, came in, she had a feeling this wouldn't be an uninterrupted meal.

Sure enough, as the kids, reeking of alcohol, were passing by
behind her, the skinny black one leaned in close and said, "Waitin'
for me all night, right, baby?" causing his Asian friend to burst out
laughing. Then they sat directly next to her, even though she'd been
the only one sitting at the counter and all the stools were free.

Geri looked at Carlos, but of course Carlos wasn't going to say
anything; why would he jump in to protect a cop? To Carlos, this was
just theater, something to hang back and watch, and make a boring
work night a little more interesting. Two drunk kids were harassing
a cop, a *female* cop; he probably couldn't wait to see what happened
next.

Geri had already had a bad day. Her investigation of a murder in
Washington Heights was going nowhere, and a potential witness, a
homeless man, had spit in her face during questioning, and she'd had
to spend two hours getting screened for TB, so the last thing she
needed now was trouble from a couple of drunk punks. She ignored
the kids, taking a bite of her BLT, hoping they would do the smart
thing and leave her alone.

But no luck there. In her peripheral vision, Geri could see the
black kid looking right at her. Then she heard him whisper to his
friend something that included the word *nasty* and his friend say,
"Go 'head" and "Just do it, man"—and then the black kid said to her,
"Yo, how's that soup, bitch?"

Geri looked right at him for the first time. The kid was smiling
in a cocky way—yeah, he thought he was a player all right. Eyes glassy,

bloodshot—definitely drunk, probably high too. The friend, egging him on, was also grinning.

Geri held his gaze for a long time, then said, "The soup's great. How's your boyfriend?"

The black kid stopped grinning, suddenly looking angry, shown up, but his friend was laughing, in a fake way, saying, "Ha, ha, ha. Damn. Oh, man. Oh . . . Oh."

The black kid wasn't laughing, though. "You got a mouth on you, don't you, bitch?" he said. "That's okay, I like that. Dirty mouth's better than a clean mouth any day. Lot more fun anyway."

Geri looked over at Carlos, who was still near the other end of the counter, relaxed, watching, like he could've been munching from a bag of popcorn.

"I'd suggest you get the hell out of here now," Geri said.

The Asian kid laughed harder, as if saying to his friend, *You gonna take that?*

"You suggest?" the black kid said. "Ha, ha, ha, that's funny. You know what I suggest? I suggest you shut your bitch-ass mouth 'less you down on your knees, looking up at me, like you're gonna be later."

Geri glared at him and said, "This is the last time I'm telling you."

The Asian kid, still laughing, said, "Check it out, J, she's your teacher now. She's gonna make you stay late after class."

"You my teacher now, bitch?" the black kid said, putting a hand on Geri's ass. "You ready to bend over your desk for me?"

On *me*, Geri was off the stool and had grabbed his hand, twisting it behind his back all the way up to his neck, and then forcing his head, face down, into her still-hot bowl of split pea soup.

Over the kid's muted wailing, Geri said, "I think you're the one who's gonna be doing the bending over tonight."

The Asian kid got off his stool, ready to help his friend, when Geri angled her hip out so he could see her holster and her gun inside it. The Asian kid's eyes widened and he backed away. He said, "Yo, man, she's a cop."

Geri said to the groaning black kid, "You're gonna keep your hands off women, right?"

The kid was gargling into the soup. Geri knew she was going too far, but she'd had a bad day and, somehow, this was making her feel better.

"I can't hear you," she said, pushing his face down harder.

Now the gargles were more agonized; he was probably straining to breathe. Geri lifted his head.

"Crazy bitch," he said. "I got rights."

She forced his head back into the soup, then lifted it again.

"Okay, okay, whatever, just chill," he said. "Just chill."

Geri gave him one last taste of the soup, then yanked him back away from the counter and let go of him. He stumbled backward, wiping soup from his face with his fingers.

"I'm gonna sue your ass," he said.

"You've got ten seconds to get out of here," Geri said, "or you can talk about your lawsuit with the judge when you're being arraigned tonight."

She wasn't planning to bring him in; she just wanted to scare him.

He looked like he was about to go after Geri. She knew it was just for show—drunk punks were usually all talk, no action—but she was ready to defend herself just in case.

But then the Asian kid grabbed his friend and said, "J, c'mon, let's just get outta here, man."

"Let go of me, man," he said, as if trying to break free, to go after Geri. Yeah, right.

"J," the Asian kid said.

After a long icy glare, the black kid said, "C'mon," and then the two kids left the diner.

Unfazed, Geri continued eating her BLT. Carlos cleaned up the spilled soup and brought a fresh bowl without saying a word.

Later, when Geri was leaving the diner, and while she was walking back to her apartment, and especially entering the walk-up, no-doorman building, she looked back over her shoulder to see if the kids were following her. She didn't think they'd be looking for any more trouble, but she knew from experience that making assumptions about people was always a bad idea. She just hated that she was in this position, that she had to be concerned, but that was just the way it was. She was a cop, yeah, but she was still a woman.

In her apartment, while she was bolting her door and pulling down the security bar, her cats came over and were purring and meowing, rubbing against her legs.

"Mommy's home," Geri said, flicking on the light.

The cats were Havana Brown males with chocolate coats, so she'd named them Willy and Wonka.

"How you guys doing?" she said, reaching down and rubbing them under their necks. "Miss me?"

Geri wasn't a cat person. She'd gotten them only because there had been a mouse problem in the building, and the brother of a cop she knew told her about a friend in the Village who had some cats to give away. Geri didn't think it was fair to have just one, with her usually gone all day, so she'd gotten the pair.

At first Geri had regretted getting them, hating having to change the litter and chase them out of her bed at night, but she'd gotten used to having the little guys around. They were good cats and didn't demand much from her. They liked to be fed, petted once in a while, and then they left her alone. As Geri sometimes joked to her friends, "They're the perfect men."

Actually the cats had been the only males in Geri's apartment lately, but she didn't have a problem with that. Unlike some single women who were afraid to be alone, Geri was perfectly content not being in a relationship, and she intended to keep it that way. At work, she used to get hit on all the time by cops, lawyers, prosecutors, even judges. Geri didn't want to get involved with anyone she worked with, so she blew off all the guys, and then rumors started going around that she was a dyke. Men and their egos—if a woman wasn't interested she had to be gay, right? But Geri didn't mind. If she told people she was straight, she'd be hit on constantly. Besides, the gay rumor gave her more time to focus on her true love—police work.

Geri came from a family of female cops. Her grandmother, God rest her, was a prison guard at Wallkill in the sixties and seventies, and then her mother was a cop in the Bronx, where Geri grew up. Geri always knew she'd be a cop one day, but she had bigger dreams—to be a detective. She'd seen the glass ceiling hold her mother and grandmother back, but she was determined not to let it stop her. She worked her ass off, working OT, determined to be the best patrol cop in the city, and volunteered to work in narcotics. Three years ago, when she'd been just thirty-four, she'd made detective at the 34th Precinct, and then last year she had moved up a grade to homicide detective at Manhattan North.

Geri's job was her husband. Even when she wasn't working, she was thinking about work or dreaming about it. When she was in the middle of a case nothing else mattered; it took over her whole life. She barely had time to sleep or eat, so how was a man supposed to fit in?

After Geri fed Willy and Wonka and gave them fresh water, she got ready for bed. Washing her face—she didn't wear much makeup; just lipstick, a little blush—she had an unsettled feeling that she got when she had unfinished business. Was it the incident with the kids at the diner? No, they were just a couple of punks and Geri wasn't concerned about them. The Washington Heights murder case was frustrating because she hadn't been able to get Carlita Morales, the only known witness, to cooperate with the investigation, but she didn't think that was it either. Then, when she got in bed, it hit her— it was the phone conversation she'd had earlier with Robert Mangel from the 19th Precinct, the detective in charge of the Olivia Becker disappearance case.

Olivia Becker was a successful thirty-eight-year-old woman who lived on the Upper East Side and owned her own graphic design company in midtown. About three weeks ago her co-workers had reported that after "behaving oddly" at work one afternoon, she hadn't shown up the next day and they'd been unable to contact her. The police had opened an official missing-person investigation but hadn't made any progress in the case. There was no credit card activity and no evidence that she'd left the city. After that afternoon at work, there was a report that she'd been seen at a bar on Thirty-fifth Street, and there was a possible sighting downtown, near Chinatown, but aside from that it was as if she'd disappeared.

Geri wasn't working the case, and it probably wouldn't have caught her interest at all if it weren't for one detail. A couple of weeks before she'd disappeared, Becker had started dating a guy named Michael Hartman whom Geri had questioned as a possible witness in a couple of strange wolf-related deaths in the New York City area. Hartman wasn't a suspect in the cases, but he had given an alibi to a person of interest in the case, Simon Burns, an ad exec who lived on

Columbus Avenue on the Upper West Side. While the police had cleared Hartman in Becker's disappearance, his possible involvement had caught Geri's attention. The way she saw it, she'd questioned this guy and then a few days later his girlfriend disappeared. Coincidence? Maybe, but it still made Geri feel unsettled.

Getting updates on the investigation hadn't been easy. The first time she'd contacted Mangel, he hadn't even bothered to return her call. He could've been busy, hadn't gotten around to calling back, or it had slipped his mind. Or maybe he had a problem with another detective, especially a female detective, moving in on his turf. Not that Geri was actually moving in, but still.

A couple of days later, after Geri had left Mangel another message, he finally called back and they spoke for the first time. Geri mentioned that she'd spoken to Hartman recently and filled Mangel in briefly about the wolf deaths, and Mangel said, "Wolf deaths?"

"Yeah," Geri said. "Remember that case last year? A Manhattan man was found mauled to death in Brooklyn?"

"No, I don't remember." Geri couldn't tell whether Mangel sounded distracted, sarcastic, annoyed, or all of the above.

"Then I was involved in another investigation," Geri said. "A man in northwest Jersey was found mauled to death outside his house. There was a person of interest in the case living in Manhattan, and Hartman was his main alibi."

"Mm-hm," Mangel said.

"Is there a better time to have this conversation?" Geri asked, not bothering to hide that she was pissed off.

"I don't get what you want me to do." Now Mangel was definitely annoyed. "Hartman isn't a suspect in the Olivia Becker case. He isn't a person of interest either."

"So what do you think happened to Becker?"

"The investigation is ongoing," Mangel said. "But if you're asking me to guess, I think she killed herself. She was unstable, had been acting bizarrely before her death."

"So where's the body?"

"I said the investigation is ongoing," Mangel said. "Is there anything else, because I'm kind of in a hurry now?"

"Yeah, can you let me know if there are any new developments?" Geri said.

"I'll be sure to do that," Mangel said. If he was trying to hide the sarcasm in his voice, he wasn't doing a very good job.

Over the next couple of weeks, Geri continued to follow the progress of the Becker investigation. She didn't have any further contact with Mangel, but through the department grapevine she heard that the police didn't have any major new leads in the case. There weren't any stories in the papers, or even online, and investigators were sticking to the theory that Olivia Becker had committed suicide. Geri wasn't satisfied, though. She couldn't shake a feeling that something was off. A happy, successful woman suddenly starts acting bizarrely and kills herself? Yeah, people sometimes have sudden psychotic breaks, but there's usually a life event that triggers it, like a divorce or getting fired. What was Becker's life event? She'd apparently been happy and successful with no history of mental illness. And why had Hartman been dismissed as a suspect? If they'd been dating seriously, at least he should have been able to supply what the life event could have been that had triggered Becker's sudden meltdown. Geri wasn't doubting whether Mangel was a competent detective. She was sure there must've been a good reason why he wasn't focusing on Hartman. Still, she wanted to know what Hartman's alibi was for the night Becker had disappeared, and if this were her case she would have at least explored whether there was any connection to any of the wolf killings. While Geri understood that none of this was really her business, that didn't stop her from wanting to know the details. God knew some parts of her life weren't perfect, but when it came to police work, she was an obsessive control freak.

So Geri kept pursuing Mangel. He hadn't returned a couple of her recent calls, but she had gotten through today. She asked him about the case and he said, "We're on it." When she pressed for details, he wouldn't give her anything substantial and then pretty much hung up on her.

Yeah, it was definitely the call to Mangel and the Olivia Becker case that was keeping her awake. The only thing Geri hated more than getting dissed was being kept in the dark. Geri had a feeling that Mangel wasn't "on" anything. After three weeks, the leads had probably gone cold, and he was willing to accept the likelihood of the theory that Olivia had committed suicide. While it was certainly possible that she had killed herself, Hartman's connection to the case still bothered Geri, and she knew she wouldn't have an uninterrupted night's sleep till she got some answers.

"You shouldn't'a put his head in the pea soup," Geri's partner, Detective Shawn Phillips, said to her.

They were in an unmarked black Charger, Geri driving them up to Washington Heights. Geri and Shawn were opposites in practically every way. He was a large black man—six five and over three hundred pounds—who had played college football at Rutgers and now lived with his wife and two kids in Queens. When they were together it looked like Shawn could squash Geri, and he probably could, but when it came to detective work Geri always took the lead, and Shawn was fine with it; he preferred being in the background. While Geri was emotional and always spoke her mind, Shawn was cool and quiet and rarely lost his temper. When they did the "good cop, bad cop" routine, Geri was always the bad cop.

"So what was I supposed to do?" Geri said. "Let a couple of punks molest me in public?"

"I thought only one of them grabbed you," Shawn said.

"One or two, what difference does it make?" Geri said, going along Fort Washington Avenue, under the overpass to the GW Bridge.

"Yeah," Shawn said, "but you provoked them."

Geri felt confused. "You're kidding me, right?"

"I'm just saying," Shawn said. "I mean based on what you're saying to me, I don't think putting his head in the pea soup was the right way to go."

"So what was I supposed to do?" Geri said. "Just sit there calmly and smile and go, 'Excuse me, would you please remove your hand from my ass and leave the diner?' Give me a break."

"What if somebody had a camera?" Shawn said. "What if it wound up on TV?"

"Nobody had a camera," Geri said.

"You don't know that," Shawn said. "These days, everybody has a camera, man. Anybody with a phone can put you on YouTube."

"There was nobody else in the diner."

"What about the guys in the kitchen? Or what about the security camera? You think that wasn't caught on film? You want to see yourself on the ten o'clock news? Or, wait, I got the headline in the *Post* . . . COP O'SOUP." Shawn laughed. "Cop O'Soup, get it? That's funny, right?"

"No, it's not funny," Geri said, hitting the gas to make a light.

"I'm just saying," Shawn said. "Sometimes you gotta think of all the consequences before you act."

At the next light she braked hard, and she and Shawn jerked forward a little.

"Okay, let's just drop it," Geri said, partly because she didn't like how Shawn was judging her, and partly because she knew he was right.

"Oooh, somebody's testy," Shawn said. "What's going on with you anyway?"

Geri didn't feel like answering.

They didn't speak again till they got to the apartment building on 184th Street where Carlita Morales lived, and Geri said, "You don't have to come."

"What," Shawn said, "you gonna leave me in the car like a dog? Keep the window open a crack so I can breathe?"

Shawn smiled; Geri didn't.

Together they went over to the tenement and buzzed Morales's apartment. They had already spoken to her a couple of times but were hoping the third time was a charm and she'd give them some useful information. There had been violence in the neighborhood lately by a Dominican gang called DDP—Dominicans Don't Play—and the shooting the other night was almost certainly drug-related as the victim, Orlando Rojas, had had a long rap sheet with multiple arrests for dealing and possession. It wasn't surprising that Morales didn't want to talk—not very many people wanted to get involved in ratting out drug dealers—but Geri still hoped she could wear her down.

"*Si?*"

The visit was unscheduled, which was probably why Morales had bothered to answer her intercom.

"Policia, Detectivos Rodriguez y Phillips."

Now Morales probably regretted answering the intercom big-time.

There was no reply. Geri was about to ring again when Morales buzzed them in.

On the second floor of the tenement Morales—heavyset, in her fifties, with bushy gray and black hair—was standing in front of the door to her apartment when Geri and Shawn arrived on the landing.

"I told you, *no se nada*."

"Cálmate, cálmate," Geri said. "We just have a few more questions for you."

"Last time you had a few more questions," Morales said. "How many times're you gonna have a few more questions?"

Thinking, *Till you start talking*, Geri said, "I promise, it won't take long. Can we come in?"

Though she didn't exactly seem happy about it, Morales let them into her apartment. It was a studio and, like the last time they had been there, it was a mess—dishes piled in the kitchen, stuff on the floor and the table. The TV was blasting *The View*.

"Que quieres? Ya te dijo todo."

"English, please," Geri said.

At their previous visit, yesterday afternoon, Geri had asked Morales to speak in English so Shawn, who didn't speak much Spanish, could follow.

"I told you everything," Morales said. "You're just wasting your time."

"You didn't give us a description of the shooter," Geri said.

"That's 'cause I didn't see the shooter. Seriously, how many times're we gonna have to do this, 'cause it's starting to piss me off? I'm busy. I got work to do today."

Geri looked toward the TV and gave Morales a look as if saying, *That's work?* Shawn had the same expression.

"Seriously," Morales said. "I don't got time for this."

"Can we sit down?" Geri asked.

"No," Morales said.

"It's okay, we don't gotta sit," Shawn said. "Standing burns more calories anyway, right?"

"All right, look," Geri said to Morales. "You were there. You made the 911 call. You told the operator that you witnessed a shooting—"

"I told you, I made a mistake when I said that," Morales said. "When I got there the guy was already shot."

"Or maybe when the cops came you decided to change your story," Geri said. "Figured, *Do I really wanna get in the middle of somethin' like this?* But let me be honest with you right now, okay? Whoever the shooter is, he or she—I'm assuming it's a he—knows what's going on. This guy shot somebody, and if he thinks you saw him he's not gonna forget about it. If he doesn't know you've been talking to us, he's gonna find out you've been talking to us, and he's gonna start making assumptions, know what I mean? Even if you didn't ID him, he'll *think* you ID'd him, so for you it's the same difference. You have family in the area, right?"

Morales, distracted and terrified and a little dazed—Geri knew she was getting through to her—didn't answer.

"She's asking you about your family," Shawn said, to jolt her out of it.

"Yes, my whole family's in the city," Morales said. "I told you that yesterday."

"So I don't have to connect the dots for you, do I?" Geri said. "If, as we suspect, this is DDP-related, I'm sure you've heard how brutal they can be, how ruthless, how . . ." Geri tried to come up with another word to scare the crap out of Morales, but went with, "You know what I'm talking about, right? So the question you gotta ask yourself is how you'll feel if somebody in your family gets hurt. Because, like I said, they could hurt someone anyway, even if you don't say a word to us. But if you help us out, we can get this guy, take him off the street before he has a chance to hurt anyone you love."

Geri furrowed her eyebrows to show how serious and dangerous the situation was, but she hoped she wasn't overdoing it, that it didn't seem like an act to get her to talk.

"And what about his friends?" Morales asked. "You gonna take them off the street too?"

"I thought you didn't see anything," Geri said.

"I didn't," Morales said quickly. "I'm just saying even if I did see something and you got him off the street, that doesn't mean I'd be safe."

"Him?" Geri asked.

"*Sabes lo que quiero decir,*" Morales said.

"What's she sayin'?" Shawn asked.

"If you saw him," Geri said, "that means he probably saw you."

"I know what you're doing," Morales said. "You're just trying to scare me."

"You're right, we are trying to scare you," Geri said, "but that's because you're in danger. I guarantee you if this guy knows you saw him, he'll come after you. Yeah, he might not be the only threat, but chances are he's just concerned about saving his own ass. It's doubtful anyone else in DDP cares about you, and the NYPD will do its very best to protect you from any threat that might materialize, including providing you with twenty-four-hour police protection. But we can only help you if you cooperate."

"Well, I'm not cooperating," Morales said, "'cause I told you everything I know and I don't know nothing else. So all you're doing right now is wasting your time."

Geri and Shawn exchanged looks, as if saying to each other, *Well, at least we tried.* They'd been through this act so many times, they had it down pat.

Then Geri said to Morales, "Fine, you want us to go, we'll go. But the last thing I'll say is if, God forbid, something does happen to somebody you love, then you're gonna have to live with your decision. Take it from me, somebody who's seen lots of people in your situation—talking is a lot better than not talking. At least when you talk you can live with yourself after." After giving Morales a long, serious glare—she deserved an Academy Award for this—she headed toward the door and Shawn followed her.

Sure enough, just as she was turning the handle, she heard:

"All right."

Geri smiled slightly, not letting Morales see, then turned back toward her.

"Okay, whatever, I'll tell you everything." Morales looked and sounded like she was about to cry. "But you better get the son of a bitch—fast."

They sat with Morales and finally got a full account of what had transpired the other night. Morales had been about to enter her building when she'd heard a gunshot. She'd seen the victim on the sidewalk and a man—in his early twenties, about five ten, medium build, wavy dark hair down to his shoulders, in a black leather jacket—standing near a double-parked car. She even gave a description of the car—a light blue economy car.

"What about the driver?" Geri asked. "Did you see him?"

"No, I didn't see anybody else, I swear."

Geri believed her.

"But the guy with the gun," Morales continued. "He saw me. He shot the guy again, I guess to make sure he was dead, then after he got in the car, right before he drove away, he looked out the window, right at me. I feel like such an idiot. I don't know why I stood there; why didn't I run into my building? If I went right in he wouldn't've seen me. I don't know why he didn't shoot me right there. I mean he could've shot me, but instead he just smiled. I'll never forget that smile—it was so calm, so relaxed, like it was a summer day and he was passing by, smiling at a pretty girl on the street. But now he knows what I look like and he knows where I live."

Morales was crying.

"Think of it this way," Geri said. "Now we can get him before he has a chance to hurt you."

"Yeah," Shawn said. "And maybe you'll save somebody else's life too."

Geri asked Morales if she would come to the station and describe the shooter to a sketch artist.

"Do I have to?" she asked.

"If you want us to make an arrest as fast as possible, yes, you do," Geri said.

Morales agreed to come back to the precinct. While Geri and Shawn were waiting in the hallway for her to get ready to go, Shawn said, "Nice one, Rodriguez," and Geri said, "How about you congratulate me after we get the guy?"

They drove Morales to homicide on Broadway and 133rd. Geri and Shawn hung around until the artist arrived and then stayed in the room while Morales described the suspect. It took almost an hour, but when the composite was completed Morales looked at it and said, "Oh my God, that's him. It's amazing, how did you do that?"

"You did it, not us," Geri said.

"What happens next?" Morales asked.

"We'll get the sketch to our officers and to the public and continue our investigation."

"We'll do our best," Geri said. "In the meantime, we'll have an officer outside your apartment, twenty-four-hour protection." Geri could tell Morales was concerned, so she grabbed her hand and said, looking right into her eyes, "You did the right thing."

Morales managed to nod.

Geri and Shawn got right to work on the case. Shawn put out a bulletin on a suspect to precincts around the city while Geri updated Dan McCarthy, her CO on the case. Dan was a ruddy, burly guy who always seemed to be sweating, even on frigid days in the middle of winter. He was on the phone when Geri entered, probably talking to his wife because he sounded rude, saying, "I told you I don't wanna talk about that." In Geri's experience, people were at their rudest and most disrespectful when they were talking to their spouses; another reason why she intended to never get married.

Geri was about to leave when Dan held up his hand like a stop sign and Geri waited at the door while Dan said, "I got somebody in my office . . . I said, I got somebody in my office," and hung up.

Not making eye contact with Geri, looking for something in the mess of papers and folders on his desk, Dan said, "What do you want?"

Geri figured that Dan's attitude probably had nothing to do with her; it was just leftover tension from his phone conversation.

"Maybe there's a better time," she said.

"What is it?" Dan said.

"We got a good lead in the Washington Heights shooting," Geri said, then explained that Carlita Morales had given them a description of the shooter.

Instead of a pat on the back from Dan, or some kind of positive reaction, she got, "Why didn't you get this sooner?"

Thinking, *Is he serious?* Geri said, "We tried to get it sooner, but the witness wouldn't talk yesterday."

"But now it's what, thirty-six hours after the shooting took place?" Dan said. "The suspect could be on the other side of the world."

"Sorry," Geri said. "Next time I'll use my psychic powers to get a description sooner."

"Excuse me?" Dan said, though he'd obviously heard her.

"We're lucky she talked at all," Geri said. "What's up with the attitude?"

"Never mind," Dan said. "Let's just move quickly. I'm under a lot of pressure on this case, okay? Washington Heights is a gentrified neighborhood; at least it's supposed to be. The powers that be don't want to see any more gang violence there."

"Yeah, they want all the gang violence to stay tucked away in the Bronx, right?"

Geri was joking, but Dan stayed serious, saying, "Exactly." Then he added, "So do you have any leads yet?"

"You mean in the four minutes since the sketch was completed? No, but the style of the killing definitely points toward DDP. The victim, Orlando Rojas, was apparently hooked on H, and a few of his friends told us that he'd seemed worried and stressed lately. As you know, DDP is big into heroin."

"What about the shooter?" Dan asked impatiently.

"DDP sometimes uses newbies for their hits," Geri said. "The shooter sounds young, maybe inexperienced; he could be a kid just off the boat. Now that we have a full description of the car we're going to take another look at video in the area. We'll also recanvass the area with the sketch and see if we find somebody else who's willing to talk. Hopefully it won't mean needing another TB screening."

"Any word on the gun?" Dan asked.

"Talked to ballistics this morning," Geri said. "We got no priors on the weapon, which isn't surprising. One thing about DDP—they aren't stupid. Even when they use newbies for their hits they give them clean weapons. We probably have a better chance of finding that gun at the bottom of a river than in some database."

"What about the car?"

"Possible make and model but no plate and no description of the driver, but hopefully we'll make some progress on that front today. I'll need as many officers as possible in the area this weekend, working the case."

"The marathon's this weekend, remember?"

"Come on, I'm talking about five to ten additional officers."

"Look," Dan said. "It sounds like you're finally making some progress. Hopefully we can make a quick arrest today and we'll all be happy. Just try to stay focused, okay?"

"Focused?" Geri was confused. "How am I not focused?"

"Look, I know the Olivia Becker case has been sucking up your time," Dan said, "but you're gonna have to let go of it."

"Wait, so let me get this straight," Geri said. "You think because I'm interested in a case that, by the way, might be related to a case that *is* my responsibility, that, what, I didn't get that info out of Carlita Morales sooner? Is that what you honestly think?"

"Drop the Becker case," Dan said. "It's in excellent hands."

"Over three weeks and no body and no leads," Geri said. "Sorry, but I have a problem with that."

"I read the report," Dan said, "and there's no evidence to suggest that the disappearance has anything to do with the wolf killings or that the investigation has been mishandled in any way. In other words, there's no reason for you to get involved."

"There're loose ends I'm not happy with," Geri said.

"You know what I'm not happy with?" Dan was raising his voice. "I'm not happy that it took you thirty-six goddamn hours to get a sketch you should've gotten a day and a half ago." His face was pink, pinker than usual, and veins were showing in his forehead. Then in a more restrained, but definitely not more relaxed, tone he said, "Please, Geri. Leave it alone."

A few minutes later, Geri was driving back up to Washington Heights with Shawn in the passenger seat, her adrenaline surging.

"You okay?" Shawn asked.

"Yeah, fine," Geri said. "Why?"

"You're just acting, I don't know . . . distracted."

That was the last thing Geri needed to hear: somebody else telling her she wasn't focused.

"I'm not distracted, okay? I'm fine."

"I was just askin'," Shawn said. "I mean I heard you in Dan's office before and—"

"It's between me and Dan."

"Seriously?" Shawn said. "'Cause I'm your partner. We're supposed to share things, right? You know, communicate."

Geri didn't answer. She was thinking about the Becker case. So what if Dan wanted her to back off? She'd back off when it was time to back off.

"What?" Geri asked. She knew that Shawn had just asked her a question, but she had no idea what it was.

"I asked if you want to stop for lunch now or get something later," Shawn said.

"Later," Geri said.

"See, that's better," Shawn said. "At least you're talkin' to me, we got some back-and-forth goin' on." A few seconds later he added, "Maybe we won't have to go to marriage counseling after all."

FOUR

Simon spent the night on the couch. He didn't *sleep* on the couch because for Simon *sleep* really meant *alert rest*. When he was asleep, he was unconscious, but he was also highly aware of his surroundings, as if every part of his body were asleep except his brain. This style of rest certainly had its advantages. For example, he was hyperaware of sounds and smells, so he was an excellent supplement for the smoke detector, and no one was going to break into the apartment without him hearing. For a while Simon had feared that with his brain so active at night, he'd never get a fully satisfying night's sleep again, but then he realized that he was waking up feeling fully rejuvenated, and sleep had never been so satisfying. He also didn't need as much sleep as he used to. He used to be cranky if he got less than seven hours of uninterrupted sleep, but now he felt great with just four or five hours of rest.

When Simon got up, at five A.M., he felt antsy, as he often did when he hadn't been active for several hours, and he immediately did about a hundred push-ups and about twenty minutes of crunches and sit-ups, just to get his blood flowing. Then he went into the kitchen and whipped up some bacon and eggs and sausage, for his daily morning protein fix. At sixish he heard Jeremy stirring, even though Jeremy's room was down the hallway and his door was closed. Simon went into his room and, sure enough, Jeremy was sitting up in bed.

"How did you know I woke up, Daddy?"

Jeremy had been asking similar questions a lot lately—*How did you hear what I was saying, Daddy? How did you hear what Mommy was saying, Daddy?* Like most three-year-olds, Jeremy thrived on question and repetition.

"I just know," Simon said, saying what he always said, like a line in a script.

"Are you a magic daddy?"

"Yep," Simon said, "I'm a magic daddy."

Jeremy stood in bed.

Simon hugged him and said, "Thataboy, kiddo," and kissed him on top of his wonderful-smelling head. Although the dominating scent was Johnson's Baby Shampoo, as far as Simon was concerned the smell of his son's hair was still the best smell in the world.

"Ow!" Jeremy screamed.

Simon was confused for a couple of seconds and didn't know what was wrong, and then he realized he was squeezing Jeremy way too hard. He let go, but Jeremy was already on the verge of crying—his little scrunched-up face was bright pink.

"Oh, God, I'm so sorry." Simon felt awful. "Are you okay? Did I hurt you?"

Jeremy was already hysterical. The screeching and crying was extremely loud, echoing off the walls of the small room, but to Simon it sounded even louder.

With his hands over his ears Simon shouted, "Will you stop? Will you please just *stop it*?"

Alison, in panties and a long T-shirt emblazoned with "Best Mommy in the World," rushed into the room and said, "What's going on here?"

Simon couldn't take the noise anymore, and he pushed by Alison and went into the bathroom in the hallway and locked the door. Yeah, like a little push lock would be any protection for his family if he turned into a werewolf.

Rinsing his face with cold water, he tried to calm down, but his pulse was still pounding. There was no pain in his mouth, like what he'd experienced that time he'd transformed. There was no unusual pain elsewhere in his body, and he checked his hands and there was no sign of increased hairiness, or of his fingers and nails changing into claws.

He remained in the bathroom for about five minutes just to make sure he was okay, and then he returned to Jeremy's room. Jeremy was sitting on Alison's lap, smiling, holding Sam, his favorite stuffed bear.

"Is he okay?" Simon asked, though he knew the question was rhetorical.

"He's fine," Alison said calmly, but by her tone Simon could tell she was furious with him. She said, "You and Sam play for a little while, sweetie. Mommy has to talk to Daddy about something."

Simon knew he was in for it, so when he and Alison got into the bedroom, he tried to nip it in the bud, saying, "It was no big deal. I just hugged him a little too hard and he got scared."

Glaring, Alison said, "He said you hurt his arms."

"Oh, come on, he's exaggerating. I barely touched him." Simon knew this wasn't true; he *had* hugged him much harder than he'd intended. But he continued, "You know how he likes to create drama, especially lately. The other day I lifted him out of his stroller at the playground and he said I was hurting his arms."

Simon was trying to do everything he could to minimize and defuse the situation, but he could tell it wasn't working with Alison, who was still looking at him like he was some vile criminal. If she'd blinked during the past sixty seconds, he'd missed it.

"I have to know if I can trust you," she said.

"Excuse me?" Simon said.

"It's one thing . . ." Alison had to take a few moments to compose herself, stifling tears. Then she continued, "It's one thing if you're going through something personal. I can deal with you sleeping on the couch, and not wanting to touch me, and your weird exercise obsessions and whatever else you need to do while you work on your . . . well, your *problem*. I'm willing to support you, and to be patient, and try to help you through this. But it's another thing if you're going to bring Jeremy into it, if you're going to start acting weird around him. I mean, if you're going to start hurting—"

"Oh, come on, can you stop it?" Simon said. "I didn't hurt him, okay? I'd *never* hurt him. I hugged him a little too hard and he got scared. That's it, end of story. You don't really think I'd ever hurt him intentionally, do you?"

Alison continued to stare at Simon, as if she were trying to see into his brain. "It's weird," she said.

"What's weird?" Simon was suddenly paranoid. Did Alison know? Could she *tell*?

"Your eyes," she said. "They look, I don't know, darker."

Simon had noticed this himself. His eyes had always been brown but now they were a much darker shade of brown, practically black.

"It's just the lighting," Simon said, because he couldn't think of a better excuse.

Continuing to stare at him in that invasive way, Alison said, "Maybe I should take off work for a while."

"What for?" Simon asked.

"Just to give you some time to . . . I don't know . . . work things out, or whatever you need to do."

"It's not necessary," Simon said.

"Maybe I can take Jeremy to California for a week or two," Alison said. "We can stay with my sister."

"Come on, let's just stop this, okay?" Simon said. "You're not taking off work. What I'm going through has nothing to do with my ability to take care of Jeremy. I'm a great dad. You know I'm a great dad."

"I'm not saying this to threaten you," Alison said. "I'm honestly not. But I have to put Jeremy first right now. I'm willing to be patient with you, but if it starts to affect Jeremy . . . I'm sorry, I'm going to have to protect him."

"What is that supposed to mean?"

Alison didn't answer, just stared at him with that penetrating gaze, then went into the bathroom and shut the door. A few seconds later he heard the shower water go on.

He was going to go after her, but he knew she was right. If their situations were reversed and she announced she thought she was a werewolf and started acting strangely, and he thought she could be a danger to Jeremy, he'd want to protect him as well. And the real situation was much worse than she ever could have imagined. She only thought he thought he was a danger. What if she knew that he actually *was* a danger? He'd definitely hugged Jeremy too hard before. What if next time he couldn't control his strength and he actually hurt his son, or worse?

While Simon was making Jeremy pancakes for breakfast, Alison showered and got ready for work. About a half hour later, Jeremy was in front of the TV watching *The Wiggles* and Simon was into another set of push-ups, when Alison entered the living room, ready for work, in a tight rust-colored dress and heels. As usual, her outfit straddled the line between pretty and too sexy.

"Well, I'm off," Alison announced. She came over to Jeremy and kissed him on the cheek and said, "Mommy loves you," then said to Simon, "Have fun today," without kissing him or even making eye contact.

When Alison left, Simon had the cold and empty feeling he'd had on a lot of mornings lately. He hated how dysfunctional their marriage had become. There was definitely truth to the adage that a couple that sleeps apart grows apart, and Simon felt like he and Alison weren't even a couple anymore. It was as if they were roommates. Or worse than roommates. They were roommates who didn't get along very well.

Simon rushed out to the hallway, wanting to say good-bye properly and to reassure her that she could trust him with Jeremy, but the elevator doors had closed and there was just the lingering scent of her perfume and body, which somehow made Simon feel even worse.

Jeremy looked so content, watching TV and eating his pancakes; he'd obviously completely forgotten about the incident in his bedroom, as if it had never happened. Still, Simon felt like he'd dodged a very serious bullet, and he knew that if he was going to continue being Jeremy's sole caretaker he'd have to be absolutely certain that he wasn't endangering him in any way. If there was one more incident where he hurt him, or almost hurt him, or felt any inclination to hurt him, he was going to do the right thing and leave, get as far away from him—and Alison—as possible. Nothing was more important than the safety of his family.

"Are you okay, Daddy?"

Jeremy was a smart kid and could tell that Simon was tormented.

"Fine, kiddo." Simon forced a smile. "How're those pancakes?"

"Yummy."

"Great. You finish up and then we're going to have a great day today. How about we go to the zoo?"

"The zoo, yay!" Jeremy raised his fork, with a big piece of pancake stuck to it, to emphasize his excitement.

After breakfast, Simon helped Jeremy get dressed and brush his teeth and go potty. Simon was hyperaware of all of his movements, careful not to be too rough with Jeremy or hurt him inadvertently. The strategy seemed to work, and, while it took a little longer than usual to get him ready to go out, at least Jeremy was smiley and giggly the whole time and there were no incidents. It gave Simon hope that if he remained mindful all the time, he could eventually get control of his condition and learn how to live with it.

It was the perfect fall day—about fifty degrees, bright sunshine, a brisk refreshing breeze. With Jeremy in the jogging stroller, Simon left the apartment building and walked at a steady pace toward Central Park. Although Simon was going for a low-key look in a Mets cap and dark sunglasses, it didn't exactly make him incognito, at least as far as attention from women was concerned. Practically every woman he passed seemed to make eye contact with him, even old ladies and the ones with guys, and some smiled at him and one woman said hello to him, which was almost unheard of on a Manhattan street. There was no doubt he was sending out some kind of vibe, or aura, because he'd never gotten this kind of attention from women in his pre-werewolf days.

They entered the park at Eighty-sixth. Pushing the stroller ahead of him, Simon started jogging along West Drive.

Looking back, Jeremy was grinning, saying, "Faster, Daddy! Faster!"

The exertion was giving Simon a rush, and he wanted more. He increased his speed, going as fast as the bicycles on the downhill, and this got a loud "Yippppeee!" from Jeremy, but then it hit Simon that he wasn't being safe. Jogging strollers probably weren't built for that kind of speed, and what if the wheels couldn't handle it and Jeremy went flying from the stroller? Simon slowed to a normal jogging pace, angry at himself for not being vigilant and almost slipping up. Was this how it would always be? Would he never be able to go ten minutes again without slipping into werewolf behavior?

"How come we can't go faster?" Jeremy asked in a whiny tone.

"Because we can't," Simon said firmly, to put a quick end to the discussion.

Passing the Ramble, Simon tried but failed to ignore the allure of the woods and the pungent aroma of mulch and dew, and the sounds of the birds in the trees and the rustling leaves and creaking branches. Nature had never seemed so seductive. He remembered how amazing it had felt to run around freely and wildly in the pitch-darkness, and then he was overwhelmed by a sickening sensation in his gut, and he stopped jogging suddenly, causing Jeremy to lurch forward in the stroller. Jeremy was fine, but Simon wasn't. He was remembering last night when he'd detected the werewolf scent. Weirdly he hadn't thought about the incident at all today—maybe he'd blocked it out—but now the memory of the odor was so clear that he became convinced he was smelling it all over again.

He looked around, sniffing frantically.

Jeremy started laughing. "Why are you making such silly faces, Daddy?"

Simon knew he probably looked crazy with his eyes darting around, flaring his nostrils. A couple passing by—they looked like tourists, maybe from Italy—were looking at him with concerned expressions. Simon forced a smile, an attempt to reassure the couple, then said to Jeremy, "Because you have a very silly daddy, that's why," as he continued to try to detect the scent of werewolf.

He didn't think he smelled anything unusual anymore and decided it was all in his imagination—now, but not last night. Last night there had definitely been another werewolf in the Ramble.

"I have a very, very, very silly daddy," Jeremy said.

Jeremy was smiling now, but kids' emotions could turn on a dime and Simon wanted to make sure he wasn't frightened.

Putting on an overly upbeat tone, like a clown at a birthday party, Simon leaned around the stroller and said, "Are you ready to have some fun today?"

This backfired, as his sudden happiness seemed to frighten Jeremy a little.

Toning down his excitement, Simon said, "I mean, we're going to have a great time today, right? Just you and your daddy at the zoo; won't it be fun?"

"Yes," Jeremy said cautiously.

Walking downtown, pushing the stroller ahead of him, Simon tried to shake the memory of last night, but couldn't. Who had been in the Ramble? Maybe it was Michael, but it could have been Charlie or Ramon. The last time Simon had seen them, Michael was biting into Ramon's neck, and that psycho werewolf Olivia had bitten off chunks of Charlie's body. It was possible Charlie and Ramon were both dead, but why couldn't there be other werewolves in Manhattan? Maybe werewolves were rampantly passing along their blood around the city, around the country, around the world. Maybe this was all some kind of raging virus, but instead of weakening its victims, it made them stronger, faster, healthier, and sexier.

"Can I have a balloon, Daddy?"

Jeremy's question jolted Simon from his swirling thoughts. He was shocked to see that they were already near the entrance to the Children's Zoo, on the other side of the park and much farther downtown, near Sixty-fourth Street. It must have taken them twenty minutes to get here, but he had completely lost track of time.

"Of course you can have a balloon," Simon said. "How about two balloons?"

"Okay!" Jeremy was thrilled.

Simon decided he had to stop worrying about things he couldn't control. He hadn't asked for any of this; it had just happened to him, and just as he didn't have any control over the past, the future was equally unpredictable. If werewolves were taking over the world, and disaster loomed, what was Simon supposed to do about it? There was certainly nothing he could do to control the situation. But what he could control was his life right now, in the moment, and that meant being a great father.

"What do you want to see first, the pigs or the goats?" he asked.

"Both," Jeremy said.

"Okay, we'll see both first," Simon said, smiling.

Simon unstrapped Jeremy and folded up the stroller. A few minutes later, as they went along the narrow dirt path, approaching the pigpen, Simon was suddenly in a great mood. In the past he wasn't a huge fan of the Children's Zoo and would go just because Jeremy wanted to. But now Simon was as excited as or more excited than his three-year-old son. The prominent odor of manure and the sounds of the pigs, goats, and sheep had an oddly comforting, familiar effect on him, as if he had been traveling for a long time in a foreign country and had just returned home.

Other kids, mainly with their moms and babysitters, were ahead of them, and they had to wait their turn to see the pigs. Although Simon didn't make eye contact with any of the women, he could *feel* the fixated attention of at least a couple of them.

Finally it was Jeremy's turn to pet the pigs. Jeremy reached over the low wooden fence, but instead of letting him pet them, the pigs cowered away to the other side of the pen.

"Why'd they go away?" Jeremy asked.

"I don't know," Simon said, but he did know. Dogs on the street and in the park had been shying away from him for weeks, so why would it be different with other animals?

They waited for the pigs to return, Jeremy saying, "Come back, piggies, come back," but they didn't.

"Let's go say hi to the sheep," Simon said.

He was hoping for a different situation, but when they were several feet away, the sheep suddenly starting bleating, making a ruckus, as they scrambled to get away from the fence. Other people nearby noticed what was going on, and a zookeeper, a young blond guy, seemed, if not alarmed, then at least concerned, as he rushed over to see what was going on. The sheep were still pushing and shoving one another, making a racket, as they tried to get as far away from the petting fence as possible. As the zookeeper went into the pen and tended to the sheep, Simon didn't wait to see if the goats would let Jeremy pet them. Instead, he cut his losses and picked up his son in one hand and the stroller in the other and made his way toward the exit.

"I want to pet the animals," Jeremy said, getting upset.

"We can't today," Simon said.

"Why not?"

"Because the animals don't want to be petted."

"Why not?"

"Because they're too shy."

"It's not fair; I wanted to pet them." He was about to lose it.

"We're going to go to the grown-up zoo, okay?" Simon said. "You can pet the animals there."

"I don't want to pet those animals, I want to pet these animals."

"You can pet a polar bear. You want to pet a polar bear?"

There was nothing like a good lie to avoid a three-year-old's crying fit.

"What kind of polar bear?"

"A big, fluffy, friendly one," Simon said.

Outside the Children's Zoo, Simon managed to get a calmer Jeremy back into the stroller. He had dodged a fit bullet, but he was still disturbed and angry by what had just happened with the pigs and sheep. He didn't want to go to the main zoo, but he knew Jeremy would lose it if he reneged. He figured they'd go in, zip around, see a few caged animals and the birds, and then Jeremy would be ready to leave. As long as they didn't get too close to the animals, Simon figured it would be fine.

They arrived just in time for a seal show. With a crowd of maybe a hundred people they watched a guy do tricks with the seals, getting them to jump up and grab fish and do other tricks. This was a much better idea than the Children's Zoo. There were more looks from enamored women, of course, but Simon did his best to focus on Jeremy and the seals. Jeremy didn't seem to be having the greatest time in the world, but at least he was watching the show and wasn't on the verge of a full-blown meltdown.

Next they went to see the bird house. The birds didn't have any unusual reaction to Simon, but he felt extremely uncomfortable in the narrow hallway, as if he were a bird himself, trapped in a cage. He'd been experiencing similar feelings of claustrophobia lately when he was in confined spaces, such as elevators, and he'd been avoiding the subway, as being underground was the absolute worst. Several times in elevators and small rooms he'd had actual panic attacks—which worried him because he didn't know whether a panic attack could potentially cause a transformation into a werewolf—and he felt much more comfortable and secure outdoors, in open space. In addition to the incredible stuffiness of the bird house, the odors of so many varieties of bird poop were overwhelming, and Simon suddenly had an awful headache. But Jeremy, out of the stroller, was enjoying himself, so Simon sucked it up and stayed for as long as he could—about ten minutes—and then said, "Let's go see the polar bear," and they went outside. The fresh air was a huge relief; Simon couldn't get enough of it in his lungs.

Imitating Simon, Jeremy was taking exaggeratedly deep breaths.

Making it into a joke, Simon said, "You have a very silly daddy, don't you?"

Jeremy, still imitating the face, didn't answer.

On the way to see the polar bear, Jeremy said, "Oooh, can we see the monkeys?" pointing toward the large outdoor space with a lake and rocks where the snow monkeys were kept. A couple of monkeys were hanging out not far from the fence, and people were watching them. Although Simon and Jeremy were about thirty yards away, the monkeys must have sensed Simon approaching because they suddenly made a mad dash to the other side of the lake.

Immediately veering away, Simon said to Jeremy, "We'll see the monkeys later. Mr. Polar Bear is waiting for us."

Simon felt comfortable seeing Gus, the famous Central Park polar bear, as he was kept a good distance away from viewers. Also, if the other animals had reacted to Simon because they sensed his inner wolf, he doubted a polar bear would be intimidated.

So he and Jeremy walked up the steps to the viewing area overlooking the rocky area and artificial lake where Gus was swimming back and forth.

"I can't see anything," Jeremy said.

Simon lifted him up onto his shoulder and said, "See, right over there. That's Gus."

"Where?"

Simon was holding Jeremy's legs. In order to point he needed to let go of one of the legs, so he did, but at the same moment Jeremy said, "I see him!" and leaned forward suddenly. Simon lost his grip and Jeremy started falling forward. They were very close to the railing, and if Simon hadn't grabbed his leg at the last moment he could have fallen over.

"God, are you okay?" Simon asked frantically.

"What?" Jeremy said.

Jeremy didn't seem to realize something had almost happened, but Simon's heart was still racing.

"Never mind," Simon said, taking Jeremy off his shoulders. "Let's go, we'll get a better view downstairs."

Simon was calming down. He was irritated with himself for losing control of Jeremy for a second and putting him in danger. It had been an accident, but the old Simon would have been more mindful and probably wouldn't have been so close to the railing to begin with. In his head Simon heard Alison saying, *I need to know I can trust you*, and Simon knew before he could legitimately convince her that he was a trustworthy parent, he would have to be able to convince himself.

There were about twenty people—a combination of grown-ups and kids—bunched in front of the Plexiglas for an underwater view of Gus.

"I want to see, I want to see," Jeremy said.

A woman in front heard this and smiled understandably at Simon, then moved aside to let Jeremy through.

"Thanks," Simon said.

The woman was still smiling, but in a different way. She was gazing intensely at Simon, with a look of restrained lust. Not wanting to lead her on, Simon looked away immediately, focusing on Gus, who, at the other end of the lake, was flipping back around like an expert swimmer and heading back toward the Plexiglas.

"Here he comes," Jeremy said excitedly.

The enormous animal was moving gracefully, effortlessly in the water, and, obviously a seasoned performer, was heading right toward the onlookers for maximum entertainment effect. Simon was focused on the bear's big dark eyes when something strange happened. A sudden sense of panic overtook Simon's body, a fight-or-flight mechanism kicking in, as if he were under attack. But he wasn't under attack. He was behind Plexiglas, watching a zoo animal perform. He wasn't in danger.

Or was he?

At the glass, instead of doing the Michael Phelps bit and flipping around and swimming in the opposite direction, Gus didn't stop. Instead, with full momentum, the tremendous animal extended himself into an upright position and pounded the Plexiglas with his huge paws and claws extended. The impact shook the glass so violently it seemed as if it might actually shatter. Then Gus backed up a bit and charged forward and attacked the glass again, his huge mouth wide open, revealing his long, sharp teeth, like some horrific Halloween mask.

Though the bear's behavior was frightening, no one, not even the children, screamed. Everyone was probably too shocked to react, collectively thinking, *What the hell is going on?* At least Simon knew why *he* wasn't reacting. He was mesmerized by a combination of fear, surprise, and disbelief over the bear's absurd behavior. After all, Gus was the star of the zoo, the old pro, and Simon had seen him maybe a dozen times over the years and he'd always been calm and playful and had never acted remotely like this. But the freakiest, most terrifying part of all of it was how as the bear continued to pound the glass, his dark eyes were fixated on Simon, leaving no doubt about who had incited his rage. Then Gus gathered momentum and slammed against the glass with such force that it seemed as if he could actually break through. Simon imagined the nightmarish scene—the water flooding out, the screaming crowd, and the crazed bear ripping everyone to shreds.

With Jeremy back in the stroller, Simon rushed away from the polar bear area, back through the zoo, toward the exit. Now he was vaguely aware of screaming and panic behind him, but it was fading as he was running away, dodging people like a running back. He wasn't running as fast as he could, but he was still going pretty damn fast.

He didn't stop until he had left the zoo and was exiting the park about five blocks farther downtown, across from the Plaza Hotel. He was aware that his behavior during the last few minutes was far from normal—so much for being mindful—and he had been so caught up in the feeling that he had to get away, that his life was in danger, that he hadn't checked to see what effect this was all having on Jeremy.

Simon checked the stroller, expecting to see Jeremy angry or crying or at least looking horrified. What he didn't expect was to see Jeremy smiling, and then, when he saw Simon, suddenly laughing giddily. Simon figured it was probably some kind of defense mechanism, his way of dealing with the traumatic experience.

"Did the bear scare you?" Simon asked. "It's okay if he did. He scared everybody."

Jeremy continued laughing so hard that it took him maybe a minute to get a hold of himself. Then he finally calmed down enough to say, "It's true."

"True? What's true?" Simon had no idea what he was talking about.

Jeremy laughed for a while longer, then added, "I do have the most silliest daddy in the world."

Maybe Jeremy was unfazed by the experience with the polar bear, but Simon wasn't. To him it was yet another indication that he was just kidding himself, thinking he could ride this out and hide from his condition indefinitely. The animals knew what he was, and eventually everyone would, unless he figured out some way to deal with it.

Simon didn't relax until he was midway into his lunch—four bunless Angus burgers at McDonald's on Seventy-first and Broadway. The protein surge energized him, which was at least a good distraction from his other problems. Jeremy was happy as well, with his McNugget Happy Meal. After lunch, Simon put Jeremy back in the stroller and pushed him uptown, and things almost seemed normal.

Jeremy fell asleep in the stroller, which was perfect because his naps usually lasted about an hour and a half and Simon wanted to run. Simon veered toward Riverside Park—as usual, around the grass and trees he instantly felt at home, at peace—and jogged downtown. To maintain a normal speed, he drafted behind another jogger, a thin young guy. It was a little annoying because Simon was full of energy from the burgers and was dying to blow past the guy, but he managed to control himself and enjoy the moment and appreciate his good fortune. After all, if Jeremy hadn't fallen asleep they probably would have returned to their cramped two-bedroom Columbus Avenue apartment. While the apartment wasn't small by New York standards—it was actually on the big side, about fourteen hundred square feet—being in there for too long made Simon anxious and edgy. But aah, jogging along the Hudson, with the open space of the river to his right and the trees, grass, and other vegetation to his left, along with the fresh air, or at least fresher air, along the Hudson, was as enjoyable as running in the Ramble in Central Park, and just about the closest he could come to bliss in Manhattan. Simon remembered just a couple of months ago telling someone at his old job how he couldn't imagine ever living outside New York City. He'd said, "I think I'd either die of boredom or shoot myself." God, had he actually said that? Wow, he really *had* changed. He could barely imagine how incredible it would be to go for a run on a country road or—oh, man—in the woods, the *real* woods? Last summer, he and Alison had gone away for a weekend with Jeremy to a B&B in the Berkshires, and she had had to practically drag him out to go for a hike. What had he been thinking, almost blowing an opportunity to experience real nature? If he lived in the country he would go for hikes and runs in the woods every day. Did the people who lived in rural areas realize how great they had it?

Lost in thought, Simon had left the pace-setting jogger well behind. Jeremy was sleeping soundly and the path was smooth so he thought, *What the hell? Why not air it out?* So he picked up the pace, taking rapider, deeper breaths, loving the rush and euphoria that overtook his body. He tried to tell himself that he was making a mistake, that he shouldn't be flaunting his physical abilities, but he was enjoying the experience too much and his thoughts faded and then disappeared entirely. Like earlier, there was a gap—or really a long, pleasant buzz—and when his awareness returned he saw he was much farther downtown, approaching Chelsea Piers. Suddenly realizing the huge mistake he'd almost made, he turned around and ran away fast, but not too fast, in the other direction, not slowing until he was maybe a mile back uptown.

He couldn't believe he'd been so thoughtless, with Jeremy in tow no less. If he'd gone another couple of miles, he could've run right by the Battery Park playground where Michael, Charlie, and Ramon often hung out with their sons.

Simon inhaled deeply but couldn't detect any unusual scents. But just because he couldn't smell the guys didn't mean they weren't there, and it didn't mean that *they* couldn't smell *him*. For all he knew they were tracking him right now. He continued trying to pick up a werewolf scent as he ran uptown. He didn't smell anything unusual and it began to set in that his reaction might have been pure paranoia. After all, he'd been miles from where the guys sometimes hung out, and he had no idea if they were even there today. And the idea that they were following him didn't make much sense either. If the guys wanted to find him, how hard would it really be? He wasn't exactly hard to track down. His number was listed and he was easy to find on Facebook and Google. Wouldn't calling him or sending him an e-mail be an easier way of getting in touch than stalking him in the Ramble or waiting for him to stumble on them in a playground? And since they could easily contact him, the bigger question was, why hadn't they?

Michael had gone to such lengths to lure Simon into his pack, and now he had completely forgotten about him? It didn't make any sense.

Then Simon shuddered as he thought, *What if they're gone?* They could have left the city, or the country, or they could even be dead. But this idea didn't give Simon any comfort because, while he was worried about the guys exposing him and trying to get him to fully join their "pack," the idea that he was alone, that he was the only werewolf in the world, somehow seemed much, much worse.

Simon had jogged the entire way back to his apartment and had been on the move almost nonstop all morning, but he was barely winded and actually was in the mood to go out to run some more. He was considering having some sliced turkey and maybe a can of tuna fish for a protein jolt and then heading out again when he noticed that Jeremy was stirring in the stroller, rubbing his eyes.

Forcing himself to be upbeat for Jeremy's sake, Simon said, "There's my big guy," and he undid the straps, lifted his son out of the stroller, and held him up in front of him so that his face was at eye level. "Did you have a nice nap?"

Jeremy didn't answer, just yawned widely; his "sleep breath" seemed particularly pungent but Simon didn't mind it. Actually, in an odd way, the stale aroma was comforting.

"I'll take that as a yes," Simon said. "Are you hungry? You want some turkey or tuna fish?"

"I just had a Happy Meal."

"Oh, that's right." Sometimes Simon forgot that he was the only one in the family whose appetite was practically insatiable.

"I have to go potty," Jeremy said.

Helping Jeremy in the bathroom and then setting him up with a puzzle on the living room floor were good distractions for Simon. He played with Jeremy the rest of the afternoon until Alison returned home from work. After she kissed and hugged Jeremy hello and told him how much she'd missed him, she said to Simon, "How was your day?"

Though she said this in a normal, friendly way, Simon detected an edge in her voice, leftover tension from last night and this morning.

"Pretty good," Simon said. "We went to the zoo."

"The zoo, wow, that must've been fun."

Recalling how Gus had been pounding against the Plexiglas as if he were rabid, Simon said, "Yeah, it was a blast."

"Good, I'm glad you did something different for a change," Alison said without making eye contact. "Don't you have a therapy appointment today?"

Simon had completely forgotten that he had a fake psychiatry appointment this evening.

"Not till seven," he said.

"Oh, well maybe you want to leave early, you're probably feeling cooped up."

Simon *was* feeling cooped up—what else was new?—but he didn't like feeling as if he were being kicked out of his own apartment.

"It's okay," he said, "I have time. And, besides, it'll be nice to have dinner together."

Alison, not smiling, asked, "Did you go food shopping today?" as she went past him into the kitchen and opened the fridge.

Alison had asked him to go to Whole Foods today to stock up on food and he'd promised he would.

"Sorry," he said, "but I can go now."

"Never mind, we'll order in Vietnamese." She let the fridge door slam shut. "What about the laundry?"

Simon had completely forgotten about this as well. He said, "I was about to do it before you came home, but I'll do it now."

"It's okay, I'll do it," she said, but she didn't sound happy about it. "Did you pay the bills?"

Simon's mouth opened as he was about to say, *I'm sorry*.

But Alison cut him off with, "This just isn't fair, Simon. I have to work all day and you're here at home. You have to do your share. I can't do everything."

"You're right," Simon said. "I've been distracted with other things lately, but from now on I'll do more. I promise."

Alison ordered the food and then went into the bedroom to get out of her work clothes. When she came out in sweats and a T-shirt, Simon had set the dining room table.

"Thank you," she said sincerely. "And I'm sorry I jumped down your throat before. It's just things get so overwhelming sometimes."

"No, I'm the one who should apologize," Simon said. "I know I haven't been the best husband in the world lately, but I'll try harder."

"Can I kiss you?" Alison asked.

"Of course you can," Simon said.

She kissed him on the lips and he distracted himself—imagining he was still running along the river—so he wouldn't get too aroused.

"What about me?" Jeremy asked. "What about me?"

Jeremy, who hated to miss out on hugs and kisses, had come over and was extending his arms, wanting to be picked up.

"Don't worry, we didn't forget about you," Alison said.

She lifted Jeremy, holding him between her and Simon; when they kissed his cheeks simultaneously he grinned widely. Simon was enjoying the family moment and was thrilled that there was a shift of focus.

A few minutes later dinner arrived. Alison had thoughtfully ordered a beef dish for Simon—*bo luc loc*. Simon did his best to eat the delicious cubes of marinated beef at normal, human pace. As he chewed the first bite ultra slowly he thought, *Don't wolf it down*, and couldn't help laughing at the unintentional pun.

"What's so funny?" Alison asked.

"Oh, um, nothing," Simon said. "I'm just enjoying the food, that's all."

The explanation didn't make much sense, but Alison didn't seem to mind, as she was involved in cutting up pieces of marinated chicken for Jeremy.

But then Jeremy started laughing and said, "Daddy was very silly today. At the zoo he even made the animals act silly."

"He did?" Alison asked. "How did he do that?"

"Oh, animals always act silly," Simon said, changing the subject. Then he said to Jeremy, "That chicken looks delicious, doesn't it, kiddo?"

For most of the meal, Jeremy was the focus. Simon and Alison were monitoring his eating and joking around with him, telling knock-knock jokes and singing Wiggles songs. Simon managed to eat his beef relatively slowly, and although he was dying to have some of Jeremy's chicken, he resisted and ate rice doused in *nuoc cham* sauce instead, figuring he'd pick up some more meat on the street later on. All in all, it was nice to have a nice, normal meal with his family, and he almost managed to forget about all of his problems.

Then, when everyone was just about finished eating, Alison said, "Oh, so I was e-mailing Stacy Rosenberg today."

"Stacy Rosenberg?" Simon had no idea who she was.

"You remember Stacy," Alison said. "I went to grad school with her. Stacy, Stacy-and-Rob Stacy? They live in Midtown East, like near the UN. We went out to a bar with them that time with those other people?"

Simon had no recollection of any of this. "Oh yeah, right, Stacy," he said.

"They have a two-year-old girl," Alison said. "Her name's Jessica and she looks adorable—blond curly hair and these big blue eyes. Anyway, Stacy doesn't work either, so I was thinking maybe you two could hang out sometime."

"What do you mean?" Simon asked, trying not to get too defensive.

"I mean a play date," Alison said. "Like maybe you could meet up at a playground sometime, or Pizzeria Uno, or maybe you could invite her over to the apartment."

"No, I mean about how she doesn't work either. I work. I got laid off, but that doesn't mean I don't work."

"Okay, you both don't currently have jobs, is that better? I was just thinking that it could be a good match, that's all. She goes to Carl Schurz Park on the East Side. She said she'd meet you there sometime."

"You mean you talked to her about this already?"

"We didn't *talk*, we just exchanged a couple of e-mails. Why? What's the big deal?"

"Is this because of what happened this morning?"

"This morning? What do you—"

"Because of what you said," Simon said, "how you don't trust me."

Alison looked at Jeremy, who was distracted, playing with a piece of chicken on his plate, and said, "It has nothing to do with that. It has to do with that Jeremy needs to be around kids his own age. It was great when you had those guys to hang out with during the day, but since you don't want to hang out with them anymore I'm just giving you another option."

Simon had told Alison that he didn't want to hang out with the guys anymore because he didn't have enough in common with them. There was no way he could tell her the truth, of course—that he had something very big in common with them, much bigger than she could ever imagine.

Continuing in a quieter tone he said, "I don't believe it. I think it's because you don't trust me. You don't want Stacy to have play dates with me, you want her to babysit me."

"That is not true," Alison said. "I just think it would be a good idea if Jeremy spent more time with other kids his own age."

"You said the girl's two," Simon said.

"Going on three," Alison said. "And girls mature faster than boys anyway. I don't understand what the big deal is, why you're acting so threatened."

"Maybe because you're threatening me."

"How am I threatening you?"

"Acting like I'm not capable, like there's something wrong with me."

"There *is* something wrong with you. That's what this is all about, isn't it?"

"What's wrong with Daddy?" Jeremy sounded concerned.

Simon and Alison looked at each other.

Forcing a smile for Jeremy's sake, Alison said, "Nothing's wrong with Daddy." Then she stood and said to Jeremy, "How about two more bites and you can have some ice cream for dessert, okay?"

Alison tended to Jeremy, acting as if Simon weren't in the room. Well, so much for nice and normal.

After dinner, while Jeremy was playing in his room, Alison came into the kitchen where Simon was doing the dishes and said, "I can do those. Don't you have a therapy appointment to go to?"

"It's okay, I can finish cleaning up," Simon said.

"No, I think you should go now," Alison said.

Simon could tell she was seriously upset, and he agreed that some time apart would do them both good, so without another word he put on his shoes and black leather bomber jacket and left.

Whenever he went out for a fake therapy appointment he walked around for a couple of hours, then returned home. As he went down Columbus Avenue, he replayed snippets of the argument with Alison, and he knew she'd been one hundred percent right. There was nothing wrong with her suggesting that he go on play dates with her friends, and he knew he'd acted oversensitively. He and Alison had been in marriage counseling for the past year or so but their problems had always been the minor issues that all couples had—pet peeves, bad communication, et cetera. But now he had a major issue that he couldn't discuss with her or anyone. He was back in a troubled marriage and he knew she wouldn't put up with his crap forever. If he didn't figure out how to change his behavior and become a better husband and father, he was going to lose his family forever.

Simon was crossing Eighty-sixth Street when it happened. He was distracted by thoughts about his troubled marriage and the admiring gazes of two women who were at the curb, facing him, when he realized he was crossing against the light. The next moment the car slammed into him from his side. It must've been speeding because he didn't have a chance to react in any way. Almost instantaneously his legs gave way and he was sucked under the front of the car with the force of a powerful vacuum. His head slammed hard against the street and at least one wheel of the car ran over his neck.

While this was happening time seemed to slow down, or vanish entirely, and he only had one dominant thought: *You're about to die.* But strangely he wasn't frightened, or even mildly scared. For years he'd suffered from hypochondria and panic attacks and, in a way, an underlying fear of death had always dominated his life, but now when he was confronted with the moment when his life was about to end, death didn't seem like any big deal.

"Hey, are you okay?"

The voice was from one of the women who'd been eyeing him. He knew this because she was kneeling next to him. She had straight dark hair and was wearing Obsession and a strong deodorant. But how did he know any of this? How could he see her and smell her if he was dead?

Now there was another voice, a man talking fast in some foreign language, probably Arabic. Simon looked over and saw a scruffy man who reeked of cigarettes next to the woman. Then Simon became aware of other odors and sounds but he didn't know why he was so lucid. And where was the pain? He'd hit the pavement so hard, it should have cracked his skull open, but he was barely dazed, as if he'd just headed a soccer ball. There was some mild achy pain in his legs, but otherwise he felt perfectly fine. Maybe he was imagining all of this. Didn't some people believe that you can hallucinate right before death? Or maybe he was having a near-death experience. Soon he'd see the bright light, reach out for the welcoming hand of a dead relative.

But none of this happened. There were just more strangers crowding around him, asking him if he was okay, and assuring him that he was going to be fine and help was on the way.

Then Simon stood up, the leg pain gone. Aside from some very slight dizziness, he didn't feel at all unusual, but that was exactly what was so unusual. A car had hit him at full speed and he should be dead, or at least very seriously injured, but instead he felt barely jolted. The people around him noticed how unusual this was as well. Everyone seemed amazed, with widened eyes, and some jaws were slacked open.

"W-what're you doing?" the dark-haired woman asked.

"I'm fine," Simon said. "I mean, I'm not hurt."

The Arabic guy next to a cab—ah, so it was a cab that had hit Simon—seemed stunned.

Simon glanced at the people, the taxi, and then at the area toward the front of the taxi where his body should have been lying with multiple broken bones and blood splattered everywhere.

"You really should sit down," the woman said.

"Yeah," a guy behind her said. "You shouldn't move till the ambulance gets here."

The word *ambulance* terrified Simon. He couldn't be taken to a hospital. He couldn't have his blood tested and have the ER doctors discover that their patient wasn't human.

"Nothing's broken," Simon said. For emphasis he shook his arms, then each leg. Then he said, "See? I'm fine."

Everyone still seemed amazed, or in shock, as if they'd just witnessed someone come back to life, which, in a way, they had.

"The car must've gone right over me," Simon said, figuring that some barely plausible explanation was better than nothing.

He forced a smile, but no one smiled with him. After an awkward few moments, he made his way through the crowd of about twenty or thirty onlookers, toward the curb. Then he walked away faster, practically running. He didn't know if he was exhilarated or terrified.

He just wanted to get away.

FIVE

Geri thought they'd caught Orlando Rojas's killer. Early Saturday morning the police received a tip via the department's 577-TIPS hotline from a caller who had seen the sketch on TV. Most tips were useless, as a lot of people treated calling in tips like buying lottery tickets—phone in a bunch and, hey, you never know, one might hit— but this one sounded legit. The caller was certain that James Arrojo, from Astoria, was the shooter, and even claimed that Arrojo drove a light blue economy car, perhaps a Ford Escort. When Queens police officers went to investigate, Arrojo threatened them with a pair of scissors. The officers were able to subdue the suspect, and he was taken to Manhattan North, where Carlita Morales was brought in to view him in a lineup.

Geri, who had been home at the time of the arrest, arrived at Manhattan North shortly after Arrojo. Well, the guy certainly looked like the sketch—dark hair, same shaped eyes, same bushy eyebrows. He didn't have any gang connections, though, and he didn't seem like the drug dealer type. He worked at a retail computer store in midtown. He had no record.

Officer Phillip Campo, one of the arresting officers, said to Geri, "When we broke down the door, he attacked us."

"Wait," Geri said. "You broke down the door? You mean you had a warrant?"

Campo smirked and said, "I thought I smelled some pot in the apartment."

A relatively new law in the city allowed police to break into apartments or houses if they smelled marijuana from outside or in a hallway. The law was designed to prevent offenders from disposing of drugs before police showed up, but some people felt the law could be used as an excuse by cops to avoid the hassle of getting warrants.

"Okay, let's see what we got," Geri said.

Geri liked a lot about her job—the detective work, the zero-to-sixty rush when things got out of control—but her favorite part of her job was interrogations—getting into the head of a perp, taking control.

When she entered, the first thing Arrojo said was, "Yo, I didn't do it. You got the wrong guy."

No surprise there. Practically every suspect—whether innocent or guilty—opened with, "You got the wrong guy." After about an hour of questioning, Geri hadn't gotten very far. Arrojo was sticking to his story that he was home with his girlfriend at the time Rojas was shot and he had no idea why he was even a suspect. He said he'd only gone for the scissors when the police arrived because he thought somebody was breaking into his apartment.

"It's one o'clock in the morning, people start breaking down your door, what would you do?"

"You mean you didn't know they were police officers?"

"Not till they were busting in my apartment," he said. "Then before I knew it they had me on the floor and were cuffin' my ass. How come I don't got a lawyer? I asked for a lawyer in the squad car and they told me to shut my ass up."

After rewording questions she'd already asked and getting the same answers, Geri left Arrojo in the room and went out to where Shawn was watching through the two-way glass and said, "He's not the guy."

"His girlfriend could be lying," Shawn said. "That's what people do when they're in love. They lie."

It was true that lovers and relatives were usually useless for alibis.

"She's not lying," Geri said.

"I'm not saying she is, I'm saying she could be."

"Come on," Geri said. "This was a drive-by and this guy sells computers. We have nothing on him except he drives an Escort and he has bushy eyebrows."

"Let's put him in a lineup just in case," Shawn said.

"Why?" Geri said. "So we can waste more time?"

"It's not a waste of time if he gets ID'd."

Carlita Morales was here and they had four guys for the lineup so Geri figured, *Why not?*

Carlita wasn't happy to be at the precinct for the second time in two days, saying, "I gave you the sketch, why do I have to be here again? And on a Saturday morning? I could be home sleeping right now."

Geri assured her that it would only take a few minutes and that none of the suspects would be able to see her. Of course Geri didn't let on that she didn't think there was a chance in hell that the suspect in the lineup was the shooter and all of this was, more than likely, a total waste of time.

A few minutes later Carlita, standing alongside Geri and Shawn, viewed the lineup. Geri gave her all the usual BS, about how to take a good look at each guy before reaching any conclusions. She was expecting Carlita to say that none of them looked familiar so she was surprised when she heard, "Wait, that guy right there."

"Which guy?" Geri asked.

Carlita pointed at Arrojo. "That guy, second from the right."

"Are you sure?"

"Yes." Then she said, "Wait, I don't know, he looks familiar, around the eyes, but I don't know. I only saw him for a few seconds, maybe less. How'm I supposed to know?"

"Take another look," Shawn said.

Seeming frustrated, Carlita stared at Arrojo for a good minute. Then she said, "I don't know. Maybe. I can't say for sure."

"But at first you said it was him," Geri said.

"So I changed my mind," Carlita said. "What do you want me to do, lie to you?"

Shawn let out an agitated breath.

"Okay, thank you," Geri said. "That's all we need for right now."

"For right now?" Carlita said. "What do you mean? I have to come back here?"

"Maybe," Geri said.

"Yesterday you said all I had to do was give you a sketch," Carlita said. "You didn't say anything about having to ID anybody."

"You're our prime witness," Geri said. "You're our only witness. So until there's an arrest in the case we're gonna need you to be at our disposal. You've just gotta be patient, that's all. And you don't have to worry, there're cops outside your apartment twenty-four-seven, and it's gonna stay that way till we get this guy. If you need a lift back to your apartment I'll get somebody to drive you."

Carlita said she wanted a lift, so they went back to near the entrance to the precinct where Officer Campo was still hanging around. Geri asked Campo to give Carlita a lift back home.

Campo didn't seem thrilled. "I was actually about to go on break," he said.

"Pick-a-Bagel can wait," Geri said.

Geri went into Shawn's office and said to him, "So what you think? Do we let Arrojo go or do we requestion him?"

"I would love to get this case wrapped up so I can get back to watching my college football games this afternoon," Shawn said, "but I don't see what we have to go on except that he has bushy eyebrows and drives an economy car. But I think we've got ourselves a bigger problem."

"Carlita," Geri said.

"What happens when we make an arrest and get her in court? She'll be like, 'Naw, that's not him. Wait, I made a mistake, it is him. Naw, I was right the first time.'"

"You think she's playing us?"

"Honestly? No, I don't," Shawn said. "I wish she was. I wish she was just afraid, trying to get off helping us, but I don't think that's the case. I think she really doesn't know what she saw."

"I'll tell Arrojo he can go," Geri said. "I just hope we're not releasing a computer salesman who moonlights as a hit man."

"I don't know about you," Shawn said, "but I need somethin' to eat or I'm gonna pass out. And I'm not talking about diet food. I need some eggs, pancakes, waffles. Wanna hit a diner?"

"Already ate." Geri had an idea. "But I'll catch you back here when you're done."

The truth was, Geri hadn't eaten since an early dinner yesterday and was starving, but she knew that Detective Mangel would be around now because she'd checked his schedule the other day. Figuring this would be a good time to chat with him in person about the other case that was gnawing at her, she drove to the 19th Precinct on East Sixty-seventh Street.

There was very little traffic, early on a Saturday morning, and she made it down and across town in about fifteen minutes. It turned out Mangel wasn't in but was expected soon, so Geri had a chance to eat after all, grabbing a ham, egg, and cheese on a roll and a coffee at a deli around the corner from the precinct. She took it to go and ate New York City–style—while walking. When she was about to go back into the precinct she saw Mangel walking toward her along the side-walk. She smiled and Mangel smiled back in a flirty way, obviously not recognizing her. He probably smiled at every good-looking woman who was twenty years younger than him whom he saw on the street.

When he got closer Geri asked, "Hey, how's it going?"

Mangel was about thirty pounds overweight, bald—well, *he* probably didn't think he was bald because his thin gray hair was combed over a big bald spot—and he had an extremely wide nose that almost looked fake. He still didn't seem to know who Geri was because she saw his eyes shift down briefly as he zeroed in on her chest. She could see the tip of his tongue between his yellowed smoker's teeth.

"Hello," Mangel said in his thick Bronx accent, his eyes finally shifting back upward.

"Rodriguez," Geri said. "Manhattan North."

Geri expected Mangel's attitude to change, but nope; if anything this seemed to be more of a turn-on for him.

"Oh, so *you're* Rodriguez," he said, taking another long, very obvious look at her body. "I had no idea."

"No idea, what?" Geri asked, though she knew exactly what he'd meant.

"Just no idea who you were," he said. "I mean sometimes you hear a voice and you get a picture of somebody in your head and sometimes the voice doesn't match the picture."

Geri hated how he was talking down to her, especially since she was technically his superior officer, but she knew that demanding respect wouldn't get her what she wanted, so she might as well play up the sex card.

"Well," she said, "I hope I live up to the hype."

"Oh yeah, you live up to it," Mangel said. "You don't gotta worry about that."

Geri noticed Mangel's thick gold wedding band, but this didn't surprise her—most married cops were bigger hounds than the unmarried ones. Did he really think he had a chance to score with her? Yeah, probably.

"Sorry to just show up," Geri said, "but you don't seem comfortable talking on the phone."

"Oh, sorry about that," Mangel said. "Things have been crazy, you know how it is."

"Yeah, I know," Geri said, making lots of eye contact. "So you think we can just talk for a little bit while I'm finishing my coffee?"

"I'd like that," he said, "but if it's about the Olivia Becker missing-person case, I told you pretty much all there is to tell."

"Oh come on, just five minutes to get me up to date," Geri said. "Most men wouldn't complain about a chance to spend five minutes with me."

She didn't know how she was able to say all this without vomiting, but Mangel seemed to believe she was actually flirting with him.

"Well, I guess I've got five minutes," he said.

They went into the precinct and down a hallway to his office. As they walked, Mangel was full of questions: *How come we never met before? How long have you been with Manhattan North? Do you live in the city?* Funny how Mangel was so interested in the details of her life. At the entrance to the office Mangel held out his arm and said, "After you."

Geri knew he just wanted her to go in ahead of him so he could get a good look at her ass. She didn't care—let him look. She even swung her hips in a more exaggerated way than she did normally, hoping it would give him an extra thrill and make him even more cooperative.

She sat across from his desk, and then he sat in his swivel chair and asked, "So, what can I do for you?"

"You can tell me where you are on the Olivia Becker case."

"If there was any news, you would've heard it."

"Come on, cut the crap," Geri said. "I'm not moving in on the case, I'm not trying to steal your glory—like there's any glory to be stolen. I just like closure with my cases, that's just the way I am."

Mangel let out a breath, then said, "Well, in this case I'm afraid there may never be closure."

"No leads on the body?" Geri asked.

"*Nada*," Mangel said.

"I didn't know you spoke Spanish so well," Geri said, trying to keep the flirty mood alive.

"One of my many talents," Mangel said, as if he thought he was winning her over.

Letting the eye contact linger, Geri asked, "So if there's no body, why do you think it was suicide?"

"Her behavior," Mangel said, twirling his wedding band. "She was definitely having some kind of breakdown. The day she disappeared she practically assaulted a client from Japan."

"What do you mean *assaulted*?"

"Maybe assaulted is too strong a word," Mangel said. "But she was coming on to him, trying to grab him. I'm telling you, it sounds like she was totally losing it mentally."

"Did she talk about any plans to kill herself?"

"Not specifically, no."

"What about her boyfriend, Michael Hartman?"

"What about him?"

"Did he have an alibi?"

"Yeah, he did. He was home that whole night."

"Who vouched for him?"

"His father."

Great, Geri thought. *An alibi from a relative.* She saw Mangel's eyes shift downward; he was obviously checking out her breasts.

Trying to act like she hadn't noticed, she asked, "And you believed him?"

"Look," Mangel said. "I'm with you, okay? A woman disappears, you check out the boyfriend, it's detective work 101. I mean, it's not like I gave Hartman a free pass. I agree there's something freaky about the guy. He has those dark eyes, talks in a kinda funny way, with some kind of accent. No doubt about it, he's weird, but being weird isn't a crime."

"What about Olivia Becker's friends?" Geri asked.

"What about them?" Mangel asked, getting distracted by a text or e-mail on his cell.

"Did Becker tell them she was unhappy or depressed?"

Mangel finished tapping out a reply, then said, "What?" as if he hadn't heard her.

Geri was about to repeat the question when, as if her voice had bounced off a satellite dish and reached Mangel by delay, he said, "No, not at all. Just the opposite actually."

"Opposite how?"

"Everyone said she'd been in a really good mood lately," Mangel said. "Falling in love, going on about how happy she was with Hartman. But you know how it is—a lot of time what you see on the outside's much different than what's going on on the inside. Some people, they do a really good job of disguising themselves. Oh, but there was this one friend that told us something weird. *Weird*, there's that word again."

"What was so weird?" Geri asked.

"Well, she said she saw Olivia . . . change."

"Change?"

"Into some kind of animal."

Geri tried to absorb this, then said flatly, "Into some kind of animal."

"I told you it was weird, right?" Mangel shook his head. "I swear I don't know what these people are smoking. Maybe that's it—there's some new drug people're on, some kind of hallucinogen. Crack and X are out so something's gotta be next, right? Yeah, an animal, with teeth, claws, fur."

"Fur?"

"*Fur.* That's what she told us. She said Olivia Becker turned into an animal and tried to attack her the day she disappeared."

"Did she have a history of mental illness?"

"Who?" Mangel asked.

"The girl," Geri said.

"What does it sound like to you?" Mangel was twirling his wedding band again. "Look, it's obvious these people aren't playing with a full deck. This girl needed some serious help and I hope she gets it."

"What was the girl's name?"

"Coles," Mangel said. "Diane Coles. She was the last one to see Becker alive, so we questioned her extensively, but there was no reason to believe she had anything to do with Becker's disappearance and she wasn't exactly a credible witness."

Just what Geri needed today—another noncredible witness. "You mind if I talk to her?"

Mangel gave her a look.

"Just to see if it has any relevance to my case, but I doubt it does."

"Don't you have anything better to do at North? Aren't you working on that Washington Heights shooting?"

Geri didn't appreciate being talked down to. "Let me rephrase that," she said. "Give me the phone number or I'm going to talk to my CO about taking over the whole case and, just for the hell of it, maybe a couple of other cases you're working on."

Mangel gave her Coles's phone number. Then, glancing at his phone again, he said, "Is there anything else? 'Cause maybe *you* have a lot of free time on your hands to work on cases that're going nowhere, but I don't."

Geri did have to get back uptown. Besides, she'd gotten all she could out of Mangel.

As she stood, Mangel got up too and said, "I'll walk you out."

Mangel held his hand out, as if saying, *After you*, and, as she walked ahead, Geri felt his gaze on her ass again.

Walking alongside her in the hallway, Mangel said, "Just want to apologize again for being so, what's the word? . . . Aloof. Yeah, aloof. I mean, I hope you don't hold it against me or anything."

Remembering how Mangel had acted like a total dick before he'd met her in person, Geri said, "No big deal. Thanks for taking the time out to talk today."

"So maybe we can get together again sometime," Mangel said. "I mean another time just to, you know, talk shop. There's this little bar I sometimes hit after work, the Subway Inn off Lex. You know where it is?"

Wow, he was inviting her out to a dive bar. Did this guy have class or what?

She didn't want to lead him on to what would definitely be a dead end, but at the same time she wanted to keep him around, in case she needed some more info. How did that expression go? Keep your enemies closer? Well, the same thing applied to sleazeball cops.

"Sounds like a plan," she said. "Let's definitely keep in touch."

On the street, she called the number Mangel had given her. After four rings, she got Diane Coles's voice mail. She was going to leave a message, but decided to just call back later.

Driving back uptown to meet up with Shawn, Geri wasn't sure what to make of the Olivia Becker case. There were still a lot of unanswered questions, but just because there were questions didn't mean there had to be answers. Becker could be alive and well—in New York or some other city. Just because she'd been having some kind of breakdown didn't mean she was suicidal. Maybe she ran away, started a new life. Or if Mangel was right and she'd jumped off a bridge, or off a boat in the ocean, there was a chance her body would never be found. Who knows? Maybe she left the city, went to Hawaii, and dived into a volcano. And even if her body was found, it didn't mean she was killed, or that it had anything to do with Michael Hartman or Simon Burns.

But something still felt off about the case to Geri. Becker's friend had claimed that she'd seen Becker turn into an animal? What the hell was that all about?

Back at Manhattan North, Geri met up with Shawn, and the rest of the day her major focus was the Washington Heights shooting. Several new tips had come in, but nothing sounded very hopeful.

Around five o'clock, Dan McCarthy came by Geri's office and said, "Guess who I just got off the phone with."

Had Mangel called him and told him she'd come by to talk to him?

Ready to get blasted, Geri asked, "Who?"

"The police commissioner," Dan said. "As you can imagine, he wasn't thrilled to hear that it didn't work out with Carlita Morales. He's losing patience and I am too."

"So what do you want me to do," Geri said, "arrest the wrong guy just to make you look good?"

"No," Dan said. "I want you to arrest the right guy to make me look good."

Geri updated Dan on the latest with the investigation, which was pretty much where the investigation had been from the get-go—nowhere.

"Look, I have faith in you," Dan said. "I really do. I know you're great at what you do and you'll eventually get a break, so please don't take this the wrong way. I just have to cover my own ass on this thing too."

Geri didn't get it. "What do you—"

"Rob and Derrick are gonna be working with you and Shawn," Dan said.

Why wasn't Geri surprised? Rob Santoro was Dan's golf buddy. Derrick Reese was Rob's partner.

"What's this," Geri said, "my punishment for making a few calls about the Olivia Becker case?"

"I'm not nearly as petty as you think I am," Dan said. "As you've pointed out, we need as much manpower as possible on the Heights case, so I'm just giving you what you want. And don't worry, you're still lead detective—for now anyway."

Dan left, and then Geri, muttering to herself, swiped some papers in front of her onto the floor. She wasn't sure what she was more upset about: Dan butting into her case or using that word—*manpower*. Yeah, like that wasn't intentional.

Apparently Dan hadn't wasted much time getting the news to Santoro and Reese or—more likely—he'd told them they were on the case before he'd bothered to tell Geri—because Dan hadn't been gone a minute when Santoro poked his head into Geri's office and said, "Meeting in two in the conference room." His expression was all business, but Geri sensed the smugness underneath.

Dan and Shawn also attended the meeting. Geri got everyone up to speed on the investigation. They all agreed that the idea that the shooting was DDP-related was still the most likely scenario. They also agreed that it was highly unlikely that James Arrojo was the killer, and Geri and Shawn expressed their concerns about Carlita Morales's reliability as a witness. After Geri was through, Dan divvied up the investigative responsibilities on the case: Santoro and Reese would focus on questioning all known DDP associates in the area and in prison, especially at Rikers, while Geri and Phillips would oversee the canvassing in the area. Geri wasn't thrilled with this, as she felt it was likely the bust would come from a known entity, not a lead that fell from the sky, but she kept her mouth shut.

Maybe her feelings were obvious, though, because Dan said, "Something wrong, Geri?"

"No, everything's perfect," Geri said. "This isn't an ego thing for me. Let's just get this son of a bitch . . . today."

Geri and Shawn spent the rest of the afternoon through the evening in Washington Heights, talking to everybody they could, but there were no breakthroughs. There was nothing from Santoro and Reese either. Geri had been working for seventeen hours, almost nonstop, and she was zonked.

At about eleven o'clock, she took the subway back down to Hell's Kitchen and went to the diner on Tenth for her BLT and pea soup. Today no kids bothered her, and Carlos, at the counter, didn't say anything about what had happened last time. They just had their usual chitchat in Spanglish and then Geri flipped though the *Daily News*. There was a story about the Washington Heights shooting, how the police hadn't made an arrest and residents were concerned that there could be an increase in gang violence. Geri read part of the article but was too frustrated to finish it. She checked her phone to see if she'd missed any messages; nope, but while she had the phone out, she figured she'd try Diane Coles again.

The phone rang a few times, and Geri was expecting voice mail to pick up again. This time she'd leave a callback number, a short message.

Then a woman answered. "Hello? Can I help you?"

"Hi, my name's Geri Rodriguez, I'm with the NYPD, homicide, I'm calling about—"

"We've had enough with detectives, okay?" The woman sounded

angry. "We told you everything we know and at this point I'd appreciate it if you respected our privacy."

"This'll only take a few minutes of your time and—"

"I told you, we're not talking anymore. And did you say you were with the NYPD?"

"That's right."

"In New York?"

"Yes."

"Why're you calling here anyway? What does this have to do with you?"

"I just have some follow-up questions about an investigation you were already questioned about. It should only take a few minutes."

"Now the NYPD wants to talk to us? This is unbelievable."

"Ma'am, I—"

"Whatever this is about, I'm sure your colleagues with the Grosse Pointe police can fill you in because I'm through talking."

"Grosse Pointe?" Geri was lost.

"Yes," the woman said, "where did you think you were calling?"

"Manhattan," Geri said. "Am I speaking with Diane Coles?"

The line was silent. Geri thought they might have been disconnected.

"Hello," Geri said.

"This is Diane's mother. I guess you didn't hear."

"Didn't hear what?"

"My daughter's dead. She was shot to death in our driveway three days ago."

Geri let the news settle. *Dead? Shot to death? What did this mean?*

"I . . . I'm so sorry for your loss," Geri finally said.

"Yeah, I'm sure you are." Diane's mother clicked off.

Geri remained, phone to ear, listening to the silence.

SIX

"Luke, I am your father."

Simon was in the master bathroom in his apartment, looking in the mirror, practicing his James Earl Jones impression. It really was incredible how deep his voice could get. He used to have a normal tone, not particularly high or low—but now he spoke so deeply he could probably sing like Barry White.

Just for the hell of it, he crooned a couple of lines of the chorus of "Can't Get Enough of Your Love, Babe." Wow, not too shabby. He knew what he was singing the next time he went to a karaoke bar.

"Simon?" Alison was in the bedroom right outside the bathroom.

"Yeah?" Simon said, his face suddenly hot, like a teenager caught sneaking a drink from a liquor cabinet.

"Everything okay in there?"

"Yeah, um, everything's fine." Simon turned on the sink. "I'm just, um, finishing up shaving."

Actually Simon hadn't started shaving yet, but he needed to badly. Although he'd shaved last night before bed, he already had what he used to consider about three days' growth.

After shaving his face, he used the grooming feature on his razor to trim his chest hair. Then he cleaned up the little strands of hair from the floor and exited the bathroom. Alison was standing near the bed, fully dressed, in jeans and a thin leather jacket.

"Oh, you're ready to go already," Simon said. "Sorry, I guess I lost track of time. I'll be ready in about two minutes."

Simon took out a pair of jeans from the dresser drawer and pulled them on.

"Were you singing Barry White in there?"

There was no way to deny it. "Yeah," he said. "I guess I was."

"Since when do you like Barry White?"

"What do you mean? I've always liked Barry White."

"Really?" Alison said. "The last time I put on Barry White while we were having sex, I think it was last year, you didn't seem to like him very much then. What'd you say? Oh right, 'The music's putting too much pressure on me.'"

Simon remembered that time when Alison, on advice from Dr. Hagan, their marriage counselor, had downloaded Barry White's "Just Another Way to Say I Love You." Hagan had suggested it as a way to create more romance and intimacy in their marriage.

"Well, I guess he grew on me," Simon said.

Simon turned away from Alison, toward the closet, as he started to put on a sweater.

"I have another question for you."

Oh no, had she noticed hair on his back? He didn't have nearly

as much hair on his back as on his chest, but there was probably more
than there used to be.

But she asked, "How did your voice get so deep?"

"Oh, I don't know," Simon said, relieved they weren't talking
about back hair. "I guess it's always been deep."

"But I've heard you sing before," Alison said. "You could never
get nearly that low. You actually sounded a lot like Barry White
just now."

"I guess it's never too late to discover new talent," Simon said.

Seeming more fed up than confused, Alison left the bedroom.

Simon was aware that there was still a lot of tension in his marriage, but it didn't affect his upbeat mood. Since the cab had hit him
yesterday evening and he'd walked away pretty much unscathed, he'd
been feeling pleasantly uplifted. Like anyone who has a near-death
experience, he had a new appreciation for life and being alive, but he
was also starting to fully understand the enormity of what he had
become.

Pretty much all Simon knew about his condition was what
Michael's father, Volker Hartman, had told him, and it wasn't much.
Volker had come to Simon once, very briefly, downtown along the
river near Battery Park to warn Simon about the threat Michael
posed. He'd told Simon that werewolves—though he'd used the German word, *wolfe*, pronouncing it "vulf"—lived longer, and he
explained to Simon that the only certain way to kill a werewolf was
to rip its head open by tearing its jaw apart. Simon had confirmed
that this method actually did work, as he'd used it to kill Olivia.
Simon saw a flash of his hairy hands prying her jaw apart, and
remembered the sound of her ligaments and bones snapping and the
warm blood shooting against his face. God, how had he actually *done*
that? After all, she'd been no slouch; Simon had seen her, or *it*, toss

Ramon and Charlie around, and even bite off a chunk of Charlie's face, but Simon had somehow fought her off and had been able to reach into her mouth and grab her lower teeth in one hand and her upper teeth with the other. The teeth were sharp wolf teeth and cut into his skin, but he'd been so determined to stop her and save the guys that he was able to ignore the pain, or block it out, and continue his relentless assault.

While the events of that night seemed foggy and fragmented, like a dream almost forgotten, Simon remembered exactly what transforming had felt like. It was a rush of confidence and strength, and, though it was extremely painful, the sudden release of human worries and fears was relaxing, even blissful. Now in his nonwolf state he was strong—much stronger than he used to be—but it was nothing compared to how powerful he felt as a full-blown werewolf. When he was a werewolf he was in total control. Nothing, absolutely nothing, could defeat him and he felt like . . . well, like he was invincible.

Simon doubted he was actually immortal. For example, if someone tore his jaw apart he knew he wouldn't survive, and if he were in a fiery plane crash or at the epicenter of a nuclear explosion he probably wouldn't walk away unscathed. But last night a cab had slammed into him at about forty miles per hour and he'd gotten up as if he'd slipped in the street in the snow, so there was no doubt he had some superhuman ability to heal from injuries and absorb trauma. This raised the question, if the cab hadn't killed him, what would? Would a bullet to the heart or the brain do the job, or if he was shot would he miraculously heal? Or what if someone stabbed him with a knife and severed a major artery? Would his arteries heal immediately? And what about dying of natural causes? If he got cancer, would he somehow be able to fight it off?

When Simon was growing up, he was obsessed with superheroes. He devoured as many comic books as he could and sometimes imagined he was a superhero himself and had to save the world from imminent destruction. After he became an adult the obsession had waned but the fascination hadn't, and over the years he'd occasionally sneak out to his favorite comic book shop on his lunch break and read the latest releases. Now, as he sat at the edge of the bed tying his shoelaces, he thought, *Could I be a superhero?* Last month, seriously asking himself this question would have been the sign of a major mental illness, but now it didn't seem ridiculous at all. He could run extremely fast, seemed to have limitless endurance, and had survived an accident that would have killed anyone else; if those weren't prerequisites for superherodom, what were? Maybe he'd been looking at this all wrong, being so concerned about his potential for hurting people. What if he put his strength to good use and *helped* people? He could fight crime, save lives, or—hell, why not?—he could become a secret weapon for the U.S. Army—move over Captain America, here comes Simon Burns. Seriously, what did any Navy SEAL have on him?

"Are you coming?"

Alison's voice snapped Simon out of his fantasy.

"Yeah," Simon said, probably smiling widely. "Let's motor."

Alison seemed confused, as if she didn't recognize him. Then she said, "You seem so happy today."

"I guess I *am* happy," Simon said. "Is that a bad thing?"

Alison still looked like she couldn't figure Simon out. Then she said, "No, happiness is definitely not a bad thing."

Alison put Jeremy in his stroller, and then they headed out for a family day. Spending some quality time as a family had been Simon's suggestion, because he'd realized that since he'd lost his job and become a full-time stay-at-home, he and Alison had been doing a lot of tag-team parenting, which probably had been having as detrimental an effect on their marriage as anything else. After all, how could they get closer if they were always apart?

One of their typical family outings was to hang out at the South Street Seaport and then have lunch in Chinatown, so they'd decided that was where they'd head today.

Leaving the building, Alison, pushing the stroller ahead of her, turned left. Simon knew she was heading toward the subway at Eighty-sixth and Broadway because that was how they usually traveled downtown. But since he'd become a werewolf, there was nothing he hated more than the dank subways.

"Um, how about a cab?" Simon asked.

Alison stopped and said, "A cab? Why?"

"Um, I don't know," Simon said. "I just think it would be nicer, that's all." Actually he wanted to run downtown, but he knew that suggestion wouldn't go over very well.

"What's nice about a cab?" Alison asked. "Besides, we said we're cutting back on cabs, remember?"

It was true that they'd crunched the numbers and figured out that, despite Simon's unemployment payments, the only way they could get by in Manhattan on one salary was if they cut down on unnecessary expenses, such as taking taxis.

"Then how about a bus?" Simon suggested.

"It'll take forever to go downtown on a bus," Alison said.

"Come on, it'll be better," Simon said. "Besides, the 1 train is always packed on weekends. It'll be a pain with the stroller."

"If you really want to take a bus, let's take a bus," she said.

She was right—the trip downtown did take forever. Well, more than an hour anyway. But Alison didn't seem at all annoyed and

Jeremy was having a great time, getting attention from both parents at once for a change. They sang songs and told silly knock-knock jokes and it was great, just like old times.

When they got off the bus, Jeremy seemed tired and after a snack of Goldfish crackers and a little box of apple juice he got silent, the way he did when he was ready to take a nap. Sure enough, a few minutes later he was out cold.

Jeremy's naps usually lasted about an hour and a half, which would give Simon and Alison a good chunk of time to themselves. Having one-on-one time felt awkward, but it was also exciting, like a first date. They had to come up with topics for conversation and figure out how to talk to each other again. Alison told him about what had been going on with her work, how her firm was going to start test-marketing a new product, and how she would have to go for a couple of days of training in a few weeks. Simon shared some anecdotes about Jeremy and his latest learning leap—the other day he'd used the phrase *May I suggest* for the first time—and they marveled about how fast he was growing up and how time was flying by.

"I have to apologize to you," Alison said. "I shouldn't've tried to arrange that play date for you with Stacy Rosenberg."

"It's okay," Simon said.

"No, it isn't okay," she said. "I've just been under a lot of stress myself, with work and everything, and I shouldn't've undermined you. You're the stay-at-home dad."

Simon got the sense she wasn't speaking her own words, that she'd sought advice from a friend, or a book on marital problems, or even a psychologist. Still, Simon appreciated that she was trying to make up.

"Thanks," Simon said, "but you're right, Jeremy should be having more play dates and there's no reason why we can't meet up with your friend just to see how it goes. I know their daughter's younger, but who knows? Maybe they'll hit it off."

Alison smiled and said, "This feels good."

"What does?" Simon asked.

"Resolving conflict so easily," she said. "We waste so much time bickering. I mean, there's no reason to be at each other's throats."

Thinking that being at her throat was exactly what he was so afraid of, he said, "Yeah, that's definitely something we should try to avoid."

Walking up Water Street, he held her hand, feeling a twinge of arousal, but it was okay—he was confident he could control it.

"Oh, I meant to tell you," Alison said. "Did you hear about what happened at the zoo yesterday?"

Ignoring a flash of the polar bear pounding against the Plexiglas, Simon played dumb. "No, what happened?"

"It was on the local news this morning," Alison said, "you know, one of those morning shows. Yesterday afternoon Gus the polar bear apparently went crazy."

Alison described what had been reported, and Simon did a good job of acting like he was hearing it all for the first time.

"Wow," he said, "that's pretty intense."

"I was wondering if you guys were there when it happened," Alison said. "I mean they said it happened a little after noon. That's around when you were there, wasn't it?"

"Um, around then," Simon said. "I guess we must've just missed it."

"Yeah, you must've," Alison said.

Was Simon imagining it or did she seem a bit suspicious?

"We should probably get a snack for Jeremy, he'll be hungry when he gets up," he said, just to change the subject.

As they turned off Water Street onto the closed-off cobblestoned mall area of the Seaport, passing bars, restaurants, and touristy shops, Simon was suddenly aware of the strong odor of urine. Some reveler last night must've taken a leak—Simon was able to pinpoint the location—against the brick wall of a building to his right. He knew it was human urine, not animal urine. He could tell the difference— human urine smelled more like, well, more like his own urine. His ability to detect smells was another power that he could put to good use. What if he could be trained to sniff out bombs? He bet his ability to discern odors was as powerful as any police dog. He could save thousands of people and thwart a terrorist attack, maybe save the whole city.

Simon was aware that Alison had asked him a question, but he had no idea what the question was.

"Sorry, what was that?"

"I said doesn't it freak you out?"

Simon was lost for a few seconds, then caught on that she was still talking about the zoo. Trying to ignore another flash of the furious bear, he said, "Doesn't what freak me out?"

"You know." She was looking at him in a knowing way. Did she know? Was she just trying to get him to open up and tell her the truth? She added, "Polar bears don't usually lose it like that. And you know what always happens in disaster movies. It's always the animals who sense the danger first."

"So is that what you really think?" Simon said. "That there's going to be some big disaster?"

He was just relieved to be having a conversation that didn't contain the word *werewolf*.

"I don't know," she said. "But if there's a tsunami tonight, don't say I didn't warn you."

They smiled together. It felt good to be joking around and enjoying each other's company.

They wove through the crowd of mainly tourists and teenagers, toward the mall, which was on a pier stretching into the East River. For years, since well before Jeremy was born, they'd been coming down here, usually on warm summer nights, to have drinks overlooking the water.

"Want to go to our old spot?" Alison asked.

"I'd love that," Simon said.

Because Jeremy was still asleep in the stroller, they couldn't take the escalator, and Alison suggested the elevator.

Elevators weren't nearly as bad as the subway, but Simon had been trying to avoid them as much as possible; still, he didn't want to put up a stink about it. So they got on, with several other people, and though the aromas of deodorants and perfumes and bodily scents were overwhelming, Simon managed to get through it. He was so much better than he'd been just a couple of days ago. There was no doubt he was getting used to sensory overload.

They went past the shops and intoxicating odors of soaps, perfumes, and potpourri, and then through the food court and all the food odors—the burning meat the most alluring—into the mini mall, where he could still smell the meat mingling with the scents of all the people.

"How about we go outside and get some air?" Alison suggested.

Simon couldn't've been more thrilled with this idea, as all of the smells indoors were overwhelming his brain and making him extremely antsy. He felt much better as soon as they went out to the long deck/outdoor eating area. There was a great view of the river, the Brooklyn skyline, and the Brooklyn Bridge. As Alison checked on Jeremy in the stroller—his head had slumped to one side and she

straightened it out so he could continue his nap more comfortably—
Simon inhaled deeply, enjoying the air near the water that was so
much more oxygenated than normal city air. He was feeling better,
more relaxed, until, suddenly, he couldn't breathe at all.

Alison was still tending to Jeremy, moving sweaty strands of hair
off his forehead, and she didn't see Simon struggling. Also, Simon
managed to turn away so Alison couldn't see his face as he tried to
calm down. This was worse than any panic attack he'd experienced
lately. Usually it was all mental—he *thought* he couldn't breathe and
was dying—but this time the reaction was definitely physical. His
throat was constricting, as if he were choking, but the most troubling
symptom was the tingling in his hands and feet. It was similar to how
he'd felt the night he'd turned into a full-blown werewolf.

But he couldn't let that happen, especially not here, in broad
daylight at the South Street Seaport. What if he couldn't control his
impulses? He might go on a homicidal rampage, mauling whoever
got in his way. Women, children—including Alison and Jeremy—
would be in jeopardy. The police would try to gun him down, but
would their bullets kill him? A speeding cab had barely hurt him
when he wasn't in a full-blown state, so what damage would a few
gunshots do? If he transformed, he'd be much stronger, and probably
harder to kill. If he could be taken down by the cops, it would probably take more than a few bullets. It would require serious firepower,
but before the backup arrived Simon would do plenty of damage.
He'd experienced firsthand what werewolves were capable of, and he
imagined himself covered in blood, wildly biting off chunks of people's flesh. He could injure or kill hundreds, even thousands, before
he was stopped.

"He's so adorable when he sleeps, isn't he?"

Obviously Alison still didn't have any clue what was going on.

Simon was still struggling to breathe. His hands and feet were still tingly. He looked at his hands; was he imagining it, or were they a little hairier? They didn't look much different than they did normally, though; well, not different enough for anyone else to notice anyway.

"He'll probably wake up in twenty minutes," Alison said. "Maybe we can go to the dim sum place we went to last time, the one on Mott?"

Simon was breathing. It still felt like he had asthma, but at least he was getting air into his lungs.

"Or, wait, is it Bayard?" Alison asked. "I always get those streets down there confused . . . Are you okay?"

Simon waited to get enough air to speak, then said, "Yes," but his voice was very faint.

Alison came over to get a look at his face. He tried to turn away, but not fast enough, and she caught a glimpse.

"Oh my God," she said, "you're sweating."

Simon hadn't realized he was sweating, but he was. He tasted the saltiness on his lips, and his shirt was practically soaked. But he was relieved that the sensation in his extremities had almost dissipated completely, and he hoped the increased hairiness was going away as well.

"It's nothing," he said, "just a little anxiety. Dr. Levinson said I might have panic attacks. It's probably just a side effect of my medication."

He hated how it was getting easier and easier to tell these lies, how invented explanations flowed effortlessly.

She stared at him, as if she were trying to see into him, and he couldn't help wondering, *Can she?*

Then she finally said, "You look really pale."

"I'm fine," he said, thinking, *Yeah, fine except I think I'm about* to turn into a werewolf in one of the busiest areas of Manhattan. "I just need a minute."

"How about something to drink?" She reached into the bag attached to the handle of the stroller and took out a juice box. "Here."

He wasn't thirsty, but drinking seemed like a good idea. Alison poked the straw into the container and handed him the apple juice. The liquid did seem to relax his throat a little.

"How do you feel?" she asked.

"Better," he said, "I'm almost back."

Since the attack had started he'd been so focused on trying to breathe and to prevent a nightmare from ensuing that he hadn't thought about what had caused the panic. But now that he was calmer he turned away from Alison, toward the river, and gazed across at Brooklyn Heights, and to the left, the Brooklyn Bridge and the trendy DUMBO area, and beyond, before a bend in the river, the old factories and warehouses near the Navy Yard, including the defunct Hartman Brewery where all of Simon's troubles had begun.

When Simon had suggested going to the Seaport today he'd made no connection that he'd been returning to the area where, for all he knew, Michael and the guys were hanging out at this very moment. Like yesterday when he'd caught himself heading toward the Battery Park playground, he didn't know if coming here was just a coincidence, or if something was pulling him unconsciously. He remembered Michael saying, *Welcome back to us,* with his weird Germanic accent, and the voice in Simon's head was so clear that it sounded as if Michael himself were here next to him, whispering in his ear.

"Maybe you should call Levinson," Alison said.

"What?" Simon was startled, thinking she'd said, *Call Hartman,* even though that didn't make any sense. Then it hit and he said, "Oh. What for?"

"To adjust your medication," she said, as if it were obvious.

"It's not my medication," he said, thinking at least this wasn't a lie since he wasn't on any medication. "It's just going to take a little time, that's all."

He had the rest of the juice box and felt almost normal. He didn't know why he'd had such a strong panicked reaction, but he took it as a positive sign that he'd been able to avoid a full transformation. It gave him hope that it was possible that he could control all of this, and he wouldn't have to live his life in constant fear.

"Simon," Alison said in the tone she had when she was very angry or very serious; it was hard to tell which was the case this time.

"Yeah," Simon said.

She looked so intense; it was hard to maintain eye contact with her.

"Is there something you're not telling me?" she asked.

He wanted to blurt it out, get it all over with, say, *Yes, there is something I'm not telling you. I don't have lycanthropic disorder. I don't think I'm a werewolf, I actually am one. And I'm terrified that if you know the truth you'll leave me and take Jeremy away, so I'm hoping, no, I'm praying, I can figure out some way to control this, to keep it a secret forever, but still live a normal, functional life.*

But instead he heard himself say, "Not telling you about what?"

Before continuing, Alison looked around. There were a lot of people nearby, but no one seemed to be eavesdropping. Most people were just hanging out, eating, resting in wooden lounge chairs, or admiring the view. Maybe twenty yards away, a boy, maybe ten years old, was begging his mother for change to put into a coin-operated telescope, which was fixed on some point in the distance, maybe the Statue of Liberty. The boy was saying, "Please, Ma, I really wanna use it," and the mom was saying, "The answer is no," and then Simon realized that the conversation was taking place way too far away for an average person to overhear.

"Do you want to be in this marriage?" Alison asked.

"What?" Simon said. "What kind of ques—"

"I just want you to be honest with me," she said. "You don't have to be afraid to tell me the truth. If you want out and this is, I don't know, your way of trying to tell me, I understand. I mean, I *don't* understand, but I won't be angry at you for telling me how you feel."

Like before, Alison didn't sound like herself; she sounded like some self-help book. Simon held her hand and pulled her toward him, trying to focus on *her*, instead of how amazing she smelled and how badly he wanted her.

"Don't be ridiculous," he said. "You know that's not true."

"How do I know?" She seemed strong, in control, but he knew she was just overcompensating, trying not to get emotional in public. "All I know is you've been avoiding intimacy and now we're spending time together for the first time in ages and it seems to give you panic attacks."

"It's not you," Simon said.

"If it's not me," she said, "then who is it?"

He knew what she was getting at. "Come on, you know there's no one else."

"I want to believe that, I really do, and you know I never get jealous. But it's hard when . . . well, when I see the way women look at you."

"What do you mean?" Simon said, but it was hard to pretend to be shocked when he knew exactly what she meant.

"Come on, I see the way women are checking you out lately," Alison said. "Just before in the elevator, that cute blonde was totally staring at you. Maybe it's just an, I don't know, available vibe you're sending out."

Simon hadn't noticed the blonde. He'd been getting so much female attention lately, maybe he was becoming oblivious to it.

Simon put his arms around her waist and pulled her in close—it was okay, he was in control—and said, "It's true, I have noticed women paying more attention to me lately, but it's not on my end, I swear. Maybe they're just attracted to my wisdom."

"Your wisdom?"

"Yeah," Simon said, smiling to show he was joking. "Maybe I'm getting better with age, like cheese."

"Oh no, now he thinks he's cheese," Alison said. "I'm not going to have to find you a psychiatrist who cures that disorder too, am I?"

They were suddenly kissing. With his nose so close to her face, the scent of her skin was even more overwhelming. While he was aware of the effect this was having on his body, he tried to accept it, to go with it. Hadn't Michael once said that too, that you just have to go with it? Or maybe not—maybe it was something he'd said to himself—but it was helpful nevertheless.

Accept it, accept it, he kept telling himself, as he continued kissing her. His tongue was rougher than it used to be—more like a dog's than a human's—but if she noticed she didn't seem to care. Going by the way she was moaning softly and moving her hips up against him, she seemed to be pretty distracted.

Then, realizing they were in public, she pulled back, not too far—their noses were almost touching—and said, "I think we need to get a room."

"Accept it." Simon didn't mean to say this out loud.

"What?" Alison was confused.

"I mean it's a good thing we already live together," Simon said, and then he got distracted, looking beyond Alison toward the area in Brooklyn, past DUMBO, where the Hartman Brewery was located. Simon was certain that Michael was there at this very moment. He was probably hanging out with Charlie and Ramon and maybe with other werewolves. Simon pictured Michael, with his thick gray hair, jet black eyes, and usual affectless expression. The vision was so clear it had to be real.

Alison must've seen something in Simon's eyes.

"What's wrong?" she asked.

"Nothing." He kissed her again, holding her tight, loving that he was able to control himself and be close with his wife. Then with his lips still against hers he said, "Nothing at all."

The rest of the day was pretty much perfect. Jeremy woke up from his nap and the family took a nice walk to Chinatown. After they had lunch at their favorite dim sum place—Simon managed not to OD on pork dumplings, even though he wanted to, by repeating his *Accept it* mantra—they bought fruit and vegetables to last a few days and then caught a bus uptown at Canal and Hudson. It wasn't a particularly exciting day and nothing memorable happened—just a lot of small talk and tending to Jeremy—but that was what made it so great. It was a family Saturday like the other family Saturdays they used to have before he lost his job and this whole werewolf nightmare started.

But now Simon felt like he had new hope. Not only had repeating his new mantra helped temper his meat cravings, it seemed to curb the attention from random women. He was still getting noticed much more than he had in his pre-werewolf days—even the older Chinese woman serving the dim sum had given him a kind of seductive look while she was doling out the shrimp dumplings—but women weren't completely fawning over him the way they'd been lately. On the bus Simon was aware of a few women noticing him, the way they would notice any attractive guy, but the attention wasn't out of control.

When they got back to the apartment, Simon suggested that Alison go to the gym. Her schedule hadn't given her much opportunity to work out lately, and she was glad to have the time to herself. Simon and Jeremy played a game Simon had invented called "apartment tag," which involved almost constant running around the apartment. They were both having a blast, but they had to stop when the doorman called up with a noise complaint from the neighbors downstairs.

When Alison returned all sweaty—God, she smelled amazing—Simon, needing to exert himself in a big way, went for a run. In the park he wanted to let loose, but his mantra helped restrain him and he was content jogging at a normal pace around the park's six-mile "big loop."

Back at home, around nine, Alison had put Jeremy to bed.

"He fell right asleep; I was surprised," Alison said. "I mean after he had that long nap this afternoon. Maybe he's growing. So how do you feel?"

Simon knew she was really saying, *Do you want to have sex?* To make her intention even more clear, Alison bit down on her lower lip seductively. She'd showered, so her natural scent was masked by odors of shampoo, conditioner, soap, and skin moisturizer, but when Simon focused he could still make out her natural scent and he couldn't help getting turned on.

"Today was nice," Alison said, moving closer to Simon.

Even if she didn't notice the growing bulge in his sweats, she sensed he was getting excited, and he could smell her excitement.

"I know," Simon said. "We should have family days more often."

"I'm not just talking about that," Alison said. "I'm talking about us. It was nice kissing you at the Seaport."

Seeing the image of Michael, watching, waiting on the roof of the brewery, Simon said, "I know, it was really nice."

"We should have a regular date night," Alison said. "I know we've talked about it before with Dr. Hagan, but this time we should stick to it. We can get Christina to babysit one fixed night a week, let's say Thursday nights because I usually don't have any big meetings on Fridays, and then we can go out. Even if it's just out to dinner or to get coffee or take a walk around the neighborhood. It's time spent together and I think that's important."

"Sounds like a great idea," Simon said. "Let's go for it."

"Okay," Alison said, moving closer to him so that their bodies were practically touching. "Going for it sounds like a good idea to me."

Simon was thinking, *Accept it, accept it*, but being so close to Alison when she was so turned on was way too arousing, and he was terrified of what might happen next.

"Just relax," she said, and he could feel the heat from her breath on his face. "I'm not going to bite you."

But I'm *going to bite* you.

"I'm sorry," he said. "I'm . . . I'm just not ready yet."

She waited, then said, "I understand," but he could tell she didn't.

"We made progress today," Simon said, realizing he was sweating badly; even his face was wet. "I mean I think we're getting there, slowly but surely."

Alison didn't seem convinced. She said, "Well, you let me know when you want me again," and then kissed him quickly on the lips and went down the hallway toward the bedroom without saying good night.

* * *

Simon understood why Alison was frustrated, but he tried to stay positive. While it was true things were a long way from normal in their marriage, and he wasn't sure he'd ever have a regular sex life again, he had to look at the bright side—he was making progress, and if he continued to make progress every day, maybe normal, or at least almost normal, wasn't so far away.

On Sunday morning, Simon was up early, and after his usual extended sets of push-ups and sit-ups, he heard Jeremy stirring in his room. He hugged him—making sure not to get too carried away like the other morning—and then set him up in front of the TV with a sippy cup of milk and a couple of waffles. While Simon could have eaten twenty sausage links, he was content with just eight. He had to eat them ultra slowly to savor the flavor, but he took this as another example of the progress he was making. Maybe soon he'd be able to get by on just three or four links in the morning, and maybe over time the meat cravings would subside entirely. Maybe he'd be happy having fruit and yogurt in the morning, and he'd get satisfaction from eating fruit and vegetables and cereal. While he couldn't imagine a meatless existence—and the whole idea of it actually seemed like torture—nothing was out of the question.

Simon let Alison sleep late, till about ten. He felt bad about disappointing her sexually again last night, so to help make up for it he prepared her a breakfast of coffee, fruit salad, and oatmeal and had it waiting for her when she came into the dining room.

"You didn't have to do this," she said.

"I wanted to," he said. "You've been working hard and I just wanted to let you know how much I appreciate everything you've been doing."

"Thank you." She smiled. "It's nice to hear you say that."

Simon sat with her while she ate. He tried to have some coffee, but the bitterness repulsed him, so he sipped from a glass of water instead.

After breakfast, Alison went on "Jeremy duty," sitting with him on the living room floor in front of the TV while drawing in coloring books with magic markers. Simon slipped away into the bathroom and did his morning shave and body-hair trim. He was trimming the hair on his right leg—he hadn't trimmed his leg hair in a couple of days and it was getting out of control—when Alison called urgently from the living room, "Simon, come out here!"

Fearing that something had happened to Jeremy, Simon left the razor and rushed into the living room. Jeremy was still happily coloring and Alison was gripped by something on TV.

"I thought it was an emergency," Simon said.

"Sorry," Alison said, "but it is kind of incredible and I didn't want you to miss it."

Simon saw that Alison was watching the New York City Marathon. He knew the marathon was today; he'd seen them setting up for it in the park last night.

"Miss what?" he asked.

"Just look," she said.

They were showing the front-runners. Two slim black guys, probably from Kenya—a Kenyan always seemed to win the marathon—and slightly in front of them a noticeably stockier, much more muscular white guy. It was definitely unusual to see a big guy like that among the leaders.

"Can you believe it?" Alison said.

"Yeah, that is pretty weird," Simon said.

"They're saying he never even ran in a marathon before," she said.

"And he's a New York City fireman. Can you even imagine how big a news story this is going to be?"

The word *fireman* gave Simon a jolt. But even though at that moment he knew what was happening and the huge effect this was going to have on his life, he didn't want to believe what he was seeing. He wanted to believe it was some mistake. It was a hallucination, he was just imagining he was watching this, or he was still asleep, he hadn't woken up yet today, and this was just a dream.

But this wasn't a dream—that reality was setting in fast. This was a nightmare, except he wasn't asleep—the nightmare *was* reality.

Alison said, "Isn't it incredible?" as Simon stared at the screen, mesmerized, watching Charlie, the fireman/stay-at-home dad from Michael's pack, taking over the lead from the Kenyans, as the race was in its final stage in Central Park—it looked like the runners were near the Metropolitan Museum of Art. Then the angle switched to a close-up of Charlie, and in his expression Simon recognized that look of total euphoria and freedom. It was so familiar, he could've been watching himself.

Simon was so absorbed watching Charlie that he lost self-awareness for several seconds, maybe longer, and then he suddenly realized he had a much, much bigger problem.

He was turning into a werewolf.

SEVEN

Something rough and wet was touching Geri's face. She woke up, startled, slapping her cheek. *What the hell?* Then Wonka jumped off of her, screeching, and Geri realized she'd fallen asleep on the couch.

"Jesus," Geri said, trying to catch her breath and orient herself. She glanced at the window—it was dawn, Sunday morning. She'd been up most of the night, reading whatever she could find online about Diane Coles's murder in Michigan and ruminating about how it could possibly be connected to the Olivia Becker disappearance. She was also obsessing about the murder in Washington Heights, frustrated that they hadn't gotten a break yet. She hated unresolved cases, and now she had two of them to deal with. Ter-freakin'-rific.

From what Geri could tell, the police in Michigan hadn't made much headway in the Coles case. Last Wednesday afternoon at

approximately two P.M. Diane Coles had returned home from shopping at a nearby drugstore. When she was exiting the car, she was
shot and killed at close range. Ballistics had determined that the gun
was a S&W .38. The police had no suspects in the shooting and no
known motive. Her parents claimed she had been "distraught lately"
and had "a lot of anxiety" perhaps over a recent breakup with a boyfriend in Manhattan. One article contained interviews with neighbors, saying the usual, about how shocked they were about the
murder, how nothing bad ever happened in the neighborhood, and
the detective involved in the investigation was quoted, basically saying that the cops had zip.

When Geri had been a patrol cop at the 34th Precinct, she'd had
a mentor, Detective Antonio Munez. Antonio—now retired—was an
old-timer, had been with the force since the seventies, and Geri had
learned everything she knew about detective work from him. Maybe
it was corny, but sometimes when she was working on a case she
heard Antonio's voice in her head, guiding her, and now she heard
one of his favorite phrases: *No hay tal cosa como coincidencias* ("There
are no such things as coincidences"). That advice had never seemed
any more appropriate than in the Olivia Becker disappearance case.
She was dating a shady guy, Michael Hartman, who was the alibi in
three murders in New Jersey, and now her best friend was killed at
close range, with no apparent motive? There had to be some connection somewhere.

Geri wasn't sure what to do next. She could go to her CO, Dan,
trying to persuade him to let her take over the investigation, but
coincidences weren't evidence, and she doubted Dan would let her
have the case, especially given how much of a hard-ass he'd been
about the Becker case. Since the disappearance was Detective Mangel's case, she could let him in on what had happened to the woman

he'd questioned, but would Mangel take it seriously? Yeah, he'd look into it, talk to the Michigan police, but without any solid link to the Olivia Becker case it was doubtful he'd start requestioning witnesses. Mangel had struck Geri as a paper pusher. He had to be in his mid-fifties, probably looking at early retirement options. Why rock the boat? If Mangel did find a link to Becker and possibly to the New Jersey murders, it could be even worse because with a killer possibly crossing state lines, the Feds would get involved. At that point, Geri would be shut out of the case completely.

Willy and Wonka were meowing, Willy rubbing his head up against Geri's leg as she sat on the toilet, peeing.

"Okay, guys, I'll feed you, I'll feed you," Geri said. "Just chill out. Mommy's got a lot on her mind this morning."

They kept meowing until she went into the kitchen and put some Fancy Feast filet mignon–flavored cat food into their bowl.

"I helped you guys out, how about you give me some help now?" Geri said to the cats. "What do you guys think I should do? Do I hand this over to Mangel so he can sit on his fat sexist ass, or do I work on it myself?"

The cats ignored her, devouring their food, and then, with horror, Geri thought, *Oh, God, was I actually talking to my cats?* Maybe it was just lack of sleep, or maybe she was going crazy, losing her mind.

But she couldn't deny that seeking advice from her cats and hearing herself out loud had solidified in her head what she had to do. She had to be uptown later in the morning, to meet about the Washington Heights case, but before then she was going to go downtown, hopefully to talk to Michael Hartman at his apartment in Tribeca. She had questioned him there before, when she was investigating the New Jersey murders. She considered calling first, to save time if he wasn't there, but she preferred to have the element of surprise in her investigations. When people were caught off guard they were more likely to slip up, sometimes leading to breaks in cases.

She cabbed it downtown, making it in good time early on a Sunday morning. Hartman lived in an industrial building that had been converted to co-ops, probably in the eighties or nineties when a lot of the gentrification in Tribeca had taken place. She remembered that Hartman had told her that he owned the entire building. How many millions was a building this size in Tribeca worth? Five, ten? His family used to own a brewery, so maybe that was where he'd gotten rich. Or, who knows, maybe he was a drug kingpin. There was definitely something off about the guy. Maybe he didn't kill his girlfriend and her best friend to cover it up, but he was probably hiding something.

After pressing the M. HARTMAN button, Geri waited about a minute. It was possible he wasn't home or was still sleeping—it was only just after nine after all. Or maybe he was home but just wasn't letting her in. There was a camera on the intercom; it could be on and he was watching her. She definitely *felt* watched. She buzzed again, waited about a minute, then buzzed a third time and waited. She was about to buzz time number four when she heard the intercom go on.

"You've come to see me," Hartman said.

Geri remembered that Michael had this weird way of talking, where he was very direct and straightforward. It was only one of the weird things about the guy.

"You remember me, huh?" Geri said, looking at the camera, uncomfortable that he could see her but she couldn't see him. It made her feel like she was one step behind, not in control, and she hated that feeling.

The buzzer beeped and Geri entered the vestibule, where the elevator's doors opened on their own for her. In the elevator, she pressed 4, but the button didn't light up, and then the doors closed very fast. She tried the button again, still no luck, and then tried the other buttons.

Muttering to herself, hoping she wasn't stuck, she continued pressing buttons. Then, after maybe ten more seconds, the elevator started moving. At the fourth floor, when the doors opened, Michael was waiting. He was maybe ten feet away from the elevator with his hands at his sides. His gray, almost white hair was combed straight back and he was wearing the same red silk robe he'd been wearing the last time she'd interviewed him. Who did the guy think he was, Hugh Hefner?

"I'm waiting for you," he said.

In addition to the weird way he spoke, he had an accent, maybe German, but it didn't really sound German. It sounded like a mix of German and something else.

"Well, I got up here as fast as I could," Geri said.

She waited for him to say something, maybe invite her into the living room area of the huge loft, which was the size of an entire floor of the building—he had all this money from a beer business that wasn't even a business anymore? Hm—but he didn't say anything, just stared at her with his very dark eyes. That was another weird thing about him—his eyes and the way he stared at her. She didn't know if he did that to everybody or if he was just trying to be a wise guy, to make her feel uncomfortable. Geri was usually good at reading people, could figure out an MO, but Michael Hartman was a total mystery to her.

"So," Geri said, "can we sit down for a few minutes? I know it's early in the morning, but something just came up that I really need to talk to you about."

"You've found Olivia," Michael said.

"No," Geri said. "Actually I'm not really working on that case, but that's actually part of the reason I'm here. Can we sit down?"

That's the way, tell him *what to do. Take back control.*

But Michael just stood there.

"Or," Geri said, "if you prefer to go down to the station and talk, we can do it that way."

"It's not your case," Michael said.

"Yeah," Geri said. "So?"

"You won't take me to the precinct to talk. You can't take me to the precinct; that's why you're here."

So much for getting back in control.

"Look, if you don't want to talk to me, you don't have to," Geri said. "But this might be my case soon, and I guarantee if I have to come back here again I won't be nearly as pleasant."

Geri was trying to regain the upper hand, the way she would with a usual person she questioned on a case, but Michael wasn't a usual person—that was becoming very clear. Nothing seemed to faze this guy. Actually Geri's threat had the opposite effect, as she was the one who felt threatened. He wasn't doing anything to make her feel in danger; there was just something about him that exuded a general feeling of menace. Maybe it was the way his dark eyes were fixed on her and his expression was entirely blank, and she had no idea what he was thinking, or what he might do next. Just in case, Geri was aware of her Glock 26, her off-duty piece, tucked in a holster right above her waist. She knew, if she had to, she could have it in her hand and fire it in less than two seconds. She'd always been a quick draw, the fastest draw in her year at the academy.

"Come," Michael said, and he walked toward the living room area, leaving her behind near the elevators.

Geri hated that she felt so intimidated; she was the cop, *she* was the one who was supposed to do the intimidating. She took a deep breath, getting a grip, then went into the living room area, where Michael was already seated where he'd sat the other time she'd been here—on a chair across from the couch. It was a wooden chair; it looked like an antique, and it was several inches higher than the level of the couch where Geri sat. Had he planned it this way so he could be above her, looking downward? Yeah, probably.

"Your son with his mother?" Geri asked, looking toward a Power Ranger Black Wolf action figure on the coffee table. She'd met his young boy during his last visit.

"You don't have children," Michael said.

"Excuse me?" The statement was so unusual that Geri was caught a little off guard.

"Having a child is the most beautiful thing in the world," Michael said. "There is nothing more rewarding than looking into your son's eyes, noticing his resemblance to yourself, knowing he's yours, that you created him."

"Yes, I agree," Geri said, deciding that Michael was probably mentally ill or at least had a major personality disorder, and she had to stop letting him get to her.

"Yet you chose not to have a child," he said. "You wanted to be alone, without beauty."

Geri had no idea how he seemed to know details of her personal life.

"Thanks for your insight," Geri said, "but I'm not here to talk about me; I'm here to talk about a woman who was killed in Michigan last week. Do you know Diane Coles?"

"Yes," Michael said.

She waited for him to elaborate. He didn't.

She asked, "How did you two meet?"

"Olivia was my lover."

"So you met through Olivia."

Michael didn't answer.

"Did you talk to Diane after Olivia disappeared?"

"No," Michael said.

Geri was frustrated that she still couldn't read Michael; she had no idea if he was lying or telling the truth.

"Were you and Diane friendly?"

"She was a friend of my lover."

"I know, you said that, but were you friends?"

Long stare, then finally, "No."

"So did you see Diane frequently?"

"Diane was the lover of a man in my pack."

"I'm sorry. Your pack?"

"Yes."

"Maybe I'm wrong about this, but you don't seem very surprised to hear about Diane's death."

"Death never surprises me." Michael was deadpan.

"Really?" Geri wondered, *Is this guy for real?*

"I'm sorry, maybe I'm just having trouble reading you," Geri said, "but you don't seem very upset about any of this actually. I told you the girlfriend of one of your friends was killed, and you don't seem to care very much one way or another."

For a long time, maybe ten seconds, Michael didn't answer. Again, Geri was aware of the menace he was emitting, and she was trying her hardest not to let it affect her.

Finally he said, "I don't feel sadness."

"Never?" Geri tried to stare at him, give him a taste of what it felt like, but she felt silly and it didn't seem to be having any effect on him anyway. Then she said, "You don't even feel sad when somebody dies, somebody close to you?"

"The woman wasn't close to me."

"But 'the woman' was close to your friend. Don't you feel bad about that?"

"Only the weak feel bad about death."

"I know some strong people who feel pretty bad when somebody dies."

"Death is natural."

"Diane didn't die of natural causes." She didn't want to mention that Diane had been shot, hoping that he'd let this fact slip himself if he was involved.

But instead he said, "Animals don't mourn the dead."

"Why does it matter what animals do?" Geri asked. "And by the way, that's not true. If a dog loses a friend, the dog mourns. Monkeys mourn."

"Mourning is weakness," Michael said.

Geri was frustrated that she'd lost control of her questioning again, that they were talking about freaking monkeys. She asked, "Where were you the night Olivia Becker disappeared?"

"You're asking this question, yet this isn't your case," Michael said.

"Please just answer the question."

"Questions only waste time. You should be direct. You don't have questions; you want knowledge. You're asking me if I killed my lover, Olivia, or if I killed Ramon's lover. I didn't kill these people. Now you have the knowledge you came for and you can leave."

Hating that she was flustered, Geri asked, "Is Ramon the guy in your pack?"

"Yes," Michael said.

"Okay then, well, if you don't mind another of my silly questions, can anybody besides your father vouch that you didn't take a trip to Michigan last week?"

"My pack knows where I was."

"Who else is in your pack of friends besides Ramon?"

"There is Charlie."

"What about your playground buddy, Simon Burns?"

Michael didn't answer. Geri was getting tired of mind games.

Then Michael said, "Yes, Simon is in my pack. But Ramon and Charlie know I was here. You must go now."

Even though she was about ready to leave anyway, she didn't like being told what to do.

"Do these guys in your pack, Charlie and Ramon, have last names?" she asked.

"I don't know their surnames," he said.

"Wait, these are your friends and you don't know their last names?"

"Names don't concern me," he said.

"Yeah, well, they concern me," Geri said. "How about their phone numbers?"

Without bothering to mention where he was going, Michael walked away to another part of the loft. He returned a few minutes later with his phone and gave Geri Charlie and Ramon's numbers.

"I have given you what you want; now leave," he said.

Smiling, thinking, *Well, this is one day I'll never forget*, she went to the elevator. When she got on, Michael stood watching her until the doors closed. Geri pressed the button for the ground level, but, like before, the elevator didn't budge for a long time, and then, without any button lit up, it moved on its own. Maybe there was something wrong with the buttons that they didn't light up, but Geri had a feeling that Michael was controlling the elevator with some remote switch. But just because the guy was weird as hell and a control freak didn't mean he had anything to do with any murders. Still, Geri felt something off about him, and she was eager to check up with his friends Charlie and Ramon. It was interesting that Michael had seemed uncomfortable at the mention of Simon Burns. Was there some kind of rift there? That was another thing to look into.

It was ten to ten and Geri needed to be all the way uptown at Manhattan North ASAP or she'd catch more hell from Dan. She figured a cab would be faster than the subway, but maybe this wasn't her day because in midtown she hit bumper-to-bumper traffic— thank you very much, marathon.

Simon rushed into the bathroom off the hallway and tried to lock the door but couldn't. His hands had already partially transformed into claws and he couldn't push the lock on the handle. The pain in his joints and bones was practically unbearable, and though he was trying to scream, he was making a loud growling sound.

"Simon? What the hell is going on in there? Simon?"

Alison opened the door to the bathroom, but only an inch or two, before Simon used his weight to slam it shut.

"Simon, what's *wrong* with you?"

"I'm okay," he said, or tried to say. He could *think* the words but couldn't speak them.

Alison was still pushing against the door, saying, "Simon, open up, Simon," and then he had an idea. He bent over—it was weird, his back felt extremely flexible and agile—and used his tongue—which had become thicker, longer, and much stronger—to push the lock shut. The whole thing was ridiculous, of course, because how could a flimsy little lock restrain him?

"What is wrong with you, Simon? Why are you acting this way?"

Simon could tell that Alison was extremely angry but also on the verge of tears. He wished there were something he could do to reassure her, but trying to talk to her only seemed to be making things worse.

Then he looked at the mirror. His first thought—it wasn't a mirror, it was a TV screen. He wasn't looking at himself—it was an actor, playing a role. But this delusion didn't last for long. He raised his right arm slightly, and sure enough the thing in the mirror moved its arm as well. Still unconvinced—or deep in denial—he flared his nostrils, and the dark, practically black wolflike nostrils of the beast in the mirror flared. Then he tried to touch his face, but he did it awkwardly, with too much force, and he hit himself so hard he stumbled back against the door.

This got another "Simon?!"

He recovered and looked at the mirror again. He'd cut his face with his claws. *Claws?* He flexed his hands but didn't have total control of them. It almost felt like he was wearing two catcher's mitts. The T-shirt he'd been wearing was stretched to its extreme, about to rip, like something out of his old Incredible Hulk comics.

Oh God, how was this possible? Then it finally set in that this was his life now, his new reality. This half-man, half-animal thing was the new him.

The door was still shaking. He could smell Alison's scent, which turned him on, but he also wanted her in another way. He wanted to dig his fangs into her, to taste her. She smelled so good, she would have to be the ultimate meal.

Craving her uncontrollably, he rammed against the door, practically breaking the hinges. Suddenly the bathroom felt like a cage, and he had to escape, be free. He charged the door again, when a voice inside shouted, *No!* He didn't really want to hurt his wife. The other Simon Burns was still inside him somewhere, but this voice was faint, muted, and overwhelmed.

"You're gonna break the door down!" Alison screamed. "Stop it! Just stop it!"

He rammed the door again, the hinges barely holding, now detecting Jeremy's scent as well. The scent was extremely strong, and Simon knew this meant fear. The crazy animal part of him wanted to break down the door and attack Jeremy, but the rational Simon voice was screaming, *No! Stop!*

Instead of ramming the door again, the Simon voice steered him into the shower stall. He wanted to get under water, cold water, but he realized that, like with the door handle, his wolf hands couldn't turn the faucet, so he bent down and tried to use his tongue. It was much harder to move a faucet, though, and to coordinate the movements of his body, and the combined scents of Alison and Jeremy were extremely tempting, making him ravenous. He didn't know how much longer he'd be able to resist busting out of this bathroom/cage and attacking them.

Then the faucet turned—slightly at first, but then he made more progress and water was coming out in a steady stream. Next he used his tongue to push the lever that shifted the water between the tub and shower, and a moment later cold water sprayed all over his head and back. The water felt especially cold, like ice—maybe in his form as a werewolf his skin had become more sensitive?—and the Simon voice wondered if this had been a big mistake. Maybe the shock of the cold water would just antagonize the werewolf part of him more and cause a deeper transformation, and the rational Simon voice would be muted completely.

Simon was leaving the bathtub when he was suddenly in pain again. It wasn't nearly as bad as before, but it seemed to affect every part of his body and was so intense his legs buckled and he fell onto the floor. Then he started spasming, as if he were having a seizure, and his Simon voice was saying, *Hold on, just hold on*, and he could hear Alison—he knew she wasn't right outside the bathroom any longer, because her scent had faded, but her voice was still clear— maybe on the phone, saying, ". . . think he's having some kind of attack . . ." and then it ended. Well, at least the spasming stopped, most of the pains were gone, and he felt almost normal. He looked at his hand and saw the end of it—his claws transforming back into fingernails. What the *hell*? But he was so happy to have his hands back, and probably in shock, that the total absurdity of what was happening barely occurred to him.

He stood, on his *normal* feet, and looked in the mirror and thanked God it was him staring back, the *real* him. He was so happy he actually started laughing, softly at first, but then with more energy, until he was looking in the mirror laughing hysterically. Then he became aware of the scent of Jeremy standing outside the bathroom, but unlike before, he wanted to hold his son and protect him, not hurt him. He opened the door and said, "Hey, kiddo!" and bent down and lifted him up. He was so thrilled to see him, he didn't notice he was crying right away.

"It's okay, don't be sad, everything's fine," he said. "See, your daddy's okay."

"Put him down."

Simon looked over and saw Alison at the end of the foyer, near the kitchen. She looked as angry as she'd sounded.

He said, "Everything's o—" and she cut him off with, "Did you hear what I said?"

He noticed she had one of her hands behind her back; was she holding something?

Not wanting to get Jeremy more upset than he already was, he squatted and let go of him.

"Go play in your room," Alison said, trying too hard to sound sweet.

Jeremy was smart, could see right through it, and said, "Why are you mad at me, Mommy?"

"I'm not mad at you, sweetie," she said. "Mommy loves you very, very much, but Mommy wants you to go play in your room now, so please go and play, okay?"

Still wasn't working; Jeremy was on the verge of tears.

"Listen to Mommy," Simon said. "I'll come in and play with you in a few minutes, okay?"

"O-okay, Daddy," Jeremy managed to say, and then went to his room.

Before Simon could say anything, Alison, fuming, said in a hushed tone, "Get out."

"Okay," Simon said, "just calm—"

"I gave you a chance," she said unsteadily, "and I told you I was serious, so please just leave without making a big scene and scaring Jeremy more than you already have."

She was still talking in a loud whisper, but Simon looked back to make sure Jeremy wasn't there, just in case.

"I had a little setback, okay?" Simon said. "But I'm making progress, I'm getting better."

"Oh, really? Acting totally insane and trying to break down the bathroom door is progress?"

Simon wanted to keep denying it, but noticing the paint chips on the floor from the hinges almost breaking, he knew he couldn't.

"This was an isolated incident," he said, "but overall you have to admit I'm getting much better. Yesterday we had a great day, didn't we?"

He was smiling, trying to win her over, but it wasn't working.

She stared at him for a few seconds like, well, like she absolutely hated him, then said, "I'm sick of all this Jekyll and Hyde crap. I don't know who you are anymore."

Simon caught a glimpse of what she was hiding behind her back. It was something shiny.

"What's that?"

"Nothing," she said.

"Is that a *knife*?"

He took a step toward her.

Now she held out the knife—the biggest one they had—and said, "Stay back, just stay the hell back."

"Come on, put the knife down," Simon said in a fake relaxed tone, trying to minimize the situation. "I'm calm now, okay? I know my little freakout was probably really scary, but it's over. You have nothing to worry about."

"Mommy."

Jeremy had come out of his room and was looking right at Alison with the knife.

The fake-calm mommy voice was officially gone. She lost it and screamed, "Get the hell back to your room, Jeremy, right now! Right now!"

Terrified, Jeremy darted back to his room.

"Come on," Simon said to Alison, "you didn't have to—"

"Just leave us alone," Alison said. "Go downstairs and wait in the lobby."

"Wait? Wait for what?" Then he remembered hearing her make that phone call. "Who did you call?"

"I trusted you," she said. "I gave you another chance, but I told you that was it, the *last* chance. I think I've been extremely patient."

"You called 911?" Simon said. "Why'd you do that?"

"You need help," Alison said. "More help than you're getting from Dr. Levinson."

Oh, God, this was the last thing Simon needed—more trouble from the police. When his boss was killed last month, he'd been a suspect, and he was brought into the Manhattan North precinct and questioned extensively. He'd really thought that detective, Rodriguez, was going to find some evidence that he was involved in the killing. But that was before he was a werewolf—well, at least before he was a full-blown werewolf. What if he was questioned again? They could pick up on something in his behavior or, even worse, make him submit to a blood test. If they found the wolves' blood in his system, there would be chaos. The discovery of a man with the blood of a wolf, the revelation that werewolf mythology wasn't mythology at all—it was real, it was actually happening—would cause the media frenzy to end all media frenzies. It would be as if alien life had been discovered for the first time—but the alien wasn't from outer space; the alien was from right here in New York City and his name was Simon Burns. And Simon would undoubtedly be treated like an extraterrestrial life form—studied, analyzed, probed—kept apart from humans, including his own family.

"Call 911 back," Simon said. "Cancel the call. Tell them everything's fine. Tell them you made a mistake."

"I can't live like this anymore," Alison said. "I can't . . . I just can't."

"Cancel it," Simon said, "for Jeremy's sake. You don't want a whole scene here, do you?"

Alison was crying now, still holding the knife in front of her.

Simon considered trying to get the knife, then calling 911 back him-self, but he didn't want to make things any worse, and besides, it was probably too late to cancel the call. She'd called them, what, five, ten minutes ago? He'd lost track of time; the cops could be here any second.

"Okay, you're right, I need help," Simon said. "I'll wait in the lobby, okay? I just don't want to have any more drama, okay?"

Alison didn't answer, but now she was holding the knife limply by her side. Simon, with his hands raised in an I'm-not-going-to-touch-you-see? way, went around her, toward the front door. As he knelt to put on his sneakers, he looked toward the living room, at the TV. Charlie had finished the marathon and there were a swarm of report-ers around him and microphones in front of his face. One reporter asked, "How long have you been training for the marathon?"

The camera moved closer on Charlie's face. He looked blissful, content, and barely winded.

"Not long," he said. "Only a few weeks, actually."

Simon cursed under his breath. Alison was watching him, tears dripping down her cheeks.

"I'll call you later and let you know how things are going," Simon said. "A little time apart'll probably do us some good anyway."

Simon wanted to say good-bye to Jeremy, to reassure him, but he knew the police could be here at any moment.

"I love you both very, very much," he was saying as he left the apartment.

EIGHT

Before the elevator doors opened, Simon smelled the cops in the lobby. He wasn't sure exactly how he was able to distinguish cops from other people, but when the doors opened, sure enough two uniformed officers were getting on the elevator.

Nonchalantly, Simon walked right by them. The doorman, James, saw him and, eyes widening, said, "Hey, those cops were heading up to your place; everything all right up there?"

"Yep, perfect," Simon said as he left the building.

When he turned onto Columbus Avenue, he started to run. Not too fast—he didn't want to attract attention—but fast enough to get some distance between himself and his building as quickly as he could.

He had no plan. He just wanted to get away, to be alone for a while, to figure out what to do next, but, maybe instinctively, he ran toward the comforting autumn scents of Central Park. The streets leading to and from the park had swarms of marathon fans, and Simon had to navigate between them. In the park, at the first opportunity, he darted into a woodsy area. Still, he wasn't exactly alone. Besides the people he could actually see, he could hear and smell people all around him. He tried to block out the sensations, but they kept gnawing on his brain, like being surrounded by annoying cell phone conversations he couldn't ignore. And despite the fact that he was away from his apartment and the cops, he didn't feel safe because it wasn't the cops who were the danger. Even if the cops had shown up while he was at the apartment and he was taken away in a straitjacket, he would have had a chance to talk his way out of it. He could figure out how to avoid a drug test, learn to modify his behavior, work on repairing his marriage. All of this was, at least potentially, within his control. No, his biggest threat was what he couldn't control which, unfortunately, was himself. He was his own biggest danger.

But none of this was a revelation to him. He knew what was at stake when he saw Charlie on TV, and when he left the apartment, and that was why he'd gone into the park and why he was running downtown toward the finish line of the New York City Marathon at the south end of the park.

As he got closer to the finish line, the sounds and combined odors of the throngs of people increased. There were lots of cops around too, but Simon wasn't concerned. A 911 call had been placed for a domestic complaint on the Upper West Side; he wasn't exactly a wanted man. But as Simon passed a group of officers he suddenly realized how he was able to distinguish them from other people—it was the scent of gunpowder. Wow, Simon was seriously impressed with himself. He might have been even more in awe of his talents if he weren't on the verge of his whole life going to hell.

Close to the Columbus Circle exit of the park, the crowd got so dense that he had to walk. He knew he was heading in the general direction of the marathon's finish line when another amazing thing happened—he could *smell* Charlie. There had to be thousands of people in the area, yet he was certain he was detecting Charlie. As he made his way through, going as fast as he could, he noticed women noticing him, some giving him admiring looks and smiling at him, and then he accidentally bumped into a big, muscular guy, and the bottle of Powerade he was holding spilled a little.

"Hey," the guy said.

He turned toward Simon, glaring angrily. Simon stopped and looked at the guy but didn't say anything. Simon didn't say anything—just looked right in the guy's eyes—and the guy's expression suddenly softened. The guy was clearly intimidated, knowing that Simon was someone he didn't want to mess with. Then the guy and his girlfriend continued away without saying another word.

Simon continued toward Charlie. The crowd was so dense that Simon had to stop, maybe fifty yards from where he knew Charlie was, near the marathon's finish line. Exhausted runners were arriving at a practically constant rate and, over the PA system, someone was announcing their times in a loud, garbled, echoing tone. While Simon couldn't see very far ahead of him, he could see reporters near where Charlie was, and a bunch of TV crews.

Oh, God, it was as bad as he'd feared—Charlie was on the verge of becoming a media sensation.

There was commotion near where the camera crews were bunched, and then people nearer to Simon began stirring. There was increased chatter, but there were so many people talking at once it was hard for Simon to make out more than snippets. He heard a woman say "to the side" and a man say "him through." The crowd

was parting and the Charlie scent was getting stronger. As the anticipation built, Simon felt strangely excited, as if something magical
were about to happen, and then it did.

Several yards ahead of Simon, Charlie appeared. Although Simon
had expected to see him, actually seeing him was still somehow
shocking. It felt surreal, like a dream or fantasy. Going by Charlie's
expression, how he seemed content and in awe, with a Zen-like smile,
he seemed to be feeling the same way.

"I knew it was you," Charlie said.

Charlie's voice sounded the same—with a slight Brooklyn
accent—but there was something different about him. Not just his
stronger-than-before scent and appearance—he was leaner and more
muscular than he'd been a few weeks ago—but his whole demeanor.
He had a new air of confidence about him, and there was something
different about his blue eyes too. They used to be light blue; now they
were darker, practically navy, and much more intense.

Simon was positive that Charlie was a werewolf.

"Wow, it's great to see you," Simon said, and he couldn't have
been making a bigger understatement. It was greater than great to
see him. It was amazing to be face-to-face with someone like himself,
and he found himself unprepared for the rush of emotion he felt. He
had an overriding sense of relief and a feeling of *Thank God I'm not
alone.*

Simon was unaware of time, and it seemed as though everything
went silent. It was just Simon and Charlie, face-to-face, and the people
and the park and the whole rest of the world disappeared.

Then they were hugging. Simon didn't know who'd hugged who
first, whether Charlie had come over to him or he'd gone over to
Charlie, but it didn't really matter. The only important thing was that
they were hugging, being unrestrained with their emotions, acting

the way they felt. He had forgotten how comforting it was to have this camaraderie, to experience real closeness, and he realized how much he'd been missing it. Simon was unprepared for the emotion he felt, as if he were reconnecting with an old family member. Ah, and Charlie's scent also gave Simon a warm, connected feeling. His aroma was particularly pungent, undoubtedly because he'd just run a marathon, but he wasn't soaked in sweat. His shirt was only slightly moist, the way Simon's shirts were after long runs.

Finally, after embracing for maybe a minute or longer, they let go.

"This is crazy," Charlie said. "How'd you find me?"

"I saw you on TV," Simon said.

"Oh, yeah, that," Charlie said. "Can you believe I ran in a *marathon*?" He sounded almost giddy about it.

Simon remembered why he'd come here, because of the danger Charlie had potentially put him in, but he was still so excited himself about reestablishing contact with his old friend that those rational concerns quickly receded.

"Well, it was still pretty surprising seeing you here," Charlie said. "I mean I knew I'd see you again eventually, but I didn't know I'd see you here, now, today."

Wondering why Charlie was so certain their paths would cross again, Simon said, "Well, it was definitely a big surprise to see you on TV, running in the marathon."

At that moment a TV reporter who reeked of cigarettes and who had dyed black hair—Simon could smell the dye—came over and said, "Excuse me, Mr. Hennessy, can we just ask you a few more questions?"

"Sorry, gotta run," Charlie said, and he grabbed Simon's wrist and led him away through the crowd.

They were heading toward Columbus Circle. Simon didn't ask

where Charlie was leading him, but he was just glad to be getting away from the hordes of people because it had been starting to get him seriously claustrophobic.

As they approached the exit near Fifty-ninth Street, Charlie let go of Simon's wrist and said, "Had to get away from there. Being around all those people was driving me crazy."

Simon had to admit, he loved that he and Charlie were on the same wavelength. Since he'd been disconnected from the guys he hadn't felt this kind of connection to anyone, and he hadn't realized how much he'd missed it.

"Where are we going?" Simon asked.

"Away," Charlie said.

Simon knew that feeling well, of wanting to get away. He'd had it for weeks.

Simon let Charlie lead the way, jaywalking through slow-moving traffic on Columbus Avenue, then past the Time Warner building, onto West Fifty-eighth.

As they approached Ninth Avenue, a man seemed to recognize Charlie and said to his girlfriend, "Check it out, it's the fireman from the marathon."

Then a couple of blocks up, another man—across the street, but Simon could still hear him clearly—said, "Hey, didn't he just run in the marathon?" and on the next block a teenage boy said to his girl-friend, "Yo, check it out, it's the marathon man."

Charlie didn't acknowledge the people who spotted him, but Simon's earlier fear seemed to be justified—Charlie was now a celeb-rity, potentially a world celebrity. He'd lost his anonymity, not just for himself, but for Simon as well.

But while Simon knew this should concern him, at the moment

he was so excited to be back with a kindred spirit, nothing else seemed to matter.

They went into a bar on Tenth Avenue and went through to an outdoor seating area. There were picnic tables set up around the backyard—most occupied by at least a few people, but there were a few empty ones toward the back. Charlie sat at one of the tables in the back corner and Simon sat across from him. Before Simon could say a word, Charlie ordered two pints of Stella and eight rare hamburgers.

"Eight?" the waitress asked, confused.

"Good point, better make it ten," Charlie said. "I just ran in the marathon, after all. And no buns."

"Oh . . . okay," she said. "Do you want these on separate plates?"

"One's fine," Charlie said.

The waitress, still seeming a little baffled, returned inside.

"You think that was a mistake?" Charlie asked.

"Actually, I'd love some meat myself," Simon said.

"No, I mean the beer," Charlie said. "I should probably be having water after running twenty-six miles, but I was in the mood for a nice, cold brewski."

"As long as it's not the family beer," Simon said.

At the brewery in Brooklyn, Michael had given the guys a "family beer" that had, in effect, prepped them to become werewolves. The beer had turned them into half-wolves, causing some werewolf behavior. Then, after they were bitten on their necks on the night of a full moon, they became full-blown werewolves.

"I don't think there's any need for that now." Charlie's blue eyes had definitely gotten darker. They were practically midnight blue. He added, "It really is great to see you, man. I wanted to come looking for you, but Michael wouldn't let me. He said it would be better if you came back on your own."

"So Michael's still here," Simon said. "In the city?"

"Of course," Charlie said. "Where'd you think he was?"

Simon remembered being at the Seaport yesterday, having the certain feeling that Michael was on the roof of the brewery, watching him.

"What about Ramon?" Simon asked.

"He's doing great," Charlie said. "Yeah, I think I've seen him with five different women over the last few weeks, and I bet there are more. They just can't keep their hands off him, and he's not exactly trying to stop them. But he's not leading anybody on, know what I mean? He's a straight shooter, and they know what they're getting into. He says he just wants to have sex—sorry, *make love* to them—and they're all okay with it."

This was yet another thing Simon had to worry about. What if Ramon blurted out that he was a werewolf to one of the women he seduced? And how did he have sex with them anyway, without transforming?

He was about to ask about this, but Charlie said, "And you look great too. You look strong, healthy. You been running a lot?"

"Actually, I have been," Simon said.

"Nothing better, right? I wish you could've run in the marathon with me. Being in front, barely breaking a sweat, all those people cheering. It was freakin' awesome."

"Well, I'm just glad you can run at all," Simon said. "The last time I saw you, you were in pretty bad shape."

"Yeah, a werewolf bit off a chunk of my face; it doesn't get any worse than that, right?" Charlie laughed. "I lost a ton of blood. I didn't think I'd make it."

Simon had a flashback of Olivia, the crazed werewolf, attacking Charlie, biting into his face with her enormous fangs.

Charlie touched his cheek, and Simon noticed a faint scar.

"I figured that if you survived you would at least be deformed," Simon said. "I know we heal quicker but you can barely tell anything happened."

"It's one of the gifts Michael gave us," Charlie said.

Simon had to do a double take. Charlie still sounded like his old self, but he never used to talk about "gifts" with a glazed-over, cultish look in his eyes.

"What did Michael tell you?" Simon asked. "I mean, how is all this happening? What did he do to us? What was in that family beer? How did he get the way he is? Does anybody else know about it? Has he told you *anything*?"

Charlie was almost smiling, as if remembering a private joke. Then he said, "No, he hasn't told us anything."

"Doesn't that bother you? He did something to you, to us, to our blood apparently, and we don't know anything about it. How do you know it won't make us sick?"

"You feel like it's making you sick?"

Simon had never felt better.

"Still," Simon said, "we don't know anything. I mean, are we the only ones? Are there others?"

"Michael said none of that matters."

"It matters to me."

"Michael says animals don't care where they come from; only humans do. When you think about it, he makes a good point. We have the gift; what difference does it make who gave it to us?"

"Yeah, it's a real gift."

"What do you mean?"

"I agree it's amazing, how great I feel and the things I can do," Simon said. "The running, and the healing, and how strong I am—in that sense yeah, it's a gift, but there's definitely a dark side."

"Yeah, like the moon," Charlie said.

"Are we talking about Michael now or Pink Floyd?"

Charlie didn't smile. "Michael says every living thing is like the moon; it has a bright side and a dark side, but only animals embrace their dark side."

"Wow, Michael definitely seems to be having a big effect on you," Simon said. "You're officially a disciple now, huh?"

"Yeah, Michael's our big boss," Charlie said, still not smiling.

"Your big boss?" Simon said. "What do you mean?"

"You know, the big boss, the leader. He calls the shots, but that's cool. I'm not one of those control freaks or anything like that."

"So you still hang out together?"

"Of course," Charlie said.

Simon had to ignore a pang of, if not jealousy, then longing. He didn't miss Michael, but he missed hanging out with Charlie and Ramon.

"With the kids?" Simon asked.

"Yep," Charlie said. "Same playground mostly, in Battery Park."

Simon remembered running along the Hudson, getting the sense that the guys were at the playground.

"Yeah, the kids're doing great," Charlie said. "Nicky's been asking about Jeremy, saying, 'When's Jeremy coming back? I miss Jeremy.' I didn't know what to tell him, you know? So how's he doing?"

Trying to block out an image of Jeremy standing in front of his room, watching Alison confront him with a knife, Simon said, "He's doing great. He's a happy kid."

Charlie was staring at Simon's eyes. It was making Simon uncomfortable.

"You really should come back to us," Charlie said.

Come back to us. It sounded like something Michael would say with his weird, slightly Germanic accent.

Charlie probably caught the slip himself because he said, "I mean, you should start hanging out with us again."

"You mean with Michael?"

"Why not? Michael's a great guy."

"A great guy?"

Charlie had no reaction.

Simon looked around to make sure no one was eavesdropping—there was a group of college-age kids a few tables away, but they were distracted and too far away to overhear anything—and then practically whispered, "Michael's a total psychopath. He killed my ex-boss and shot two innocent people in cold blood. He's probably killed other people too. He tried to kill me, and he's the one who did all of this to us."

"That's why I love him," Charlie said.

"Because he's a killer?"

"No, because he gave me this gift. Did you see how fast I was running today? Do you know how amazing it felt?"

"Yeah, I know exactly how amazing it feels, but what happens when the world finds out that we're . . ." Simon was going to say *werewolves* but said instead, ". . . different. What happens then? We'll be treated like total freaks. Will you think it's a gift then?"

"No one'll find out," Charlie said.

"You were on national television today." Simon had raised his voice. Quieter, he continued, "You don't think people'll wonder how a fireman won the New York City Marathon?"

"I didn't win."

"What?"

"I didn't win. I faded at the end and finished ninth. I *could've* won if I wanted to; I could've set a freakin' world record. But I was smart. I knew winning would be too much."

"Ninth, first, it doesn't matter," Simon said. "How many interviews did you just do? How many people are tweeting and Facebooking about you right now? Don't you think people'll find it strange that a nonrunner was able to finish ahead of so many top-class athletes?"

"I couldn't help it, I had to run, I had to feel what it was like. Come on, you don't feel that way sometimes? Like you can do anything?"

Simon flashed back to that day in the gym when he'd benched 360 pounds, the muscle heads surrounding him, chanting, "Go, go, go . . ."

"What if they test your blood?" Simon asked.

"Michael said our blood's normal," Charlie said. "Well, when we're normal humans anyway. When we're wolves, it's different."

If this was true, it was the best news Simon had gotten all day. He'd thought he'd have to avoid doctors and blood tests for the rest of his life. He'd been afraid a blood test could potentially prevent him from getting a job too.

"It's still a crazy risk," Simon said. "Not just for yourself, but for all of us. Did you tell Michael you were running in the marathon?"

"No, and he'll probably be pissed off about it too. It's against his rules."

"Rules? What rules?"

Suddenly Charlie looked uncomfortable, avoiding eye contact, as if he'd said something he hadn't meant to. "I shouldn't really be talking to you about any of this; that's against the rules too."

"I don't understand what you're talking about," Simon said.

"Forget about it." Charlie seemed even more uncomfortable.

"Forget about what?"

Charlie hesitated, then said, "Michael told me and Ramon not to try to find you. He said you'd come to us when you were ready. But maybe you are ready. Maybe that's why you showed up today."

"No, I showed up because I saw you on TV."

"Yeah, but you didn't have to come find me. What made you come?"

Remembering how horrific he'd looked in the bathroom mirror, Simon said, "I was just . . . concerned."

"Well, I'm glad you came," Charlie said. "Seriously, when I saw your face, I couldn't believe it. I've been wanting to thank you for weeks."

"Thank me? What for?"

"You saved my life. If you didn't kill Olivia, she would've killed me."

Simon looked around nervously, but the college kids still weren't looking over.

"You know she was Michael's girlfriend, right?" Charlie continued. "He said he was her soul mate. But he was glad you got rid of her too. She would've been trouble for all of us, that's for sure. I mean, she was out of control."

"I didn't kill her for Michael," Simon said. "I killed her to save you and Ramon."

"Yeah, and that's why you're a hero," Charlie said, "as big a hero as me, or anybody I work with, and you didn't just save my life either. You know what they say? Save one life, save a million lives."

Simon had never heard of this expression, if it actually was an expression. He said, "I'm not sure I understand."

"You saved me and thanks to you I pulled a kid, nine years old, out of a fire last week. See? Being a hero, what's it called? *Heroism.* Yeah, heroism, it trickles down. That kid might save people when he grows up. He might become a doctor or find a cure for cancer, and it's all because of you, Simon Burns."

"What if the kid grows up to be a mass murderer, the next Hitler. Was I a hero then?"

"It doesn't work that way," Charlie said. "You saved a million lives. That's the bottom line."

The waitress arrived with the beers.

Charlie raised his glass and said, *"Prost."*

Since when did Charlie toast in German?

"Prost," Simon said, and took a sip.

"Ah, you didn't look me in the eye when you said *prost,*" Charlie said. "Michael said that means you'll have seven years of bad sex."

"How about seven years of no sex?"

"Yeah," Charlie said, "like that's gonna happen."

"It's happening already," Simon said.

Charlie put down the glass, looking concerned. "You're joking, right?"

"What?" Simon said. "You mean, you can have sex without . . ."

"A condom?"

"No," Simon said. "I mean without . . . you know . . . trans-forming."

"Oh yeah, I wolfed out a couple times. That's what Ramon calls it—*wolfing out.*" Charlie smiled. "But Michael helped us out with it. I don't mean actually helped us out, but he taught me how to deal with it. You know, gave me strategies."

"What about when you get angry and excited?"

"What do you mean?"

"Well, like today. When I saw you on TV, I was surprised, as you can imagine, and maybe my heart rate surged, and I . . . well, I at least started to turn. It was terrifying. I thought I'd kill my wife and son. I didn't know what to do."

"So what happened?"

"Nothing," Simon said. "I mean, I somehow stopped it. I turned on the shower, got under cold water, and that made me change back."

"It probably wasn't the water," Charlie said.

"Really? Then what was it?"

Charlie was about to answer, and then his expression changed, as if a new thought had suddenly come to him, and he said, "That's why you need Michael; that's why you need us. You should come to the brewery tonight. We're meeting up at, like, nine o'clock."

Simon shook his head and couldn't help laughing. Go back to the brewery? Where he'd killed that crazy she-wolf, Olivia? Where he'd had the most horrific night of his life? And hang out with Michael, the homicidal maniac who'd caused it all?

"As appealing as that sounds, I think I'll pass," Simon said.

"Sorry to hear that." Charlie was suddenly avoiding eye contact again, looking concerned. He took a long swig of beer, finishing the pint, then said, "I really shouldn't be here. Michael told me not to see you." He closed his eyes and flared his nostrils. Then his eyes opened and he said, "He's not here, but it was still a big mistake." He stood.

"Where're you going?" Simon asked.

"Gotta get outta here," Charlie said. "My ex wants me to take Nicky tonight. But do me a favor? If you see Michael again, I mean *when* you see him again, don't tell him I saw you today, okay? And definitely don't tell him I told you anything about the brewery. Let's keep this our secret, okay?" He sounded like a child who'd done something wrong and was afraid he'd get in trouble for it with his parents.

"It's not a big deal," Simon said.

"It is a big deal," Charlie said seriously, raising his voice.

The college kids looked over, and then the waitress came out with a tray of plain hamburgers. Charlie's nostrils flared again, and Simon's probably did too.

"Here you go," the waitress said. "Ten rare burgers, no buns, no fries."

When she placed the tray on the table, Charlie sat back down and grabbed one of the burgers and ate it in two bites. Simon was eating with his hands as well, devouring the meat as if it were the first meal he'd had in weeks.

In silence they polished off the other burgers, completely focused on the chewing and swallowing of the food, not looking up from the plate. Simon felt as if the rest of the world disappeared, and it was just him and the food, but when he swallowed the last bite he saw that they had put on quite a show. Everyone in the garden was watching them, including the waitress, and a couple of the guys from the kitchen had even come out to watch. At first Simon was confused—what was the big deal about two guys eating some meat?—and then it kicked in that to most people two guys wolfing down burgers like they were going to the chair probably seemed pretty weird.

Simon tried to explain the behavior away with a wide smile, as if saying, *It's okay, nothing to see here, it's all under control.*

Yeah, like anyone believed that.

Finally eyes shifted away as people in the garden resumed their conversation and the staff resumed going about their business.

"I should really get going," Charlie said, tapping the side of his running shorts, realizing he didn't have his wallet. "Oh, shoot, I left my wallet home, couldn't run a marathon with it."

"It's okay, it's on me," Simon said.

"Thanks, bro," Charlie said.

He came around the table and extended his arms as if about to hug Simon. Simon was anticipating the hug, the security of Charlie's strong arms around him, pulling him in close.

But then Charlie backed away and said, "Hope to see you soon," and left without looking back.

NINE

"Did your husband give you any idea where he was going?"

Alison Burns was in the living room on the couch and two cops; one stocky with a receding hairline, Officer Granger, who was asking all of the questions, and a taller, younger officer, Roberts—who barely seemed to be paying attention, chomping on gum—were on chairs across from her. This was the third time the stocky cop had asked her if Simon had told her where he was going, and it was getting pretty annoying.

"I told you," she said, "I have no idea."

"Is there someplace he usually goes when you have a fight? A bar? A diner?"

"Maybe the gym. That's the only place I can think of."

She'd already given them the address of the New York Sports

Club where Simon worked out, but the cops hadn't seemed very interested.

"Look, honestly, at this point there's very little we can do, ma'am," Granger said. "If I were you, I'd call around to some places and see if you can find him, but even if we find him there's really not much we can do."

"Can't you get him help, at least hold him for twenty-four or forty-eight hours, or whatever the law is?"

"Not without just cause. If he's causing a public disturbance we could take him in, or if you want to file a formal complaint, but do you really want to go down that route? Do you really think you're in danger?"

"You saw what he did to the bathroom door," Alison said, "and you should've heard him, growling like an animal."

"I understand, ma'am, but he didn't actually do anything to you, or to anyone. And you said he's under the care of a psychiatrist, right?"

"Yeah, but it isn't helping. He's crazier than ever."

"What exactly's wrong with him? I mean officially. Is he schizophrenic, manic-depressive . . . ?"

Alison uncrossed her legs, then crossed them again. "No, he has a, well, behavioral disorder. Or he might have one anyway."

"Behavioral disorder? What does that mean? He's on meds?"

"Yes."

"Has he been violent before?" Granger asked. "I know you said he's never hit you or been abusive in any way, but does he have a history of violence in other relationships?"

"No, his problems have been pretty recent." Alison paused, figuring out how to explain this, then went with, "You see, I think, or *we* think he has something called lyncanthropic disorder. It's a condition where a person believes he's a werewolf."

This got Officer Roberts's full attention.

"A werewolf?" Granger said, smirking.

"Yes," Alison said, ultra serious. "You see, his ex-boss was killed—it was a big story in the news last month—and Simon felt responsible. This is what we believe anyway, and he's been trying to deal with it in therapy."

Roberts laughed, then said, "When you think you're a werewolf it definitely sounds like it's time for some therapy."

Granger laughed too.

While it annoyed Alison that the cops didn't seem to be taking this seriously, she understood that, out of context, what she was describing probably sounded pretty bizarre.

"It seemed like he was getting better," she said. "I mean, he was able to relate to me better, and was starting to have more normal behavior, but this afternoon it was so awful. Just to see him act that way was just so disturbing and terrifying."

Granger was looking away toward the dining room table, where Alison had left the large knife she'd threatened Simon with.

"Did your husband take that knife out?" Granger asked.

"No." Alison didn't want to tell them what she had done, fearing it would make her look like the crazy one, and they'd be less likely to help her. "The knife has nothing to do with it. I was just cutting something, some vegetables, and left it there." She ignored the cops' skeptical expressions. "Look, the important thing is I'm afraid, okay? I don't know who my husband is anymore, or what he's capable of. And I'm really worried about my son; he was right there when it happened. Can you imagine what it was like for him to hear his father raging like that? Excuse me, one sec."

Alison went down the hall to Jeremy's room. He was sitting on his bed, calmly, Indian-style, playing with his Leapster.

"Mommy's almost done, sweetie, okay?"

Either Jeremy didn't hear her or he was ignoring her.

"Mommy loves you, sweetie."

Still no reaction.

Alison left, angry at Simon for putting them through all this—it was so selfish, just so damn selfish—when she saw the officers near the front door about to leave.

"Wait," she said, "where're you going?"

"I'm sorry, ma'am," Granger said, "but we have to go now."

The "ma'am" talk was getting annoying, especially when he wasn't being at all helpful.

"But you can't *leave*. What if he comes back? What am I supposed to do?"

"I don't know, but you might want to reach out to his shrink, see if he has some ideas," Granger said.

"But I'm really afraid. What if he comes back here raging again?"

"I don't know what to tell you."

"Why can't I get a restraining order or something?"

"If he hasn't hurt you or threatened you directly, you won't be able to get an order of protection," Granger said. "But if he does hurt you or threaten you, call 911."

"So what're you saying? I have to wait to get hurt before you'll do anything?"

"We don't arrest people for the crimes they might commit," Granger said. "And I'm afraid growling in the bathroom and pretending to be a werewolf isn't a crime."

Roberts was smiling again.

"But he could hurt someone or hurt himself," Alison said. "He's unstable."

"This is New York," Granger said. "If we arrested unstable people there'd be nobody left. Look, I hope the situation resolves on its own. If it doesn't, give us a call."

"Have a great day," Roberts said, still smirking.

When the officers were gone Alison bolted the door with both locks and put on the chain. This was horrible, feeling threatened by her own husband. And it wasn't as if she'd married some violent, dangerous guy—or at least he didn't use to be dangerous. If anything, he used to be on the wimpy side. He used to avoid conflict, had once told her he'd never even been in a fight. Once they had seen a mouse in the apartment and he'd jumped on a chair, terrified. And now this was the man she was afraid of, from whom she felt like she had to protect herself?

She had to get a grip, be logical about all this. Was Simon really a danger to her? Okay, so he'd lost it in the bathroom, acting like an animal, but as Granger had said, he hadn't actually threatened her or hurt her. He was probably more of a danger to himself right now than to her, Jeremy, or anyone else. Besides, it wasn't like she was in a horror movie, trapped in a house in a remote location with a crazed killer after her. She was in a luxury co-op apartment building in one of the biggest cities in the world and her husband was having an emotional breakdown. No one was out to get her.

She checked on Jeremy again. He'd stopped playing with his Leapster and was lying on the bed on his back, blank-faced, staring at the ceiling.

"Jeremy, sweetie, what's wrong?"

Alison realized the ridiculousness of her question. What's wrong except his father thought he was a werewolf and he'd just seen his mother threaten his father with a knife?

Sitting next to Jeremy, gently moving strands of hair away from his face with her fingers, trying to come up with the words to undo the trauma and make it all better, she said, "Sometimes mommies and daddies fight, but that doesn't mean they don't love each other."

But even this seemed hypocritical and fake. Sure, mommies and daddies fight, but what was going on in the household lately was way beyond typical marital fighting.

"Everything's going to be okay," she said. "I promise."

She still felt like a liar. How could she really promise anything? How did she know that things would get better? What if things were as good as they were going to get right now, and there was only more dysfunction and misery in store for them?

Figuring distraction might be a better strategy, Alison played with Jeremy for a while. At first he wasn't responsive, but he gradually got into it and even laughed a little. Three-year-olds were so resilient; Alison wished she had some more of that quality herself. Though she was trying to hide it the best she could from Jeremy, she was still feeling very emotional about the whole situation and felt as if she'd overreacted. Yes, Simon's behavior had been disturbing and selfish, but she regretted going for the knife and threatening him the way she had. Jeremy shouldn't have had to see that, and she might have pushed Simon further over the edge. How could she have done that? Despite all the craziness of the past month, he was still Jeremy's father, he was still her husband, and she still loved him very much. Bottom line, she wanted Simon back; she didn't want to push him further away.

She went to her purse, took out her Droid. She was about to call him, to make sure he was okay, when she thought, was calling the right thing to do? What if that just antagonized him even more?

She had a better idea—she'd call his psychiatrist. Dr. Levinson would tell her what to do, and he should probably be informed about what was going on anyway.

Because she'd put Simon in touch with Levinson—she'd called dozens of psychiatrists in the city and he was the only one who'd actually treated a patient with lyncanthropic disorder—she had his number programmed into her cell. She got his voice mail—ughh, that's right, it was Sunday. But, wait, he had an emergency contact number. This definitely seemed to qualify as an emergency.

She called and heard five or six rings. She was trying to think of the message she would leave when the call connected and he—she recognized his voice—said, "Yes?"

"Hi, Dr. Levinson, this is Alison Burns. My husband is a patient of yours."

"I'm sorry, who is this?" He sounded almost out of breath.

"Alison. Alison Burns."

"And what's this in reference to?"

"My husband, Simon, is a patient of yours. Simon. Simon Burns."

"Simon?"

"Yes, Simon Burns." She spelled: "B-U-R-N-S."

"I'm sorry, I don't have a . . . Oh, wait, yes, right, I'm sorry. Simon, that's right. I haven't seen him in quite a while, though. How's he doing?"

Within a few seconds Alison went from confused to upset to enraged.

"Hello?" Levinson asked.

"I'm here," Alison said, fuming. "What do you mean, you haven't seen him in quite a while? He had an appointment with you a couple of days ago."

"I think there must be some mistake," Levinson said. "I haven't seen your husband in, let me see, about a month."

"I see." Alison's face was burning.

"I saw him once," Levinson said, "but then he canceled his next appointment and never showed up again. Why? Did he lead you to believe he was still seeing me?"

Feeling like an idiot, as if she'd been totally duped, she said, "Something like that."

"And I take it there's some crisis or you wouldn't be calling me on my emergency line."

"Yes, there is a crisis," Alison said. "I think that's a very accurate way of describing the situation."

As calmly as she could, she explained what had happened this morning with Simon and described his behavior of the past few weeks.

Levinson was quiet throughout except for occasional *mm-hms*—did all therapists learn to say that in grad school? Was there a *mm-hm* class they all took?—until she was through talking, and then he said, "What about his medication? Do you have any idea if he's been taking it?"

"No, I don't," Alison said. "I feel like I don't know anything anymore. I can't believe he lied to me about seeing you."

"Well he certainly seems to be in denial about his condition, which is actually par for the course," Levinson said. "He had difficulty expressing himself during our session and seemed rather uncomfortable. I'd be very surprised if he was taking his medication. From what you've described it doesn't sound like he was anyway. It also sounds like he needs treatment."

"If he wasn't seeing you, why didn't you call me?"

"Excuse me?" Levinson asked.

"Why didn't you call me?" Alison was raising her voice. "Why didn't you let me know? I mean, didn't you think it was strange that he just stopped showing up?"

"You're not the patient, your husband is," Levinson said calmly. "And I have to respect my patients' confidentiality. Many patients come to me for one session and then start seeing another therapist. Is it possible that's what happened with your husband?"

"No, he said he was seeing you specifically." Alison knew it wasn't Levinson's fault; she'd just been lashing out. "Sorry," she said, "I didn't mean to snap at you."

"It's okay, I understand," he said. "If your husband wants to continue his therapy with me, I'd be happy to see him. Or if he wants to talk today, I could be available for a phone appointment later on. I can't talk any more right now, though. I'm at a wedding, actually, and I don't want to miss the ceremony."

"Thank you, Doctor, I appreciate your time."

Levinson was gone, but Alison held the phone up to her ear, still stunned. He hadn't been going to his appointments? Seriously? What about all those times she'd asked him how therapy was going and with a straight face he'd say *Levinson said this* and *Levinson thinks that*. And if he was lying about going to therapy, what else was he lying about? How did she know what was true and what wasn't anymore? And why was he lying anyway? What was he trying to hide?

Alison wasn't sure what to do next, but she was certain of one thing—her marriage was over. She couldn't trust her husband anymore and when you lose trust, what else is there? She wanted to call a divorce lawyer immediately, but it was Sunday so she'd have to wait till tomorrow morning.

"I'm hungry, Mommy."

Jeremy had come out to the living room, holding Sam, his stuffed bear.

"It's time for lunch," Alison said, smiling, upbeat, trying to put on a good front for Jeremy. She picked him up, carried him into the kitchen, opened a food cabinet, and said, "What do you want, noodles and cheese?"

Jeremy shook his head.

"Spaghetti?"

Jeremy shook his head.

"Peanut butter and jelly?"

Jeremy shook his head.

"French toast?"

"Noodles and cheese," Jeremy said excitedly.

"Noodles and cheese coming right up," Alison said.

It was good to be a mommy again, to put some normalcy back into Jeremy's life and hopefully undo a little of the trauma he'd experienced this morning. For a while, tending to Jeremy was a great distraction, but she couldn't shake her anger toward Simon. How could he do this to her? How could he do this to *them*? And it was all because of what, because he was having a psychological reaction to losing his job? He thought that gave him the right to act out like this—raging like a madman, scaring the hell out of his son, ruining his marriage? She needed to get away right now—if not from him, at least from the apartment. There were too many memories of him here.

"I know," she said when Jeremy was finishing up his lunch. "Let's go to a movie."

"I don't want to."

"Come on, there has to be something playing you'll like. We'll go to a 3D movie; you'll get to wear those glasses."

"Why can't I play with Daddy?"

Alison suppressed a cringe. "Daddy had to go away today, sweetie."

"Why?"

"Because that's what daddies do sometimes. They go away."

"I want to play with Daddy today. He promised he'd take me to a playground."

Alison could tell he was on the verge of a meltdown, and after everything that had happened so far today, she was on the verge of a meltdown herself. Maybe what she needed was some time on her own. The last thing she wanted to do was blow up at Jeremy and make the situation even worse.

"How about Christina? Do you want to play with her?"

Jeremy liked Christina. Well, not as much as his old full-time babysitter, Margaret, whom they'd had to fire after Simon lost his job, but he always had fun with her.

But Jeremy wouldn't let go of what he wanted that easily. "Why not Daddy?"

"Because Daddy's busy today."

The finality in Alison's tone sealed the deal, because Jeremy acquiesced, saying, "Okay, I'll play with Christina."

Alison didn't know if Christina was even available today. She texted her—though she lived right across the hall, texting always seemed less intrusive than ringing a doorbell—and Christina texted right back that she was available. Alison, afraid that Simon might come home, asked if she could drop Jeremy off at her place—"My place is a total mess"—and she said that would be fine.

About ten minutes later, Alison dropped Jeremy off. Christina was twenty-three, slender, with short blond hair. She had graduated from NYU over a year ago and lived with her parents, to whom Simon and Alison said hi on the elevator but that was about it. Alison wasn't sure of her parents' names—maybe the mother was Felice, but that could've been totally wrong. Anyway, Maybe Felice and Whatever the Dad's Name Was weren't home.

Alison explained to Christina that she was going out for the day and would be back around dinnertime.

"Is Simon coming home then too?"

Alison felt awkward and wasn't sure how to answer, especially with Jeremy right there.

"No, Simon won't be home until later," Alison said. "Much later."

Leaving the building, heading toward Broadway—maybe she'd go shopping or see a movie—she replayed the exchange with Christina. Why was Christina asking when Simon was coming home anyway? Maybe the question wasn't so abnormal, but she usually didn't ask specifically about Simon, and when did she start calling him Simon? Didn't she use to call him Mr. Burns?

Suddenly Alison was enraged again; was it possible Christina and Simon were having an affair? It was so cliché for a man to screw the babysitter, but clichés were clichés for a reason. Fighting off an image of Simon and Christina in bed, her skinny little chicken legs wrapped around his body as he was thrusting into her, Alison muttered, "Skinny little slut."

Okay, okay, she knew she had to dial it down; her imagination was taking a giant leap. She didn't even have circumstantial evidence that they were having an affair. She'd never seen them flirting, and Simon had never shown any interest. But maybe he was just great at hiding it from her. After all, he definitely seemed secretive lately, so maybe Christina was the big secret. They had plenty of opportunity to see each other, what with Alison working full-time. Maybe they screwed during Jeremy's naptime. While it was hard to imagine Simon stooping that low, she never would have imagined him locking himself in the bathroom and acting like a werewolf, so how could she rule out any perverse behavior? As for Christina, Alison had never thought of her as the husband-stealing type, but come to think of it she'd had older boyfriends. Hadn't she been dating that guy last year who looked like he was about thirty? At thirty-nine, maybe Simon wasn't so far out of her range.

Alison was on her cell, waiting for a call to connect. She'd made the call with little thought. She was just tired of feeling manipulated and used and wanted to somehow get back in control.

"Hey, Alison," Dr. Vijay Rana said.

Vijay was a client of Alison's, a gynecologist who had an office in midtown but lived on the Upper West Side, in Morningside Heights, near Columbia University. They'd gone out to dinner a couple of times, and to see a show once, which wasn't unusual because part of Alison's job was to schmooze with her doctor clients. But over the last couple of weeks they'd become friendly outside work and had gotten together once for coffee. Vijay had told Alison all about his recent divorce, and she'd let him in a bit about her problems with Simon. She knew she was crossing a line, getting personal, but she didn't have many close friends in the city, and Vijay had a naturally supportive personality. Alison always felt better, more relaxed, after spending time with him. Maybe he wasn't a great-looking guy— he was a little dorky actually with his thick glasses and the way he always wore his shirts with the top button buttoned—but he was extremely nice and supportive and Alison thought his wife was crazy for divorcing him. He said his wife had complained that he was a workaholic. Was that seriously her main problem? Let her marry a guy with lycanthropic disorder and she'd find out what real problems were like.

"Sorry to call you on a Sunday," she said. "I know you're probably busy."

"Not busy at all actually," he said. "I was just here relaxing, watching the end of the marathon. Did you hear about the fireman?"

Alison remembered calling Simon into the living room to see the fireman on TV, right before he went berserk in the bathroom.

"Yeah, I saw," Alison said.

"It's unbelievable," he said. "He never ran in a marathon before, his friends said he'd never even been a recreational runner until recently, and he finished ninth in the New York City Marathon. He must be some freak of nature."

"Can we meet for coffee?" Alison hadn't meant to blurt that out. "Sorry," she said. "I mean I know it's out of the blue—"

"That's fine," he said. "I'd love to meet. Are you in the area?"

"I'm heading toward Broadway."

"I have an idea; how about you meet me at my place, then we head out from here?"

Going to a client's apartment? Was this a good idea?

"Sounds great," she said.

He gave her directions to his place on Riverside Drive. She expected that as a successful physician he'd have a killer apartment, but she didn't know that he lived in a penthouse of the nicest building on the block.

When she got out of the elevator, he was waiting in the hallway in front of the open door to his apartment, smiling widely. He didn't look as geeky as he did in a work setting. He had dimples, nice black wavy hair.

"Hey, Alison, it's great to see you." He kissed her on the cheek. "Please come in."

"Thank you."

It was such a relief to be in the company of a normal man, who wasn't raging and trying to break down bathroom walls.

"Can I get you something? Coffee? Cappuccino? Is it too early for wine?"

"Wine sounds great."

"Chardonnay okay?"

"Chardonnay's perfect."

Alison went toward the terrace and looked through glass doors at the incredible panoramic view of New Jersey. In the reflection, she watched Vijay, pouring the wine. Classical music was playing; it sounded like Tchaikovsky.

"You can sit on the couch," he said.

Alison sat on the plush white sofa. When Vijay came in he sat next to her when he could have sat across from her on the chairs. She felt he was pushing the boundaries of their relationship, definitely coming on to her a little, but she didn't care.

She knew she'd made the right decision coming here.

TEN

As Simon left the bar, it set in that he had nowhere to go. After calling the police on him, Alison probably wasn't ready for him to come home to make up. He figured she'd need a cooling-off period, maybe a day or two, before she'd even be willing to talk, and the cops were probably looking for him too. She'd probably told them that he was mentally ill, had some kind of breakdown, was potentially dangerous. What if they arrested him, ran medical tests, took blood, discovered what he was? Hopefully what Charlie had said was true, that their wolves' blood was undetectable, but Simon couldn't take the risk.

Keep moving. That was his overriding desire, the impulse that seemed most important at the moment and that would somehow make everything okay.

Okay, so he was moving, but now he had to figure out which

direction to head in. He went downtown, all the way to Soho, but he didn't want to get too close to where Michael lived, in Tribeca, or too close to the playground in Battery Park, so he headed to the Lower East Side, to near the Williamsburg Bridge, but now he wasn't far from the brewery in Brooklyn—it was right across the river. So he jogged uptown alongside the FDR Drive, which was nice for a while because there was a cool steady breeze against his face and not too many people around—but then, approaching the Thirty-fourth Street heliport, he detected the scent of cops—at least two of them—up ahead. While he seriously doubted a domestic complaint had caused a citywide manhunt for him, he didn't want to take any chances. So he headed back west, toward midtown, but the more polluted air and busy streets made him feel even more trapped and hopeless. He wasn't in a city, he was in a maze, a caged maze, and every direction he headed led to another wall.

He couldn't take the congestion any more so he went uptown, avoiding the UN, and then veered back toward the East River, uptown along the promenade. He really wanted to leave the city, to find real space in the country. Being away from people, from all people, would be the ultimate escape. He considered doing it, just running north, through the Bronx, to Westchester, until he found some woods. Ah, freedom.

There was really only one thing keeping him in New York right now—his family. Even if Alison wanted to kick him out permanently, he had to be close to Jeremy, to protect him. He didn't know what he had to protect him from, but this was how he felt.

At around East Eighty-third Street, he entered Carl Schurz Park. It wasn't exactly like being in the wild, but it was better than midtown. At least there were trees and it was somewhat of a reprieve from the odors and noises of the city. Carl Schurz was a smallish park, about the width of a city block and only about ten blocks long. He avoided the playground and basketball courts and went into the less populated middle of the park. It was late afternoon and there were still plenty of people and dogs around, but Simon found a woodsy area that was somewhat sheltered.

He remained in the park for a few hours, jogging back and forth, almost constantly moving. Near dusk, hunger set in and he headed over to York Avenue in search of his next meal. Naturally he gravitated toward meat, so he wound up at a bagel store and ordered two pounds of roast beef and two pounds of corned beef. He took the meat back with him to the park and ate while leaning against a tree. Gobbling up the lunch meat, surrounded by trees, was a very safe, familiar experience. While Simon was aware that this behavior wasn't normal, he didn't know how to change it. He was who he was.

Into the last slice of corned beef—chewing it slowly to savor the taste—he felt his cell vibrate in his front pocket. He took out the phone—one new message. Was Alison trying to get in touch? Did she want him to come back home?

Already imagining opening the front door, Jeremy leaping into his arms and saying, "I love you, Daddy"—the scent of the Johnson's Baby Shampoo seemed so real—he opened the text. The letdown set in when he saw the text was from Dave, an old college friend:

Yo yo what up? How's daddyhood? Let's hang soon! D

Dave was a pasty white guy from Westchester but had talked in a pseudo-ghetto way since college, and this habit had carried over into his texting.

Upset that the text hadn't been from Alison, Simon gobbled up the last of the corned beef. He wanted to call her, see how she and Jeremy were doing, but he wasn't sure it was the best idea. He knew his wife, how emotional she got. She needed a cooling-off period before she'd be willing to have a normal conversation. So instead he decided to text her:

> I love you and please tell little bear I love him too. I promise some-
> day you'll understand EVERYTHING.

He sent the note, but it only made him feel worse. Could he really promise she'd ever understand? And he knew she wouldn't respond. She could get stubborn when she thought she was right about something. How had his life gotten to this point? He understood the steps—losing his job, meeting the guys in the park, drinking the beer, becoming half wolf, then a full wolf—but none of that seemed to explain why he was letting his animal-like urges and impulses control his life. What kind of husband was he? What kind of father was he? He'd thought getting fired was the ultimate failure of his life, but this was so much worse.

He had to move again. Movement was the answer. Movement would make everything better.

He paced back and forth in the park until it got dark, and then he returned to the streets. He was hungry and needed another meal, but he also wanted more space to roam and, as it was a Sunday evening, the city streets were emptying out and it didn't feel nearly as claustrophobic and oppressive. After a pit stop for a few bunless burgers at Burger King on Eighty-sixth, he continued walking. He preferred the side streets, so he zigzagged downtown, going along a side street to Second Avenue, then back toward Third along another. This made the trip downtown much more time consuming than it would've normally been, but it wasn't about time, it was about movement. He was terrified of staying still.

Though he wasn't sure what time it was, he figured it had to be close to nine, when Charlie said he was meeting with Ramon and Michael at the brewery. While it was great seeing Charlie, and Simon would have loved to catch up with Ramon, there was no way he was going to hang out with Michael and become even more involved with that maniac than he already was. Yeah, he felt completely alone and isolated, but that didn't mean he had to go back to Michael. There had to be another way.

He still didn't have a plan beyond movement. Eventually he would have to rest, but he didn't want to check into a hotel. The idea of being in some small room all night seemed like total agony. Besides, if he checked into a hotel, under his name, he was afraid the police would find him. He didn't have any close relatives in the city, and his friends had families of their own. He was better off on his own, until he figured out how to control his behavior—if he could figure out how to control it.

It must've taken him an hour, maybe much longer to get down to the East Village, and then—avoiding the scents of potpourri and pot and lots of bad BO at St. Mark's Place—he headed toward the West Village along the less busy Tenth Street. He was at Tenth and Broadway, near the old church he'd passed hundreds of times but didn't know the name of, when it happened.

It started in his extremities—tingling sensations in his feet and legs, like when you come in from the cold after playing in the snow and start to defrost. But then the tingling became pain, and there was pain in his mouth too. This couldn't be happening again. It had to be all in his mind, a fantasy.

But it wasn't a fantasy.

The pain was spreading slowly, to his joints, and then he saw that his fingernails had little stubs of claws. But the other times he'd been angry, shocked, or sexually aroused, and he'd been convinced that there was some emotional component to it. This time, though, he'd been in a normal, calm state. A little stressed out, but he'd been more stressed at other times, and stress alone didn't seem to bring on an emotional response.

"You okay?" a young guy asked.

Simon ignored him, walking away quickly before the guy could get a good look at his face—in case his face showed any changes. But where was he supposed to go? There were people everywhere—he was near NYU, for God's sake. Even on a Sunday night, there were plenty of people on the streets. If he had to pick one area in Manhattan where he absolutely did not want to turn into a werewolf, this would be near the top of the list.

He needed to get away from people and get to cold water. Maybe he could go to a bathroom—there was a bar right up the street. But, no, a bar wouldn't work. Too many people at a bar. What if he lost control and went on a rampage? He had to get to open space—a park.

He ran toward Union Square. Running helped, or seemed to. He still knew he was transforming and was at least halfway toward fully turning, but maybe the exertion was slowing the process, because he didn't feel any worse. He sped across Fourteenth Street, keeping his head down, avoiding making eye contact with anyone. As long as he could somehow avoid a full transformation and no one saw the changes in his facial features, he'd have a chance to get to safety. He went past a subway entrance, into Union Square Park, but there were so many people around he didn't feel any more secure.

He ran faster, zipping through the park, past a playground, leaping over a small fence with ease. Then, when he reached the empty concrete area where there was a farmer's market on some days, he glanced up at the sky, above the W Hotel, at the bright almost-full moon, and at that moment he knew, intuitively, exactly what was going on, without having to process anything. It explained why Charlie had let it slip about the guys meeting at the brewery tonight and why Simon had started to transform spontaneously without any impetus. It was because of the moon, of course. The moon had been full the first time Simon had turned into a werewolf, and this was the first full moon since that night. But the moon wasn't full now—he could see with his naked eye that it probably wouldn't be full until tomorrow night—but there was no doubt that Simon was starting to turn. Going by the way he felt, he had a few minutes, tops, before he experienced a full transformation.

He had to get to safety as fast as possible, and the only safety he knew of was the only real woodsy area in Manhattan: the Ramble in Central Park. The problem was he was over forty blocks, or two miles, from the southernmost entrance to the park. He cut over to Broadway and ran uptown as fast as he could without attracting too much attention. While he wanted to get to the park quickly, he was afraid that after Charlie's display of speed in the marathon, the spotting of another seemingly normal-looking guy running at world-class speed would become newsworthy. But none of this would matter if he turned into a werewolf in midtown Manhattan, and, approaching Herald Square, he feared that was on the verge of happening. He had increased pains in his joints, and the pain in his mouth was excruciating, like a bad trip to the dentist.

After Herald Square, he veered uptown on Sixth Avenue, picking up speed. He considered ducking into Bryant Park, but the open space and practically leafless trees on the perimeter made it a less-than-ideal place to turn into a werewolf. With about seventeen blocks to go, it was Central Park or bust.

But after several blocks it was clear he wouldn't make it. He was trying to ignore the pain, hoping that ignoring it would make it go

away, but it was impossible not to feel it. Then he knew it was happening, he was beyond the point of no return, and sure enough seconds later all the pain was gone. He was running almost effortlessly,
seemingly gliding along the pavement, with long, fluid strides. He
noticed that his feet had grown as they became clawed, tearing his
sneakers partially apart. His T-shirt had stretched as well, but his
sweatpants had enough space to handle the growth in his legs. A
glance at his transformed hands confirmed the obvious—he had
become a full-blown werewolf.

As he passed Radio City Music Hall, where there were plenty of
people around, he reduced his speed and kept his head down, avoiding eye contact, trying to attract as little attention as possible. If someone looked directly at him, all hell would break loose. From a
distance, he could pass for human. Though he was leaner and more
muscular than most humans, the hairiness was concealed by his
stretched-out clothes. If someone looked directly at him and saw the
animal features, he would have a serious problem.

Going at a steady pace, he continued uptown, through the East
Fifties. At the intersection of Fifty-sixth he sped up to make a light
and not have to stop at the intersection, but he couldn't avoid bump-
ing into a guy crossing at the opposite side of the street.

He was a thin, older guy, maybe sixty years old, and he was holding two shopping bags. Simon didn't knock into him very hard, but
it was hard enough to jolt him off balance. The guy glared right at
Simon and he had to see, he had to. Simon was waiting for the reaction of shock and horror. Would he scream for help? Run? Just stand
there mesmerized and in awe?

What Simon didn't expect was for the guy's face to cringe in
anger and for him to say, "Hey, watch it," as if anyone else had
bumped into him.

It was dark out, okay, but not *too* dark. This was Sixth Avenue, after all, and there was plenty of light from lampposts. As Simon continued uptown he didn't know if the guy hadn't gotten a good look at him or if he was just too lost in his own world to care that the man who'd knocked into him wasn't human. Or maybe it just took more than a werewolf to shock a jaded, self-absorbed New Yorker.

Simon managed to make it to Central Park South without attracting too much attention. Well, except when he was entering the park and a horse from a horse-drawn carriage reared up and almost unseated the driver and the tourist passengers. Maybe the humans couldn't recognize what he was, but animals apparently could.

But Simon didn't care because for the first time as a full-blown werewolf he was in the park. The experience was more than exhilarating; it was total joy. Maybe it was similar to the nothingness Buddhists experience when they're in their deepest meditative states. He was at one with nature, with the universe, and his thoughts and feelings didn't matter anymore. The feeling of being caged was gone, and all that mattered was his need to be free.

With the glee of a live fish tossed back into the ocean, he sprinted through a woodsy area of the park, jumping branches. As a wolf, he found that his sonarlike ability to avoid objects and humans seemed more refined. Without thinking, he knew exactly in which direction to head and, if he got too close to the scent of a human, he would stop instantly and go in another direction. No wonder some wild animals could survive in populated areas for their entire lives without ever being seen by human eyes. If Bigfoot or the Loch Ness Monster existed—and given everything Simon had experienced lately, it was hard to be skeptical about anything anymore—it was understandable how they could survive undetected for years.

Simon went across a baseball diamond, and in the middle of the outfield he stopped and looked up at the bright full moon. He experienced a strange, unexplainable attachment to the moon, as if the moon were a parent he'd been separated from a long time ago, and to show his love and appreciation he couldn't resist howling at it. He didn't let loose, knowing that loud howling could put him in danger. But he howled as loud as he could, at a level he knew no humans could overhear. As he howled, inner love and peace overtook his body—it was just him and the moon and it was intimate and beautiful.

Then he was running again—across a path, veering to avoid human scents, climbing and leaping over a fence with ease. At a road, he waited behind a tree until a jogger and a few bicyclists passed. He detected scents of a man and woman—maybe twenty yards away—but he didn't want to wait any longer and dashed across, into an area with grass and trees near the Central Park Lake.

He made his way across the perimeter of the lake, going slower because of the dense bushes and because he had to stop and alter his course occasionally to avoid humans and a couple of dogs. Then he reached an open area and ran at full speed, over rocks, climbing even the tallest ones with ease, using the suctionlike grip of his clawed hands to propel himself. He leaped from a rock onto a small bridge and, finally, he was in the Ramble.

Over the past several weeks, running around the Ramble in human form had been exhilarating, but it was nothing like this. With the energy of a puppy he ran around in the woods, shifting directions, jumping over branches, climbing trees, and howling gleefully whenever he knew he was fully out of human earshot. There was nothing better than this; this was pure joy and he couldn't get enough of it.

He must've been running around almost nonstop when he detected a familiar scent. It was an animal, but it wasn't human and it wasn't canine. Then he knew, but by then it was too late to react because it was already nearby, right behind him.

He turned around and, though it was pitch-dark aside from faint moonlight shining through tree branches, he knew he was standing face-to-face with a werewolf. He knew why the scent was so familiar as well because it was the same werewolf scent he'd detected in the Ramble a few days ago.

Simon didn't sense any danger. He knew the werewolf was here in peace, and he also knew that it was older and wiser. There was an overwhelming calming, safe, protective energy coming from the other werewolf, not unlike the feeling Simon had had while he was howling at the moon.

Then it hit—the werewolf was Michael's father, Volker. This explained why Simon hadn't been able to place the scent last time, because he had never met Volker in his werewolf state before, and human and werewolf scents in general were very different, like two different species. But from a close distance Simon could identify the scent as Volker's.

"Hey, it's great to see you," Simon tried to say, but it came out as a loud howl.

Volker got the meaning, though. He howled back, *Hello*, and then howled again, telling Simon to get naked.

Simon wasn't sure he understood so he asked, *What?* and Volker repeated, *Get naked*.

Simon was uncomfortable in his clothes anyway, so he stripped.

Then Volker howled again and ran away. Simon knew he was saying *Follow me* and, without giving it any more thought, he did as he was told.

ELEVEN

"**I** got some bad news for you."

Geri heard this from Shawn moments after she'd arrived at the Manhattan North precinct. Her first thought was that it had to do with Diane Coles. Detective Mangel had found out she'd been killed in Michigan and was reopening the investigation. Maybe the bad news was Dan wasn't going to let Geri take over the case.

"About Diane Coles, right?" Geri asked.

"Who?" Shawn said.

Then Geri figured it had to do with the Orlando Rojas murder case. Maybe Dan had added more detectives to the case, or taken Geri and Shawn off.

"Oh, not more drama," Geri said. "Am I gonna have to sit down before I hear this?"

"Yeah, you probably will."

Shawn seemed very serious, which got Geri concerned.

"So what is it?" she asked.

"It's about Carlita Morales."

"What about her?"

"She's dead."

At first, the words had no effect. They just seemed like part of mindless conversation. Instead of *She's dead*, Shawn could have said *It's a beautiful day today* or *I like your shoes*.

Then the meaning suddenly hit. Geri was breathless, her legs weak.

"What do you mean she's dead? The hell're you talking about?"

"She was shot in her apartment."

"Shot? What does shot mean?" She understood, but she didn't want to believe it.

"It happened early this morning. Somebody came in, they think through the fire escape, and shot her."

"What? The apartment faces the street. There were cops right outside the building. How's this possible?"

"Maybe you wanna go sit down before you hear the rest," Shawn said.

"Tell me what the hell's going on!" Geri shouted.

A few other cops nearby, and the receptionist, looked over.

"The protection order was removed last night," Shawn said.

"*What?*" Geri said.

"I couldn't believe it myself," Shawn said. "It was 'cause of the marathon. They needed more cops downtown, so—"

"There was supposed to be twenty-four-hour protection till there was an arrest in the case. Who the hell removed that order?"

Shawn was looking beyond Geri, toward the entrance to the main part of the precinct. Geri looked back and saw Dan McCarthy standing there.

"Let's take it easy, okay?" Dan said.

"*You* did this?" Geri was walking toward Dan.

"I said let's—"

"You had no right to do that. I promised that woman protection."

"Okay, let's take this inside."

"I want to know what the hell's going on here."

"Inside, I said."

Geri was so furious—her brain swirling, thinking about so many things at once—that she didn't remember going down the corridor with Dan to his office. She just seemed to wind up in there, screaming at him, "How could you do this? How could you?"

"Hey, just shut up, just shut the hell up and listen to me," Dan said. "I've had it with you causing scenes here, all right? This is a police station, not a goddamn playground."

"Tell me why," Geri said, trying her best to stay calm. "Just tell me why."

"We were undermanned for the marathon."

"Come on, they couldn't get some cops from Brooklyn and Queens who wanted triple pay?"

"She wasn't a credible witness," Dan said.

"Whoever shot her thought she was credible, and now she's dead and the killer's still out there."

"She was useless at the lineup yesterday," Dan said. "I don't believe she was ever planning to help us, she was just busting our balls."

"That wasn't your call to make."

"As the commanding officer at this precinct, actually it *is* my call to make. But before I made my decision I consulted with Santoro and Reese."

"You didn't consult with me."

"You weren't here."

"Come on, that's bull—"

"Look, I'm as upset about this as you are. You think I'm not upset?"

"The only thing you seem upset about is protecting your own ass."

"Look, Rodriguez, I've just about had it with you—"

"I gave that woman my word, goddamn it," Geri said. "I told her we would protect her, and now because of your . . ." She was going to say *your stupidity* but caught herself and said, "This isn't right. I told her we would protect her. I promised her."

"You shouldn't make promises you can't keep."

"The hell's that supposed to mean?"

"You knew we could only protect her for a limited amount of time. If the case went unsolved for a month, for a year, you knew we wouldn't have cops out there forever, she wasn't going into the freakin' witness protection program. Eventually she was going to be on her own."

"It was two days after she agreed to talk to us," Geri said. "Two days."

"Look, I agree this is an unfortunate situation; it sucks, okay, and despite what you think, I am extremely upset about it. But the fact remains, the past is the past and there's nothing we can do about it now except deal with it."

"Yeah, well I want to hear you explain to her family why this *unfortunate* situation went down the way it did. And I want to hear how you explain it to the press too, because you know when word gets out that a witness who was supposed to be under police protection was murdered, they're going to be all over this."

"I won't have to explain it," Dan said. "You will."

"Excuse me?"

"As lead detective on this case you'll go to the crime scene in Washington Heights and make a statement on behalf of the department. You'll explain why we made the decision."

"If you think I'm taking the fall—"

"You aren't the NYPD," Dan said. "I'm tired of your attitude that you're in this alone. You're part of a team."

"I wasn't part of the team that made this decision."

"You're still part of the team and lead detective on the case. One thing I won't tolerate around here is an atmosphere of finger pointing and blame."

"You expect me to go out there and lie?"

"No, I expect you to go out there and do your job."

"Yeah, do my job, so you can cover your own ass."

"I'm not asking you; I'm giving you an order, is that understood?"

"What if I don't take it?"

"That would be the biggest mistake of your career."

Geri glared at Dan, using every bit of restraint she could muster up not to go ballistic on him, and then she stormed out of the office, passing Shawn, who was sitting and eating a Pop Tart, saying, "Let's get the hell out of here."

Driving uptown on the Henry Hudson Parkway, Shawn next to her, Geri put the siren on, not only because she wanted to get to Washington Heights in a hurry, but because she wanted to speed, let out stress. An angry driver to begin with, she was out of control, going eighty, cutting over two lanes to pass an SUV.

Shawn, still holding a chunk of Pop Tart, said, "Take it easy, will ya? When I die I don't want it to be closed casket, know what I'm sayin'?"

Geri didn't slow down, pushing the needle past eighty-five.

"Hey, look, I know you're pissed off," Shawn said, "but you wanna be a cop, sometimes you gotta roll with the punches."

"I can't do that."

"You'd better do that. It's called a pecking order."

"Pecking order my PR ass," Geri said. "If it wasn't for my ethnicity, if I wasn't a woman, you think we'd be having this conversation? Dan had a problem with my promotion to begin with, and this is how he's taking it out on me. And he's like, 'What can she do about it?' 'cause he knows it's like I'm on probation one more year till I move up a grade. He knows I can't rock the boat 'less I want to walk off the plank."

"I don't know about walkin' planks," Shawn said. "All I know is you're gonna kill both of us if you don't slow the hell down."

Realizing ninety on the Henry Hudson was getting out of control, Geri slowed to seventy-five.

"Good, now we're at open casket again," Shawn said. "Least my kids can see me one last time before they put me in the ground." Then he said, "But you think I didn't have to take hits on my way up? Nobody makes it without getting past the bumps in the road. And if you don't like it, then quit. Be a security guard, work the door at a strip club. You walk away, trust me, there'll be cops lining up to take your spot, you can count on that."

In Washington Heights, when they turned onto 184th Street, they saw news trucks from the major networks double-parked in front of Morales's building. There were also several marked and a couple of unmarked police cars, and reporters, cops, and dozens of bystanders milling around the area.

"Guess these cops had to leave the marathon early," Geri said sarcastically.

When Geri and Shawn got out of the car they were intercepted by Annabelle—Geri couldn't recall her last name—a media relations person for the NYPD whom Geri had met a couple of times before.

"When do you want to make a statement?" Annabelle asked.

"Gimme a few," Geri said.

Reporters shouted questions as Geri and Shawn bypassed them and went into the building and up to Carlita's apartment. Santoro and Reese were there.

"Sorry about this," Santoro said. "I really am."

Geri didn't want to hear any apologies. Though she had a feeling Santoro was being sincere, she didn't say anything.

"So what do we got?" Geri asked.

"What you see is what you get," Santoro said. "Perp may have entered via the fire escape. Apparently the victim was in the bathroom at the time. No sign of struggle, seemed to be surprised, two gunshots to the head, and then he was gone."

"What's forensics saying?" Geri asked.

"Not much, unfortunately. Might have partial prints on the fire escape, but apparently kids were playing on the fire escape yesterday, so that may turn out to be nothing."

"What about witnesses?" Geri asked. "Wait, lemme take a wild guess, nobody saw or heard anything."

"Nobody saw or heard anything," Santoro said.

"Gee, what a surprise," Geri said. "One witness gets taken out and nobody else wants to talk. Gee. I wonder why."

"Nobody wanted it to go down this way," Santoro said.

"It didn't have to," Geri said. "So why'd you agree to getting rid of protection? And please don't tell me it had to do with getting cops down to the marathon."

"We can't protect everybody who gives us a tip or a sketch," Santoro said. "You know that. But, just so you know, I told Dan I didn't feel right about throwing you out to the sharks on this. I was fully willing to shoulder the responsibility, but it wasn't my call."

Geri could tell that Santoro, unlike Dan, seemed legitimately upset.

"Whatever," Geri said. "Guess it's all part of my initiation, right? Last in, first to take the fall."

One of the forensics workers, a young black guy, came in, and Santoro told him to check the roof and the roofs of the other buildings on the block.

When the forensics guy left, Santoro said to Geri, "We're still trying to figure out how the perp gained access to the apartment. Even if the perp came through the window, he had to get into the building somehow. He probably just bypassed the double door security; somebody could've buzzed him in."

"The entrance to the roof locked?" Geri asked.

"No, lock's been broken, the super said. Of course he could've entered through another building and dropped down the fire escape, but one thing is the perp probably did his recon; he seemed to be pretty familiar with the building."

"Well, guess it's time to face the storm," Geri said.

She was leaving the apartment when Shawn came over and said, "I'll talk to them with you if you want."

"Nah, it's okay," Geri said. "I can handle it. But I appreciate the offer."

Geri went downstairs, noticing when she got to the vestibule that there were a lot more reporters there than there had been ten or however many minutes ago. Any hopes that this wasn't going to be a major news story were fading fast.

As Geri exited the building, Annabelle asked her, "You want to go over anything first?"

"Nah," Geri said. "Think I'm just gonna wing it."

With mikes and a few TV cameras aimed at her, she gave an official police statement about the incident. While she was tempted to tell the truth, that this murder could have been avoided and had nothing to do with her, she spoke in a formal "police-ese" tone, saying, "Yesterday we made a decision to remove police protection of Carlita Morales, which had an unfortunate result." She went on, explaining what had happened, hating that she had to be so cold and unemotional.

She kept the statement short and sweet and was dying to get away, but she had to take a few questions.

"Were there any direct threats?" a reporter asked.

"No, there were not," Geri said.

"Do you have any leads in the shooting?" another reporter shouted.

"I can't comment specifically on anything regarding the investigation itself at this time," Geri said.

"Are there threats against anyone else?" a reporter in the back of the group asked.

"No, we're not aware of any at this time."

Thankfully Annabelle cut in, rescuing her. Geri was heading back into the building when a man to her right, several yards away, behind the police barricade, shouted to her, "My sister died 'cause of you!"

Geri stopped and looked over at the young Latino. He looked

familiar, probably because he looked so much like Carlita. It was
startling, actually. They had the same big brown eyes, same narrow
nose with the little bump in the middle.

"I'm really truly sorry," Geri said.

"Sorry ain't gonna bring my sister back!" he shouted.

An officer came over, in case he had to restrain the guy, but Geri
nodded to the officer as if saying, *It's okay, don't worry.*

Geri said to the young guy, "We're gonna find out who did this,
I promise you."

And the guy said, "I want my sister back, that's all I want, can
you promise me that? Can you?"

Geri held his gaze for a few seconds, then entered the apartment
building. On the stairwell she had to take a moment to control herself,
and then she went up the stairs to Carlita's apartment. Shawn was in
front and said, "You ready for round two of bad news?"

"What is it?"

"While you were down there, Dan called; he's taking us off the
case."

"What?" Geri wasn't expecting this at all. "That's ridiculous, after
I go out there and suck it up for the department?"

"That's just the way the timing worked out."

"Yeah, right."

"He said the order came from the police commissioner himself."

"So I have to be part of the team," Geri said, "till a head has to
roll, and then I'm on my own."

"Your head's not the only one rolling; my head's rolling too."

"You didn't go out there to take blame for something you had no
part of only to get kicked in the ass again two minutes later."

"You gotta just chill right now. He said it could've been worse,
we could've got suspended. Since you're not full grade, he could've

made you a patrol cop again. I mean, that wasn't gonna happen, but I'm just sayin'."

"Saying what?" Geri said. "Now we've got a killer out there and they take the cops who had the best chance to catch him off the case?"

"Sometimes you gotta just roll with the punches," Shawn said. "That's what I'm sayin'."

"This isn't why I became a cop," Geri said, practically yelling.

Forensics workers and cops looked over, including Santoro. By Santoro's expression it was obvious he knew what had gone down.

"Well, good luck," Geri said. "You're gonna need it."

Geri and Shawn left the building, ignoring the reporters' questions. As she got into the Charger, Geri looked at Carlita's grieving brother, realizing she'd made yet another promise she wasn't going to keep.

G eri wasn't in the mood for another confrontation with Dan, and besides, today was supposed to be her day off anyway, so after she dropped Shawn and the Charger back at the precinct, she headed back home on the subway, figuring she'd get some shut-eye and try to sleep this day off.

Back in her apartment, Willy and Wonka, maybe sensing that she was in a bad way, didn't come to greet her at the door and rub their heads against her legs and purr the way they usually did. They didn't even bother to get up from the couch.

Geri lay in bed, knowing there was no chance of getting to sleep. Her mind was way too active, replaying events of the day. She had anger and resentment, yeah, but the worst was how powerless she felt. A family had lost a daughter, a sister, and Geri couldn't do anything to make things right.

Then her thoughts drifted to the Diane Coles case—a family in Michigan had suffered a loss and wanted closure too. She reached for her cell and called Michael Hartman's friend Ramon. She got his voice mail—no message, just Julio Iglesias crooning, "Besame Mucho." Shaking her head, Geri ended the call. She didn't like to leave messages, especially when she was working on a case, because she wanted to be in a position of control. She didn't want to be the one waiting around for the phone to ring. She'd rather keep calling back, and her number was private so no one could see it on Caller ID.

So she waited a few minutes and called again. He didn't answer, so she hung up and then called a third time. It took about ten calls before a man picked up and said, "You my secret admirer?"

Geri was thrown off—she wasn't sure why—and said, "Um, is this Ramon?"

"Depends who's calling," the man said, trying to be suave.

"I'm Detective Geri Rodriguez with Manhattan North Homicide."

"That case, I guess you *are* my secret admirer. I mean, I had eleven missed calls; you must want to talk to me pretty badly."

Was this guy for real?

"I wanted to talk to you about a case I'm working on," Geri said.

"I heard it's not your case," Ramon said.

Geri wasn't in the mood, especially today, for his smart-ass attitude. But she wanted to stay in control, not play his games, so she kept it professional, saying, "Then I guess you spoke with your friend, Michael."

"He said you might call me, yeah."

"Well, actually the case is related to a case I've been working on, so it *is* my case."

"Whatever you say," Ramon said. "Whatever you say. I won't argue with a pretty cop."

Had Michael told him she was pretty? Or was Ramon the type of smooth talker who told every girl he met she was pretty? Either way, Geri had had enough of this nonsense.

"I'd rather talk to you in person," Geri said.

"Sounds good to me," Ramon said. "I like to keep things more physical myself."

Rolling her eyes, Geri asked, "Are you home now?"

"Actually I'm at rehearsal for a play, but I'm gonna be off in about a half hour."

"Where's your rehearsal space?"

"Theater district," Ramon said. "It ain't Broadway yet. But gimme a couple months; I'll get there, baby, I'll get there."

So he thought he was God's gift to women *and* a great actor. As long as this guy wasn't cocky.

"I'm actually in the area," she said. "So I can come by."

He gave her the address, at a theater space on Forty-sixth near Ninth, which was only a few blocks from her apartment. She wasn't looking forward to questioning some smart-ass, but it felt good to be back working on a case, and more important, she hoped she could help get some closure for Diane Coles's family.

When Geri arrived at the old, tenement-style building, she went up a few flights of stairs, then didn't have to figure out where to go because she could hear the actors performing. It was a small theater—maybe fifty seats. There were only a few people in the audience in the front row, and Geri counted twelve people on stage, including Ramon. Although she'd never seen him she recognized him right away, before he said a word. He looked like he'd sounded on the phone—cocky, suave, smoldering—the kind of arrogant good-looking guy who knew he was good-looking and wanted to flaunt it. But Geri was surprised because, while Ramon looked and acted like the slick, phony

kind of guy who normally repulsed her, instead of resenting him she
had a sudden, strong attraction that she couldn't explain or deny.

Geri couldn't follow what was going on in the play—something
about poisoned water, or a conspiracy or something, but even though
the language was old-fashioned the actors were talking like they were
from Long Island. But the main reason she couldn't follow the plot
was that Ramon was way too distracting. The guy had an aura about
him. He was cocky, yeah, and he was strutting like he thought he was
a combination of Antonio Banderas and Javier Bardem, but he was
somehow able to pull it off and actually come across as the sexy,
irresistible Latin lover he was trying so desperately to be. Geri didn't
know if it was star quality, charisma, or the X factor, but whatever it
was, this guy had it.

It was as if the other actors had disappeared and Ramon were
acting in a one-man show. Staring at him, Geri crossed and uncrossed
her legs a few times, then discovered she was actually getting aroused.
When had just watching a guy, a stranger, ever had this kind of effect
on her? She was getting so turned on, she was afraid it was getting
obvious, and she was about to go out and wait in the lobby when
Ramon—maybe he sensed Geri was about to get up?—asked the
director, the heavyset woman in the front row, if they could take a
break.

"Okay, let's break for fifteen and then I have notes," the director
said.

Ramon strutted—yes, *strutted*—over to Geri and, with a wide
grin and dark smoldering eyes, said, "See, I was right, you are beautiful."

Geri felt wetness on the insides of her thighs, and she felt something else she hadn't felt in ages around a guy. She actually felt
nervous.

"You must be Ramon," Geri said, feeling like she was fumbling her words. What was going on?

"The one and only," he said. "You like the play?"

"Just saw a bit; it was hard to get into."

"Ibsen, *Enemy of the People*," Ramon said. "We're setting it modern day, New York City, but the themes resonate." Ramon hadn't stopped looking at her eyes. Was he sniffing her? He said, "You smell wonderful. I love your perfume."

"I'm not wearing perfume," she said.

He leaned in a little closer, maybe to get a better whiff, and said, "Even better."

Geri's face was hot and she had to uncross and then cross her legs again. What was she doing, flirting with a potential suspect in a murder case? Like when she was questioning Michael, she felt as if she didn't have the upper hand, as if they were tangoing and he was leading, and Geri usually never felt this way at work. What had happened to the tough chick detective who was the bad cop in "good cop, bad cop"? Maybe they were right for taking her off the Washington Heights murder cases. Maybe she was losing her edge.

"Is there, um, someplace we can go to talk?" she asked, afraid that it had come out all wrong. She wanted to go someplace else, figuring a change of location would help her get her act together, but the way she said it, it sounded flirty, as if she wanted to go someplace where they could be alone.

"There's a coffee place across the street," Ramon said. "They got couches, dim light. We can sit in the corner where it's nice and quiet and—"

She sensed he was about to touch her hand. She stood up quickly and said, "Okay, let's go."

On the stairway down, he said, "After you," and she knew he was checking out her ass. But unlike when Detective Mangel and other creeps checked her out, she couldn't help liking it this time. Instead of grossing her out, it made her feel sexy.

Outside, she asked him how long he'd been an actor. Again, it came out flirty, like they were on a freaking date, but she was glad because it gave him a chance to do all the talking and she could try to get control of herself.

At the quaint little coffee shop that Geri had passed many times but never gone into, Ramon said, "Let's go to the back where we can be alone," and even though she was tempted, she said, "No, the counter near the door's fine."

"What're you having?" he asked.

"It's okay, I can pay for my own," she said, and went to the counter with him.

Waiting for the coffee, he asked her where her family was from, and she said her mom was from San Juan.

"*Mi familia es de San Juan tambien,*" Ramon said.

When they got their coffees and sat at the counter, Ramon started talking fast and excitedly in Spanish about Puerto Rico, and how he'd spent every summer in San Juan when he was growing up. Like before, Geri didn't like the direction the conversation was going. She also didn't like talking in Spanish, as she felt it was too intimate.

In English she said, "Did Michael tell you about Diane Coles?"

"Ooh, getting all coplike," Ramon said. "I like that."

"Did he?" she asked, aware that his leg was practically touching hers and that she wasn't trying to shift hers away.

"Okay, okay, I'm sorry, I'm sorry, I'll be good, I'll be good." Ramon smiled. "For now." Then his expression suddenly shifted and he got very serious and said, "Yeah, he told me. I was devastated. Diane was a wonderful woman, had everything going for her. I couldn't believe it. I mean, for her to go like that, it just ain't right."

Ramon seemed sincere, even a little teary eyed. But he was an actor, after all.

"And you can vouch that Michael was in New York last Wednesday?"

"Yeah, we were with our kids at the playground all morning, then we took 'em to Shake Shack for lunch."

"And you're not just saying this to protect him, right? If I look at that Shake Shack video I'll see Michael there, right?"

Leaning closer, looking right into her eyes, he said, "One thing I won't ever do is lie to you."

Geri couldn't help feeling weak inside. What was it about this guy?

"So you were in town all last week?" she asked.

"Yeah, of course," he said. "Come on, I know you don't really think I had anything to do with this. You're just asking because you gotta be all cop with me 'cause it's your job, right?"

Geri couldn't help smiling a little, then said, "So somebody can vouch for you being in New York?"

"Yeah, somebody can vouch," Ramon said. *"Mi madre."*

"You were with your mother all week?"

"I live with my mother," Ramon said. "After my father died she was lonely and didn't want to be alone, so I had her move in with me. It works out with me, especially since I've got a kid. My kid's mom left, so . . ." He seemed to be getting emotional. "Anyway, it's nice to have my mother around to help out."

Geri didn't think he was acting anymore. Despite his ladies'-man persona, he seemed like a genuinely good guy. She also couldn't help noticing that he smelled nice too. It wasn't deodorant or cologne, it was just him, but it was arousing. She noticed he was looking right in her eyes again.

"You're staring at me," she said.

"Sorry," he said. "When I look at something beautiful it's hard to look away."

Normally, a line like that would've grossed her out or made her laugh, but she was getting aroused again. Desperately trying to keep it professional, she said, "Did Diane tell you why she was moving to Michigan?"

"No, she just kind of started blowing me off, you know? Maybe she was upset 'cause her friend disappeared or maybe she thought it wasn't working out, but that was cool. I'm not the kinda guy who puts pressure on a woman, know what I mean? If it ain't workin' out, that's chill, I let them be."

"So you didn't talk on the phone at all?" Geri asked.

"No." Ramon was giving her that look again. "Sorry," he said, "I can't help it."

Crossing her legs, Geri asked, "What about Olivia Becker? Did Diane mention anything that was going on with her?"

"Just that she was worried about her, thought she was acting weird."

"Weird how?

"Maybe *weird*'s the wrong word," Ramon said. "Crazy. She thought Olivia was going *loco*. And I only met Olivia a couple times."

"Did she tell you about any problems Olivia was having with Michael?"

"No, and trust me, the problem was Olivia, not Michael," Ramon said. "I mean I know Michael can be kind of weird himself when you first meet him. He has that whole strong, silent type thing going on, and that funny accent. But once you get to know him you find out how chill he really is. You got a boyfriend?"

"What?" Geri said.

"Tienes un novio?"

"I heard you," she said.

"Sorry I'm staring at you again, but I just can't help myself," he said. "I just love looking at your eyes too much. And they tell a story."

"What story is that?" she asked weakly.

"About a girl," Ramon said. "She acts tough, works all day long, but when it comes down to it, she just wants to be loved, like everybody else."

"I should probably go now," she said, but she didn't get up.

"I know you're feeling our connection right now," Ramon said. "I see it in your eyes, the way you're looking at me right now, and I feel it too. You're the one I've been waiting for my whole life. I know what you're thinkin' right now—he probably says that to every beautiful woman he meets, and I'll be honest with you, I have said it before. But I never meant it the way I do right now. I don't care if we just met and we hardly know each other. Like Michael says, 'You can hide hate, but you can't hide love,' and I know this is the real thing and you know it too. I know you know it."

Geri knew this was wrong. While she didn't believe that Ramon had had anything to do with Diane Coles's murder, he was still a witness, a potential suspect, and she shouldn't be flirting with him. But she couldn't deny that she did feel an unusually strong connection with him. It was crazy, but she felt it.

"When am I going to see you again?" he asked.

"If I have any more questions, I'll be in touch," she said.

He reached out and grabbed her hand.

"I don't mean that," he said. "You know what I mean. I mean just the two of us, one-on-one, someplace where we can be alone."

She wanted to move her hand, but then she didn't want to anymore. His hand felt good and she thought maybe this wasn't so wrong after all. Yeah, she was questioning him, but was he really a witness? She had no evidence that he had any connection to the deaths of Olivia Becker and Diane Coles, and besides, this wasn't even her case. She could've met him on the street or at a bar, and would anything be wrong with it then?

"Come on, I know you want to see me again," Ramon said. "You can't hide from it. You gotta admit it. You gotta be free."

His dark eyes were like magnets, pulling her in, but she wasn't afraid, not anymore.

"I'm free tonight," she heard herself say.

Into their second glass of Chardonnay, Alison was telling Vijay about her troubles with Simon when their legs touched. Alison could've shifted away, but she didn't, wanting to see if Vijay would move any closer. She was glad that he didn't.

"Maybe it's just a phase," Vijay said.

"No, I don't think so," Alison said. "I thought so at first, but it's gone on too long, almost a month. I don't know. It's so crazy."

Alison knew she was rambling, but she couldn't help it. She was too distracted by the feel of her leg against Vijay's, wanting to be closer to him. With the top buttons of his shirt open she could see his smooth tan chest.

"And you really think there's someone else?" he asked.

She realized she was staring at his chest and shifted her gaze back toward his eyes. "I don't know," she said. "Yes, probably. I mean, his

behavior has changed so much, there has to be someone. That's
what I thought originally, but I think I've just been, I don't know, in
denial. I thought it might be Christina, our babysitter, but that's probably crazy. I don't know. I just don't know."

Alison started crying. She didn't want to cry—it made her feel
weak, and she hated feeling weak—but the stress that had been building up all day was too much and she needed a release.

Vijay took her wineglass from her and placed it on the coffee
table, then put an arm around her and pulled her in close against his
chest. She hadn't cried with the motive of getting Vijay to hold her,
but she was glad it had worked out this way. Being close to him felt
so good, so right, and then they were kissing. She didn't know who
kissed who first; all she knew was that she was kissing this solid,
supportive man and it felt great.

As they kissed, Vijay had his hand on her right leg, just above her
knee, and he was kneading her with his fingertips. She wanted him
to move his hand higher and, as if he could read her mind, his hand
moved to the inside of her thigh, and she had a hand on his chest and
she was biting on his lip, sucking on it, while she was thinking, *I want
more, please give me more.* Responding, he had his other hand under
her shirt, feeling her hardening nipple over her bra, and she moved
her hand lower, over the bulge in his jeans. She wanted him to
attack her, to tear off her clothes and pin her down to the couch, or
maybe the floor, yes the floor, and feel his naked body on top of her.

Then she heard, "I don't think this is a good idea."

She was so caught up it took a moment or two to register that
they weren't making out anymore, and he'd shifted away from her
on the couch.

"Okay." It was hard for her to get a full breath. "I mean, if that's
what you want."

"It's not a matter of what I want," he said, "it's a matter of what I think is right. You're an extremely beautiful, exciting woman and I love spending time with you, but you have to figure out what you're doing in your marriage; that has to be your priority right now."

She knew he was right, but she still wanted to be under him on the floor.

"That makes sense," she said. "I mean, I get what you're saying."

They finished their wine and, holding hands, talked about other things. Vijay told her about a recent trip to Italy and how he'd love to go back. It was easy to imagine being in Rome with Vijay, taking long walks and having romantic dinners. Then they talked about recent shows and movies they'd seen, music—they both liked live jazz—and about Southampton, where Vijay owned a summer house. It was easy to fantasize about falling in love with Vijay, marrying him, and having a normal life in the city. Maybe they could even have a child together. The idea of another kid with Simon had been off the table for a while, but since he'd lost his job it had officially been shelved, since making it with two kids in the city on their current income was a financial impossibility. But Vijay had mentioned a few times how much he loved children and how he couldn't wait to be a dad someday. Alison wanted another kid too, and her clock was ticking, and she had no doubt that Vijay would make a wonderful father.

Alison was dying to kiss him again.

He must have sensed what she was thinking, or maybe he just saw her staring at his lips, because he asked, "So what do you think you're going to do?"

She knew he meant about her marriage, and she said, "I don't know. I really don't know."

"Well, all I can say from the point of view of a guy who's divorced is if you decide to leave him you should do it with a good conscience, especially when there's a child involved. You want to make sure you've done everything you can to save the marriage before you leave, and that if you leave you're leaving for the right reasons."

"We've been in counseling for a long time and it hasn't helped," she said. "We've tried everything."

"But you still don't know what's going on with him, so the question you have to ask yourself is, do you really want to know?"

"What do you mean?"

"Have you considered hiring a PI? If you're right and there is someone else, then you'll know you left for the right reasons. Then again, you might prefer not knowing."

"No, I definitely want to know," Alison said. "I've thought about hiring a PI, but maybe you're right. Maybe I should just do it and find out once and for all."

"I have an old friend who's a PI, has a big agency here in the city," Vijay said. "His name's, don't laugh, Stephen Tyler."

Alison laughed.

"He spells it with a *ph*, not a *v*," Vijay said. "Anyway, he's here in the city and he's very discreet and professional. If you give him a few days he'll tell you what's going on and, one way or another, you'll have a much clearer picture. Just don't make any Aerosmith jokes, he's heard them all."

After all the chaos and weirdness she'd endured lately, the concept of "a clearer picture" was very appealing to Alison, so, figuring she had nothing to lose, she took Stephen Tyler's contact information. She didn't want to overstay her welcome, so she said she should probably get going now. At the door she told him she had a great time, and Vijay said he had a great time too, and they kissed good-bye. She didn't want the kiss to end.

Several minutes later, she was wandering downtown on Broadway, fantasizing again about being with Vijay in Rome, when her cell phone buzzed. She hoped it was Vijay, telling her what a wonderful time he'd had because that was what she was planning to text him, but the message was from Simon:

I love you and please tell little bear I love him too. I promise some-day you'll understand EVERYTHING.

Annoyed, Alison deleted the message and typed a happy one to Vijay.

TWELVE

Simon ran with Volker all night. While it was a thrill to have a companion, a fellow werewolf, to run with, it was also a great learning experience. Despite his age—as a human Volker had deep wrinkles and appeared to be at least ninety years old—Volker was a very fast, agile werewolf. He was much quicker than Simon, but this was mainly because Simon still wasn't fully comfortable in his wolf's body. That started to change, though, after several hours of running with Volker. Simon learned how to trust his new animal instincts and to use more of his speed. He also learned how to be a great tree climber. This was more amazing because, in his normal human body, he'd never been a very good climber. When he was growing up, his friends could climb to the highest branches of trees, but he was always the one who was too afraid to climb very high. But following Volker's lead, Simon was able to climb to the highest branch of a tree, where, because he was certain there were no humans in the area, he howled as loud as he could.

At one point, Volker stopped running and squatted. Simon was confused until the odor hit and he knew Volker was pooping. When Volker was through, he buried the poop in the ground using his feet/claws as shovels, and then he indicated that it was Simon's turn. Simon had to go, so he pooped and then buried it the way Volker had. While Simon was vaguely aware that this was weird, mainly he felt very normal pooping in the woods, as if he'd been doing it forever.

In the middle of the night, probably around four in the morning, the brightness of the moon faded, and Volker settled to rest. Simon lay next to him, feeling, strangely, as if he were part of the ground, that when he inhaled, his breath went into the earth, and when he exhaled, air from the earth left his mouth. If he'd been on drugs this would have been a seriously good trip.

When he opened his eyes it was dawn. Volker was gone, but his intense werewolf scent lingered. Simon felt achy and a little dizzy and then he looked at his normal human hands. He had some cuts and bruises on his arms and legs, but he knew they'd heal within minutes. He was sad that he wasn't a werewolf anymore—he mostly missed the carefree abandon—but his disappointment was overtaken by panic as he realized he had bigger problems. He was naked and, worse, he smelled a human, very close by, and heard footsteps—crunching twigs and dried leaves.

Simon scrambled to put on his clothes but only managed to get underwear and part of his T-shirt on when he heard, "Hey."

It was a man's voice and it wasn't a friendly *hey*. It was a *Hey, what the hell are you doing here?* hey.

With his back to the guy, Simon froze with the T-shirt over his head and on one arm and said, "Um, not much."

"You sleep here all night?"

Simon put on the rest of the T-shirt, then looked at the middle-aged black guy—in a City Parks Department uniform.

Knowing that being in most parts of the park at night was illegal, he said, "Nope, I, um, just got here."

The guy was looking around. "Who're you here with?"

Simon got the implication, as the Ramble had a reputation as a gay hookup area.

"No one, I swear," Simon said. "I was just, um, hiking, and I thought I got poison ivy, so I was just checking, that's all." He realized this explanation was ridiculous, but, on the spot, it was the best he could come up with.

"There's no poison ivy around here," the guy said.

"See, that's good to know," Simon said. "I wish you were here five minutes ago. You would've saved me a major panic attack."

Simon smiled, trying to make it into a joke, but the guy wasn't amused.

"Just get dressed and get the hell out of here," he said, "or I'm gonna call the cops."

"Definitely," Simon said, pulling on his pants. "Have a great day."

The guy walked away, shaking his head.

Simon put on his socks and sneakers. The holes in the socks and rips in the sneakers reminded him of what had happened last night. It all seemed like a dream or a fantasy, but he knew it was real.

Then, he was checking his cell phone—still nothing from Alison—when he heard a crash behind him. Simon had a strong jolt in his chest and his breath was gone; he actually thought he was having a heart attack. Then he saw Volker—the human version of Volker—standing a few feet away after his leap from a tree branch above them. Volker was dressed in black—black shoes, black pants, black turtleneck—and for such an athletic guy he looked astonishingly old. Though he had very thick white hair, his face looked like someone had carved lines it, reminding Simon of some of the last photos of Mother Teresa.

"You just scared the hell out of me." Simon caught his breath. "I thought you left."

"I wouldn't leave you," Volker said with his strong German accent.

Simon put his phone away and patted his pockets, making sure he had his wallet and keys. Then he said, "We should probably get going. That parks guy might get the wrong idea."

"He is gone," Volker said.

Simon breathed deeply—it was true, the scent had faded. He said, "Yeah, I guess you're right." Then, aware of his lingering queasiness, he said, "How do you feel? I mean I feel a little nauseous."

"Nausea is normal," Volker said.

Simon looked at Volker's very dark, practically black eyes, which were eerily similar to Michael's, then realized he was staring and said, "Sorry, it's just a little freaky seeing you here; I mean, I didn't think I'd ever see you again. Where did you come from?"

"I'm from Germany."

"I know *that*. I mean, I didn't think I'd ever see you again myself. How'd you find me? Did Charlie send you?"

"No one had to send me. I have been tracking you for days."

"Days?" Simon said. "How's that possible? I mean, I picked up a scent here the other night, but if it's been days I would've picked up on something else."

"I can be more than a kilometer away from you on a city street and still be able to track you."

Simon didn't know the metric system very well, but he knew a kilometer was about two-thirds of a mile—pretty damn impressive.

"Wow." Simon was seriously impressed; his own ability to detect scents didn't seem nearly as powerful. "That's amazing, I mean that you can do that in Manhattan; with all these scents, it can be overwhelming sometimes."

"It's not overwhelming for me." Volker was emotionless.

"How is this all possible?" Simon asked. "I mean, I get it now, I know I'm capable of these incredible things now, but where did it come from? How am I able to change? Does it wear off? Is there a cure?"

"A cure." Did Volker sound disgusted? "You talk as if you have a disease."

"Well, it's like a disease," Simon said. "It was given to me, I didn't ask for any of this, and I have a right to know what's going on with my body. I mean, I know it came from you and Michael, but how did you get this way? What's in my body? Will it make me sick? Am I going to die from it?"

"No, you won't die for another one hundred years, perhaps longer."

"If you think this is a joke, I'm not laughing," Simon said.

"Does it seem like a joke?" Volker paused, staring, then said, "To answer your other questions, my father made me who I am, and unfortunately I made Michael who he is. Are there other wolves? Maybe. I've heard rumors, but I've never encountered one. But *werewolfe* are excellent at disguising themselves, at assimilating. That is something you must learn if you are to survive in the human world. Right now, you are like an animal raised in captivity. You don't have the skills to survive in the human world."

Simon's brain was overloaded, trying to process all this—*Fathers?*

Assimilating? Captivity? "Look, I want answers, real answers," he said, raising his voice. "Where did all this start? What happened to my body? What's making me act the way I'm acting? How does my body change?"

"Why are these questions so important to you?" Volker asked.

"Are you kidding me?" Simon said. "Why wouldn't I want to know?"

Volker waited several seconds, then said, "Fine. If you insist, I'll tell you what you want to know. Maybe it will help you understand what's at stake." He let that hang there, then asked, "Do you want to sit down?"

Simon had too much energy. "No, standing's fine," he said.

"Very well." Then Volker was quiet again, staring blankly for a long time. Finally he said, "It is impossible to explain about Michael and me, if I don't first tell you about my father. His name was Heinrich Hartmann, spelled the German way, with two *n*s, and he was a very cruel man. Every day when he came home from work he would beat my mother and me mercilessly. My earliest memories are of my father's violence. Sometimes when I close my eyes I can hear my father yelling at me and my mother, and I can feel the pains of his fists against my face and his belt against my back. Although this happened nearly 140 years ago, the memories are fresh in my mind."

Simon was shaking his head.

"Is something wrong?" Volker asked.

"It's just what you keep saying about your age."

"What about my age?"

"Come on," Simon said, "you really expect me to believe you were around a hundred and forty years ago?"

"I was born in Freiburg, Germany, in the year 1871," Volker said.

It was clear that he wasn't kidding, or at least he believed it was true.

"Wow, I guess you must have some pretty good longevity in your family," Simon said.

"Strength and healing aren't the only gifts of the wolf," Volker said. "You and the others will live longer than humans as well. Well, this is depending, of course, on what sort of survival skills you learn. Michael was born in 1921 and he's still healthy and quite strong."

Normally Simon would've dismissed Volker as a demented old man with an excellent imagination, but after experiencing what he'd experienced last night, and witnessing Volker's remarkable strength and agility, how could he discount anything?

"So what does your father, Heinrich, have to do with this?" Simon asked. "Was he a werewolf too?"

"No, not initially," Volker said, "but one day something happened to him that would change the course of our family forever. It began like any other day. My father went to work, and when he returned he was drunk and began beating my mother. I came to my mother's defense, but I was just a young boy and my father was a very large man, at least twice as large as me, and I couldn't hurt him with my fists, but when he grabbed me and was going to hit me I bit his arm. This enraged him further and I knew I'd made a huge mistake, that he would beat me mercilessly.

"Then he grabbed me by my ear and pulled me outside behind our house. I was screaming very loud and he didn't want the neighbors to hear so he pulled me farther into the woods, where no one could hear my screams. Then he told me to take off my shirt and turn away from him. I knew what was coming and I just wanted it to end as soon as possible. I didn't want to think about the pain, but I couldn't help it. He beat me with his belt harder than he ever had before, and my screams must have echoed through the woods. I prayed to God for a miracle, for the pain to end, and then the wolf appeared.

"I saw it in the woods, in the distance ahead of me. It was big and gray and very majestic and it was watching my father whip me. My father didn't see the wolf, or he would have stopped beating me, I'm sure of it, but I sensed the danger and ran away. My father yelled for me to come back and chased after me. Usually my father could catch me easily, but I was so frightened of the wolf that I ran faster than I'd ever run before. I was running through the woods, trying to get home, and my father was chasing after me, and then I heard my father but he wasn't screaming my name—he was screaming in agony. The wolf was attacking him, biting into his flesh with its huge teeth. There was blood, so much blood, and my father was defenseless. It was a wonderful thing to see. After all the abuse I had suffered, I loved seeing my father feel some of my pain. I wanted the wolf to kill my father, to get revenge for my mother and me.

"I ran home and I was so happy I was probably laughing out loud. My mother asked where Father was and I lied to her. I said my father had gone for a walk in the woods and sent me home. I was afraid if I told her the truth she would send men into the woods to try to save my father. That night, my father didn't return, and it was the happiest night of my childhood. I imagined him in the woods, his body torn to shreds by the wolf, and that my mother and I would never have to fear him again. I hoped there was a hell and my father was in it and would feel the pain of the wolf forever.

"In the morning, there was a search for my father. They found his blood, but not his body. We were told that the wolf probably dragged his body somewhere and that my father was almost certainly dead. Although my mother cried, I knew they were tears of joy, that she was as happy as I was that my father was gone forever. So you can imagine how surprised and terrified we both were two weeks later when my father returned from the woods stronger and healthier than ever."

Simon could tell that Volker was so caught up in the story that, in his mind, he was back there in the woods, watching the wolf attack his father. Meanwhile, Simon felt like he was at a campfire, listening to an old man tell an eerie story. But the fact that he knew this wasn't a story, that this related to his life and his future, made him even more anxious to find out what happened next.

"So where did your father say he'd been?" Simon asked.

"He said he had been lost in the woods," Volker said. "The authorities concluded that the blood that was found must not have been his, and everyone in the village was glad my father was alive—well, everyone except my mother and me. I, of course, knew the truth, but I was afraid to tell anyone. I also knew that as soon as he had the chance my father would beat me mercilessly for leaving him in the woods to die.

"But my father didn't beat me, which surprised me, but I knew something about him had changed. There was a darkness in his eyes that I had never seen before, and I feared him more than ever. At night he would leave, sometimes not returning until morning. He was eating meat constantly and was always restless, and he grew a thick beard and had more hair on the rest of his body as well. He was very strong—one day I saw him chop down a thick tree with a single swing of an ax. People in town thought he'd gone mad from being in the woods for so long, but I knew he wasn't crazy. And then, on the night of a bright full moon, it happened."

Simon couldn't doubt Volker anymore; how could he? The

description of Heinrich's behavior after getting bitten was so similar to what Simon had experienced.

"What happened?" Simon asked anxiously.

"I heard him and my mother in their bedroom," Volker continued. "It was the sounds of lovemaking at first. I was ashamed to listen, so I put a pillow over my head, but the pillow couldn't block out what came next. My mother was screaming, as if she were being attacked, and it sounded as if there were an animal in the room with her. I had no idea what was happening, but naturally I wanted to save my mother, so I went to their room and opened the door and saw my father attacking her. But it wasn't my father—it was my father as a wolf. He was chewing her flesh, his animal face covered in blood, and my mother's silence told me it was too late to help. Then my father turned toward me and before I could run he was upon me, biting into my neck. I was certain I was going to die and, in a way, I suppose I did die, because my life as a complete human ended that day."

Volker was quiet for a few moments, and then with new energy he said, "Everything went black. When I opened my eyes it seemed like only an instant had passed, yet I wasn't in the bedroom, I was in the woods with my father, and the gray wolf was there too, the one who attacked my father. I should have been frightened, but I wasn't. I felt very calm, very at peace. My father explained that he had given me the greatest gift—the gift of the wolf. At first I didn't understand what he meant, but soon I discovered how powerful I was. I also felt bonded to my father for the first time, and I knew it was a bond that could never be broken."

Volker paused again and looked away, in the direction of the Central Park Lake, as if reflecting. Simon couldn't tell if he was sad or just tired from talking so much.

"Are you okay?" Simon asked.

"Yes, I'm fine," Volker said. "I just haven't spoken of this in many, many years."

Simon gave Volker a few minutes to collect himself. He didn't want to check the time on his cell phone, but he figured it had to be about six A.M. Soon there would be people all around the Ramble.

"If you're too tired to continue, maybe we can meet up another time," Simon said. "Maybe later in the day or over the weekend. We can set up a time to—"

"No," Volker said. He let it hang there, then added, "I want to answer your questions. Maybe it will help you understand."

"Okay, that's great," Simon said. "Actually there is something I'm not sure I understand. You said you saw your father kill your mother, but after your father bit you, you felt a strong bond with him."

"An unbreakable bond," Volker said. "There is no bond stronger than sharing the blood of the wolf."

"But didn't you hate him for what he did to your mother?"

"Yes, of course I hated him."

"That's what I'm not sure I understand. How can you hate him and feel a bond with him at the same time?"

"A bond is not the opposite of hate," Volker said. "You can have a bond and still have hate."

"But I don't feel any bond with Michael," Simon said.

"Yes, and that's precisely what makes you different from the others," Volker said. "You weren't bitten directly by Michael. You were bitten by the woman, Olivia. That's why the others feel a loyalty to Michael that you don't."

Simon hated that this made sense, because the more it made sense, the more real it became. And the more real it became, the more terrifying it became.

"So how did Michael get the way he is?" Simon asked. "I mean, was he born a werewolf?"

"No, the children of a werewolf are all born human," Volker said. "Before Michael created his beer to prepare you and the others for the bites, the only way to pass the blood of the wolf was by a bite to the neck, a deep bite that lasts about one minute. And it could only be transferred along the same bloodline."

"So you bit Michael?" Simon asked.

"Yes," Volker said. "And it was the most regrettable mistake of my life. But I'm jumping ahead; that occurred much later. After my father bit me I had to learn how to assimilate in the world with humans. I was very much the way you are now—I was lost, I was alone, and I didn't know how to control the craving."

"The craving for meat?" Simon asked. "Yeah, I've been getting that all the time. I wish there was some way to—"

"No," Volker said, "I am speaking of the craving for human flesh."

Simon didn't know why he was waiting for a sign that Volker was joking because it was obvious that he wasn't joking about any of this.

"Oh, okay," Simon said. "So did you—"

"I did many horrible things, yes. I was a killer as vicious as Michael. When I had a craving, I couldn't resist it. I had to satisfy it. And the craving could come at any time. I was totally at its mercy."

Simon remembered being in the bathroom, partially transforming, having to resist the urge to break down the door and attack Alison and Jeremy.

Horrified, Simon asked, "So how . . . how did you learn how to control it?"

"My father was my teacher," Volker said. "Without a teacher it is impossible to learn. It is like learning to talk when you can't hear voices. I had the ability within me, but I needed someone to show me how to utilize it properly."

"But once you learned, you were okay?" Simon said. "I mean, the craving went away, right?"

"No, the craving never goes away," Volker said. "The craving is part of who you are now. But, yes, I did learn how to control the craving. I was able to assimilate in the world of humans and I had my normal human life, and my life as a wolf."

"So you mean you didn't turn into a werewolf spontaneously anymore?" Simon said. "You could control it when it happened?"

Instead of answering, Volker took a couple of steps back and, though Simon sensed what was about to happen, it was still shocking to see Volker turn into a werewolf. Although Simon had been with the werewolf version of Volker all night, watching his facial features change, hair grow, and claws develop was still surreal.

Not sure if what he was feeling was awe or fear, Simon said, "Okay, okay, I get it, I get it. Can you turn back, please? *Please.*"

Within seconds, Volker was back in human form.

"Wow," Simon said. "How the hell did you do that so fast?"

"You can learn that as well," Volker said.

"Okay, so what about when the moon's full?" Simon asked. "Do you automatically turn?"

"No, that is a myth," Volker said. "Is it easier to transform when the moon is full? Yes, during a full moon and a day or two before or after, it is easier to become a wolf. Do I have to transform when the moon is full? No. But for you, right now, because you have no control of the craving yet, resisting transformation during the time of the full moon would be more difficult."

"But you said the craving doesn't go away completely, right?" Simon asked.

"That is correct," Volker said. "But you can control the craving and satisfy it in other ways. For example, instead of craving human flesh, you can crave the flesh of other animals. You can go into the woods and hunt deer or rabbit or even squirrel and that will satisfy the craving."

"And this is what you did?"

"Yes, and I was able to fully assimilate into the world of humans," Volker said. "My father opened a brewery in Freiburg and I worked there. During World War One, the brewery was converted into a clothing factory, making uniforms for German soldiers. After the war, I had a wife and two beautiful daughters and one son, Michael. For many years we were happy, even as our country suffered a great depression. I had my life with my family and my secret life as a wolf. In the meantime, my father was getting older and I was afraid for what would happen when he died. Not only did we share a bond, we shared a secret, and I was terrified of having to keep the secret alone."

Volker was looking at Simon with a lost, maybe confused expression. Simon thought he might have lost his train of thought and was about to say something when Volker continued:

"So, when Michael was eighteen years old, I took him far into the woods where no one could hear his screams and I gave him the gift of the wolf. I thought it would cure my fear of loneliness and that we would share the same bond that I shared with my father, but it turned out to be the biggest mistake I ever made. You see, I had assumed that the blood of the wolf would have the same effect on Michael as it did on me, but that was not the case. I could control the craving, but Michael was different—Michael *became* the craving. He didn't care how many human lives he took or how much misery he caused. Men, women, children—it didn't matter to him. People disappeared all over Germany, and elsewhere in Europe, and he was responsible.

One afternoon, he took my wife and beautiful daughters into the woods, far enough that no one could hear them, and he . . ." Volker paused for a few moments, then added, "It looked like they were mauled to death by a wolf, which was true, I suppose."

"Wait," Simon said. "So you're saying Michael killed your family and you didn't do anything?"

"What could I do? Tell the police? If Michael was arrested, what would happen to me? I had killed too, of course. I was as guilty as he was."

Simon understood Volker's dilemma, as it was similar to why Simon couldn't call the cops on Michael right now. If Simon turned Michael in, it would be like turning himself in.

"But you bit Michael," Simon said. "Weren't you his leader, or in control of him, or however you want to put it? Couldn't you tell him what to do?"

"I tried to control him, of course," Volker said. "But Michael's craving was too strong and our bond was too powerful. I couldn't bring myself to kill him, although part of me wanted to. My father tried, though. He was a very old man, but he knew that Michael had to be stopped. There was a battle in the woods one night. My father tried, but ultimately Michael defeated him."

"You mean Michael killed your father?"

"Yes. He tore his jaw apart and ripped his head open."

Simon cringed, remembering the awful sound a jaw makes when torn apart, the ripping of ligament and bone and the splattering of blood.

"After my father died, I felt an even stronger bond with Michael," Volker said. "We only had each other, we were our only family. We had the brewery, but we mainly lived a secluded life. But this was during World War Two, of course. So Michael joined the army. It was like a dream for him—a chance to kill without fear of punishment."

"Wait," Simon said. "So you're saying that Michael fought in World War Two for the Nazis?"

"Yes," Volker said. "But rest assured, nationality means nothing to a wolf. Michael killed many Russians, Americans, French, and Germans during the war. He had a great advantage, as his wounds, even from gunshots, healed faster, and no one was stronger than him. And his thirst for blood was infinite."

"I just want to get this straight," Simon said. "So you want me to believe that during World War Two, during battles that have been documented and recorded in history, Michael transformed into a werewolf and killed people?"

"Yes, but by this time, you must understand, Michael had learned to assimilate," Volker said. "He would never kill as a wolf around a witness—at least not a witness who survived. If humans were in the area, he could detect them. But Michael loved to kill with weapons as well, and in the heat of battle there were many opportunities to kill friends and enemies. He had a craving for blood that was never-ending."

Not sure anymore how much of this he believed and didn't believe, Simon asked, "So when did you come to New York?"

"When the war ended," Volker said. "We didn't want to leave Germany, but we had no choice. There were rumors in Freiburg and cities and villages near the Black Forest, and we decided it wasn't safe for us to stay."

"Rumors?" Simon asked. "Rumors about what?"

"What do you think?" Volker said. "*Werewolfe.* Most people thought they were myths, but some bodies Michael had left in the forest had been discovered by hunters, and locals in the town noticed there was something different about us—people who knew us when we were young wondered why we appeared to be no older than their sons and grandchildren. We knew it was too dangerous to stay; we had to leave, and many people were immigrating to America at the time and New York seemed like the perfect place to blend in. So we purchased the brewery in Brooklyn and have lived here since."

"Has anyone gotten suspicious about you here?" Simon asked.

"Occasionally, yes," Volker said. "Michael's craving has ended many lives. Sometimes he'll travel around the country in search of victims and people disappear, many without a trace."

"So Michael's like a serial killer?"

"No, not a serial killer," Volker said. "Michael isn't crazy. He doesn't kill because he wants to kill, he kills because he *has* to kill, because it's his nature."

Simon didn't get the distinction, but he asked, "And how did he have his son . . . Jonas?"

"Jonas came many years later, of course," Volker said. "As the years went by, Michael had the desire to form a bond and pass along his blood to a son. I understood this desire, of course, but I also knew it would be a mistake, that Michael's craving was too strong and unpredictable. But I was getting older and Michael was terrified of being alone—a wolf has no greater fear than the fear of loneliness. So Michael took a lover in Manhattan and had Jonas. I knew what Michael was planning to do next, because he had no use for the woman, he only wanted the boy. I tried to warn the woman that she was in danger, but she refused to listen, and she paid for this mistake with her life."

"Wait," Simon said. "So Jonas is a werewolf?" He was horrified that he'd taken Jeremy on play dates with that boy.

"Not yet," Volker said, "but Michael intends to give him the gift of the wolf when he is eighteen years old. He fears that if he bites him when he is too young, even if he had the beer as preparation, that the wolves' blood would kill him. And he's probably right."

"Okay, so someday he'll have Jonas," Simon said. "He'll have another werewolf to feel a bond with. What does he need us for?"

"For Michael, having Jonas wasn't enough," Volker said. "He wanted a pack of men to share the bond of the wolf with, and he wanted Jonas to have a pack someday as well, so Jonas wouldn't have to live his life in fear of loneliness. I understood this desire, as it is the nature of the wolf to want a pack, but for most of my life I thought it was impossible, as I knew it was impossible for the blood of the wolf to be passed along outside our family to a group of strange men.

"Then, just several years ago, after we closed the brewery for good, Michael went to Canada and spent a winter with a pack of wild wolves in a forest in Saskatchewan. When he returned I knew something had changed. He had a look in his eyes, a new darkness I had never seen before. He spent hours at the brewery in Brooklyn. I knew something was happening there, but I had no idea what. Then one day he announced he had created a beer that could turn men into wolves. I didn't believe him at first. I thought he had gone mad in Canada and was inventing stories. Then he had a few men drink the beer, but it didn't work—when Michael bit them, they died. But then he perfected the formula and had you and the others drink it."

Simon was shaking his head. "Okay, okay, look," he said. "I've been going along with you on this, I mean I've been listening to what you have to say. I'm willing to believe you're a hundred forty-one years old and a wolf bit your father, and I'm even willing to believe that Michael is a Nazi werewolf serial killer. But now you're saying that a pack of wolves in Saskatchewan told Michael how to make the beer that he gave to all of us, that turned us into werewolves?"

"You'd be surprised what secrets you can learn from wolves." Volker held Simon's gaze for a few moments, and then suddenly he was looking around anxiously. "We must go now. There're people everywhere now."

When Simon sniffed he couldn't detect any human scents, but he was willing to take Volker's word for it.

"Wait, I need to know more," Simon said. "Why us? I mean of all the guys in Manhattan he could have had in his pack, why me, Charlie, and Ramon? Why were we chosen?"

"I don't have that answer; only Michael does," Volker said. "But he must've seen something in each of you, perhaps a weakness he could exploit and use for his own gain. Michael does nothing that is not for his own gain." Volker looked behind him—Simon still couldn't detect any scents—then said, "I told you all of this so you would understand properly what is at stake. The others were bitten directly, so he'll have a great influence on them; he'll teach them to enjoy the craving as much as he does. Before long, there will be mayhem, and many innocent people will die, unless Michael dies first."

"I knew this was what you wanted, and the answer's no," Simon said. "I'm not a killer."

"You've killed already," Volker said. "You have the craving."

"That was different. That was self-defense."

"If you kill Michael you'll be defending many, many lives. I don't have the strength or I would kill him myself. Despite our bond, I know it's time for my son to die."

"Look, the answer's no, okay?" Simon said. "I was already a suspect in three murders thanks to Michael, and now I'm trying to get my life back together, not get in any deeper than I already am. I appreciate you taking the time to talk to me and help me, but I'll figure this out on my own."

"You won't survive on your own," Volker said. "It's impossible. Either Michael will kill you or you'll kill someone you love. You don't know how to control the craving yet."

"Look," Simon said. "I'm all for you teaching me how to control the craving or whatever you want to call it. We can meet up here at a regular time and you can give me lessons or training, but that doesn't mean I'm going to go kill somebody."

"Do you want a chance to be human again?"

Now Simon could smell a human—the park worker who'd come by before. The scent was faint, but getting stronger. Simon said, "What're you talking about?"

"When the beer didn't work correctly the first few times, Michael created another beer, a remedy beer that he said could correct the effect of the other beer."

"I thought you said there's no cure for this," Simon said.

"Not a cure, a remedy," Volker said. "Michael told me he experimented with it once and it worked—it reversed the symptoms of the *wolfe* and effectively removed the *wolfe* serum from the subject's blood. I suspect he also adds new ingredients, perhaps an exotic grain, during the steeping process. You see, when it comes to beer making, Michael is a genius. Now I'm not certain the remedy would work on you, since you have already been bitten and are a full *wolfe* now, but I don't see why it wouldn't. Perhaps you would need to take it in a larger quantity."

Simon still had a lot of questions, but the park worker's scent was getting stronger, so he asked the most important one: "Okay, so how do I get this remedy?"

"It's at the brewery, I'm sure," Volker said. "I'm sure he has a quantity of the beer itself, but he should at least have the recipe. I think you would learn to enjoy your life as *wolfe*; it is so much more satisfying than a life as human, and you won't want to abandon it. But if you want to be human again, I believe you can."

"So you're saying I can go to the brewery, take this remedy, and that's it, my problems will be solved."

"No," Volker said. "Michael would certainly kill you if you took the remedy, and as a human you would be defenseless. Michael won't let you live with his secrets and risk revealing his pack, and you'll be unable to hide from him. You saw how easily I tracked you. Well, Michael is even better at it than I am. And he won't just kill you—he'll kill your entire family just for his pleasure."

"Okay, I get it, I get it," Simon said. "So what use is a remedy if I can't take it?"

"You can take it *after* you kill Michael," Volker said. "Return to him, tell him you are ready to join his pack. Tell him you made a mistake and you want him to teach you the way of the wolf. You must be convincing. When he trusts you, you can find an opportunity to get the remedy."

"So basically you're telling me I have to get the Wicked Witch's broomstick," Simon said.

Volker didn't seem to understand.

"Whatever," Simon said. "So how'm I supposed to convince Michael I'm on his side? The last time I saw him we were trying to rip each other's heads apart."

"It won't be easy," Volker said. "He will be suspicious, but you can do it, and then you will have access to the remedy."

"And what about Charlie and Ramon?" Simon said. "What do you expect me to do, kill them too?"

Volker considered this, then said, "Perhaps you can persuade them to take the remedy as well. It will be difficult because they were bitten directly by Michael and they both seem to be enjoying the life of the wolf very much. They may resist, but it is important to remember that when Michael is dead you will be their leader. You will have the power over them; you will be in control."

Volker was walking away through the woods.

"Wait, how can I find you again?" Simon asked.

"I can find you," Volker said, "that's more important."

"Wait a second!"

But Volker had already zipped away through the trees and was gone.

"Hey, jerkoff."

Simon turned and saw the park worker facing him, hands on his hips.

"Who're you talking to?" the guy asked.

"Sorry, sorry," Simon said as he hurried away.

THIRTEEN

Stephen Tyler looked nothing like Steven Tyler. Not that Alison really expected that a PI would look like a rock star, but that was the image she'd had in her head. But this Stephen Tyler was Vijay's age, fortyish, and preppy-looking with wavy blond hair and a very tan face. He was in a red pinstriped shirt tucked into beige slacks. The office was another surprise. It was a normal office building, but the office itself was a big space, divided into cubicles, and his "office" was one of the cubicles. Vijay had said Tyler owned "a big detective agency," hadn't he?

Tyler invited Alison into the cramped space that had barely enough room for a small desk, then told her to wait a second and returned with a chair for her to sit in that he'd borrowed from another office.

"Sorry it's a little messy," he said, pushing a few boxes out of the way with his foot so there was room for the chair. "Actually I just moved here."

"Really?" Alison said. "Where did you move from?"

"Oh, just the other side of this office," Tyler said, smiling. "Yeah, it was a little tight over there, so it's great to be able to spread out a little."

Alison looked around at the space, which was probably about ten square feet. Meanwhile, Tyler sat at his desk, moving some more boxes off the desk onto the floor.

"I'm just a little surprised," Alison said. "Vijay said you owned a large agency."

"Oh, it *is* pretty large," he said. "I have twelve people working for me, and I'm looking to hire a couple more. Most detective work is done from home nowadays. It's not Sam Spade and Philip Marlowe running around in fedoras anymore, it's a bunch of geeks in their underwear on their Macs. So you said on the phone you work with Vijay?"

Alison fought off an image of Vijay kissing her, their hands in each other's hair, and said, "Yes, we're, um, colleagues."

"Are you a doctor too?"

They hadn't discussed her profession when they spoke on the phone, and now Tyler seemed intrigued, maybe because he thought he could get away with charging a wealthy doctor more?

"No, I work in pharmaceutical sales," Alison said. "Vijay is one of my clients."

"Oh, okay, I get it," Tyler said. "Like Grace."

"Grace?" Alison was confused.

"Vijay's ex," Tyler said.

Alison didn't know why she'd blocked this out. She knew Grace was Vijay's ex-wife. She just didn't know she had also worked in pharmaceutical sales. Why hadn't Vijay ever mentioned that?

"That's right, Grace, of course," she said.

"Well, I don't know what Vijay told you about me," Tyler said, "but I'm not your ordinary PI. I took a sort of unorthodox route to detective work. I have a master's in psychology from the New School. I worked in forensic psychology for a few years, then got into the investigation biz. So what I'm saying is I have a unique understanding into the psyche of my clients. In other words, I'm sympathetic to what you're going through. I get it."

Alison already had her own therapist and a marriage counselor. The last thing she needed was more therapy.

"Thank you," she said. "I appreciate this, but I really don't need any emotional support. I just want to find out if my husband's cheating on me."

"You don't mean *if*," Tyler said.

"Excuse me?"

"Honesty is the most important thing in a detective-client relationship," he said. "Eighty percent of women who come in here who suspect their husbands are cheating turn out to be right. Unfortunately that's just the way it is, and in my experience it's best to be up front and honest about that reality. I know how difficult divorce can be, coming to terms that your marriage is over."

So much for not having another therapist.

"Well, I think the jury is still out on this case," Alison said. "My husband's behavior has been pretty, well, unusual, but I don't know for sure he's cheating."

"Unusual how?" Tyler asked.

After taking a full breath for energy, Alison explained how Simon had lost his job and then started acting strange until he finally claimed he'd become a werewolf. Tyler absorbed it all, until she mentioned the word *werewolf*, and then he started laughing.

"Sorry, I shouldn't laugh," he said, "it's wrong. I mean, I know this is a traumatic situation for you." Tyler tried to maintain a serious expression, and then laughter burst out again. "Sorry, I'm really sorry. I mean, it's just you think you've heard everything and then . . ." He laughed again. "I'm really truly sorry."

"No, go ahead and laugh," Alison said. "I know how funny it could seem if it's happening to someone else. If I were you I'd probably be laughing too. Everyone thinks it's funny, even the police."

"Police?" Tyler wasn't laughing now.

"Simon had an incident yesterday morning," Alison said. "I guess you could call it a breakdown. Anyway, we had a fight afterward and he left the apartment and I haven't seen him since."

She left out the part about how she'd threatened him with a large knife, figuring this was a detail that didn't really matter.

"You have any idea where he went?" Tyler asked.

Alison shook her head. "He texted me yesterday, but I didn't respond. I guess he's in the city somewhere. I mean, he had to sleep somewhere, so it's either a hotel or at someone's apartment." *Someone* was purposely full of accusation and bitterness.

"Is there a hotel he frequently stays at, or has relatives stay at?"

"No, not really," Alison said.

"No or not really?" Tyler asked.

"No," Alison said.

"What about other women in his life? Is there someone he works with who's been calling? An ex-girlfriend? Somebody he texts with, chats with on Facebook?"

"No, the only one I'm kind of suspicious of is our babysitter, this girl Christina."

"Girl?"

"Well, she graduated from college but lives with her parents across the hall. Actually she's with my son right now, but I don't think she's really having an affair with Simon. I think it's just paranoia."

"If you're paranoid, there's usually a reason for it," Tyler said. "It sounds like things have been rough for a while between you two."

"No, not really," Alison said. "I mean, we used to have problems, like all couples, but nothing like this. Our problems really started when he lost his job and became a stay-at-home dad and met these other dads in Battery Park. That's when he really changed and started developing all of these problems. I think they were a bad influence on him, especially this guy Michael. But maybe I'm wrong. Maybe it has nothing to do with them. Maybe he's been cheating on me for years and I've just been oblivious."

"Well, I'm going to find out what's going on," Tyler said, looking right at Alison's eyes. "I guarantee that."

Alison liked Tyler's confidence. It made her feel secure, like she had an ally.

"Thank you," she said. "That's all I want at this point. Some kind of closure."

"Well, here's what I want to do," Tyler said. "I can try some of the likely hotels, but it'll be faster if I can just tail him and see what he's up to. You said he texted you?"

Alison nodded.

"Great," Tyler said. "So here's what we do. Text him back. Tell him you want to talk to him. Phrase it however you want, just leave it vague, and tell him something that'll make him want to meet you somewhere."

"But I don't want to meet him."

"You won't," Tyler said. "Pick a busy spot, like Grand Central Station; can't get more public than that, right? You won't show up, but I will, and then I'll tail him. Does your husband, Simon, know where the bar at Cipriani is?"

"You mean the one up the steps?" Alison said. "Yeah, we've been there before."

"Perfect," Tyler said. "Tell him you want to meet him there sometime today, as soon as possible, five o'clock would be perfect on my end. I'm working on a couple of other things right now, but I want to get right on this today, and five's as busy as it gets at Grand Central. So you arrange a time to meet him, and then I find out who he's with, where he's staying. If all goes well, in a few hours you can have the closure you're looking for."

He made it sound so simple.

"You make it sound so simple," Alison said.

"Hey, that's why you came to me, right?" Tyler smiled. "So why don't you text your husband right now and see what he says?"

Alison typed, then deleted a few texts, then fiddled with the wording in one and finally sent:

I really want to talk to you today, away from Jeremy. How about five at Cipriani in Grand Central?

She thought he'd think it was unusual to suggest meeting at Grand Central and might suspect it was some kind of setup, especially considering she'd called the police on him yesterday. But she thought mentioning that she wanted to see him away from Jeremy made sense—it was the best explanation she could come up with, anyway.

While they were waiting to see if Simon wrote back, Tyler went over his fee. He explained that he normally charged five hundred dollars a day plus expenses, but because she was a friend of Vijay's he'd do it for four fifty. He estimated it could take anywhere from one to three days to get the information he needed, but they agreed they would talk again if the case seemed to be dragging. All of this seemed reasonable to Alison. Tyler asked for the first day's fee up front, and Alison charged it on her Amex.

Still waiting for some response from Simon, Alison and Tyler talked about what a great guy Vijay was, and Tyler told a funny story about how in college Vijay got lost on a road trip to Syracuse and wound up in Buffalo. Then he asked about her work, and he seemed genuinely interested in what she had to say. It had been ages since Simon had asked her about her work, and lately he had been completely self-absorbed. It was such a relief to be with normal guys like Vijay and Tyler, who were attentive and supportive. It made her realize how much had been missing in her marriage.

Alison's phone vibrated, announcing an incoming text.

Reading from her phone she said, "He said he'll be there at five."

"Perfect," Tyler said. "When he texts you, asking where you are, say you couldn't make it, something came up, but don't cancel until he texts you. I'll be in touch later on and let you know how it's going. How does that sound?"

"That sounds wonderful," Alison said.

"All I need is a photo of your husband," Tyler said. "Hopefully you have one on your phone or online somewhere."

"I have pictures on my phone," Alison said.

She found a couple of photos of Simon that were taken last month when they'd taken Jeremy to Central Park together. It was shortly after Simon had lost his job and his weird behavior had started. She remembered how a few minutes after the photos were taken he'd climbed with Jeremy to the top of some very high rocks and then jumped off, leaving Jeremy up there alone. He'd been so careless, so irresponsible, but now she realized that the behavior had foreshadowed everything that had come later—how he'd checked out, abandoned the family, gone off in his own crazy fantasy world.

"Everything okay?" Tyler asked.

"Yeah, fine." Alison forced a smile. "What's your e-mail?"

Tyler gave her his address, and then, as she was sending the pics, he said sincerely, "I promise. It *does* get better."

Leaving the office building, Alison was excited. Soon she'd get the closure she needed and find out what big secret Simon was hiding. At this point it was only a matter of time.

Simon had left the Ramble and was heading across the romantic Bow Bridge when a man with a heavy Italian accent said to him, "Will you take a photo?"

The guy was young, in his twenties, obviously a tourist, out for an early-morning stroll in the park with his wife or girlfriend, also twenty-something.

"Sure," Simon said.

The guy handed Simon his camera, wincing a little when he got close. Funny, Simon was so adept at detecting scents—for example, the scents of the guy's cologne and the girl's perfume were prominent—but was oblivious to his own body odor. After a night of running around the Ramble as a werewolf he doubted he smelled very pleasant.

"Where do I press?" Simon asked, embarrassed, wanting to get this over with as soon as possible.

The guy showed him where the button was, and Simon took a shot of the happy, smiling couple posing with the buildings of Central Park West, including the Dakota, above the trees in the backdrop.

"Perfect," Simon said.

"Thank you very much," the man said, wincing again as he took his camera back.

"Yes, thank you," the woman said.

Simon noticed the woman was wearing a small, shiny diamond ring. They were probably newlyweds, on their honeymoon in New York. As they walked away, giggling and holding hands, obviously in love, Simon remembered how he and Alison—back when things were good—would take long walks in the park, holding hands, never running out of things to talk about. She still hadn't responded to the text he'd sent yesterday. The image of her wielding the knife was still fresh in his mind and, though he wanted to go home, he knew going back now would probably be a bad idea, especially if it caused another scene in front of Jeremy. Besides, he knew he couldn't trust himself around his family, not until he somehow got hold of the remedy Volker had mentioned. While much of Volker's story about Nazis and werewolves had seemed bizarre, given what Simon had experienced himself and how similar it was to most of what Volker had described, he had no reason to doubt any of it. If Michael had invented a beer that could turn men into werewolves, why couldn't there be another beer that could turn them back?

There was a public bathroom, Simon remembered, adjacent to the Boat House restaurant, on the other side of the lake. A few minutes later, Simon arrived there. At the early hour, the restaurant was closed, but there were a few homeless guys in the restroom—two were washing up in the sinks, and the other was sprawled, asleep, next to a urinal. All the men had very pungent, very distinctive scents. Simon waited until one of the guys was through at the sink, then took his turn, splashing water on his face and then bending over and dousing his whole head.

"Man, you stink," one of the homeless guys said to him.

Simon knew if this guy told him he smelled, then he must really stink. In addition to his stench, the T-shirt he was wearing was torn at the seams, thanks to his transformation, and his sneakers had holes in them from where his clawed feet had poked through. Feeling his hairy face, he knew he needed a shave desperately. He hadn't shaved since yesterday morning and had the equivalent of what used to be a week's growth of facial hair.

He took off his shirt, noticing that his chest was very hairy as well, and splashed water over his armpits and then rinsed the shirt and wrung it out the best he could. Then, wearing the damp shirt, he left the bathroom, wondering, *How has my life come down to this?*

He took out his cell and texted Charlie:

OK, I'm ready to meet you guys

Less than a minute later he got:

Awesome. Come to the playground.

Simon was typing a text to ask what time when he got:

@10

It was seven twenty-eight now, which gave Simon plenty of time. He would have loved to go to an H&M or wherever and get some new clothes, but stores probably wouldn't open till ten or eleven. Besides, he had a more pressing need—to eat meat.

He exited the park at West Seventy-second and frustratingly couldn't find a place with any decent meat—there were just coffee shops and bakeries filled with carbs. *Carbs.* How could anybody want carbs? Simon had no idea how he used to have a scone or muffin for breakfast and feel satisfied.

Heading straight, toward Broadway, he passed a newsstand—the *Post* and *News* both had pics of Charlie crossing the finish line of the marathon on their front pages. The *News* headline was BLAZING FAST and the *Post*'s was ON FIRE. Simon shook his head but was too hungry to stop and read either of the articles.

Finally, he found a diner. He went in and sat at a booth, planning to order a big plateful of bacon and sausage. He must've really built up an appetite from running around as a werewolf last night because the odor of the mingled meats was so intense Simon had to resist an urge to barge into the kitchen and gobble up whatever meat he could find.

Then an older, gray-haired Greek guy came over and said, "Sorry, you're gonna have to leave."

"What?" Simon was confused.

"Come on, out of here," the guy said.

Simon didn't understand what was going on until he noticed that the guy was wincing the way the Italian couple had been wincing. He realized that what with his partially ripped, wet T-shirt, overgrown facial hair, and reeking body odor he probably seemed like some crazy homeless guy.

"Oh, no, you don't understand," Simon said, trying overly hard to enunciate his words as a lame attempt to prove that he wasn't some kind of bum or drug addict, that he was actually educated and together. "I live in the neighborhood. Well, uptown. Not *too far* uptown, on Columbus and Eighty-ninth."

"You gotta go," the guy said.

"Wait, look." Simon took out his wallet and showed he had credit cards and cash. "I can afford to buy food here. You have to serve me."

"I don't have to serve nobody I don't wanna serve," the guy said. "Now get the hell outta my diner before I call the cops."

Simon was going to insist on being served, but he was afraid if he got too angry he might turn into a werewolf. So he left the diner and went into a deli, to the first meat he saw—beef jerky—and bought two big handfuls, charging whatever it cost on his Amex. Then, resting on a bench in Verdi Square, near Seventy-second and Broadway, he tore into the jerky sticks, engulfing them almost as fast as he could open the wrappers. He was completely absorbed in eating—he had fifteen or twenty of them—and then noticed a woman passing by with her daughter, maybe ten years old. The daughter was staring at him, and then her mother noticed and pulled her along. When they were farther ahead the woman assumed they were out of earshot and whispered to her daughter:

"Never stare at crazy people, sweetie."

As Simon continued to swallow partially chewed pieces of the jerky, he decided there was one thing that Volker was wrong about— being a werewolf wasn't a gift.

It definitely wasn't a gift.

A little before ten, approaching the playground in Battery Park, Simon was missing Jeremy terribly. Although he hadn't been a stay-at-home dad for a very long time, he'd gotten used to the routine of being with his son every day, and it felt especially weird to be at a playground alone, as if he were going to a party he hadn't been invited to. The joyous sounds of other kids' laughing and screaming only made Simon feel more out of place.

Then, among all the other strong scents in the area—people, dogs, mulch, rotting garbage—he could smell Charlie, and was it Ramon? He looked toward the bench they usually sat on but didn't see them there. Suddenly he had a buzz of anticipation, but he couldn't tell if it was excitement about hanging out with Charlie and Ramon again, or fear of seeing Michael again.

"There's my man," Ramon said.

Simon turned to his right and saw Ramon and Charlie walking toward him, both smiling widely, pushing along their sons in baby carriages. Ramon was sharply dressed in jeans, a white T-shirt, and a black blazer. Charlie had cleaned up well since the marathon, in jeans and a tight white long-sleeve shirt accentuating his lean, muscular body. Looking at them, it was hard to believe they were living secret lives as werewolves. They looked like a couple of normal, good-looking dads out spending a beautiful fall morning with their sons in the park.

"Hey, it's great to see you," Simon said.

Simon couldn't resist rushing up to Ramon and hugging him tightly. Ramon was hugging him back, and neither of them wanted to let go. Simon had forgotten how good this felt; he wanted the hug to last forever.

Then Charlie said, "What, I don't get some too?"

Simon stopped hugging Ramon and hugged Charlie, saying, "Don't worry, there's enough to go around."

After about thirty seconds, Simon ended the hug with Charlie, knelt down, and said to Ramon's son, Diego, and Charlie's son, Nicky, "And how about you two little guys? How're you doing?"

"Good," Diego said, but Nicky looked away shyly.

"Good is good," Simon said. "Good is better than bad, anyway."

Seeing the other kids made Simon miss Jeremy again.

As if reading his mind, Ramon asked, "Where's your little man at?"

"Oh, um, he's with his mom today," Simon said.

"So you came down here just to see us?"

"Yeah," Simon said. "Actually."

"That's cool," Ramon said. "You're makin' me feel so special."

"Can we get out, Daddy?" Diego asked Ramon.

"Yeah, I wanna go uppy," Nicky said to Charlie.

Ramon and Charlie unstrapped their kids, who then ran off to play. Then the three men went into the playground—getting admiring, even lustful, looks from practically every mom and babysitter—and sat on their usual bench. Simon breathed deeply but didn't smell Michael.

"Looks like somebody was wolfin' out last night," Ramon said to Simon.

Simon wasn't sure why Ramon said this, but then realized it had to do with the torn shirt.

"Oh, yeah." Simon looked at Charlie. "I think you forgot to mention something about that to me."

"Sorry about that, bro," Charlie said. "I wasn't allowed to, but I did invite you to come to the brewery."

Simon didn't know what *I wasn't allowed to* meant but assumed it had to do with Michael being the leader of their pack.

Simon wanted to be angry at Charlie, but it was hard when Charlie was such a nice guy.

"Whatever," Simon said. "I avoided disaster last night anyway."

"Where'd you hang out?" Ramon asked.

"Central Park," Simon said.

"Cool." Ramon was excited. "Bein' in the trees and woods, damn, that must've been awesome."

Simon remembered how amazing it had felt, running with Volker as a wolf.

"Yeah, it was definitely an experience," Simon said.

"Maybe next full moon you can hang out with us," Ramon said.

Thinking that in a perfect world, by the next full moon Michael would be dead and they'd all be human again, Simon said, "Sounds like a plan."

"Or maybe we can all run together in the park," Ramon said, "or up at Michael's house."

"Michael's house?" Simon asked.

Ramon looked at Charlie, as if wondering if he'd said something he wasn't supposed to say. Charlie shrugged.

Then Ramon said to Simon, "Yeah, he has a summer house. Upstate, but not too far up, like an hour and a half outside the city."

Simon couldn't deny that running as a wolf in the woods had to be the ultimate experience, but why hadn't Volker mentioned that Michael had a house upstate?

"Have you guys been up there yet?" Simon asked.

Ramon said, "Nah, not—" and then Charlie cut him off with, "Michael said we're not ready to go up there yet. But when the time's right we're definitely gonna let him take us."

"Yeah, well, that sounds like it'll be a lot of fun," Simon said.

Ramon suddenly appeared very serious, which was unusual, because he usually had a wide, engaging smile. He asked, "So why'd you come back here anyway?"

Simon had prepared an answer for this. He said, "Last night taught me a lesson, I guess. I didn't want to be alone anymore."

Ramon absorbed this, then put an arm around Simon and said, "Well, you're not alone anymore, man. Stick with us, all your problems'll be solved."

"Yeah," Charlie said, also putting an arm around Simon.

It felt good to be sandwiched between the two guys, breathing in their warm, familiar scents. He noticed some women in the playground staring at them, but he couldn't tell if it was because they noticed or sensed there was something unusual about the three guys with their arms around one another, or if they were just uncontrollably attracted.

Ramon said to Simon, "So I heard you were having some problems downstairs."

"Downstairs?" Simon asked.

"You know," Charlie said. "Your problems in bed."

"It's not a *problem*," Simon said. "Everything's working fine down there; too fine, if you know what I mean."

"Oh yeah, we know," Charlie said.

"No, I meant I heard you been wolfin' out."

"I almost . . . wolfed out." Simon felt funny saying that. "I mean I had a few close calls, so I've been avoiding intimacy."

"Hang with us, all your worries'll go away," Ramon said. "Before you know it, your only problem'll be you'll be wantin' it too much."

"Yeah, so how is this gonna happen?" Simon asked. "Is there another beer or something I'm supposed to drink?"

Simon was hoping Ramon or Charlie would give away some info about the remedy beer.

"Nah," Charlie said. "It's more like a, you know, behavioral type thing."

"Yeah, and trust me," Ramon said, "when the floodgates open you won't know what hit you. I mean, check it out, right now, all these women here in this playground, they want our bodies. Even the old ladies can't resist us."

Simon noticed a woman with a walker, probably eighty-five years old, who was taking a rest on a bench across from them, staring at the guys like they were slabs of meat on a rack.

"I could get any of these women I want," Ramon said. "I know, I used to be the same, but it was never like this. Before, I had to work it. I had to have the right look, right clothes, say what they wanted to hear, but now, forget about it, bro, now it all just happens naturally. I get women proposing to me every day, like I'm, I don't know, Derek Jeter or something. You think that happened to me before I got bitten? When I was just an unemployed actor living with my mother in *el barrio*?"

At the other end of the playground, a very attractive young blond woman, probably a babysitter, was giving Simon a come-hither look.

"I've definitely been experiencing that part of it," Simon said.

"But you know what the funny thing is?" Ramon asked. "When you can get anything you want, know what happens? You don't want it anymore. You want one thing, one solid thing you can hold on to forever. And that's what happened to me last night."

"Oh no, here we go," Charlie said.

Ignoring Charlie, Ramon said to Simon, "She was like an angel that dropped from the sky and showed up at my doorstep. She had the silkiest black hair I'd ever seen, and when I looked in her eyes I wanted to get lost in them and stay lost forever."

"We've only heard that a gazillion times before," Charlie said.

"Last night was different," Ramon said. "Last night was the real deal. Last night I fell in love for eternity. And want to know the funny thing? She's a cop."

"A cop?" Simon hoped he was joking.

"Yeah, you believe it?" Ramon said. "I've met so many beautiful women in my lifetime, but I never would've thought the one I would want to be with forever would be a cop. But, yeah, Geri's the one for me."

A cop? Geri? A sickening feeling was building in Simon's gut.

"Wait," Simon said. "Her last name isn't Rodriguez, is it?"

"Yeah," Ramon said. "She talked to you too?"

Simon's throat was closing up. Well, not really, but that was what it felt like.

"You okay, bro?" Charlie asked.

"Yeah, I know her," Simon said to Ramon. "She was the detective who questioned me when my boss was killed in New Jersey."

"Oh yeah, that makes sense," Ramon said. "She might come talk to you again, so just be ready."

Now Simon had full-blown nausea. Suddenly he didn't feel comfortable with Ramon and Charlie's arms around him. He felt trapped between them, and their arms were like clamps, locking him in.

"Is that how you met her? She *questioned* you?"

"Yeah," Ramon said. "Don't worry, nothin' to do with your boss. My ex-girlfriend Diane was shot and killed in Michigan."

Simon knew Diane. She was a friend of Olivia, the woman/werewolf Simon had killed. Simon had warned Diane to leave New York because she knew too much about Michael and the pack, but apparently someone had found her.

"When did this happen?" Simon asked.

"Last week," Ramon said. "But what can you do? When your time's up, your time's up."

Simon had only been there about five minutes and he already felt like he was getting sucked back into a nightmare.

"Tell me the truth," Simon said. "Did you do it?"

Charlie removed his arm from around Simon and said, "Whoa, that's not cool, bro."

"I just want to know the truth," Simon said. "I don't want to be in the dark anymore about anything. If I'm going to hang out with you guys, I need to know the truth about what's going on."

Simon realized that he wasn't making much sense, but this was the best he could come up with.

Ramon moved his arm off Simon as well and said, "Of course I didn't kill her. She was a wonderful woman. It sucks that she had to die."

Noticing that Ramon didn't exactly seem torn up that his ex-girlfriend was dead, Simon said, "What do you mean, 'had to die'?"

"He didn't mean anything by it," Charlie said.

"I just meant it was a tragedy," Ramon said. "But I guess that's just the way God is sometimes. He's got a plan and he sticks to it even if it means good people get hurt."

Simon couldn't read Ramon. He had no idea whether he was lying.

"Okay, if you didn't do it," Simon said, "what about Michael?"

"Nah," Ramon said. "Michael was with us the time Geri said Diane was killed."

"So you're Michael's alibi," Simon said.

"Yeah," Ramon said. "I guess we are."

Simon was still trying to accept the idea that Diane was dead, actually *dead*. She had to have been in her midthirties, so much life ahead of her.

"Look, I honestly don't believe that you guys are killers," Simon said. "But I think you have a craving now, a craving that you may not be able to control. And I know that Michael must be fueling that craving for you. He wants to make you behave the way he behaves, and I don't think you can help yourselves because he's the leader of your pack, so of course you have to respect him, and do what he wants you to do."

"You have anger."

The deep, familiar voice had come from Simon's left. Then he looked over and saw Michael standing there with his son, Jonas. Michael's graying hair was combed straight back with no part, and his face was smooth and affectless. Though his big, extremely dark eyes were a little freaky looking, he looked damn good for ninety-one years old. Simon hadn't detected Michael's scent, so he was surprised to see him appear next to him. Weirdly, Simon couldn't even smell Michael right now, with them only a couple of feet apart.

"Hey," Simon said as he stood to face Michael. Though Michael had startled him, he didn't feel at all intimidated. He said to Jonas, "And how're you doing?"

"Fine," Jonas said.

Jonas looked like a mini version of Michael. They even had the same eyes.

"You're angry at me," Michael repeated to Simon.

Deciding not to let Michael's weirdness intimidate him, Simon said, "I guess you heard what I was saying, huh?"

Michael, staring, didn't answer.

Simon said, "No, I'm not angry at all, actually." He knew he had to get Michael to trust him; that was the whole reason why he'd come here today. "Honestly, I'm just concerned more than anything. I know we're all in this together now, and I don't want things to get out of control, that's all. I guess I'm hoping you can give me some kind of second chance."

Michael's black eyes fixated on Simon.

Michael said, "You fought me. You wanted to kill me. You had rage."

Simon knew Michael was referring to the last time they'd seen each other, when they'd fought as werewolves on the rooftop of the brewery.

"I'm sorry about that," Simon said. "I guess I was afraid. I didn't get what was going on or what I was getting into. I admit I had issues with you and some of the things you've done, but now that I've lived with this awhile and I see what it's all about, I realize I need you. I want to learn from you."

Simon was trying to act as sincere as possible, but he didn't think he was convincing enough. Michael was going to tell him to leave and that would be it—Simon would be on his own as a werewolf. And Volker was probably right—Simon didn't think he'd last long on his own. He'd hurt someone and the secret would be exposed or Michael would kill him. Those would be the only possible outcomes.

"Never apologize for rage," Michael said. "Rage is natural. Rage is who you are."

Simon didn't get exactly what Michael meant by this. "Okay, you're right," he said, because he didn't know what else to say. "I won't apologize for it again."

"You have rage," Michael said.

"Yeah, you're right," Simon said. "I have rage."

Michael and Simon stood face-to-face. Had Simon said the wrong thing? As usual, Michael was impossible to read, but Simon wasn't going to back down, figuring at this point he had nothing to lose. He was locked in on Michael and wasn't looking at Charlie and Ramon or anyone else in the playground, but he sensed that everyone was watching, even the kids. There was the tension of a schoolyard stand-off, people waiting to see what would happen next.

Finally Michael said, "Welcome to your pack," and extended his arms as if to give Simon a big hug.

Was it a trick? Would he give Simon a bear hug and crush him to death in a crowded playground? It seemed unlikely, but then again Michael was apparently a psychopathic, Nazi, serial-killing werewolf, so why was anything beyond him?

But figuring that he had no choice, Simon moved forward and let Michael hug him.

Simon hated that he liked it.

The four guys were sitting on the bench, just like old times. Simon was next to Michael, and to Michael's left were Charlie, then Ramon. Charlie and Ramon were doing most of the talking—mainly about their kids. Nicky's fourth birthday was coming up next month and Charlie was planning to have a party at his apartment in Turtle Bay, and then they had a discussion about preschools. Though the kids wouldn't be going until next fall, in Manhattan preschools were hard to get into and you had to start visiting and applying early. Charlie commented about how awesome it would be if the kids could go to school together next fall.

Simon had been dreading having to see Michael again and had been expecting to be uncomfortable next to him, but he didn't feel that way at all. Despite knowing about some of the horrific things Michael had done and put him through, Simon felt close to Michael. Not close in the sense that he felt love, or even respect, but there was definitely an underlying attachment, a connection, the way he might feel connected to a second or third cousin. Was this the bond between werewolves that Volker had gone on about? Simon hoped so, because if the bond was true, then maybe everything Volker had told him was true, including that a remedy beer existed and that there could be a supply of it in the brewery in Brooklyn.

After a lull in the preschool conversation, Simon said, "So Ramon was telling us about a woman he met. I think it's someone you're familiar with, Michael."

Simon thought this topic would make Ramon uncomfortable, but Ramon said eagerly, "Yeah, she's that homicide detective, Detective Rodriguez."

"I sent her to you," Michael said.

"Yeah, she told me you did. I gotta thank you for that, bro. That woman is stunning; I can't stop thinking about her. I think I found my soul mate."

"You told her I was in New York when the woman in Michigan was killed," Michael said as a statement.

"Yep, told her the truth, man," Ramon said.

"She didn't talk to me," Charlie said to Michael, "but I would've backed it up too, boss."

"So it's true?" Simon asked Michael. "You really were in New York? You really had nothing to do with it?"

"I would never lie about a killing to a member of my pack," Michael said.

Simon realized that Michael hadn't exactly answered the question—what else was new?—but he also realized it was probably as close to a denial as he was going to get.

"Look," Simon said, "I was just telling the guys before, if I'm going to hang out with you guys again, I just want to be more in the loop. I understand that we're different now, and we behave differently, but I don't want to be one step behind, in the dark, you know?"

Simon waited, maybe thirty seconds, for Michael to respond, but he was just staring straight ahead, watching Jonas, Diego, and Nicky play on the monkey bars. Simon knew there was no reason to repeat himself—this was just Michael being Michael.

Then Simon continued, "I mean, I guess what I'm trying to say is, doesn't anyone here agree with me that Ramon dating a cop is a bad idea. I mean of all people, why a cop?"

"She's my soul mate," Ramon said.

"Come on," Simon said, "there're eight million people in New York. You can find another soul mate."

"Actually I don't think you can," Charlie said. "Isn't that why they call it a soul mate? Because there's only one of them?"

"Seriously, I think it's dangerous," Simon said. "Like Charlie running in the marathon. I think it potentially exposes us, and they're risks not worth taking."

"I'm having sex with a woman tonight," Michael said.

"Yeah, who?" Ramon was excited.

Simon was aware that the subject had been changed, but what could he do?

"You know the big boss doesn't like to kiss and tell," Charlie said.

"I'll be having sex with her all night," Michael said. On that he stood and said, "We'll meet here again tomorrow at ten," then, pushing the stroller ahead of him, walked away toward where Jonas was playing.

Simon went up to him and said, "Hey, wait a sec."

Michael stopped. Simon was facing him.

"Now that I'm back with your pack, can you teach me some things?" Simon looked around to make sure no one was eavesdropping, then continued, "I mean, can you teach me how to control my transformations so I don't wolf out, like Ramon says, in public? I think it's in all of our interests if I learn how to do that. I'm sure there're other things you can teach me, and I'm ready to learn everything."

"You will learn when you're ready to learn," Michael said, and continued away toward the monkey bars.

Michael said to Jonas, "Get in," and Jonas, without a single pro-
test, obediently got into the stroller. Michael fastened the straps and
wheeled his son out of the playground like a normal, competent
stay-at-home dad.

Simon rejoined Charlie and Ramon, who were back to talking
about minutiae about the kids. All the kid talk and being on a playground was making Simon miss Jeremy terribly. He checked his cell;
still nothing from Alison.

"Something wrong?" Charlie asked.

Charlie and Ramon both had concerned expressions. Simon
didn't see any reason why he had to hide anything from them.

"My wife and I, we've been having some problems." Simon didn't
intend to get emotional but felt his eyes welling up a little.

"Yeah, we knew it, bro," Ramon said.

"You did?" Simon said. "How?"

"It was pretty obvious," Charlie said.

Simon didn't know what had given it away, but he said, "Honestly,
it's one of the main reasons I came here today. I'm losing my family
because of all this."

It felt good to talk about his predicament out loud. He hadn't
realized how much keeping it all to himself was stressing him out.

"If it's because of the wolfin' out, I promise you, you'll get it under
control," Ramon said.

"That's part of it," Simon said, "but at this point we have so many
problems I don't know if we can work them out. We had a bad fight
yesterday. I may have to move into a hotel."

"No way you're staying in a hotel," Charlie said. "Not when I have
an empty pullout couch in my living room."

"Thanks," Simon said. "I really appreciate the offer but I can't do
that."

"You don't have a choice," Charlie said.

"He means it, man," Ramon said. "No point arguing with Charlie when he wants to do somethin' for you 'cause he always gets his way."

Simon realized that staying with Charlie could work to his advantage. Maybe Charlie could help him learn how to control transformations, and if he was going to pull this all off—kill Michael and find a werewolf remedy—he had to get the guys to trust him, so it made sense to stay as close to them as possible.

"If you really don't think I'm putting you out, that sounds great," Simon said.

Ramon announced that he was in a rush, that he had to drop off Diego uptown "with his *abuela*" and then head back down to the rehearsal of an Ibsen play in the Village.

Simon left the playground with Charlie and Nicky. Charlie said he also found subways oppressive lately, so Simon and Charlie jogged uptown together, Charlie pushing the stroller. A bunch of people recognized Charlie from the marathon and the subsequent publicity and waved and said hi, and Charlie even stopped and signed autographs for a group of giggly teenage girls.

In the Thirties, they cut over to the east side. It was lunchtime and they couldn't run along the crowded streets, but they jogged as fast as they could. More people spotted Charlie and asked for autographs, but Charlie didn't stop to sign.

"Now I get why famous people can be total jerks," he said. "A few times it's fun, then it gets to be a pain in the ass."

When they arrived at Charlie's place in Turtle Bay, there were a few reporters waiting in the lobby of the modest postwar apartment building.

"Can't talk now, sorry," he said, passing by them to the elevator.

When he entered the apartment, Simon saw that Nicky had fallen asleep in his stroller.

"Make yourself at home," Charlie said, then went right to the fridge and took out a few huge packages of chop meat that looked like they must have been purchased at Costco or some superstore. He asked, "How do you like your meat?"

Was Simon drooling? He felt like he was.

"Rare," Simon said.

"Is there any other way?" Charlie said.

Charlie turned on the countertop grill and began forming the chop meat into patties. The smell of the raw meat was so tantalizing that Simon wished he could devour it all right now.

"I gotta admit, it's awesome having you here," Charlie said. "It's like we're Frederick and Oscar."

"You mean Felix and Oscar," Simon said.

"Right, Felix and Oscar, the Odd Couple. Two divorced guys sharing an apartment in Manhattan."

"Yeah, only I'm not divorced," Simon said.

"Yeah, but we are pretty freakin' odd."

Charlie and Simon laughed. Then they stopped, but when they looked at each other they started laughing all over again. This happened a few times. It was like they were two kids in the back of a class in middle school, unable to control themselves. Simon couldn't remember the last time he'd laughed so hard. It felt like it had been years ago.

When they were through laughing, Charlie said, "I didn't mean any offense, what I said about you being divorced. I just meant two guys, been married, in an apartment. Not been married, I mean . . . You know what I mean."

"No offense taken." Simon had to go into the living room to get away from the chop meat scent or he wouldn't've been able to resist attacking one of the packages.

Putting the first patties on the grill, Charlie said, "Hey, and let me tell you, if God forbid your marriage doesn't work out, I just want you to know the grass isn't green on the other side, it's bright green. Especially after what happened to us now, with all the attention we get from women. Trust me, you wind up single, you're gonna have the time of your life."

At that moment Simon got a text from Alison:

I really want to talk to you today, away from Jeremy. How about five at Cipriani in Grand Central?

Grand Central? Why would she want to meet there? And what did *away from Jeremy* mean? Was she going to ask for a divorce?

But the questioning didn't last for long. She wanted to see him, that was the important thing, and once they were together he'd at least have another chance to apologize to her and convince her that things were going to change. He'd also have a chance to hit an H&M first, buy some new clothes.

"Here they are, just like you like them."

Charlie was holding a plate with four rare burgers.

Within a few seconds an entire one was on its way down Simon's throat.

FOURTEEN

Had Stephen Tyler played the whole Alison Burns thing perfectly or what? He'd laid the crap on big-time, telling her how he was different from other PIs because of his background in psychology—how hadn't he lost it then?—and how he really cared about his clients. Seriously, sometimes he didn't know how he could say this stuff without coughing up puke. But it worked—oh, man, had it worked. Alison seemed to trust him big-time, and one thing Stephen had learned in the PI business—getting a vulnerable divorcing woman to trust you is the same thing as taking her panties down.

Yeah, Stephen knew it was only a matter of time before he scored with Alison, and what would that be? The seventh client of the year he'd banged? And it was only November. After he was through with Alison he still had a month and a half and could easily nail a couple more, especially when Christmas came around, when the cheated-on women got particularly vulnerable. If he could nail ten clients this year, that would beat out his previous best record of nine clients, which he'd set two years ago. All in all, since he'd gotten his PI license four years ago he'd banged twenty-seven chicks. And if he was including blowjobs, the number would have to be double that. This was so much better than online dating and going to bars. Someday he was going to write a book about his life as a PI and it would sell millions of copies, he was sure of it.

The beauty of Stephen's womanizing was that the women didn't even realize they were being womanized. As far as they were concerned, Stephen was doing them a service. He was providing them the truth about their lowlife, scumbag husbands so they could break away from their miserable marriages with peace of mind, and then, as a bonus, he gave them an opportunity to get revenge. Not violent revenge, *emotional* revenge, which was so much more satisfying. Seriously, what better way to break away from a guy who screwed you over than to go out and screw somebody else? And Stephen wasn't just anybody else—he was the guy who had given them their freedom, so having sex with him wasn't just to get back at the ex, it was to *give back* to Stephen. Yeah, they were paying him, but they wanted to do more, to show him how truly appreciative they were, so what was Stephen supposed to do, stop them? They were getting what they wanted and Stephen was getting what he wanted, and the best part? Nobody got hurt.

Alison Burns wasn't reeled in yet, of course. She was nibbling on the line, though—tonguing the worm, getting set to bite the hook. The bite always came suddenly—a rush of emotion when Stephen presented the damning evidence. At the moment when everything the woman had once believed was perfect about the world blew up in her face, she'd clamp down on the hook and it would be a done deal. That was why location was so key. They couldn't be in a public space because Stephen had to seize the moment. There was a ten, fifteen-minute window when a woman was at her angriest and most vulnerable, and Stephen had to make sure he seized it. His office wasn't good because there were too many people around, but even a private office wouldn't work. No, he had to deliver the goods on the woman's turf, preferably in her apartment, where she felt most comfortable and, more important, most in control. He'd call her, say he needed to talk to her in private and that it might be a good idea if the kids—if there were any kids—stayed with a sitter. That was perfect because it showed the woman, subliminally, that he was a sensitive guy, that he cared about her feelings, which made her even more likely to want to hook up. Bottom line, Stephen knew if he was alone in a room with a scorned woman in a fifteen-minute window, there was practically a zero percent chance he wouldn't get laid or at least get a blowjob.

And the best thing about the Alison Burns case was that it was so damn easy, such a slam dunk. Her husband, Simon, sounded like a real freakazoid, thinking he was a werewolf. That was Stephen's only real slip-up, when he'd laughed when Alison had talked about that; he should've been more composed, but how was he supposed to keep a straight face? But any guy who was making up werewolf stories had to be hiding something—Stephen didn't have to be a shrink to know that. Alison had said Simon had spent last night somewhere and Tyler was willing to bet it wasn't at a hotel. He was staying at his girlfriend's place and at five P.M. today he was going to lead Tyler right to the love nest.

Stephen spent the rest of the afternoon organizing his new office space and making follow-up calls for other active cases, but mostly he was fantasizing about Alison Burns. That was the best part of a score—the fantasizing, the buildup. You meet a woman and she's cute, yeah, you want to nail her, but what does she look like naked? What is she going to do in bed? Stephen had a feeling Alison was going to be a total animal in the sack, because the ones who didn't look wild were always the wildest. Stephen loved how proper, how put together Alison was. She had the short bob haircut, stylish clothes, totally had that whole kind of Upper West Side, working woman, cougar thing going on. If her marriage weren't about to blow up, Stephen wouldn't have had a chance with her.

Deciding that some thanks in advance were in order, Stephen texted his old college bud Vijay:

Thanx for sending over the tang. I owe you one, man!!

Stephen and Vijay had always—well, since they were frat brothers at Colgate—had a thing going on where they would try to one-up each other with women. It had toned down when Vijay got married but had picked up again when Vijay got divorced. Whenever one of them was dating a new chick, they'd send pics back and forth, compare war stories. For a while, Vijay had been doing better than Stephen because he had that whole doctor thing going on. Vijay cleaned up with patients, nurses, hospital staff, but his big wheelhouse was drug reps. This had been another near slip-up with Alison—when she'd mentioned she worked in pharmaceutical sales. A pretty woman in pharmaceutical sales; it made Stephen wonder, had Vijay gotten to her first? Not that he was opposed to taking sloppy seconds from an old frat bud, but still.

Less than a minute after he'd sent his text, Vijay wrote back:

HANDS OFF!!!

Stephen smiled. Ooh, so Vijay hadn't gotten to her first. Stephen was surprised Vijay had sent over a chick he liked; didn't he know who he was dealing with?

Stephen texted:

Don't worry, doctor, I'll be gentle with her ☺

Then Stephen got:

I'm serious!!!

Right as he was sending:

I'm kidding, I won't tap her, I won't tap her

Stephen sent the text, then added:

I promise

Vijay didn't respond. Stephen knew there was no way Vijay believed that *I won't tap her* crap. Poor guy was probably regretting big-time sending Alison over to him, but it wasn't like there wasn't enough to go around. After all, they'd shared women before. Stephen would be Alison's shoulder to lean on, and then Vijay would step in. What was the problem?

At four fifteen, Stephen freshened up—well, put some extra Speed Stick under his arms and around his crotch—and then walked up Madison to Grand Central Station.

It was early still, just past four thirty. Stephen didn't want to be an easy mark in case Simon suspected it was a setup and was scoping the place out. Stephen doubted this was the case. Cheaters usually didn't think too far ahead and were cocky as hell too, believing they could get away with anything.

Stephen bought a copy of the *Post*. At a few minutes before five he positioned himself at the bottom of the stairs leading up to Cipriani, the bar/restaurant in the west balcony of Grand Central's main concourse, and acted like he was waiting for somebody, or for a train, and was reading the newspaper. He read the lead story about that fireman who'd finished ninth in the marathon yesterday. It was weird how some nonprofessional runner had run so fast, and Stephen wondered if it was going to come out that the guy was on steroids, or took a subway and jumped into the race when the cameras weren't on. There had to be *something* going on that people didn't know about.

He skimmed the rest of the paper—looked like some woman NYPD detective had messed up big-time, pulling a protection order on a woman in Washington Heights—and the Knicks and Rangers had both lost. Then, at five almost exactly, Simon Burns walked right by Stephen and headed up the stairs. He didn't look much like the picture Alison had given him—if the guy was growing a beard, why hadn't she mentioned that? He also looked leaner, more muscular than he had in the photo. He was in jeans, a black T-shirt, and what looked like a new thin black leather jacket.

Now it was just waiting time. It could take a half hour or longer before Simon realized Alison wasn't showing and he decided to bail.

Simon was looking around, checking his cell, glancing over at the big gold clock above the information booth in the middle of the main concourse. He seemed extremely antsy and agitated, more antsy than he should have been. Well, Alison had said he had a mental disorder; maybe this was one of the symptoms.

At a quarter after, Simon seemed more restless, and he texted somebody—probably Alison. Stephen didn't want to be noticed, so he left where he'd been at the bottom of the steps and walked to the information booth in the middle of the terminal. There were hordes of rush-hour commuters, but from Stephen's position he could still see Simon clearly at the top of the stairs. He was pacing, checking the bar area, and then he made a call. After no one picked up, he lowered the phone. He still seemed unusually agitated, and then, suddenly, he walked away to Stephen's left, toward the entrance to the Campbell Apartment, another bar at Grand Central. The problem was there was an exit over there, out of Stephen's view, and when Simon couldn't find Alison he might just take off through that exit and Stephen would lose him.

Stephen pushed his way through the crowd, nearly knocking down a few people, and then rushed up the stairs. He was heading frantically through the bar of Cipriani, feeling like an idiot for letting Simon get out of sight, and bumped into a waiter who said, "Watch it, sir." Then Simon was walking toward him—he was sweating badly and seemed distraught; there was definitely something wrong with him, something medical. Stephen ignored Simon, looking straight ahead, as if he were trying to find someone himself. Then he stopped near the bar and watched Simon return to the supposed meeting spot with Alison.

After Simon checked his phone a couple of more times for texts and made another unsuccessful call, he headed down the stairs to the main part of the station and Stephen discreetly followed, staying a good twenty or thirty feet behind, but making sure not to lose him in the swarm of people. Was Simon going to look for Alison in another part of the terminal? Maybe he thought he had the wrong location somehow? Nope, he continued out to Forty-second Street— it had gotten dark out but the street was mobbed with rush-hour crowds—and stood on the curb, leaning over with his hands on his hips, as if trying to catch his breath. Was he having some kind of anxiety attack? That was what it seemed like.

Stephen stayed inside the terminal, holding up the *Post* but watching Simon through the doors. He expected that Simon would walk away, but instead he suddenly had his hand out, hailing a cab. Stephen cursed as he rushed outside the terminal. Simon was in the cab and it was starting to pull away. Stephen darted out to the street— barely avoiding a collision with a speeding bike messenger—and tried to hail a cab. Meanwhile, the cab Simon was in was stopped at the light under the Park Avenue Viaduct.

All the cabs were full; it was hopeless, but wait, an older woman was getting into a cab down the block toward the Hyatt. Stephen sprinted over there, holding a twenty-dollar bill out, and said to the woman, "Here."

The woman was confused.

"Here, I'm buying your cab from you."

"What?" the woman said.

"My wife's in the hospital, she's dying," Stephen said.

The confused woman took the twenty and Stephen got into the cab.

"Follow that cab," Stephen said to the driver, feeling ridiculous as soon as the words left his mouth.

The foreign driver said, "What?"

Stephen didn't know if the guy didn't hear or didn't understand, but it didn't matter. The light at Park had turned, and Simon's cab was moving.

"That cab, up there!" Stephen was shouting. "Follow it now!" He held up some bills. "I'll give you a fifty-dollar tip. Fifty dollars!"

"Why you want—"

"Just do it, fifty dollars! I'll give you fifty dollars."

The cabbie hit the gas and said, "What cab? I don't see no—"

"That one, right there, the one heading toward Fifth!"

"You're crazy."

"Here." Stephen gave the driver two twenties and a ten. "Here's your fifty, now just don't lose that cab, okay? Follow it, just keep following it."

The cab continued downtown on Fifth, then headed back to the East Side.

"I don't know where he's going," the driver said.

"It doesn't matter where he's going, I'm paying you," Stephen said.

"Crazy, you're crazy," the driver muttered.

Simon's cab got on the FDR, heading downtown, prompting the driver to whine, "He's taking FDR."

Stephen ignored this.

Traffic was bumper-to-bumper. Stephen's cab was a few cars behind Simon's but well within view. Then Simon did something weird. He was leaning his head out the window and seemed to be gasping for breath, with his tongue even exposed, hanging from his mouth. Wow, when Alison said Simon thought he was a werewolf, she wasn't kidding. He definitely seemed like he thought he was a dog or some kind of animal. Stephen was actually glad to see that Simon was such a psychological mess because it would make Alison even more likely to want to have some fast rebound sex. After all, compared to her screwed-up, train-wreck husband, Stephen would come off as the greatest guy on the planet.

Finally the traffic broke and Simon's cab got onto the Manhattan Bridge.

"He's going to Brooklyn," the driver complained, as if Brooklyn were the other side of the world.

Stephen wasn't surprised that Simon was going to Brooklyn. Simon had the beard, the identity crisis; maybe he was becoming some kind of hipster. Maybe he was shacking up with a wannabe werewolf chick in Williamsburg, Stephen thought, and almost started laughing out loud.

But Simon wasn't going to Williamsburg. He took the first exit off the bridge and then into an industrial area in the Navy Yard.

"Jesus Christ, this is crazy," the driver whined.

Okay, so maybe Simon's hipster werewolf broad had an apartment down here. The neighborhood didn't exactly look residential, but nowadays you never knew, there could be some renovated old building with condos in it.

Simon's cab turned down a deserted-looking street near the river, then slowed at the end of the block.

"Pull over right here, right here," Stephen said to the driver. Their cab had just turned the corner, and he wanted to stay a safe distance from Simon.

Stephen watched Simon get out of the cab and head toward a building. He seemed to yank on the door for a few seconds and then entered. Stephen paid the fare and then rushed along the sidewalk. He saw on the building above the entrance:

HARTMAN BREWERY

This didn't look like a freakin' condo. Then Stephen noticed that the new-looking padlock on the door had been busted. Was that what Simon had been doing before he entered the building? Busting the lock? No, it was impossible, the lock must've already been broken.

Stephen considered waiting outside to see if Simon exited with some chick but decided it was too risky. There could be another exit to the building and he could lose the tail. So he waited a few minutes until he was sure he didn't hear anything, then opened the door very slowly and slipped into the dark, dilapidated building thinking, *The hell?*

The room was dark, the only light coming from the door Stephen had just entered through. Was Simon hiding somewhere here? If he was Stephen would've been screwed, but at this point he had nothing to lose. He went to the flashlight app on his Droid and shined the beam around the room. No sign of Simon, thankfully—just boxes, old newspapers, paint cans, and other junk strewn everywhere. What the hell was Simon doing here, in some old run-down brewery?

Stephen shined the beam on the door. He went over and saw that it opened to a staircase leading up. This seemed to be the only place Simon could have gone. Stephen hesitated for a moment, getting a bad feeling about this, then thought, *Oh, stop being such a wuss*, and headed up the stairs.

Of all the places Simon had been since he'd become a werewolf, Grand Central Station was by far the most unpleasant. The thousands of human scents were overwhelming enough, but to Simon's ultrasensitive ears the noise was like being in front of a speaker at a rock concert. He wasn't sure why Alison had wanted to meet him here anyway. Maybe it was because there were so many people around and after their fight yesterday she was afraid to be with him alone. Well, he couldn't blame her for that.

At five fifteen he knew Alison wasn't going to show up. For as long as he'd known her she'd been late only a handful of times, and she was usually early. Why would she blow him off when she was the one who'd suggested they meet? That wasn't like her either; she always told Simon to "do what you say you're going to do." He just hoped everything was okay with Jeremy, that there hadn't been some kind of medical emergency or something.

At five thirty he texted her:

Leaving. Please let me know all is well with u and J. ttyl xoxox

He gave it another few minutes, and then that was it—he had to get out of this hellhole. When he left Grand Central it was a relief to be able to be outside, breathing in fresh air; well, if you considered the air on Forty-second Street fresh. He figured he'd walk back to Charlie's, but then he had a better idea. Michael had said he had a date tonight, right? And Charlie was working a twenty-four-hour shift at the firehouse and Ramon had a rehearsal for the Ibsen play, so this would be the perfect time to go to the brewery and search for the remedy beer.

Without giving it any more thought, Simon hailed a cab to Assembly Road in Brooklyn. The cabdriver didn't know where the address was, so Simon had to get a map up on his phone to show him. Afterward, since he had his phone out, he decided to Google *Hartman Brewery*, just to see if the information jibed with what Volker had told him. There was a short Wikipedia entry for the brewery that described its history—how the brewery was opened in 1914 in Freiburg, Germany, by Heinrich Hartmann, how Volker Hartman had expanded the brewery's operations to Brooklyn, New York, in 1949, and how the brewery had officially shut down in 2006. Of course, this was Wikipedia, and it was possible that Volker himself had created the entry, but it all seemed legitimate.

While Simon was surprised that so much of Volker's story seemed to be true, he was also excited. After all, if the history of the

brewery was accurate, maybe the rest of Volker's story—as implau-
sible as it had sounded—was accurate as well, including that there
was a werewolf remedy beer hidden somewhere at the brewery in
Brooklyn.

The cab meandered through the midtown streets and then got
on the FDR. The traffic made Simon particularly restless and claustrophobic, and he had to stick his head out the window for air. He
was seriously tempted to just get out and run, but especially now he
didn't want to do anything weird that would attract too much attention. Hopefully he didn't have too much time left as a werewolf, but
in the meantime he wanted to be as safe as possible.

Finally the traffic broke and they made it to Brooklyn. Being near
the brewery was bringing back lots of bad memories, but Simon tried
to focus on the positives—there was a finish line in sight, he had hope,
this nightmare was going to end soon.

Simon got out of the cab and saw that the door was padlocked.
He wasn't expecting this. He tried to think of some other way in—
through a window? around the back?—when he remembered he had
superhuman strength now. With minimal effort he tore the lock
apart. Wow, that was pretty cool, but he was going to need that
strength and more if he was going to tear Michael's jaw apart.

But first things first—he needed that remedy beer, if the remedy
beer was even here. The brewery building was huge, and he had no
idea where to look for it. Though he'd been to the brewery a couple
of times before, he'd only been on the top floor and on the roof, and
the building had ten floors. Ten big, industrial-size floors, as the
building occupied about a quarter of the block. And Simon had no
idea what he was even looking for. What, was there going to be a big
bottle with the label WEREWOLF REMEDY on it? Whatever he was

looking for could be hidden somewhere in the building, or not in the building at all.

He went up the dark stairwell to the second floor. It was pitch-black, but he was somehow able to find his way around. He couldn't see objects, but he knew where they were without thinking about it. He sensed some movement to his left. It was something alive, with an animal scent, probably a rat or a mouse. Weirdly, the thought of a live rodent in his vicinity made him hungry, and he had to resist an urge to go after it.

He veered off into some large room. There was stuff—boxes mainly—in his way. But avoiding knocking into things wasn't good enough; if he was going to actually find this remedy beer he was going to need some light. He felt along the wall near the door and found the switch. Would've been great, except when he flicked the switch, nothing happened. Avoiding some more objects, he made his way to the other end of the large space, to the opposite wall. After some searching he found another set of switches. He flicked all of them and one light in the room went on.

The room, like the rest of the building, had an art deco style and several large chandeliers—one was lit. The space was filled mainly with boxes and other junk. Going by all the cobwebs and dust every-where, it didn't seem like anyone had been here in a while. Struggling with that trapped, claustrophobic feeling again, Simon checked some of the boxes—some were empty, some filled with other boxes. If he went box to box, it would take hours to search the room, and he couldn't handle being in here that long. He tried to harness his abil-ity to detect scents, trying to hone in on a beer scent. For several minutes, he continued checking boxes, not smelling any beer, but then he did pick up something. It was very faint, though, and it seemed to be coming from one of the far corners of the room. He made his way over there and realized the scent wasn't coming from the room, but from a vent in the ceiling. Okay, there was definitely beer somewhere in this building; now he just had to find it.

With some renewed hope, he shut off the light, then went back out to the dark stairwell and climbed the stairs to the third floor. The beer odor was definitely stronger up here, which encouraged him. He flicked some light switches and this time they all went on—the sudden brightness was startling, even a little painful, and he had to shield his eyes for several seconds before they adjusted. This was definitely where the beer odor was coming from, because he was in what had been a beer manufacturing area. *Had been* for sure because there were stainless steel beer-tapping tanks and what looked like bottle-filling machines and other equipment, all covered in dust and cobwebs, that seemed as if they hadn't been used since the brewery had shut down. As Simon walked through an aisle between the equipment, it was becoming increasingly clear that this wasn't where Michael had concocted any types of beer recently.

Then it hit him that he was going about this all wrong. Instead of trying to find a beer scent, he should be trying to find Michael's scent. After all, it figured that if there was an active brewing area in the building where Michael had spent a considerable amount of time, and perhaps hung out there recently, then the remedy beer might be in the same area. Buzzed about this new strategy, Simon did a cursory look around the rest of the room, not detecting Michael's scent, then left and went up to the next floor.

This was another seemingly inactive part of the brewery with a layout and equipment similar to the floor below. He couldn't make out Michael's scent here either, but just to make sure he gave the space a quick walk-through. He was inspecting the back of the room, where most of the tanks and other brewery equipment were concentrated, when it happened. There was the noise of footsteps coming from the floor he'd just vacated. He didn't know how he knew this because the floors and walls in this building were thick, and with normal human hearing it would've been impossible to actually make out footsteps from a lower floor, but Simon didn't have normal human ears and he was certain of what he'd heard. Then he heard another noise; someone laughing?

He went to the entrance to the room and shut off the light. Now he could hear the shallow breathing of the person and make out his strong manly scent. It wasn't Michael; he was positive of that. It was a completely unfamiliar scent. But why was he trying to be silent, as if he didn't want to be discovered in the brewery?

Simon couldn't deny that the scent was igniting a hunger in him, the way the scent of the rodent had. He was about to shout, *Hey, who's there?* when the realization hit:

Someone had followed him here.

Stephen was in a large dark space with a lot of boxes everywhere, some kind of storage area or something, when he saw lights go on above him. Okay, Simon was upstairs, doing whatever he was doing with whomever. Stephen would just sit tight here for a while, then wait to see what the hell was going on.

The idea that this place was some kind of love shack for Simon and his girlfriend was fading fast. But Simon had something going on here he was trying to hide, that was for sure. Maybe this was some kind of brothel or something. Maybe upstairs there was a madam and a slew of Russian girls. Or maybe it was something that needed to be more hidden away, like a perverted sex club with underage kids.

The thought disgusted Stephen, but the bright side was it would disgust Alison even more. Yeah, it was only a matter of time till she was on her knees, thanking the man who'd rescued her from her sick, child-porn-obsessed husband.

Then the lights went off upstairs and Stephen was in pitch-darkness again. Stephen heard footsteps going up to a higher floor, so, after waiting awhile, he went up to the next landing. He noticed a light on the floor above him, so Simon for some reason seemed to be going floor to floor. Stephen explored the floor he was on with the beam from his flashlight app. It looked like there was lots of dusty industrial-like equipment; well, the place had been a brewery, right? *Hartman Beer.* Wait, it was starting to ring a bell now. Wasn't Hartman that skank beer he and the frat guys at Colgate used to drink? But they used to call it Fartman. Inadvertently, he laughed out loud.

Well, Stephen wasn't sure what Simon was up to now. It didn't seem like an underage brothel was going to materialize here soon. And why was Simon going floor to floor; was he searching for something? Maybe this was a crack den and he was looking to meet his dealer here. That would explain why Alison said he'd been going crazy. Didn't crack addicts have mental problems?

Stephen was heading back toward the stairwell when the light on the floor above him went off. Stephen cut the light on his phone and was in darkness again. Okay, he'd wait here until Simon went up to the next floor or wherever he was going to go. He was thinking about Fartman beer again, trying not to laugh out loud, and then it was on him.

It because he had no idea what was attacking him, or what the hell was going on—one second he was smiling in the dark, the next some animal—*animal?*—had him pinned to the floor. It was growling and clawing at Stephen's face and oh God, the pain in his face. Was it *biting* him? Yes, it was biting his cheek, his nose. He tried fighting it off, raising his right arm to push the thing off, but then there was sudden excruciating pain in his arms and, Jesus, it wasn't there anymore, his arm was *gone*. The thing was biting into his neck, his face, and there was nothing but pain, the whole world was pain, and he was screaming, but he knew no one could hear him, and then it didn't matter because he couldn't scream anymore anyway.

FIFTEEN

"What do you got to smile about today?"

Shawn had just walked into Geri's office at the Manhattan North precinct, where Geri was at her desk, trying to get some work done. Trying, because she was too distracted to focus, and kept seeing flashes of last night with Ramon.

"What's the matter, a girl's not allowed to be happy?"

"This the same girl I was with yesterday, I had to keep from trying to attack the police commissioner, the mayor, and anyone else who got in her way?"

"Yeah, well, that was yesterday," Geri said.

When Shawn left, Geri tried to get back to work, getting some info together on a past case for a prosecutor downtown, but in her mind she was still in bed with Ramon, making love. Oh God, how many times had they done it last night? Did it really matter? There were really no *times*—the whole night was just one long-lasting experience, like one long orgasm that she didn't want to ever end. It really was amazing how instantly connected they were in bed because, seriously, when had that ever happened to her before? It usually took being with a guy at least a few times before she even started to feel comfortable, but with Ramon she felt familiar with his body from the get-go and he was the same way with her, touching her exactly the right way, as if he had access to her brain and knew exactly how to turn her on.

And to think, she'd almost canceled and missed out on the most sensuous night of her life.

When she'd left the coffee shop yesterday afternoon and had some space away from Ramon, she wasn't quite as, well, under his spell as she had been, and she felt stupid for falling for his whole Casanova act. Because that was what she was convinced it had been, an act, because the guy was an actor, right? He had a bunch of lines and, okay, he was convincing at the time and Geri had felt something, but that was what actors did—they made you feel something in the moment, but that didn't mean the feelings were real.

But every time Geri tried to call him to cancel the date, she couldn't go through with it. One time she actually pressed send and the call connected, but she ended the call before it rang. As much as she was convinced that he was a player, she kept remembering what it had felt like to be near him, to feel that heat between them. She'd never experienced that kind of intensity with a man before and, even if it was an act, she was willing to be entertained.

They had arranged for Ramon to come to her place to pick her up at seven. At exactly seven the buzzer rang and she buzzed him up. She was planning to give him a quick tour of the apartment—how long would that take? from the front door you could practically see the whole place—and then they'd head out.

Geri had gotten dressed up—well, dressed up for her. She was in a nice pair of jeans, heels, and a low-cut blouse, and she put on makeup, actually taking her time with it. She opened the door just as Ramon arrived, and she was as mesmerized as she'd been at the coffee shop. Just looking at him made her feel hot and a little woozy, as if she were a teenager and he were a rock star or something.

He took her hand and kissed the back of it, the way a sleazeball in a movie would, then said, "You look magnificent tonight." He even made a corny line like that sound sexy.

"Come in, I'll show you my place," she said, aware that she was so flustered that her voice was unsteady.

Normally Willy and Wonka were curious about visitors and came over to at least sniff them, but when Ramon entered, both of their tails immediately stiffened, as if they were in danger, and then they darted under the couch.

"That's so weird," Geri said, "they never get like that."

When Geri turned around, Ramon had moved closer to her, invading her space. But instead of getting creeped out, she liked it. He craned his head lower, as if to kiss her, but didn't. He just stayed like that, looking in her eyes, so close she could feel his breath on her face. She knew what he was doing. He was teasing her, making her want him, but knowing what was going on didn't make her want it less; it had the opposite effect. After a while, when her desire for him was almost unbearable, he picked her up and carried her into the bedroom, and they stayed there for the rest of the night.

Now, at her desk at Manhattan North, she heard herself actually moan. Okay, this officially had to stop. Thankfully no one had heard her.

She went down the corridor to the kitchen area, poured a cup of black coffee, and gulped some of it down. Fatigue wasn't her problem, though; the problem was that she was dying to see Ramon again, and that couldn't happen. She had to break away from whatever hold he had over her before it did serious damage to her career. He was a potential witness, or even a person of interest, in a series of possibly related murders and one disappearance, for God's sake. Getting involved with him on a personal level was wrong and could even be a violation of her ethics as a police officer. She had to figure out a way to break away from him and forget that last night had ever happened.

Back at her desk, she finished getting the prosecutor what he needed, then tried to distract herself with more work. One problem was that she no longer had a current major case to focus on. She had been obsessed with the Washington Heights shootings and now she had nothing to focus on except Ramon and how goddamn sexy he was. She didn't even know what was going on with the Washington Heights case. She'd been avoiding Dan all morning, and she knew that getting an update would be frustrating whether they were making progress or not, because if there was a hot lead she would want to be a part of the investigation, and if the trail had gone cold she would want to get out there to find the son-of-a-bitch killer.

Geri hadn't even read the papers this morning, or read anything online about the case, because she didn't want to know and because she didn't want to relive the humiliation of having to take a fall to save Dan's ass. It had felt so awful to have to get up there in front of all of those reporters and basically lie. Even worse, she'd had to act like it was her fault to Carlita Morales's family—well, her brother, anyway.

Something about the encounter with Carlita's brother had stuck with Geri. It wasn't just how angry he'd been; there was more to it than that. For some reason Geri had a feeling she'd seen him before, and she rarely forgot a face. But she'd been intermittently racking her brain and had been unable to remember where she'd seen him. Eh, whatever, she thought. She'd probably just seen him on the street or someplace random and it had no connection to anything.

Moments later, she was back, fantasizing about Ramon. The flashes seemed so real, it was as if she were practically there. She tried to rid the images from her mind, but, really, what was the point?

She knew she had no choice; this was the new her. She was going to keep obsessing about Ramon, maybe forever, but she decided to just go with it.

The human scent was getting stronger; maybe the man was afraid, or maybe because Simon was just so tuned in to it. The scent was everywhere—it seemed to fill up the entire brewery—and Simon sensed that the man, whoever he was, was an enemy and was out to get him. Could it be a police officer? If so, it wasn't Detective Rodriguez, because Simon had no doubt the scent belonged to a man.

Then Simon heard the attack. A werewolf was growling ravenously, relentlessly, but how was this possible? Werewolves—or at least all the werewolves Simon had encountered—had strong, definitive scents, but the only scent Simon could detect was the scent of a human body, and now of his blood as well. Then there were a couple of faint, agonizing wails of a man being mauled to death.

In an instant—or it seemed—Simon had descended the flight of stairs. In the pitch-darkness, he knew exactly where to go and he was trying to free the man from the werewolf's grasp, but the werewolf whipped its arm back at Simon with tremendous force, and he slammed against something. Perhaps the impact ignited something in him, triggered a fight-or-flight mechanism, or his own anger was the impetus, but he was suddenly transforming. He felt the now-familiar pains in his face and extremities, but unlike the other times when it seemed to take about a minute to go from human to werewolf, this time it happened within seconds. Several yards away from him, the attack on the man was still taking place and was more ferocious. The growling was louder and more violent, and the scent of blood much stronger and more prominent.

Simon leaped onto the werewolf, digging his claws into its hairy back. He wanted to attack it, kill it, but then the scent of the human blood ignited something else in him. The potential meal was so close, and the thought of indulging was more enticing and alluring than a juicy steak dinner. He didn't just want to devour that body and taste the blood, he *had* to do it, and then, without giving it any more thought, he sank his fangs into the man's side, biting off a chunk of salty flesh. But it wasn't enough—he wanted more, he *needed* more, he had to fill his body up. He felt as if he hadn't eaten in weeks, and he wouldn't eat in weeks, and for all he knew this was the last food he'd ever have. But the other werewolf was ravenous as well, and, like two seagulls attacking a fish that had washed up on a beach, they competed for the meal. Simon took another bite of the man's side, and then another. Then he worked on the arms, found some tasty meat there, then worked up to the neck and face. The other werewolf was lower, biting through the man's jeans, over his crotch. Simon was swallowing faster than he could chew, digging his fangs into the flesh, spitting out bits of bone, tearing the body apart, knowing, as he devoured the man, that this meal alone wouldn't be enough. It could never be enough.

SIXTEEN

Simon opened his eyes, but he was still in the dark. He prayed that what he'd just experienced had been a nightmare, that he had never returned to Michael's brewery, but this hope faded fast, as the scent of human blood was everywhere and he could tell by other scents that he was still in the room with the brewery equipment.

He got up slowly on his feet—his *human* feet—and went to the light switches he'd found earlier and two of the large chandeliers went on. Then, near the exit to the stairwell, he saw the remnants of the man he and the other werewolf had eaten. He gagged a few times, horrified by what he'd done, about what was *inside* him now, but he didn't throw up. He knew that whoever had done this, and whatever horror was inside him now, didn't belong to him. A craving for flesh and blood had caused this, a craving he couldn't control. But Simon Burns didn't have the craving, Simon didn't do this, Simon Burns wasn't responsible. Something else, a visitor in Simon Burns's body, was the psychopath, and that person would be leaving soon.

The victim didn't look human anymore. The remains were an accumulation of torn-apart, chewed-on bones with little bits of meat and fat on them, like a leftover T-bone, that could have belonged to any random mammal. Some of the skeleton was intact, but most of it wasn't. The body looked like it had been attacked by wild animals, which, in a way, it had. The head was still attached to the body—well, the bones of the head, anyway—but most of the flesh and even the eyes and brain were gone.

The salty taste in Simon's mouth made him gag a few more times. Then Simon reminded himself that he didn't kill the man, that the man had been dead already. Yeah, as if that made it any better.

Staring at the remainder of the head, Simon had a flashback to digging his fangs into it while head-butting the other werewolf out of the way as they competed for the tastiest flesh.

The other werewolf. Where was he?

Simon looked around frantically, and looked up—Volker had been in a tree, hadn't he?—but he didn't see it anywhere. It could be hiding somewhere, so he called, "Hey!" His voice was hoarse and gravelly. He swallowed a couple of times to clear his throat, but the taste of blood in his mouth sickened him, and this time no amount of rationalization could prevent him from throwing up. When he saw the chunky red and gray product of his vomiting on the floor in front of him, thinking about what it contained, it made him throw up again, more violently.

When he was through, it set in that remaining here, at the scene of a grotesque murder, was stupid and dangerous. At any moment, the police could arrive, and he'd spend the rest of his life in prison, probably on death row. But he didn't care about dying so much as about what it would do to his family. His marriage was on life support already, but getting arrested for cannibalism would have to be the final bullet. But most of all he was terrified about the effect it would have on Jeremy. Having a cannibalistic werewolf father was bound to give a kid serious psychological problems. Oh, God, he just wanted to be back with Jeremy, having a normal day like they used to have together. He'd push him around in his stroller, go to the playground, kick a soccer ball around, and go to the Discovery Room at the Museum of Natural History. He wanted to go back to one of those simple days and live it over and over again forever.

"You're awake."

Michael's weird Germanic voice jolted Simon from his fantasy. Simon saw Michael, on the other side of the remains, near the stairwell. He looked clean, dapper. His gray hair was perfect and appeared blown dry, and he was in stylish black pants, a pressed black shirt, and an expensive black sport jacket. There was no evidence at all that his werewolf self had recently slaughtered and helped consume a man.

"So it *was* you," Simon said.

"You enjoyed your meal," Michael said.

Simon had to be careful—as much as he hated Michael, the fact remained that he needed him.

"Yes, I did," Simon said. It was easy to lie when he wasn't actually lying. After all, a part of him had enjoyed devouring the man; he couldn't deny this was true. He added, "But how did you do it? You didn't have any scent. It was like you weren't even here."

Michael didn't answer; what a surprise. Though his expression was blank, Simon sensed that he was trying to figure out—was Simon with him or not?

Simon said, "Well, I guess you'll reveal your trick whenever you want to reveal it. In the meantime, we have a much bigger problem. I think this guy followed me here."

"He's dead now," Michael said.

"Really?" Simon said. "You think?"

"He isn't your concern anymore," Michael said.

"Okay, look," Simon said. "I get that there's an animal side to us that we can't control, that's abundantly clear right now. I also get that there're no rules or laws or boundaries, but when we're human that's not the case. There're police and DNA and prisons, and even if we get rid of this body there'll be bits of blood, hair, and whatever else here. And we don't even know who this guy is or what he wanted. What if he was a cop? What if we just ate a cop?"

Simon realized the absurdity of what he was saying, but he didn't find it at all amusing.

"My father sent you," Michael said.

"What?" Simon was trying to sound shocked, but he was actually worried. Had he said something to slip up?

"You came here to find something," Michael said.

Did Michael know that Simon was looking for the remedy beer?

"What do you mean?" Simon said. "What're you—?"

"His scent was on you at the playground," Michael said. "I knew you had been with him."

Michael sounded like a wife accusing a husband of an affair. But Simon knew he couldn't deny it. He had to try another tack.

"Look, it's true I talked to your father, but he just made me realize I couldn't survive without a pack. That's why I came to the playground this morning, so you could teach me how to control this, so I can assimilate better. But you wouldn't tell me what to do, so I came here to see if I could figure it out on my own." Simon said all this with conviction; he thought he sounded convincing. He added, "You saw what I just did with you. You think I would've done that if I wasn't with you?"

Simon had no idea if this appeased Michael or not. The guy was unreadable.

"Trust me, you don't have to worry about that," Simon said. "You have to worry about whoever sent this guy here. What if people know he was here? You don't think they'll come looking for him?" Then Simon spotted something off to the right. "What's that?" From a distance it looked like torn-up rags, but as he got closer he saw it was the remnants of bloody clothing. He squatted near it—being close to the blood, Simon felt the craving; he was already getting hungry again. He lifted part of what used to be the guy's jeans and saw a bloodied wallet. He opened it and saw the driver's license in the window: Stephen Tyler. Struck by a horrific thought, he said, "Oh God, it can't be. We didn't just eat the lead singer of Aerosmith, did we?"

Michael didn't seem concerned. The lunatic would probably maul Steven Tyler and the rest of the band to death if he had the chance.

Simon searched frantically through the wallet. He found a credit card, then said, "Wait, it's spelled differently, with a *ph*. It's not the actual Steven Tyler. Thank God." Then he found a business card: STEPHEN TYLER, LICENSED PRIVATE INVESTIGATOR. He said, "He's a PI. See, it's just like I thought. I don't think you understand what kind of danger we're in. Someone was suspicious of you, of this place. See, you're not immune to the threats. The police won't just magically avoid finding you."

"I have no fear," Michael said.

"Well, you should have fear," Simon said. "Someone else might show up here, his partner or whoever hired him. Maybe a relative of one of your victims hired him. Maybe it was my ex-boss's wife from

New Jersey, or how about Diane, the woman who was killed in Michigan? Maybe her parents hired a PI. Wait, is that his phone?" Under
another piece of his jeans there was a corner of something shiny and
black—yep, it was a smartphone. Simon picked it up, woke up the
screen, and saw:

ALISON TANG:
I did what you told me to, ignored texts and calls. Please call with
update as soon as u can. Thnx!!

Alison Tang? At first Simon didn't think the message had any
relevance, but then he read it a couple of more times and wondered
if Alison could be *his* Alison. It had the right spelling, with one *l*, but
he still had no idea what *Tang* meant. He clicked on the message, then
checked the contact info, and sure enough saw Alison's number
pop up.

"You have fear." Michael's nostrils flared.

"Yeah, I have fear," Simon said. "My wife hired a PI." Simon
looked at the driver's license again, at the photo. "I recognize him
now. He was at the bar at Grand Central. That was why she didn't
show up to meet me before."

Simon didn't know why he was wasting his breath, because it was
obvious that Michael wasn't listening, or he didn't care; did it really
matter which? Simon didn't know how he'd let this happen, how he'd
managed to let himself get sucked back in, deeper than before. After
the killing of Olivia, Simon had promised himself that he'd never get
involved in any way with Michael again, but here it was, only a month
later, and it was worse than last time—much worse. After all, there
was a big difference between a self-defense killing and eating a PI.

"Come with me," Michael said.

Maybe Simon had seen too many Mafia movies, but he couldn't help wondering, was this a hit? Was Michael going to take him away to whack him somewhere? Was he Michael's next meal?

"Where to?" Simon asked.

"Come with me." Michael's tone allowed for no argument.

Simon knew he didn't have a choice. He had to go, to continue to show his loyalty to Michael.

So he followed Michael up the stairs to the top floor of the brewery. This was the area Simon had been to before, and it brought up some disturbing memories. The first time he had gone here, Michael had had him drink the "family beer" that had started the nightmare, and the last time was the night Simon had killed a werewolf. What would happen this time?

The top floor looked nothing like the rest of the building, mainly in that it was immaculate with high ceilings, art deco décor, and floor-to-ceiling windows with an amazing view of the lower Manhattan skyline. Simon followed Michael down a hallway to a room with a pool table that he'd been in before as well, and then through a door into a long corridor to a part of the brewery where Simon had never been. Simon was starting to get seriously anxious, which wasn't necessarily a bad thing, he told himself, because maybe if he felt threatened or attacked he'd transform and have a chance to defend himself. He had to hope so, anyway.

At the end of the hallway Michael stopped in front of a large stainless steel door that looked more like the door of an industrial-size refrigerator than the door to a room.

"You enter first," Michael said.

Simon felt uncomfortable having his back to Michael, but he did as he was told.

The room was large, clean, well lit, and completely empty. Michael entered behind Simon and the door slammed shut.

"Get naked," Michael said.

"Ex-excuse me?" Simon said.

"Get naked," Michael said.

Panic was setting in big-time, but the werewolf transformation was nowhere in sight.

Then Michael pushed a button on the wall near the door, and a door to the right opened, revealing a large shower.

"You will get in the shower," Michael said.

"Oh, okay." Simon was relieved. "So you just want me to clean up. That makes sense."

Michael pressed another button, and a door to the left opened to a room that had racks and racks of clothing. It looked like the warehouse of a fashion showroom.

"You will choose clothes to wear," Michael said.

"Wow," Simon said. "You're prepared for this, aren't you?"

"Get naked," Michael said.

If there was one thing Michael lacked, it was a sense of humor. Or maybe he was laughing his ass off inside and the big joke was on everybody else.

Simon started to undress, and Michael held open a large Hefty bag and said, "Clothes here."

When Simon was naked—holding just his wallet, keys, and cell phone—Michael left the room. Simon, eager to get clean and dressed, went into the shower but hesitated before he turned it on as he thought, *Wait, a shower?* How did Simon know gas wouldn't come out instead of water? He turned the handle slowly—there was a hissing sound, and then, thank God, water sprayed down.

After showering, Simon dried himself with a big clean white towel Michael had left, and then on the sink Michael had left a new toothbrush and toothpaste. So downstairs the place was an abandoned dump and upstairs it was like a hotel with amenities.

After he brushed his teeth, he went to the clothing racks to choose an outfit. Though he wasn't exactly a style maven, he could tell the clothes were stylish and hip and were major labels—Ralph Lauren, Burberry, Armani. Weirdest of all, there were multiple sizes of everything. A fashion warehouse at a defunct brewery? What the hell?

Simon dressed and looked at himself in a full-length mirror. He had to admit, he looked damn good for a guy who'd just been a werewolf and helped consume a man. The memory of what he'd done brought up another wave of nausea that he had to fight off by telling himself, *That wasn't you. That wasn't you.* He felt a little better—at least he didn't feel like he was going to throw up anymore—but he knew he couldn't take much more of this.

Then he saw the door near the mirror. He had no idea where it led, but he realized that this could be his best chance to explore this part of the brewery. Was it possible Michael had the remedy stored up here?

He opened the door and saw that it led to a large closet or storage area, but there was nothing stored in it, just empty shelves. He continued through till he reached another door and went in, entering into a large kitchen. This was probably the room Michael had gone into that time when he brought out steaks and beers for the guys. There was a large, industrial-size stove, the kind that would be used in a restaurant. There was a large fridge. It was empty inside, though, and didn't seem to be plugged in.

Simon continued through the kitchen, not sure what he was looking for. Maybe there was a keg or some sort of container or something that would hold beer. There were a couple of large cabinets along the back wall. He opened one—nothing inside. He checked the next one—nothing as well—and when he closed it he felt a hand on his shoulder. Startled, he turned and saw Michael standing behind him. He seemed to have come out of nowhere.

"You scared me," Simon said. "Sorry, I was just looking for you . . . It's easy to get lost in this place."

"You'll leave now," Michael said.

Simon's heart was thumping. If Michael hadn't been suspicious about him already, he was now.

"Okay, great, I need to get going anyway," Simon said.

When Simon left the bathroom Michael was waiting, holding open the door for Simon to exit ahead of him. In the corridor on the way to the pool table, Simon smelled it.

"There's someone here," Simon said. "You can smell a scent, can't you?"

"He's not an enemy," Michael said.

Simon was confused but knew that asking more questions would be pointless. Besides, he just wanted to get the hell out of there.

The stairwell was well lit now. As they approached the floor where they'd killed the detective, the human scent got stronger and then Simon saw a young black guy, in his midtwenties. He was in jeans and a hooded sweatshirt but had a large mask over his mouth and nose, like the ones doctors wear, and he was wearing thick leather gloves and holding an old rusty shovel. Simon could also detect the scent of the blood of the PI, but it was much less odorous than before.

"Hey, what's up?" the black guy said.

Simon didn't know what else to say so he said, "Hey."

"Leave now," Michael said to Simon.

Simon knew he should leave as soon as possible, but he said, "Wait, who is this guy? What's going on here?"

"Eddie is my driver," Michael said.

"Your driver." Simon had to repeat it. "So why is your driver . . ." Simon noticed that the body was gone; there was just a faint red stain on the floor. "What did he do with it?"

"Don't worry, it's taken care of," Eddie said. "That's what I get paid to do."

"What do you mean, taken care of? What does that mean?"

"The bones are in the oven," Michael said.

Suddenly Simon had thoughts of Nazis again.

"Oven? What oven?"

Michael looked at Eddie.

Eddie said, "It's down in the basement."

Simon noticed that the elevator door was open and there was a big rusty wheelbarrow in it with the detective's remains. Simon had to look away or he would've gagged.

"Looks like you wolves enjoyed your meal, huh?" Eddie said. "Hardly no meat left at all, just bone. That's cool. Makes it easier for me to clean."

Eddie scraped the last bits of the body off the floor with the side of the shovel.

"Are you serious?" Simon said to Michael. "You think if the police investigate they won't know what happened here?"

"I'm good at cleanin' up after a job," Eddie said. "I have lots of experience."

Simon couldn't see Eddie's mouth, but his eyes narrowed as if he were grinning.

"This is the twenty-first century," Simon said. "Maybe burning bodies worked fifty or sixty years ago, but it won't today. There's probably detectable hair and blood all over this place. And what if the police find the oven? You really think they won't figure out what's going on?"

"You will leave now," Michael said.

Simon was looking around—at the elevator, at Eddie, at the stain on the floor—in disbelief.

"When the man says it's time to go, it's time to go," Eddie said.

Realizing that trying to be logical was pointless, Simon followed Michael downstairs.

On the ground floor Simon said, "Okay, so what happens next? Are you going to teach me how to assimilate, to control my behavior? If not, I'm warning you, I'll screw up. I'll turn at the wrong time, when people can see me, and you know what a disaster that'll be."

The only light was filtering in from the stairwell area. Still, Simon could see the outline of Michael.

"You want to kill me," Michael said.

Simon didn't know what to say. It seemed as if Michael was always a few steps ahead.

"You can't hide from your desires," Michael continued. "I see it in your eyes right now."

Simon didn't know how Michael could see anything in this light.

"It's not true," Simon said. "I—"

"It is true." Michael wasn't yelling—he never yelled—but his tone was insistent. "You are like me now. You share my blood, you share my desires, but until you admit your desire to kill, you won't be able to control the wolf inside you. The wolf must be free."

"I thought I proved it to you today," Simon said.

"No," Michael said. "Today you shared a meal, but you didn't kill. You must kill to prove you are one of us."

"I'm not sure what you're getting at," Simon said.

"You will kill the detective," Michael said.

"But the detective's already dead."

"The woman detective," Michael said. "Detective Rodriguez."

Simon had to smile. "Come on, I know you don't joke around, but you're joking this time, right?"

"She's a threat to the pack," Michael said. "She must be killed immediately."

Not smiling anymore, Simon said, "Come on, seriously, we're not going to kill a cop."

"I won't kill her," Michael said. "*You* will, and the pack will share in the feast. That is how you will prove you are truly with us."

"Look," Simon said, "we . . . I mean, I can't kill a cop. First of all, the police are relentless when cops are killed. I'll never get away with it."

"If you don't kill her, I will, and then I will kill you, but I won't share you with the pack. I will feast on you alone."

Simon knew he had no choice, at least for right now. He had to agree to this craziness and figure out a plan later.

"Okay, fine, I'll do whatever you want," Simon said. "But how do you want me to do it? I mean, am I supposed to attack her at her desk in the police station?"

"We'll come for you," Michael said.

"I'm sorry, what does *we'll come for you* mean?"

"You will leave now." He opened the door for Simon to exit.

Then, when Simon stepped outside onto the dark street, Michael let the door slam.

SEVENTEEN

Alison was trying her hardest to be patient. It had been only about four hours since Stephen Tyler had started following Simon, and she knew she couldn't expect instant answers. Still, knowing *something* would have been nice. Even a quick text from Tyler to let her know where things were at would've been great, but she'd texted him twice and so far she'd heard absolutely nothing.

It didn't help that Jeremy had been in a mood all day. When Alison had returned home from meeting with Stephen and relieved Christina from babysitting duties, Jeremy had a fit—probably because he hadn't napped and hadn't had much lunch—clinging to Christina's leg when she was leaving and then crying for her when she was gone. Jeremy had always had more separation anxiety than most kids—that was just the way he was—but Alison had been in enough therapy to realize that this was just his way of dealing with all the stress he'd been through lately, trying to get attention or control over the situation.

Alison wished she could have a fit herself, let out stress, because she was wound up and overwhelmed. Besides having to deal with Jeremy's tantrums and waiting for Tyler to call, she was thinking about her busy schedule tomorrow. She'd taken a personal day from work today, but tomorrow she had to go in and she had back-to-back meetings from eight thirty A.M. on. Christina wasn't available for sitting, so luckily Alison had been able to arrange for Jeremy's friend Matthew's babysitter to watch Jeremy tomorrow, but Matthew lived downtown on West Sixty-seventh and the earliest she could drop off Jeremy was eight fifteen, so she'd have just fifteen minutes to make it to her first appointment, all the way back uptown on the East Side at Mount Sinai Hospital. Even if she got Jeremy up, dressed, and out the door by eight, it was going to take a minor miracle to find a cab and make it to her appointment—that she couldn't be late for—on time. And tomorrow was just one day. What was she going to do the day after tomorrow, and the day after that, and the day after that? Now that it seemed as if Simon, for whatever reason, had officially checked out of this marriage, it was hitting Alison that she was going to be a single mom, something she was completely unprepared for. She'd have to find some kind of day care for Jeremy, maybe try to hire back their old babysitter, Margaret, but that would mean going into savings and she wouldn't be able to afford it for long. If she got divorced, she'd have to sell the apartment and move to a smaller apartment or to an outer borough.

Alison needed a drink. There was a bottle of Chardonnay in the fridge. She didn't know how old it was, but did it matter? She poured a glass and drank it in a couple of gulps. She didn't feel any more relaxed, though—just a little sick on top of being stressed out.

She put Jeremy in bed, read him *Where the Wild Things Are*, then went out to the living room, checked her phone—still nothing from Tyler—and did some research on one of the drugs she would be pitching at her nine o'clock.

"Mommy, I think there're bugs in my bed."

Jeremy had come out of his bedroom, clutching Sam, his stuffed bear.

"Sweetie, Mommy has a lot of important work to do now, okay?" Alison said. "So can you please be a good boy and go into your room and go back to sleep now?"

"Will you lie in bed?

He made his adorable pouting face that was impossible to say no to.

Alison figured that if she didn't get into bed with him, he would be going back and forth out of his room for the next hour, which she definitely did not have patience for. So she lay in bed next to him, and within a few minutes he had fallen asleep, and maybe the wine was finally kicking in because she was sleepy, falling asleep as well, and then her phone, which she had brought into the room with her, vibrated, indicating a text message.

Jolted awake, she checked it, angry that it was from Simon:

I know you're angry at me, that's ok. I just wanted to make sure Jeremy is okay. Please let me know.

Where was Simon texting from? Was Tyler following him or not? Why wasn't Tyler getting back to her?

Now she was wide awake again, way too agitated to sleep or get any work done. She went back out to the quiet living room and suddenly felt like this was a glimpse of her future. Going forward, this was how her evenings would be—she'd be stressed out, alone, overwhelmed. She checked her phone again and angrily deleted the text from Simon. She wanted to call Vijay. She hadn't spoken to him since yesterday at his apartment and hadn't texted him since afterward when she wrote to tell him she'd had an amazing time with him and he'd texted back: *Yeah, it was awesome.* She'd been hoping he'd text her first today, even just to say hi, but he hadn't, which wasn't really a big deal since it had only been one day and he was a busy doctor, after all. But she also felt a little ridiculous waiting for a text from him. They were adults, colleagues—well, kind of colleagues, but still. Why not just call him?

Without further debate she called him, got his voice mail after four rings, and left a message: "Hey, it's me, Alison. Just wanted to say hi and see how you're doing today. I had a wonderful time last night and . . ." She couldn't think of anything else to say; she had to end this quick. "Anyway, well, talk to you soon. Bye-bye."

She clicked off—loving the first part of the message, hating the second part. *Bye-bye?* Ugh. She wished she'd thought it through first, but whatever, didn't she have enough to stress about?

As she washed up and got ready for bed, she couldn't stop fantasizing about Vijay. It had been nice, even soothing, just to hear his voice mail. He had such a calm, down-to-earth demeanor, like a bedside manner, and always seemed to make her feel happy. Maybe she'd been overstressing about her whole situation—maybe her single, post-Simon life wouldn't be so dismal. She and Vijay could start spending more time together, maybe even become a serious couple. They both had busy lives, but lived in the same general neighborhood; it could be the perfect situation. And they definitely had great chemistry and a strong connection. He'd mentioned he wanted kids someday, and she certainly wasn't opposed. Okay, so she knew she was getting way ahead of herself now, but so what? She imagined living with Vijay, maybe moving into his place, at least temporarily, until the baby was born. Jeremy would have a sibling, which would be great for him, and she would have a solid, dependable, attractive, successful husband.

Her ringing cell phone jarred her from her thoughts. Toothpaste in her mouth, she rushed to the phone she'd left in the living room and saw that the call was from Simon. Irritated, she let the call go to voice mail. Was he going to keep texting and calling all night? She wished she could turn her phone off so he'd get the point that she didn't want to talk to him, but she didn't want to miss a call from Tyler or Vijay.

She finished brushing her teeth, then decided to nip it in the bud and text Simon back. She didn't think Tyler would have a problem since so much time, about five hours, had lapsed since the "meeting time" at Grand Central. Besides, if she didn't respond, Simon might show up at the apartment, and the last thing she needed now was another traumatic scene in front of Jeremy.

Keeping it short and sweet, she texted him:

Jeremy's fine

She hoped that would be the end of it but then got:

Thank u

Then:

I miss u

The *I miss u* seriously pissed her off. How dare he miss her when he was God knows where with God knows who doing God knows what. He was playing twisted head games, that was what he was doing, and she was so over his silly, immature crap. She wanted to be in a real relationship, with a real man.

She was in bed when the phone rang again. She grabbed the phone angrily, assuming it was Simon, but brightened when she saw that Vijay was calling.

Smiling widely, she sat up and said in a kind of sexy, flirty tone, "Why hello, how are you?"

"Hey," he said, "sorry I didn't get back to you sooner; it's been a crazy, hectic day."

"I know, I figured," Alison said. "I just wanted to say hi, see how you were doing."

"No, actually I'm very glad you called," Vijay said. "I was going to call you too, to apologize."

"Apologize?" Alison was confused. "Apologize for what?"

"For putting you in touch with Stephen," he said. "I guess I didn't really think it through all that well. My mistake."

Even more lost, Alison said, "I don't get it. Everything went great with Stephen. Actually I'm just waiting to hear from him to see how things are going with his investigation."

"He wasn't inappropriate with you?" Vijay asked.

"Inappropriate? What do you mean?"

"Never mind," Vijay said. "I was just concerned, that's all. Stephen is like a frat boy who never grew up, and sometimes he can . . . Anyway, I'm glad to hear that all went well on that front, but the main reason I wanted to talk is I've been doing some thinking about what happened with us last night, and, well, I really don't think it's a good idea for us to see each other again."

"Oh." Alison had to absorb this. "Okay."

"I think you're a wonderful woman, don't get me wrong," Vijay said, "but you're going through a lot right now, and I don't want to be a distraction for you."

"You're not a distraction," Alison said.

"I just don't feel comfortable with the situation," Vijay said. "I'm sorry."

Alison felt the letdown.

"No, it's okay," she said. "I understand."

"Thank you, I really appreciate that," he said. "I also think someone else at your company should take over my account. Just so there isn't any conflict."

"Oh, that isn't necessary," Alison said.

"I'd feel more comfortable," he said. "If you don't mind."

A few minutes later, Alison was sitting up in bed, tears trickling down her cheeks. She wasn't upset about losing Vijay—they'd barely gotten involved and he was right, starting something now probably wasn't a great idea—but she still couldn't help feeling an overwhelming sense of loss. She'd already lost her husband and her family, and Vijay had been a nice escape. Without him, the future suddenly seemed lonely and bleak and terrifying.

Geri was heading up the stoop to her apartment building on West Forty-eighth when she heard:

"Hey, beautiful."

She was used to getting catcalls from guys on the street, and for a second she thought it was some guy hanging off a garbage truck. Then she looked back over her shoulder and saw Ramon in a double-parked red Toyota Camry, smiling widely.

"What're you doing here?" she said, excited to see him.

"I missed you, baby," he said. "You know I can't stay away from you."

A laundry delivery truck was trying to squeeze past the Toyota but couldn't fit, and the driver honked the horn.

"Come on, get in," Ramon said.

"Now?"

"Yeah, come on."

"Where're you going?"

"A mystery ride, come on."

The truck honked again.

Geri didn't know why she was hesitating—it was either hang out at home with a couple of cats or go for a drive with a guy who had turned her on the way no guy had ever turned her on before.

She got in the car and they drove away. It was amazing, how just being next to him excited her. She was already getting turned on.

"You look incredible," he said.

Although Geri had barely slept last night and had been working all day and just rode home on a hot, crowded subway, she believed him.

"Thank you, so do you," she said, and she meant it as well. In jeans and a tight black T-shirt, Ramon looked smoldering. "I wasn't expecting to see you tonight."

"I guess I'm just full of surprises," Ramon said.

They drove past Eleventh Avenue.

"So is this your ride?" Geri asked.

"Nah, I just rented it at Hertz," Ramon said.

"You rented a car just to take me on a mystery ride?"

"Yeah, I guess I did."

"Well, that's kind of romantic," Geri said. "I mean, it's not exactly a horse-and-buggy ride in Central Park, but yeah, it is pretty romantic."

She reached out and gently rubbed Ramon's right thigh. She was dying to have her hands all over him.

"So are you gonna give me any clue where we're going?" she asked.

"If I did, it wouldn't be a mystery ride," Ramon said.

"That's not true. Mysteries have clues. Take it from me; I am a detective, after all."

"You'll find out soon, baby, you'll find out soon. Why don't you just chill out and enjoy the ride?"

He turned on the radio to a Latin station—a cheesy Spanish love song that somehow seemed romantic and perfect.

"I was thinking about you all day today," Geri said. "You're very distracting, you know that?"

"You know I was thinking about you, right?" Ramon said. "You drive me crazy."

"Crazy is a good way to describe it." Noticing the big bulge in Ramon's jeans, she continued to rub her fingers against the inside of his thighs, saying. "I mean, I usually don't get like this with guys. I mean, I *never* get like this with guys. I don't know what it is about you that turns me on so much, but no guy has ever had this kind of effect on me."

"That's 'cause you never met the right guy before," Ramon said.

"You really believe that? That there's one person for everybody in the world?"

"Yeah, of course I do. I was telling the guys today at the playground that you're my soul mate."

"The guys?" Geri asked. "You mean you saw Michael today?"

Ramon didn't answer at first. Then he said, "I'll explain it all to you soon, I promise."

Geri stopped kneading his thigh but left her hand there. "Explain what to me soon?"

"You don't gotta worry about anything," he said. "I got it under control."

They were on the West Side Highway, going uptown, toward the Upper West Side. She'd figured he'd rented a hotel room somewhere, and maybe they'd have a fun night with room service and robes and hot sex, but now she was starting to get concerned. Ramon, looking out at the road with a very serious expression, suddenly didn't seem like himself.

Geri stopped touching his thigh and said, "If something's going on, you should tell me what it is."

"You trust me, right?" Ramon asked.

"I want to trust you," Geri said. "But I hardly know you."

"You know me," Ramon said. "Just because we just met, that doesn't mean you don't know me. Love's about feelings, not time."

"Whoa, love?" Geri said. "Did you just say love?"

"What's wrong with love, baby?"

"Look, I admit I feel something for you that's strong, okay?" Geri said. "It's an attraction, a desire, but love is something else."

"You're just afraid to admit it."

"I'm not afraid, I'm—"

"I know you feel it," Ramon said. "You don't have to tell me. I know you love me just by the way you look at me. I knew it when you walked into that theater yesterday and sat down. You couldn't take your eyes off me. The whole stage disappeared, the whole world disappeared. It was just me and you, alone, floating in space. That's what love is."

Geri knew Ramon was being corny, but it was true, she had felt something different when she saw him for the first time. Was it love? She'd never been in love with anyone, never let herself go like this before, so how did she know? Besides, the past twenty-four hours had been so crazy, she wasn't sure how she felt about anything anymore.

She didn't say anything for a while, listening to the cheesy Spanish love song. Then she realized that they had passed the Upper West Side and were heading toward the GW Bridge.

"Wait, seriously, where're you taking me?" Geri asked. "Are we leaving the city?"

"You really have to stop asking questions, baby," Ramon said. "You gotta relax and have faith in me. If you do that, everything'll be okay, I promise."

Geri decided Ramon was right—well, about relaxing, anyway. She was probably taking the whole thing too seriously. So what if they left the city for a few hours? He was probably taking her to some romantic dinner spot in Westchester, maybe Dobbs Ferry by the river or something. Was it really such a big deal?

Then, riding along the Henry Hudson Parkway, they passed Washington Heights, where Orlando Rojas and Carlita Morales had been killed, and Geri was distracted by other thoughts. She wondered if Santoro and Reese had made any progress on the case, but she doubted they had. They were playing catch-up, probably rehashing a lot of leads that Geri and Shawn had already checked out, and, more important, they didn't understand DDP the way Geri did. Meanwhile, Geri still had a nagging feeling that they were all missing something about the case, something obvious.

After Washington Heights came Inwood, the northernmost neighborhood in Manhattan. Geri had worked on a few cases there during her career, including one last year that involved DDP. A kid had been shot and killed in front of a bodega and local gang violence was suspected, so there had been a large-scale investigation, but the case had remained unsolved.

Then it hit her—the Devon Carter murder, of course.

Geri took out her cell and called Tim Stappini in IT at Manhattan North.

Ramon saw her making the call and, looking over, concerned, asked, "Hey, what're you doing, baby?"

Tim said, "Hey, Geri, what's going on?"

"I need you to look up something for me."

"Can it wait? I'm in the middle of—"

"It can't wait."

"'Kay, what you got?"

"I need a full search on Manny Alvarez," Geri said.

"Who?" Ramon asked.

Geri held up a hand to Ramon like the stop sign and stage-whispered, "Wait."

"'Kay, let's see what we got," Tim said. "I got a Manuel Alvarez."

"Age?"

"Twenty-nine."

"On Isham Street?"

"Yeah," Tim said. "Juvie at Tryon, three at Rikers for possession with intent."

"Gang association?" Geri asked, knowing she'd nailed it.

"Yeah, DDP," Tim said.

Going for the clincher, Geri asked, "Siblings?"

"Jeez, what do you think I am, some kinda computer geek?" Tim said. "Yeah, one sibling, a sister, Carlita Alvarez-Morales."

Thinking *Bingo*, Geri said, "Thanks, I owe you one. You can go back to drafting your fantasy football team now."

"Ha, ha," Tim said.

Geri ended the call and, noticing they had crossed the Harlem River and were in the Bronx, said, "You gotta drop me back in the city right now."

"What's goin' on?" Ramon asked.

Geri was trying to decide if she should call it in . . . why do a favor for Dan? He was protecting his ass; who was going to protect hers?

"It's just a work thing. Come on, you gotta get off at the next exit."

"Why?"

"Just do it."

"We can't right now," Ramon said.

"What do you mean, can't?" Geri said. "This is police business. I'm working on a case."

"This is more important than your case."

"Look, this is fun," Geri said. "I think it was romantic, you showing up and taking me on this mystery ride, and I agree I feel something with you, something different. I don't know if it's attraction or obsession or what, but I have an emergency now, I have to go, okay?"

"You don't get it," Ramon said. "You can't go now."

Geri didn't know what to do. She had to get back to the city, she was *going* to get back to the city. She didn't want to threaten Ramon, but she would if she had to.

"Why?" she said. "Why can't I go?"

Ramon shook his head, looking out at the highway.

Then he said, almost reluctantly, "'Cause if I let you go you're gonna die tonight, that's why."

EIGHTEEN

Simon was running. He wanted to get away from Michael and the Hartman Brewery as fast as he could, as if by leaving it behind, he could escape what had happened there, or at least make it into a bad memory. He was sprinting along the Navy Yard area by the East River, maybe running faster than he'd ever run before, despite the Ferragamo loafers, until he reached the outskirts of DUMBO. There were lots of people around, many staring at the guy sprinting in designer clothes, so he slowed to a jog and then walked toward the pedestrian entrance to the Brooklyn Bridge, because he didn't want to attract attention and because it had set in that he couldn't escape from the horror by running away because the horror was inside him.

Walking across the bridge, he saw that the moon—to his left toward the Statue of Liberty—was still almost full, which, according to Volker, would make it easier than normal for him to turn into a werewolf tonight. Great, now Simon had something else to worry about, but his most immediate problem was Michael. Simon had no doubt that Michael was serious about his threat to kill him and Detective Rodriguez if Simon didn't kill her himself, but Simon had no idea what to do about it. He had to stop Michael, but what was he supposed to do, try to kill Michael by ripping his jaw apart? Even if he was somehow successful, where would that get him? Michael would be dead, but since Simon hadn't found the remedy yet, it meant he and the other guys would be werewolves for the rest of their lives.

Simon couldn't handle this alone. He needed Volker's help, but he had no idea how to contact him. At a point on the bridge where there was no one around, he yelled, "Volker! Volker! Where the hell are you?" but his voice was drowned out by the cars speeding by, and he also felt ridiculous yelling for someone who wasn't even here. What was he expecting, that Volker would just materialize? What had Volker told him this morning? Oh, right; *I can find you, that's more important.* What the hell was that supposed to mean?

Then Simon decided that his only hope was to look for Volker at the Ramble in Central Park. Though the fastest way to get there would probably be to run, he didn't think running all the way uptown the way he was dressed was a great idea. The FDR Drive looked like it was backed up, and there was a lot of street traffic, so he figured the subway was his best bet.

At Brooklyn Bridge/City Hall, he boarded an uptown 4 train. The train wasn't packed, but it was crowded enough that some claustrophobia and panic set in. He was taking deep breaths, trying to relax, afraid he would turn. He was aware of several women on the car staring at him, and it wasn't with concern because he seemed to be slightly in distress—no, they were clearly checking him out because they were attracted to him. He realized that in his expensive clothes, and with his scruffy face, and the usual werewolf aura he projected, he probably seemed like the sexiest guy in the world to them. Simon wondered what they'd think if they knew the truth about what he'd done and what he was capable of. Would they be repulsed or would they still be infatuated?

To avoid eye contact, Simon turned to face the subway door and stared at his reflection. In the distorted dirty glass he didn't look like a monster that had an uncontrollable craving for human flesh. He didn't look much different than he used to look a couple of months ago, when he was an ad exec, a normal *human* ad exec, returning home after a long day at the office. It gave him some hope that maybe the old Simon Burns was still in there somewhere, that he wasn't dead completely.

At Fifty-ninth Street, Simon exited the subway and walked as fast as he could a few blocks west to Central Park. In the park, he let loose and sprinted, trying to enjoy the freedom of running, but he was so terrified of what he'd become and what he might do that it was hard to appreciate the positives of being a werewolf.

Past the lake, he veered off the road and entered the Ramble. He went to the area where he'd met Volker last night, and although he couldn't detect Volker's scent, that didn't mean Volker wasn't neces-sarily there, since he had the ability to mask his scent. Simon inhaled to make sure that there were no humans in the vicinity, and then he yelled, "Volker! Are you here? Volker!"

For the next hour or so, Simon walked around the Ramble, screaming Volker's name when it was safe to do so, but his desperate pleas received no response.

Finally Simon gave up and left the park with the sick, helpless feeling that he was in this alone.

*   *   *

Simon returned to Charlie's apartment, entering with the key Charlie had given him. He hadn't eaten anything since Stephen Tyler and he was starving. He went right to the fridge and, God bless Charlie, saw it was stocked with meat—chop meat, sausage, ham, and in the back a couple of steaks. Too impatient to cook the steaks, he tore open the packaging and ripped into them, standing by the sink. The meat tasted good raw, but eating a steak as a human wasn't nearly as satisfying as eating a human as a wolf. Oh, God, it was true what Volker had said—Simon did have the craving.

Though he managed to finish the rest of the raw steak, he didn't really enjoy it, feeling as unsatisfied as he used to feel after having a bagful of cookies.

Cooped up in the apartment, he felt restless. Pacing in the living room like an animal in a cage, he checked his phone—still no response from Alison to the message he'd sent from Grand Central.

So he sent:

I know you're angry at me, that's ok. I just wanted to make sure Jeremy is okay. Please let me know.

He continued pacing, and then, maybe five minutes later, his phone vibrated.

From Alison:

Jeremy's fine

He was relieved. He missed Jeremy so much, he would've given anything to pick him up and give him a big, tight hug and tell him how much he loved him.

Teary-eyed, he texted:

Thank u

Then:

I miss u

He was hoping she'd respond with *Miss u 2* but he knew this was beyond wishful thinking—it was hopeless thinking. After all, this was a woman who was so angry that she had hired a PI to follow him. A few years ago, when things were good, the idea of Alison hiring a PI would have been unimaginable. It hit Simon, really hit him, how far he had pushed her, and even if he found the remedy and it worked, he knew he had his work cut out for him if he was going to get her to ever trust him again.

Figuring that getting some rest would probably be a good idea after an extremely eventful day, he was pulling out the couch when he heard the elevator doors open and then smelled Charlie. He was surprised because Charlie had said he was working a twenty-four-hour shift.

A key turned in the lock, and then the front door opened and Charlie entered and said, "Good, you're awake, we gotta get out of here."

Charlie was usually relaxed, low-key. There was an urgency in his tone Simon hadn't heard before.

"What's going on?" Simon asked. "What's wrong?"

"The boss said you know," Charlie said.

Now Simon knew, but he was praying he was wrong. The poorly chewed steak was suddenly heavy in his gut.

"Know about what?" Simon said. "I don't know anything."

"Look, this isn't my business, all right?" Charlie said. "The boss said he discussed it with you and you'd know what's happening tonight. He just wants us both downstairs in five minutes."

Simon hadn't expected this at all. He thought he'd have time, at least a few days, to figure out what to do. But obviously Michael wasn't planning to give him a chance to come up with a plan.

"Downstairs?" Simon said. "What do you mean, downstairs? In the lobby?"

"No, in front of the building. A car's coming to pick us up."

"Wait, we can't go," Simon said.

"What do you mean? We gotta go." As Charlie glanced toward the kitchen, his nostrils flared. "Did you eat all the steak?"

"You know what he wants me to do, right?" Simon said. "I mean, he told you."

"It's okay, I got more in the back of the fridge."

"Listen to me. I can't do it, I can't kill a cop. And if he does something, we're all involved, including you."

"Come on, we gotta get going," Charlie said.

Simon moved closer to Charlie and said, "I get it. You have a bond with Michael, and you have a craving. I know, trust me, I have it too. But I still know it's wrong and I want to stop myself; I don't want to hurt anybody else. Don't you want that too?"

Charlie held Simon's gaze for a few seconds, then said, "Come on, the boss is waiting for us; we don't wanna piss him off."

Simon knew that trying to win Charlie over completely, at least while Michael was alive, was a waste of time. But that didn't mean he couldn't get some help from him.

"Okay, I'll go with you, but can you at least tell me how you control yourself, how you don't 'wolf out' at the wrong time?"

"You gotta learn that from Michael," Charlie said.

Simon grabbed Charlie by the forearm and said, "Please. I know you're a good guy, and you like me. Please, as my friend, tell me how to do it."

Simon could see something in Charlie's eyes; he wasn't unreachable.

"I shouldn't be saying this," Charlie said, "but you have to love it."

Releasing his grip, Simon asked, "Love what?"

"Who you are," Charlie said. "At first me and Ramon, we were fighting it too, but when you love it, you control it." Then, looking serious, he said, "Forget I told you that; let's go."

Charlie opened the front door and waited for Simon to grab his Armani sport jacket. Simon hesitated, then decided he had no choice but to go. If he didn't go, Michael would just kill Detective Rodriguez on his own, but if Simon went, at least he had a chance to prevent it.

Outside the building, a black Lexus SUV was waiting, double-parked. What with the tinted windows and the glare of streetlights on the windows, Simon couldn't see inside. He was able to make out the scent of a human; was it Eddie? Yeah, it was Eddie. There were no other scents coming from the car, but Simon sensed danger, a threat, and knew Michael was in there too.

Charlie opened the door, and sure enough Michael was sitting in one of the plush leather seats. He was in jeans, a perfectly fitting black shirt tucked in, with the top few buttons open, exposing his gray chest hair.

"Come join us," he said.

With a certain feeling that this night wasn't going to end happily, Simon got into the car.

Simon, Charlie, and Michael sat in the back, while Eddie drove. For a long time, maybe a half hour, nobody said a word. They were going north—FDR, then eventually across to the Saw Mill. Simon wanted to know where they were going, of course, but he didn't see the point in asking about it.

As they left the city, Simon had to admit that despite his anxiety and fear, it was exhilarating to be out of the city, breathing in the fresher air that was seeping into the car, and to be surrounded by trees and actual woods. Like a kid passing an amusement park, he was dying to get out of the car and run around and be free.

But Simon's anxiety kicked back in full force when Michael said, "You will kill the detective tonight."

Simon glanced at Charlie, who had no reaction at all to this. Then Simon said to Michael, "Look, I still think this isn't such a great idea. I mean, she's a cop and I guess I don't get why you want to get rid of her anyway. There doesn't seem to be any formal investigation going on, and if she's gone it's not like the police suddenly stop investigating. It might give them more reason to investigate you and us if she's killed working on a case."

"We'll be there soon," Michael said.

"I feel like you're not listening to me," Simon said. "Why her? Because Ramon's dating her? How about just telling Ramon to break up with her; doesn't that sound a little less drastic? Or, wait, does this have to do with Diane? Did you actually kill her in Michigan? Is that what you're afraid of?"

"I don't have fear," Michael said.

"Okay, whatever," Simon said, "is that what you're concerned about?"

"I didn't kill Diane," Michael said.

"I want to believe that," Simon said, "but it seems like it has to be connected. Diane was worried that you'd be afraid she'd talk about the things she'd seen, so it makes sense that you'd want to keep her quiet about it."

"Hey," Charlie said, "he said he didn't kill her."

"Okay, then who did?" Simon asked.

"I did," Eddie said.

Simon saw the driver's dark, shadowed eyes in the rearview mirror.

Simon wasn't expecting that, and it took him a few seconds to absorb the possible implications.

"*You* killed her?" Simon asked, because he couldn't think of anything else to say.

"Yeah," Eddie said, "drove to Michigan and waited for my shot at her. Waited for my shot at her, that's funny, right?" Eddie laughed. "Ha, I crack myself up sometimes."

Simon remembered the night he'd met Diane, when he'd tried to warn her about the pack and had encouraged her to run away to Michigan. She'd seemed like such a nice, pretty, innocent woman, and now she was dead, thanks to these psychopaths. And then, with a shudder, he thought, *And how am I any better?*

Getting hold of himself, Simon asked Eddie, "So are you a werewolf too?"

Eddie laughed again, more boisterously, as if Simon had just said the punch line of a hilarious joke. Charlie was laughing too, and—though Simon couldn't tell for sure—it seemed like Michael was almost uncharacteristically smiling.

"Me a wolf," Eddie said between guffaws. "Oh, man, that's funny." He howled a couple of times and laughed even harder.

Then, when Eddie's laughter had tapered, Michael said, "Eddie is my employee. He's a killer like me, but he prefers to kill with a gun."

Simon looked toward the darkness outside, getting the strange feeling that he had just become a part of it.

"Die? How am I gonna die?"

Geri was waiting for Ramon to answer, but he was looking at the road, acting like he hadn't heard her, but she knew he had.

"Look, I don't know what's going on here," Geri said. "Maybe you think this is some kind of game or something. Going on a mystery ride, having some fun, and it probably would've been fun, but there's an emergency now and you have to pull over." The next exit was coming up, maybe one hundred yards away. She said, "This exit, right here, you gotta get out. Are you listening to me?" They were almost at the exit. "Okay, slow down, I said slow down!"

Ramon sped up, passing the exit.

"Jesús, ¿qué diablos es tu problema?" Geri said. "You think I'm playing? You see me laughing?"

But he was pretending not to hear her again.

Geri wasn't sure what to do. She had to get back to the city to, hopefully, make a bust in the Washington Heights shootings, but how was she supposed to force Ramon to turn around? She had her gun in her holster, but what would she do, aim a gun at him while he was speeding down a highway? This was a guy she liked; she didn't want to get so extreme. Besides, she didn't take threatening people with guns lightly. Like she told rookie cops whenever she spoke at the academy, "When you point your gun at somebody, there's a possibility it's gonna go off, so don't point your gun at somebody if you can't live with the consequences."

Her best bet was to keep trying to reason with him.

So she said, "Look, I'm working on a case, okay? Two people have

been killed, two innocent people, and I think I know who's responsible. But if I don't get there now, somebody else could get killed.
Every second counts, you understand what I'm saying?"

"You got a partner, right?" Ramon said. "Why don't you call him?
Tell him to go cover for you."

She'd considered this. She didn't mind handing it over to Shawn,
but would Shawn follow it up? It was basically just a hunch, after all,
and they weren't even supposed to be working on this case. He could
get suspended if Dan found out he was investigating on his own, and
Geri couldn't hand something to Shawn just to have it blow up in his
face.

"That won't work," Geri said, "and I really don't have time to
explain any of this right now. I just have to get back to the city immediately."

"I told you, I can't let you do that," Ramon said. "If you go back
you're gonna die, and I'm gonna have to live with that my whole life."

"Why do you keep saying I'm gonna die?" Geri asked. "Are you
just trying to scare me?"

"I wish I was, baby. I wish I was."

Geri thought about going for her gun, then said, "This is the last
time I'm asking you. How am I gonna die?"

"Right now, it's better you don't know, and just let me handle it,
all right?" Ramon said. "I got a plan, okay? But meanwhile we gotta
do what he told us to do."

"He? Who's he?"

Ramon was shaking his head as if he'd slipped up, said something
he hadn't intended to.

"Who?" Geri raised her voice.

"You don't get it," Ramon said. "You got to know what you're dealing with. You gotta trust me. You gotta believe that you're my soul mate and I'd never let anybody hurt you."

Seeing a road sign illuminated by the headlights of the Camry, Geri said, "Look, there's another exit coming up in half a mile. Just get off there. Stop somewhere and we can talk about this, okay?"

"We're not stopping," Ramon said.

Geri let out a frustrated breath, then said, "Who is he? Who're you talking about?"

Ramon didn't answer.

"Who?!" Geri shouted.

"Michael, all right?" Ramon pounded the dashboard with his fist. "See? Now you got me talkin' about things I shouldn't be talkin' about."

"Is it because of Diane Coles?" Geri asked. "Did he kill her?"

"No," Ramon said.

"Or Olivia Becker," Geri said. "Does he think I—"

"No—"

"Or the wolf murders in New Jersey?"

"No," Ramon said. "See? That's what I'm talkin' about. Some murders? That's nothin' compared to what's going on here."

With her hand gripping the handle of her Glock, she asked, "What do you know about Michael that you haven't told me yet?"

"You know nothing about Michael, I'm tellin' you."

"So tell me," Geri said. "Tell me what I don't know."

"You know how you want my body, right?" Ramon said.

"What does that have to—"

"You know how you want me, right? You know how you can't resist me? You know how you feel something with me you've never felt with any guy before?"

Despite how angry and frustrated she was, Geri couldn't deny that all of this was true.

"Okay," Geri said. "So?"

"So I've always been good with the ladies, but something happened to me, something Michael did to me, and it made me even better with women. I'm irresistible now."

Thinking this was getting weirder and weirder, Geri said, "What does that have to do with—"

"You don't get what I'm tryin' to say," Ramon said. "I was . . . I was *changed* by Michael."

"Changed? Changed how?"

"You won't believe it if I tell you."

"And I still don't get what this has to do with why Michael wants to kill me."

"You'll think it's crazy," Ramon said. "Only way anybody ever believes it is if they see it for themselves."

"See what for themselves?"

"What we are," Ramon said.

Geri saw that the next exit was coming up fast, too fast to make.

"What?" Geri said. "What are you?"

As they sped past the exit, Ramon shouted, "Werewolves, all right? We're all goddamn werewolves!"

No one said another word until the SUV stopped on a country road about an hour and a half outside the city, somewhere in Dutchess County, near Pawling, New York, and Michael said, "Get out."

Despite his fear, Simon was eager to get out of the SUV and breathe in the fresh country air. He stepped out onto the dirt road, then onto a grassy area, and looked up at the still mostly full moon and inhaled. Nothing could have prepared him for how invigorating his first breath of country air was, as if he were a newborn baby filling his lungs with air for the first time. He got a head rush that had to have been better than the feeling any drug could provide, and it was more addicting. He took more breaths, inhaling and exhaling as fast as he could; he couldn't get enough of it.

"You will walk ahead," Michael said.

Still affected by the wild rush to his brain, Simon said, "Walk where?"

"Into the woods," Michael said.

There was a woodsy area up ahead, visible in the moonlight, but even if Simon hadn't been able to see it, he would have known exactly where it was because coming from that direction, mingled with the cool, crisp air, were the dense aromas of evergreens and mulch.

So Simon headed toward the woods, wishing he were running, not walking. Following him were Michael and Charlie.

"Enjoy y'all selves," Eddie called after them, but he remained near the car.

Simon entered the woods with Michael and Charlie trailing, the sounds of their shoes crunching twigs and leaves and their breathing the only noises. Again, Simon wished he could break free and run or, better yet, get naked and transform into a wolf. To run in the woods would feel like being an animal released from a zoo and set free in the wild. There was a whole new world to explore and, walking with Michael and Charlie, he couldn't help feeling restrained, as if he were in shackles, a prisoner on his way to be executed.

When they finally reached a clearing, or at least an area that was mostly free of trees, Michael said, "Stop walking."

Simon stopped and turned to face Michael and Charlie, who was

lagging a few feet behind. There was plenty of moonlight in the clearing, and their faces almost seemed to be glowing. Simon suddenly
had a much stronger feeling of potential menace than he'd had in
the car.

"So what're we doing here?" Simon asked.

"You stole the beer," Michael said.

Simon had no idea what Michael was talking about. Michael was
always an enigma and spoke in non sequiturs, but this made no sense
at all.

"Beer?" Simon asked. "What beer?"

"When you were at the brewery," Michael said.

The remedy beer? Did Michael think he'd found it?

"I didn't take any beer," Simon said. "I swear to God I didn't."

Charlie, annoyingly, was just hanging back, as if he were
Michael's bodyguard or something. Simon got that Charlie had a
bond with Michael that was hard to break, but he didn't get why a
bond had to make him so unemotional, so robotic.

"You want to save her," Michael said.

"Save who?" Simon asked. "Rodriguez?"

"That's why you came with us," Michael said.

"It's true, I'd rather we didn't kill a cop, but—"

"You aren't with us," Michael said.

"That isn't true," Simon said. "I am with you, that's why I'm—"

"You will be slaughtered with the woman tonight and my pack
will share the feast," Michael said.

Simon was aware of other scents in the vicinity—Ramon, definitely Ramon, and a female, probably Rodriguez. Simon was determined not to go without a fight, but he didn't know how he was
supposed to fight when he was outnumbered. It would be hard
enough to fight Michael alone, but if Charlie and Ramon assisted

him—and Simon didn't see why they wouldn't—then the task would be even more difficult. But the biggest problem was that Simon had to turn into a werewolf if he was going to have any chance of defending himself, and if it didn't happen spontaneously, he had no idea how he was going to make it happen. Supposedly it would be easier to turn when the moon was near its fullest, but was the moon full enough tonight to help him out? It definitely wasn't a completely full moon as there was a noticeable sliver missing on its right side.

Then Ramon and Detective Rodriguez approached from the opposite direction that Simon, Charlie and Michael had come from. It was weird seeing Rodriguez, the cop, arrive willingly to this meeting spot in the middle of the woods in some remote part of Dutchess County. What had Ramon told her that she agreed to come here? Or maybe she was the one playing him, or playing them. Maybe she had a team of cops in the area, a whole SWAT team ready to pounce at a moment's notice—although Simon knew it was unlikely that any more humans were nearby or he would've been able to smell them.

When Ramon and Rodriguez were about ten yards away, Michael transformed and pounced on Rodriguez. The transformation and attack happened so fast that Simon barely had time to react or respond. One moment, he was facing Michael in the moonlight, and the next moment Michael was a werewolf, his expanded body stretching and tearing his slacks and sport jacket, as he was pinning Rodriguez to the ground and digging his fangs into her neck.

Simon tried to pry Michael off Rodriguez, but as a human he didn't have enough strength. He tried as hard as he could to transform, but nothing happened. His impotence was terrifying. Had he lost the ability to transform, or was consciously trying making it more difficult?

He tried to go after Michael again, growling, as if maybe growling would help, when Ramon grabbed him and threw him to the ground. Wasn't Ramon in love with Rodriguez? Then how could he just stand there and let her get bitten to death?

Simon went after Michael again—well, tried to, but a clawed hand, or paw, grabbed him and flung him down hard onto the hard ground. Then he looked up and saw Ramon as a werewolf, drool dripping down his hairy chin. How come everyone could transform at will but him? Charlie was still standing off to the side, in his human form, but when Simon tried to get to Michael again and tussled with Ramon, Charlie transformed as well. Great, three werewolves against none; the nightmare scenario that Simon had feared had come to fruition.

While Charlie was distracted with Simon, Ramon charged toward Michael, leaping in the air and landing on his back, and they tumbled together off Rodriguez. Blood was gushing from Rodriguez's neck and she was trying to crawl away to safety—as if there were any safety to crawl to. Charlie left Simon and went to help Michael fight off Ramon. Simon wanted to help Ramon, but he needed to transform, right now, or he'd be useless.

He tried to do what Charlie had told him to do, to *love it*, but nothing happened. Had Charlie just been messing with him? How could loving it, whatever that meant, control the ability to become a werewolf? Then he thought maybe that was the problem—he was trying too hard, he had to just let it happen. Maybe that was what Charlie meant by *love it*, because you can't try to love, love just happens.

So Simon tried to clear his head, the way he did the times when he'd attempted to meditate, but instead of repeating a mantra, he focused on the word *love* and, like when he was trying to meditate, other thoughts intruded. He was thinking about running, with the wind in his face, and then he saw that day with Alison and Jeremy at the Seaport. They were so happy riding on the bus downtown that day; things were so normal, and later that day he had told himself that he had to accept it. Wasn't that the same as loving it? He had to accept who he was, and love who he was, and he was a wolf now. This was his new reality.

Whatever Simon was doing was working because the transformation began, faster than it ever had before. In the past, there was a slow, extremely painful buildup, but now the pain through his body came suddenly and ended suddenly, and he felt the power and confidence of the wolf overtake him.

Simon leaped, claws extended, and landed on Michael's back. He bit into the back of Michael's neck, tasting his blood, which only made him hungry for more.

Charlie and Ramon backed away to let Michael and Simon fight it out alone. Simon felt stronger than the last time he'd battled Michael, more prepared and sure of himself. He clawed at Michael's gray wolf face, trying to get his paws into his mouth so he could stretch his jaw apart. But Michael lashed out with a ferocious bite that might have decapitated Simon if he hadn't managed to avoid it. Simon saw an opening and clawed at Michael's midsection, splattering blood, and by the way Michael groaned Simon knew he'd hurt him. Sensing he'd gained an upper hand, Simon went for Michael's face again, clawing at his big black eyes, and then with a violent surge he was able to tackle Michael to the ground. They were on a slight incline, though, and rolled together a few times and then Michael was suddenly on top, back in control.

Michael was slashing and gnawing at Simon's face, and Simon was desperately trying to defend himself against the onslaught, and then he felt tremendous pain in his mouth. At first he was so involved with fighting back that he wasn't sure what was happening, but then he realized that Michael's claws were in his mouth and that his mouth was being stretched apart. He tried to grab Michael's arms, but it was hard to grab something with claws, and Michael's claws were affixed in Simon's mouth like clamps. He tried to flip Michael over, but Michael was too strong, and the pain of the corners of his mouth ripping open was making it hard to focus. He heard the crunch of torn ligaments and knew it wouldn't be long before he couldn't resist at all and his jaw would tear apart, his head would split open, and he'd die instantly.

Then Simon was free. It happened so suddenly he thought he had to be imagining it, experiencing some sort of psychosomatic defense mechanism to avoid the pain of his pending death, the way a man dying of thirst in a desert might imagine that he's drinking from a cold waterfall. But no, this wasn't his mind playing tricks; Michael actually wasn't pinning him down anymore as someone, another werewolf, had come to Simon's aid and was now fighting with Michael.

Was it Ramon or Charlie? Charlie was still standing off to the side, and Ramon and Detective Rodriguez had left and Simon couldn't detect their scents. Then Simon inhaled deeply and looked more closely at the werewolf battling with Michael and saw that it was Volker.

Simon had no idea where Volker had come from but figured he must've followed the guys here or knew where the confrontation would take place and had been waiting here. Now the father and son were assaulting each other viciously. This was a side to Volker Simon had never seen before. When Simon had run with him in the Ramble the other night, he'd seemed lean, elegant, even gentle, but now he was vicious and relentless. He was on his hind legs, growling, as he clawed at Michael's face and chest. Volker seemed to be using every bit of energy that his 141-year-old body could muster, but Michael was stronger and much younger and seemed to be unfazed by the onslaught. Then, in one swift movement, Michael lunged forward, maneuvered his paws into his father's mouth, and was trying to tear the jaw apart.

Simon rushed over, practically flying as he leaped into the air, maybe ten feet, and landed on Michael's back. Michael was able to shake Simon off, though, and Simon tumbled onto the ground. He was about to launch another attack on Michael but knew it was too late when he heard the loud, sickening sound of bones and ligaments being torn apart, and then he smelled the blood—oh, God, the wonderful scent of werewolf blood—and knew that Michael had torn his father's head open.

Though Simon knew he should be horrified, the aroma of the blood of the dead werewolf was so intoxicating, and he couldn't focus on anything else. It was clear that Michael felt the same way, as he was licking his father's blood off his claws as if a human had dipped his hands into a vat of the best-tasting chocolate. Simon was jealous— he wanted to taste the blood too. Michael was still holding Volker's bloody remains, and Simon was on his hind legs, lapping up as much blood as he could, and then Charlie came over and he was also licking and nibbling on the corpse as well. The werewolf's blood was so addicting that nothing else mattered. Simon—and the others—forgot what they had been fighting about and who hated who. All that mattered was the craving, and satisfying it. Then Simon took his first bite of werewolf flesh, which was so much tastier than human flesh, and he was in heaven. Volker was by far the most satisfying meal Simon had ever had.

NINETEEN

When Geri opened her eyes she had no idea where she was. She squeezed the mattress—no, it was a cushion, a couch cushion—and then sat up.

She was in a living room. There was a chair, a rocking chair, a coffee table with a toy tractor-trailer on it, and on the wall a couple of tacky oil paintings of landscapes with mountains and rivers. She patted her body—same clothes she'd been wearing. She also checked, made sure she still had her Glock in her holster.

"Look who's up already."

Ramon came into the living room, ultra relaxed in just black boxer briefs. He looked buff, and was his chest a little hairier since the last time she'd seen it?

Wanting him badly, Geri managed to say, "Where the hell am I?"

"My place." Ramon had that electric smile. "I'm surprised you're awake. I thought you'd sleep till morning for sure."

Geri tried to stand up, realized she was a little dizzy, and sat back down on the couch.

"What . . . what happened?" she asked.

Ramon had come closer to her. He said, "You blacked out, but don't worry, it's normal to black out after you drink the beer."

The beer. That's right, it was all coming back. In the car, driving through Westchester with Ramon, him telling her that he was a were-wolf. She thought it was a joke, he was out of his mind or just messing with her, but she had to get him to stop the car somehow so she could go check out Manny Alvarez in Inwood, so she went with her last resort and took her gun out, demanded he pull over. That didn't work, of course, because what was she going to do, shoot him? He knew she wouldn't and didn't stop the car for another hour, when they arrived somewhere near Pawling, New York. She wanted the car keys, but he insisted she didn't know what she was dealing with, and when she lunged to get the keys, that was when he did it. Her first thought was: *This can't be real.* It had to be a trick, but what kind of trick could there be to actually change into an animal, or part animal? And it happened right in front of her; she *saw* it. Then he turned back and she was so stunned she probably looked sick and he was like, "Here, drink this." So she drank from a thermos he gave her, and she was so shocked she didn't realize she was drinking some kind of thick warm beer till she had gulped down most of it.

Now she asked, "What was in the beer? Some kind of roofie?"

"I'll explain it all to you later, don't worry," he said.

Geri checked her clothes again—nothing seemed torn or indi-cated that she'd been raped. But what was on the back of her right hand? Was that *blood*?

"What the hell happened? Tell me now," Geri said. "Did you assault me?"

"Assault you?" Ramon said. "Why would I have to assault you? I mean, getting you in bed ain't exactly a problem, is it?" Ramon smiled.

Geri felt a pang of desire, but she didn't let it take over. She said, "I want to know where this blood came from. Is it my blood?" She went past Ramon, over to a mirror near the dining area, and saw a wound on her neck. She felt it—most of the blood was congealed and there was even some scabbing, as if the wound were a few days old. She said, "How the hell did this happen? *When* did this happen?"

Ramon looked tongue-tied but relaxed.

Turning back toward the mirror, feeling the wound again, Geri asked, "Wait, this is a bite. Somebody bit me." Looking at Ramon in the mirror, she said, "Did you bite me?"

"No, but I had to let you get bitten," Ramon said. "It was the only way I could save you."

Ramon sounded crazy again, the way he had in the car when he was talking about werewolves. But, wait, hadn't she seen him turn into a wolf? Was that real, or was it some kind of dream? She wasn't sure about anything anymore.

"Okay, so if you didn't bite me, then who did?" Geri asked.

"Michael," Ramon said.

"Michael?" Geri said, confused for a second, then getting it. "Michael Hartman bit me?" Geri's first concerns were AIDS and hep C—she was going to have to get tested. Then she said, "Why the hell did he bite me, and what does this have to do with a beer and saving me?"

"It's complicated, baby," Ramon said. "But I promise I'll sit down with you and—"

"No, I'm gonna sit down with *you*, right now," Geri said. "I'm taking you in and you're gonna tell me what's going on with you. And that animal thing didn't really happen, did it? I just imagined it. . . . Wait, what day is it?"

"What day is it?" Ramon said.

"Yeah, what day is it?"

"It's Monday. Well, Tuesday now."

Then Geri saw the clock on the cable box below the TV: 12:42. She remembered about Manny Alvarez and his possible involvement in the Washington Heights shootings.

"Where are we?" Geri asked.

"We're on earth," Ramon said.

"Seriously," Geri said.

"My place, I told you. Hundred Sixteenth Street."

"You still got that car you rented?"

"Yeah, I got it, but—"

"Gimme the keys."

"I don't think—"

Geri aimed her gun at Ramon's face.

"Gimme the damn car keys."

"Okay, okay, they're right over there." Ramon gestured with his chin toward the kitchen counter.

Geri grabbed the keys and asked, "Where's the car parked?"

"'Cross the street, but—"

"I'm not through with you yet," Geri said. "I'm gonna have more questions for you later, and I'm gonna have your friend Michael in too." She headed toward the door.

"You're making a big mistake," Ramon said. "We should get in bed and chillax together and I can explain everything to you."

Ignoring an urge to stay and be ravished by Ramon, Geri said, "I'll be back," and left the apartment.

She found the red Camry across the street, up the block a little. As she drove uptown, she took out her cell—damn, one bar left—and called Shawn. The first time voice mail picked up, so she called again and this time he answered.

"Yeah?" He was obviously half asleep.

"Get your ass dressed; you're meeting me uptown."

"What? . . . What's up?"

"I think I've got the shooter in the Washington Heights shootings."

"Excuse me?" Now he was wide awake.

"Come on, I don't wanna waste any more time on this."

"Since when're you, *we* back on the case?" Shawn asked.

Geri heard Shawn's wife asking, "Time's it, baby?" and Shawn telling her, "Go back to bed."

"We're not," Geri said. "I mean technically."

"Techni . . ." Shawn said. "Are you out of your goddamn mind?"

"Maybe, but I'm telling you, I think I got him," Geri said. "And we gotta bring him in before he kills again."

"We?" Shawn said. "You think I'm crazy? Workin' a case you were taken off is a good way to lose your badge."

"So you want to let a killer walk?" Geri asked.

"If you think you got a lead, call it in," Shawn said.

"So Dan can take care of it, like he took care of Carlita Morales's police protection?"

"Come on," Shawn said.

"I'm texting you the address; be there," Geri said before Shawn could say anything else.

After Geri sent the address to Shawn, she drove uptown, going the speed limit and stopping at lights because she figured this would save more time than if she got pulled over and had to explain she was a cop.

She arrived at the apartment building on Isham Street where Alvarez lived and double-parked. Normally she would have waited for backup—in this case, Shawn—to arrive before she went to confront a potentially armed-and-dangerous perp, but for some reason she wasn't concerned about the possibility of danger. She got right out of the car and strolled up to the building, where a group of teenage gangbangers were hanging out in front. Again, usually, she'd worry about her personal safety in a situation like this, but not tonight. Tonight she was fearless.

"Anybody here live in the building?" she asked.

Although she hadn't displayed a badge, the guys seemed taken aback, intimidated. None of them wanted to answer—exchanging looks to see who would take the lead.

Finally a guy with long dreads said, "I do."

"So what're you waiting for?" Geri said. "Open the goddamn door for me."

The guy, obviously feeling shown up in front of his friends, seemed like he was about to snap back but then reconsidered and let Geri into the building.

Geri had no idea where her bravado and ability to make potentially dangerous guys cower was coming from, but she was liking it. A lot.

She took the stairs to the sixth floor, not winded at all, and rang Manny Alvarez's doorbell again and again, till he opened the door in gym shorts and wifebeater, squinting because of the hallway light.

"Hell's goin' on?"

"Forget me already?" Geri asked. "I'm insulted, it's only been one day."

He forced his eyes to open a little wider, then said, "Oh yeah, the cop. You find out who killed my sister yet?"

"Yeah, actually I think I did," Geri said, and she gave him a little shove to push him back into the apartment. Well, she meant to give him a little shove, but he went straight back, his feet actually leaving the floor, and slammed against the wall in the foyer area. Geri had no idea how she'd been able to do that, as Alvarez was a big, stocky guy, must've weighed more than two hundred pounds.

Enjoying this too much and not wanting to question any of it, Geri went into the apartment and stood over Alvarez, who was sitting, looking up at her, dazed.

"I gotta admit, that was pretty clever," Geri said, "hanging out in front of the building yesterday, pretending to be the angry brother who wants justice. Guess you didn't think you'd run into a cop who'd recognize you, though, huh? What was it, four and a half years ago? After that shooting on Sherman Avenue. I was a cop back then, so I didn't question you directly, but I never forget a face."

"Bitch, you crazy," Alvarez said. "I didn't do nothin'."

He was trying to get up and she kicked him in the head, again much harder than she'd intended, and his head snapped back hard against the wall and blood gushed from his nose.

"Carlita saw you shoot Orlando Rojas," Geri said. "That's why she was so torn about cooperating with us, because she didn't want to turn in her own brother. You were threatening her, weren't you, telling her you'd kill her if she talked. Then she gave us a sketch that wasn't accurate to try to throw us off. Gotta give her credit, she had some family loyalty, not like you. You'd kill your own sister to save your own ass, wouldn't you? That's why there was no sign of a break-in in the apartment, 'cause she let you in. She probably thought you were gonna thank her for trying to throw us off, but you weren't gonna take any chances, were you? You wanted her dead, shut up for good, didn't you?"

He didn't answer. Geri kicked him in the face again, and more blood gushed. She was loving this. And, was she imagining it, or could she *smell* his blood?

"Okay, okay," he groaned. "So I shot her. So what?"

On *what* there was a gunshot, and Geri felt the pain rip through her leg. She saw the shooter—an African American woman in a bra and panties—off to the right. As Geri went for her piece she heard three more shots in quick succession, but they all missed, and then Geri fired a shot from about twenty feet away that went bull's-eye, right between the woman's eyes, and then the whole room seemed to be immersed in the aroma of gunpowder and the wonderful, alluring scent of blood.

Shawn arrived at the crime scene at about the same time as local cops, EMS workers, and crime scene investigators. Manny Alvarez was treated for his injuries, including a broken nose, at the scene, and then he was taken away, under police protection, for more treatment with possible murder charges pending. The remains of Alvarez's girlfriend, Danielle Howard, were being analyzed by investigators and crime forensics workers.

Although Geri had been shot in the leg and lost a good amount of blood, somehow most of the pain had already subsided. The wound itself didn't look as bad as it had immediately after she was shot; was it possible she was already healing? She also noticed that the bite wound on her neck that she'd gotten earlier was almost gone completely. And what about her strength, how she'd kicked the crap out of Alvarez without exerting much energy? And what was up with her sense of smell? Aside from the blood, with all the police and medical personnel around her she was hyperaware of all of the perfumes, colognes, and deodorants. Obviously something very strange was going on. She remembered Ramon telling her when she was leaving his apartment that he could explain everything, and now Geri was eager to hear that explanation herself.

When Detectives Santoro and Reese arrived, Geri explained what had transpired. Her only embellishment was that Alvarez had grabbed her before she'd beaten the hell out of him.

"What made you enter the premises alone?" Santoro asked.

"I thought the perp might try to run," Geri said.

Santoro didn't seem to buy this lame explanation, but Geri really couldn't care less.

"You should've called this in," Reese said. "Right now all you've got is a confession, an unrecorded confession, so you better hope they find something here linking Alvarez to the shootings, or your ass is gonna fry."

As if on cue, a young Asian forensics guy came out of the bedroom holding an evidence bag with what looked like an S&W inside it.

"Good news, we got the gun," he said. "We'll have to check it out, but I'm willing to bet this is the weapon."

"Congrats, Rodriguez," Santoro said to Geri.

Reese almost seemed disappointed.

Several minutes later, Dan McCarthy arrived on the scene. Santoro updated him on what had happened at the apartment, including the discovery of the probable murder weapon.

Dan took Geri aside and said, "I can't say I'm happy about how this went down. You shouldn't've been here, especially on your own, and you're going to have to explain to me exactly how Alvarez, who was apparently unarmed, sustained injuries that hospitalized him.

That said, I owe you one, Rodriguez. This case was rapidly turning into an albatross for the whole department, for the whole city, and the most important thing is that a killer will be brought to justice."

Geri and Dan shook hands. Geri squeezed too hard and Dan winced.

"Sorry," Geri said.

"Hey, I just got one question for you," Dan said, flexing his fingers. "If you got shot in the leg at close range, how is it that you're walking around?"

Geri shrugged, said, "Must've just grazed me."

In the hallway outside the apartment, there was a lot of police activity and neighbors standing in front of their doors.

Shawn came over to Geri and said, "Hey, sorry I didn't get here sooner, but I guess Super Woman didn't need me, huh?"

"You know I can't do it without you," Geri said.

"But seriously, we've been partners, what, over a year? I've never seen you do that kinda damage to somebody's face before. Seriously, where'd that come from?"

She remembered the crazy night with Ramon—seeing him turn into an animal, or just imagining he had, and then drinking the beer, and that weird bite mark on her neck. Was it related to how she was suddenly stronger, more confident, and felt like she was practically invincible?

"I guess something just came over me tonight, that's all," she said.

Leaving the building, she saw that there were already several reporters outside, a couple she recognized from yesterday in Washington Heights. After the humiliation she'd suffered, having to take the fall for ending the protection order that had allowed Carlita

Morales's murder to take place, she never expected she'd have a chance to redeem herself so quickly.

As the reporters shouted questions, she smiled widely and took a deep breath. Yeah, she was going to milk this one for all it was worth.

TWENTY

Alison just wanted to get through this day. After she'd left Jeremy with his friend Matthew's babysitter on West Sixty-seventh, she was late to her first appointment at Mount Sinai, and then she was only able to talk to the doctor for maybe ten minutes before he was called away for surgery. She'd managed to make a follow-up appointment for next week, but the doctor was so busy he'd probably cancel, and timing was so important in sales, and Alison feared that the time to close this deal had passed her by.

The bad Mount Sinai appointment set the bleak tone for the rest of the day. She was off her game at her ten thirty and thought there was a good chance she'd lose what had been a steady client to a competitor. After the appointment she got a call from Matthew's babysitter that Jeremy had been acting up, crying, and complaining that he wanted to go home. Alison had appointments stacked up all day and couldn't go over there to help calm him down; the babysitter sounded pissed off, and Alison knew this was the last time she'd be able to get coverage there for Jeremy. In between her twelve thirty and one o'clock appointments, Alison didn't have time for lunch because she was on the phone, trying to find a babysitter. She tried their old baby-sitter, Margaret; she'd found another job but was nice enough to give referrals to two other babysitters whom Alison called and made appointments to interview later in the week. She called Stephen Tyler because she still hadn't heard a peep from him since leaving his office yesterday afternoon. She'd left several messages, calling late last night and this morning, but the calls kept going straight to voice mail. Alison was getting seriously pissed off. He'd said he would stay in touch; was this what he called staying in touch? She had no idea if he'd even been able to follow Simon, but if she didn't hear something from him today, that was the end, she was going to fire him. She wanted to give him the benefit of the doubt right now, but maybe that was why Vijay had warned her about him. Maybe the guy was a total flake.

Alison was still sad about the whole Vijay situation. She knew not getting involved with him was for the best, but she wished she hadn't mixed business with pleasure in the first place. She and Vijay used to have a friendly working relationship, and now he wasn't even her client. As per his request she'd handed him off to Chandra, one of her co-workers. Chandra had been thrilled of course—Vijay was a lucrative, influential client—and now Alison had lost a friend as well as significant commission income.

The rest of the day, Alison tried to focus on work, but she was still a mess. Her afternoon appointments didn't go any better than her morning ones. She was distracted, kept losing her train of thought, and just didn't feel like being around people. She always told young salespeople that ninety percent of this job was personality based, engaging with doctors on a personal level, often in very short periods of time. Doctors were busy and often had only five or ten minutes to meet, and if you weren't having a good day, if you were in a bitter, edgy mood, your chances of making a connection were almost nil. After all, doctors had enough stress during their work-days. Alison even had a bad meeting with Dr. Morgan, a super nice Park Avenue gynecologist—older guy, early sixties—who was one of her longest, steadiest clients. Dr. Morgan had known her for years; he'd noticed she was stressed and asked her if she was okay. She got defensive, afraid that her personal life was intruding in her profes-sional life, and snapped, "I'm fine," and changed the subject, and then the meeting ended awkwardly. Leaving the office, Alison regretted her curtness and sent an e-mail apology. Dr. Morgan was such a great guy she didn't think there would be any long-lasting tension, but she knew she had to get her crap under control or it would seriously affect her job, and one thing she couldn't lose right now was her job, espe-cially in this economy.

At a little after six, after her last appointment of the day, she took a cab back across town, figuring she'd change out of her work clothes before she had to zip out again and pick up Jeremy. What she would've really loved to do was hit the gym, but when would she have time to work out again? With full-time work and solo child care at night, she wouldn't have time to do anything for herself. She already felt like crap, forgetting to eat, and was losing way too much weight. She hadn't weighed herself in a while, but going by how most of her clothes were loose on her, she figured she must've lost seven or eight pounds over the past month. If her life became more difficult and stressful and she lost another five pounds, it would push her danger-ously close to anorexia territory.

When the cab dropped her at Eighty-ninth and Columbus, she feared that today was just a preview of the rest of her life, that things would get worse. She was going to be alone, stressed out, broke, exhausted, and anorexic. And what about Jeremy? What kind of life would he have with a miserable single mom taking care of him?

Then Alison entered the lobby and saw Simon standing there. Her first thought was, *That's my husband?* He looked good, better than he'd looked in years, or maybe ever. He was lean, toned, and his skin had a healthy glow. He was also extremely well dressed in a stylish suit, an expensive-looking black dress shirt, and new black loafers—were they Ferragamos? It took a few seconds before she remembered how angry she was at him, how he'd put her through hell lately, and how she'd hired a PI to find out who he'd been screwing lately.

Putting on a serious, pissed-off expression, she said, "What the hell're you doing here?"

"I'm here to be honest with you about everything," he said.

Honest? Was he going to confess an affair? If so, how come Tyler hadn't let her in on any of this? Was he following Simon or not? And there was something different about Simon, but she couldn't quite figure out what it was. He was in clothes she'd never seen before—a clean shirt, tucked into beige chinos—but it wasn't that.

"Sorry," Alison said. "I'm just . . . surprised to see you here."

"How's Jeremy?" Simon asked.

"Fine," Alison said. "He's at Matthew's. I have to pick him up in a few minutes."

"This won't take long," Simon said, "but maybe we can do it upstairs."

Simon motioned with his eyes very quickly in the direction of James the doorman. James, organizing some packages that had been dropped off, didn't seem to be eavesdropping, but doormen were *always* eavesdropping. If you lived in a doorman building in Manhattan, you never wanted to have a dramatic confrontation in front of a doorman, as it was the equivalent of having the confrontation broadcast to every apartment in the building.

But Alison was wary of being alone with Simon after his bizarre behavior the last time she'd seen him and said, "I don't think that's such a good idea."

Simon glanced at James, then whispered to her, "I promise, nothing bad will happen. I just want to clear the air and be honest about everything that's been going on."

Alison stared at him, still getting that vibe that something had changed about him; there was an intensity in his eyes she had never seen before, but she believed he was sincere about wanting to get things out in the open and, after so much confusion these past several weeks, she was eager to hear what he had to say for himself.

"Okay, fine," she said. "But it'll have to be quick; I really have to get Jeremy."

Before they got in the elevator, she looked back through the glass windows, toward the street, wondering if Stephen Tyler was out there somewhere. If he hadn't been able to tail a man to his own apartment, he had to be the worst PI in the world. Or maybe he'd lied to her, and he wasn't even working on the case. Either way, unless he had some incredible explanation for what had been going on lately, she was going to ask for her retainer back, every cent of it.

In the elevator Alison said to Simon, "I'm warning you, if you start growling like a crazy person again, that's it, I'm calling the cops."

He was looking at her in a seductive way, as if something amused him and aroused him at the same time, and then he said, "I've missed you."

She couldn't help feeling a desire for him, though—she told herself—maybe it wasn't actual desire, maybe it was just vulnerability because of how rough things had been lately. Maybe she had a need to connect with someone and wasn't thinking it through clearly enough. Wasn't that what had driven her to Vijay?

At the apartment, Alison made sure that Simon entered ahead of her and she was between him and the door.

Heading past the dining area toward the living room, he said, "Ah, it feels so great to be home."

"Right here's fine," Alison said.

Simon stopped and turned back toward her.

"Okay," he said, "we can do it here."

She wasn't crazy about the ambiguity of *do it here*. But while she was concerned about her safety, she also felt weirdly protected at the same time.

"So you said you're going to tell me the truth about what's been going on, so let's hear it," she said.

"Okay, well, I guess the main thing is I don't have lycanthropic disorder," Simon said.

Alison took a moment, as this wasn't the direction she'd thought this conversation would go, then asked, "Then what disorder do you have?"

"I don't have any disorder," Simon said.

So this was what this was about? More games?

Suddenly angry, Alison said, "Look, I don't see what this is accomplishing. If you have something productive, something new, to tell me, I'm all ears. But if you—"

"You don't get it," Simon said. "I don't have a disorder where I think I'm a werewolf, because I'm *actually* a werewolf."

Simon seemed excited, almost giddy about all this, as if he'd just made some incredible revelation.

"Why are you doing this to me?" Alison asked. "Why do you keep playing these sick, twisted games with me? What're you getting out of it?"

"Because I want you to know the truth finally," Simon said. "I want you to love me for who I am, the same way I decided that I have to love who I am. I mean, if I couldn't love myself, I couldn't expect you to love me, right?"

She thought, *My husband's insane. And he's farther gone than I'd ever imagined.*

"I have no idea what you're talking about," she said. "I think you need help. Serious long-term help."

Then his face became the face of an animal. His face was hairy and his nose and eyes looked like the eyes of a dog or, no, a wolf. This happened so quickly that at first her brain simply accepted it, as a fact. But then the panic and disbelief and a swarm of other emotions hit her with full force. No, no, this wasn't possible. She was just imagining it. It was a fantasy, or hallucination, because of all the stress she'd been under lately.

She was shaking her head violently back and forth and heard herself whimper, "No . . . no . . ."

Then she saw that his face wasn't all that had changed. His body had expanded, stretching his clothes, and his arms were hairier and had claws.

His arms have claws.

"N-n-n . . ." she said.

She closed her eyes, telling herself it wasn't real, none of it was real. She was the one who had the disorder, she was the one going crazy.

But then she opened her eyes and saw the animal face staring back at her, and then everything went dark again.

Simon had expected Alison to have a strong reaction to the truth, but what could he do? He felt he couldn't go on like this any longer, living a lie. If he was going to get his family back, he had to open up about everything, put it all on the table, and deal with the fallout.

After devouring Volker in the woods, Simon wasn't sure what would happen next. The meal was pure pleasure, but when he transformed back into his human form the horror and disgust set in. How could he have done that to Volker of all people, the one person, or wolf, who wanted to help him? How could he keep rationalizing that his uncontrollable craving for blood and flesh wasn't a part of him? How could he deny responsibility for the awful things he had done?

Simon was expecting Michael, and maybe Charlie, to attack him next. While Simon had felt bonded to Michael when he was a wolf and they were feasting on Volker's flesh, as a human Simon didn't feel any bond or loyalty to Michael at all, and Michael had to realize this. And after Michael had killed and eaten his own father, why would he spare Simon?

Simon was ready to defend himself, and fight to his death if he had to, but Michael seemed disinterested. Maybe he was satiated from his meal and had lost the urge to kill Simon, or maybe he had another agenda. One thing Simon had learned over the past month or so—trying to figure out Michael's agenda was pointless, as his actions rarely seemed to make any sense, or at least any sense to a rational human being.

Eddie, who apparently was a jack-of-all-trades—driver, hit man, body disposer—was hard at work, digging a hole in the woods. After he shoveled Volker's remains in and filled the hole back up with dirt he returned to the car with Michael, Charlie, and Simon in tow.

Simon's guard was still way up, as he was still expecting a surprise transformation and attack from Michael, but the four men got into the car, as if it were a normal evening and they were on their way home from an outing together, like a sporting event. In the car there was even some small talk from Charlie and Michael—mostly Charlie— about play dates, and times they would get together over the next week or so. The only indication of the horror that had just taken place in the woods was the lingering odor of Volker's blood on their breath and blood in their hair and on their skin and partially torn clothing.

When they arrived in the city, it was clear that they were bypassing Manhattan.

"Um, so where're we going?" Simon spoke his first words since the mauling of Volker.

"The brewery," Charlie said. "We gotta change."

This made some sense to Simon, but he still feared a hidden agenda. Maybe he was going to be ambushed in the brewery, consumed there the way Stephen Tyler, that PI, had been.

Simon's fear was at its peak when they were all walking up the dark stairwell, but no attack came. They went right to the room with the shower and took turns washing up. Michael collected their bloodied clothes in a Hefty bag, and then they selected new snazzy outfits. Feeling healthy and spiffy, Simon left the brewery with Charlie.

Michael, who'd walked them down, said to Simon, "You will return soon."

Simon didn't answer.

Eddie was waiting with the SUV—the seats had been cleaned and now there was only a very faint odor of blood—and drove Charlie and Simon back to Charlie's place in Manhattan.

It was still dark out and the moon had almost set. It was hard to believe that only four hours had gone by since Simon and Charlie had been picked up and taken to the woods upstate. Despite the horror of what he'd done to Volker tonight, Simon felt like he'd taken a giant leap toward if not resolving his situation, then at least learning to cope with it. He understood what Volker had been trying to tell him in the Ramble that morning: that he was at the mercy of his cravings and he would have to embrace the animal part of himself if he wanted to have any chance to survive. Already he'd learned how to transform faster, and he was confident that he would become even better at detecting scents, and maybe he'd be able to hide his wolf scent from others the way Michael could. Maybe, if he worked on it, he could even have sex again without fear that he would "wolf out" in the middle of it.

Charlie left for work, to resume his shift at the firehouse downtown, and Simon rested on the couch. Finally dawn came. Despite the eventful night, Simon was alert and, for the first time in ages, excited about the future. Even if he could never find the remedy, he was confident that he could learn how to fully assimilate as a wolf in a world with humans. As time went on, he'd be able to understand his cravings and learn how to control them, and if he continued to gain control of his wolf powers he could keep Michael under control, or kill him if necessary. But mostly he was excited because learning how to control his cravings meant that there was a chance he could get his human life back, and he could be a husband and a father again.

Simon was giddy the rest of the day. Not only could being honest about what had happened to him repair his relationship with his family, it would also relieve a tremendous burden on himself. There was nothing more stressful than keeping a secret, and he was eager to let go of it.

But now, after he transformed back into his human form and knelt down, tending to Alison's unconscious body, he knew that with honesty there was always risk. All he could do was show her who he was, and try to explain, but he couldn't control her reaction. He hoped that she would be willing to give him a chance, to have an open mind about what she'd just seen, and accept him for who he was, and help him through it, but there was also a major chance that their relationship had become too damaged and that she'd have the opposite reaction. She might freak out, reject him, scream like a maniac, run for her life.

Simon knew that her initial reaction after she regained consciousness would be crucial, so he didn't give her a chance to have one.

As her eyes opened he moved in very close to her and, in the most reassuring voice he could muster up, said, "It's okay. Shh, shh, it's okay."

She looked panicked, as if she were about to lose it. He put a hand over her mouth.

"Please, just give me a chance," he said. "I know you're scared, you must be terrified right now, and that's okay, but I promise you, I'm not going to hurt you, I'm never going to hurt you in any way ever again. I had to be honest, that's all. I had to show you who I am now—well, who I am part of the time. I had to let you in on what I've been going through all these weeks, because I love you and I don't want to lose you. And I know it's going to take time for you to understand, for you to accept, to comprehend all this, but that's okay. It took me time too, and there're still times I can't believe it's really happening. But it is happening—werewolves exist."

She shuddered.

"I know," he said. "If you're scared, how do you think I felt? I've been tortured, dealing with this alone. I was terrified, afraid I was going to die or kill somebody, but there're some wonderful things about it too. Wait till you see the things I'm capable of; you won't believe it. But I get it, okay? I know it's a process. It took me time to accept it too; I'm still learning about it, and I'm not expecting any miracles here. I'm just asking you to be open, for you to give me a chance to explain to you what's been going on in my life. Can you do that? Can you try to do that?"

There was still terror in Alison's eyes. She was shaking.

"Okay, okay, I understand, I understand," Simon said. "I know this is a lot for you to take in at once. Believe me, I know. But the main thing is, as you saw, I don't have a disorder. I just told you that, or let you believe it, because I didn't want you to leave me. I thought I could figure out a way to deal with it, to get rid of it on my own, and now I think I have figured something out. It's a learning process, but I don't think I'm a danger to you or Jeremy anymore. This is just something I have to live with, like a disease. Yes, think of it as a disease, and we said we'd stay together in sickness and in health, right? Well, that's how I need you to think of this—that I'm sick, but I'm getting better. There's hope now. I might even find a remedy and become human again, but even if I can't, I can survive. I can have a normal, happy, functional life, and I can go back to being a husband and a dad too. Those are the most important things—you and Jeremy."

Alison was trying to speak, but her voice was faint, not even a whisper.

"I'm sorry, I can't hear you, sweetie," Simon said.

Continuing to shake, she tried to speak, and finally got out: "J-J-Jeremy. I—I—I have to get Jeremy."

"I know," Simon said, "but maybe I can call Matthew's and they can watch him awhile longer so you can rest."

"No." Alison sat up. "I—I have to go. I have to get Jeremy now."

"Okay, that's fine," Simon said.

He knew he couldn't keep her, that ultimately she'd have to make a choice.

He followed her to the door, saying, "I know you're still afraid, and that's okay, but I need you to think about two things. Think about the strength it took for me to tell you all this, to show you this. And think about the risk I'm taking. If you run to the police my life'll be ruined, and your life will be too. You know what kind of media event it would be if a real live werewolf were discovered in Manhattan? And it would have consequences for you as well—you'll be known as the wife of a werewolf. And what about Jeremy? Think about the effect it would have on him if this went public. So, please, just give me a couple of days to prove to you that I have a handle on this now. A couple of days, that's all I'm asking for."

At the door, Alison, still shaking, but not as badly, turned and looked right at Simon. She looked terrified and wasn't blinking at all. Then she rushed out of the apartment.

Well, Simon knew it was out of his hands now. He'd done what he'd felt he had to do, and he had no regrets. If she came back, he would work on his marriage and try to get his life back. If she went to the police, it meant he didn't have much to live for anyway, so it was better to find out sooner than later. This was the way he was rationalizing it, anyway.

He waited, pacing back and forth. He expected that she'd gone

to the police; why wouldn't she? She'd just seen her estranged husband transform into a werewolf. What reason would she have to have
any faith in him now?

He heard the elevator doors open. Maybe there was a SWAT team
out there. They'd break down the door, arrest him, and his hellish
future would commence.

But, wait, he only smelled Alison in the hallway, and . . .

Could it be true?

The door opened, and Alison and Jeremy entered. Jeremy's face
lit up when he saw Simon.

"Daddy!"

Jeremy's excitement was priceless, and so was Simon's.

Jeremy ran to Simon, and Simon lifted him up and hugged him
tightly, determined that he would never, ever let go of him again.

While Simon was thrilled that Alison had returned with Jeremy,
he knew he still had a long way to go before he fully regained
her trust. But this wasn't so uncommon. Every guy in a troubled
marriage where a betrayal had taken place had to regain his wife's
trust before love could return. They were just dealing with what
everybody else went through, on a much, much larger scale.

All in all, it was a pretty normal evening at home. The focus was
on Jeremy, and Simon, so elated to be with his son again, wasn't
thinking about anything else. But after Simon put Jeremy to bed—
Jeremy fell asleep during the second reading of *Madeline*—he joined
Alison in the living room, where they had a long talk.

Alison, who still seemed traumatized, had a lot of questions
about Simon's condition, and he answered all of them as fully and
honestly as he could. He explained how Volker and Michael were

werewolves from Germany, but he didn't tell her how long they'd lived, figuring it was important to dole out some of this information slowly. He did tell her how Michael had chosen four men to be in his pack, including him, and how it had all started the night Michael had given him a pint of his "family beer" and how it had caused physical and behavioral changes. This part of Simon's story seemed to resonate with Alison as she realized that pieces of the puzzle that she'd been trying to put together in her head were finally fitting into place. Simon didn't tell her much about the violence that had taken place, especially the violence he'd been involved with, figuring at this point that it would be way too much for her to handle.

Omitting all the violence, he summed up most of what had happened during the past, including how he had spent a night with Volker, who had told him about his history in Germany and about how he'd been learning to control his werewolf side, and how he was confident that going forward he would be able to avoid accidental transformations.

Alison absorbed most of what Simon had to say silently, only occasionally asking a question. When he was through, though, she said, "I don't know what you expect me to say. I mean, what you're saying sounds so bizarre, so insane, and yet I saw you. I saw you."

She was quiet after that, looking away toward the windows and the view of the rooftops of tenements and the moon—not full—and Simon decided not to push it any further.

Simon slept on the couch, which was fine with him, because at least he was home. It felt great to be surrounded by the scents of his wife and son, knowing they were close by and he could protect them.

In the morning, Alison was hesitant to leave him alone with Jeremy, but he insisted that she had nothing to worry about, that Jeremy was safer with him than with anyone in the world. He must've been convincing because she agreed, but she insisted that he update her every hour with texts.

It was a perfect, sunny November day, and Simon and Jeremy had a blast together. They didn't do anything special—a couple of playgrounds, pizza, kicking around a soccer ball—but the mundane- ness was perfect and just what Simon needed. He noticed that with his new attitude of accepting that he was a wolf now, rather than fighting it, he had much better control of his behavior. He wasn't craving meat as badly and even managed to eat a couple of slices of pizza—okay, with extra sausage and pepperoni—and feel satisfied. He also noticed that he wasn't getting quite as much attention from women as he had been recently. He caught a few women checking him out during the day, but when he focused on the love he had for his wolf side it seemed as if women became less interested. And there seemed to be some physical changes as well. His voice wasn't quite as deep and, when they returned to the apartment later in the after- noon, he noticed that his body hair wasn't growing as quickly. If this kept up, he could probably get away with grooming himself every other day instead of twice a day as he had been lately.

When Alison returned from work, there was still a lot of tension, but it wasn't nearly as bad as last night. She had more questions about werewolves and Simon's behavioral changes. Simon told her about his increased strength and ability to heal faster. When he demon- strated his abilities by lifting the dining room table easily with one hand and pricking his finger with a knife and then showing her how the wound healed within several minutes she was amazed. Like last night, Simon didn't mention anything about the murders and cannibalism that had taken place. Simon was surprised that she wasn't suspicious, or at least curious, but he got the sense that, at least for right now, she didn't want to hear much about the dark side of being a werewolf. She just wanted to feel confident that Simon had it under control, that he wasn't going to hurt her or Jeremy, but she didn't want to know any gory details. Simon wasn't going to push it; if Alison wanted to have a "don't ask, don't tell" policy about werewolf-related violence, that was perfectly fine with him.

Later, Simon got a text from Charlie, saying the guys were planning to meet tomorrow afternoon at the playground in Battery Park. Simon had a strong urge to be with his pack again and texted back that of course he'd be there. Unlike a week ago, he didn't feel like he was getting back into anything by hanging out with the guys. He didn't feel like Michael was manipulating him in any way. He wanted to see the pack because he understood that they were a part of him now and he couldn't deny it anymore.

Simon was concerned about the police, though, especially Detective Rodriguez. Simon hadn't seen her leave the woods, and for all he knew Ramon had taken her somewhere and slaughtered her, eaten her flesh, and buried the remains. But wouldn't the disappearance of an NYPD detective be a major news story?

On his laptop Simon did a search for "Detective Rodriguez NYPD" in Google News and shuddered when a series of news items appeared. But, wait, they weren't about a disappearance; they were about how she'd single-handedly made a major arrest in a couple of drug-related shootings. The arrest had apparently taken place on Monday evening. How was that possible? On the evening the guys had gone to the woods upstate? Simon had seen Rodriguez unconscious, being attacked by Michael, and then a couple of hours later she's taking down a drug dealer?

Simon was confused, but he was happy that Rodriguez was alive and apparently very well.

The next day, Simon took Jeremy downtown to Battery Park. Jeremy was thrilled to be back playing with his old friends and, as always, they played well together with no fighting or arguing or trouble of any kind. Simon enjoyed being with the guys as well. They gave him something he couldn't get anywhere else. It was a feeling that he belonged, that he was a part of something much, much bigger than himself. Charlie and Ramon were chatty and friendly and, though Michael was typically aloof, Simon felt a bond with him as well, but he was well aware that the bond with Michael was temporary at best. Simon hadn't forgotten Volker's warning about Michael's desire to grow his pack, and to someday involve the kids, and Simon knew that it was up to him now. Though Volker was dead, his determination to stop Michael from causing more mayhem was still alive in Simon. If a werewolf remedy existed, Simon was determined to find it. In the meantime, Simon would stay in the pack and embrace his dark side, but he'd be watching Michael closely, and if Michael looked like he was a threat to anyone, Simon would do whatever he had to do to save lives.

That night, Simon was enjoying a quiet night at home with his family, when he had a major scare. The doorbell rang and he smelled cops in the hallway. He thought it had something to do with Detective Rodriguez, or perhaps Volker, so he was shocked when the detectives, whom he'd never seen before, announced that they had come to talk to Alison, not Simon.

Stephen Tyler, the PI Alison had hired, had been missing for several days, and Alison had been one of the last people to see him alive. The questioning was basically an information gathering— Alison didn't seem to be an actual suspect. But since Alison had hired

Tyler to follow Simon, the detectives wanted to know if Simon had had any contact with Tyler. Simon swore that he hadn't, and the detectives seemed satisfied and left after only about fifteen minutes.

Simon knew that Alison must have at least suspected that he was lying about something, that he might have come into contact with Tyler or knew something about his disappearance that he wasn't sharing, but if she did have suspicions, she was keeping them to herself. It seemed to Simon that she was serious about this "don't ask, don't tell" thing, and if that was the case he was happy to go along with it.

As per their routine lately, around eleven thirty, Alison went into the bedroom to get ready for bed and Simon settled in on the couch. But tonight Alison came back out to the living room in a new slinky black lace bra and matching panties and said, "Want to join me?"

It was the first time they'd attempted to make love in weeks, but it seemed like it had been years. Simon was very tentative at first, as if they were virgins in high school. He'd done a great job of learning how to control his basic urges, but he didn't know if this would carry over to sex. What if he lost it and mauled her to death? Oh, God, and with Jeremy in the next room.

Simon was on top of Alison, pinning her down. Her scent was so strong and he wanted her so badly. He kissed her neck, resisting an urge to bite through her skin, and then he felt the tingling in his extremities that he experienced before transformations.

Sensing something wrong, Alison said, "Oh, no, what is it?"

Simon was focused on the love he had for the wolf inside him, and he let go of the resistance. Then he realized he was doing it—he was making love to his wife again. It felt so great to be inside her, to be one again, to be connected.

He had to be the luckiest guy in the world.

*   *   *

Simon was loving his double life. He was a husband and a stay-at-home dad, and he was also a member of a pack of wolves. It was as though he had two families with which he felt a strong bond and connection, but in very different ways. He was doing a good job of controlling his urges. He wasn't perfect yet; occasionally there were minor slip-ups and he still had cravings for meat many times during the day, but all in all he was successfully assimilating into the human world.

In early December, a full moon was coming, and the guys agreed to meet at midnight in the Ramble in Central Park.

Simon explained to Alison what was going to happen and, God bless her, she was cool with it.

"Have a great time," she said. Then, after she kissed him good-bye, she added, "Just be careful."

It was the perfect night to be a werewolf. The temperature was just around freezing, the moon was big and bright, and the first snow of the year, an inch or two, just enough to coat the ground and tree branches, had fallen during the day.

At midnight the guys found each other easily by their scents, and then they stripped naked and transformed into werewolves. Running bare-clawed in the snow as a werewolf reminded Simon of when he was a kid, playing in the new snow in his backyard. Somehow, as an adult human he'd lost that sense of wonderment and abandonment, but as a werewolf it all rushed back. As he kicked up snow and leaped over rocks and fallen tree branches, he couldn't get his werewolf face to smile, but inside he was grinning madly.

Simon and Charlie raced each other, back and forth, through the woods, and then Charlie climbed to the highest branch of a tree and

Simon followed him up. They must've been thirty feet from the ground. Charlie was panting, the shiny light brown coat on his face shimmering in the moonlight, and then, with no hesitation, he leaped off the branch, landing on his four feet. Simon had never leaped from such a height, but he knew he had to accept the challenge and he had no fear. He jumped and it was thrilling, falling, accelerating through the chilly night air. He didn't land perfectly, though, falling onto his side, and then Charlie jumped on top of him and they rolled around, clawing and biting each other, but in a playful way, not deep enough to cause any major wounds. Then Ramon rushed over and joined the pile and the play fight continued until Michael came over and growled menacingly and Simon knew what was going to happen next.

Charlie and Ramon moved away, leaving Michael and Simon face-to-face. It was as if the bully in the schoolyard, Michael, had come over to confront the new kid, Simon. Michael, high up on his hind legs, looked angry and menacing, but Simon didn't back down. He looked right at Michael, staring at his faint reflection in Michael's pitch-black, moonlit eyes. Then Simon sensed something different in Michael's attitude, something he'd never sensed before. Was it fear? Respect? After maybe a minute, Michael ran off with Charlie and Ramon, and then Simon followed. Simon had definitely proven something to Michael, but it was clear that Michael was still in charge of the pack.

For a long time, the four werewolves ran around in the Ramble, chasing and tackling one another, and then Simon detected another scent nearby—but it wasn't human; it was the scent of a fifth werewolf. He knew the other guys must have noticed it as well, but they didn't seem at all surprised or concerned.

Then, moments later, she appeared—a stunningly attractive female werewolf with a slender physique, a beautiful dark brown coat, and a wonderful scent. She sidled up to the other werewolves, taunting them with her beauty, and her scent got stronger, more mesmerizing, like the most alluring perfume in the world. Simon had never smelled anything more appealing, and he felt a rush to his brain, a sensory overload that made him dizzy and excited. But why did the scent seem vaguely familiar? He'd never been around a werewolf with this scent, but it reminded him of a much fainter human scent. Then, as she sashayed by again, within inches of the pack of male werewolves, it clicked and Simon knew he was looking at the werewolf version of Detective Rodriguez.

Suddenly what Simon had witnessed in the woods upstate that night made total sense to him. When Michael bit Rodriguez he was giving her his werewolf blood, but the bite didn't kill her because she had been prepared for it with Michael's family beer. That was why Michael had accused Simon of stealing a beer from the brewery—but he hadn't meant the remedy, he'd meant the family beer. Michael had assumed that Simon had taken the beer to save Rodriguez, but actually Rodriguez herself had, or, more likely, Ramon had taken the beer and had Rodriguez drink it.

But if Michael was upset with Ramon for saving Rodriguez, he hadn't shown it lately; at the playground they had seemed as friendly as ever. It made Simon wonder if Michael had actually orchestrated all of it. Maybe he knew that Ramon would try to save Geri, but the whole purpose of the night was to lure Volker, whom he considered his biggest threat, to the woods so he could be eliminated and consumed by the pack. Simon had no idea if there was any validity to his theory, and he also knew that racking his brain trying to figure out Michael's MO was always a pointless endeavor. Michael was a mystery that couldn't be solved, and Simon always had the disturbing feeling that he was at least one or two steps behind him.

Simon didn't know if a werewolf cop would ultimately be good or bad for the pack, but it was clear that Ramon and Geri were in love. Geri ran with all the guys for a while, but then Geri and Ramon paired off and ran together toward the moonlit lake. Seeing the werewolf lovers together was beautiful, but it also made Simon a little jealous. He couldn't imagine how amazing it would feel to run with a werewolf whom he was in love with, and he imagined what it would be like if Alison were a werewolf. They could transform together on full moons, make love together as werewolves, and take trips together to remote forested parts of Canada, or the Black Forest in Germany. If they shared the ultimate bond, there would be no more secrets to keep, and they could have a deeper, more connected marriage.

Simon ran alone to the highest point of the Ramble, where he climbed a rock, stood on his hind legs, and howled at the moon.

Having a werewolf lover of his own was just a fantasy, unfortunately, and it would have to remain a fantasy.

Well, for now, anyway.

AVENGERS VS X-MEN
MARVEL
AvsX
ROUND 1
AVAILABLE NOW!
#AvX
AVX.MARVEL.COM
TO FIND A COMIC SHOP NEAR YOU
VISIT WWW.COMICSHOPLOCATOR.COM
TM & © 2012 MARVEL & SUBS
Buy AVX #1 and thousands of other Marvel
digital comics now via the free Marvel Comics App.
Visit: www.marvel.com/marvelcomicsapp
MARVEL